PRAISE FOR
YOU'RE MINE

"Somer Canon delivers a gripping tale of doomed love and the dark twisted need to control."

- **Ali Seay**, author of GO DOWN HARD and TO OFFER HER PLEASURE

"I loved this novel! A blend of occult horror, suspense, and coming-of-age, the story kept me in its grip from the first page to the last. A cautionary tale about the dangers of power, magic, and the desire to be loved, this is one of Somer Canon's finest books."

- **Regina Garza Mitchell**, co-editor of THE BIG BOOK OF BLASPHEMY and two-time Golden Apple Writer-in-Residence

"Twisty, dangerous, sexy, and tense, YOU'RE MINE will seize you by the throat and tighten its stranglehold until the very last page. Somer Canon is a fantastic storyteller with a fearsome, unforgettable voice."

- **Jonathan Janz**, author of THE SIREN AND THE SPECTER and MARLA

"Somer Canon is a vibrant, vital voice in the horror genre today, and YOU'RE MINE is proof why. Creepy, cool and unforgettable, you'll descend into the world of Ioni and Raber as they fall for witchcraft and each other, all with disastrous, devilish consequences. Read all of Somer Canon's work, starting with this killer book."

- **Gwendolyn Kiste**, Bram Stoker Award-winning author of THE RUST MAIDENS and RELUCTANT IMMORTALS

YOU'RE MINE

SOMER CANON

To all who are lost and looking for their path:
Find it yourself. Don't be led.

PART ONE

CHAPTER ONE

The public school cafeteria of the United States is a place that tends to bring physical reactions to those who have been through them. Oddly scented, not always terribly clean, and full of one's peers, hostile and otherwise, it's a place that sends adults into fits of nostalgia while the hapless students look on with a mixture of comfortable familiarity and self-esteem shriveling anxiety.

On no other day were those anxious feelings more prominent than the first day of school. Well, except maybe that *last* first day. The last time one experiences that first day can be bittersweet, but for some, for those who would laugh derisively at the notion that high school contains the best years of your life, that final first day marks a great relief. With adulthood and independence on the horizon, and the desperate hope that one will no longer have to suffer the forced society of public school, that last first day is actually pretty fucking incredible. Freedom was less than a year away, and the world opened up with endless possibilities for those new graduates. At that age, with inexperience allowing optimism to rule, people tend to think that time is limitless and all things are possible. Experience teaches which of those things is true and which is absolute soul-sucking bullshit.

On this last first day, the cafeteria was noisy with excitement as students milled in and sorted themselves into their appropriate social groups. Colorful clothing adhering to style standards detailed in popular magazines washed through the large room. There were the style anomalies, of course. In Stearnsville, a town that boasted an almost twenty percent

1

poverty rate, there were more than a few tattered shirts and hole-riddled pants that weren't made so on purpose. Even with those stylistic aberrations, one's eye was inevitably drawn to one particular table in the room. The weirdo table.

Calling the high school seniors seated at the table "weirdos" was a broad enough description (and insult) for the small, mostly white town to handle. Heavy, black eye-makeup, piercings, and tattoos adorned the four as did surprising flashes of color in either clothes or hair dyes that contrasted with their mostly black wardrobes. Where most of the other students were exuberant and energized, the four at the weirdo table were more subdued, talking among themselves privately. They weren't goths, really, a style that still had a sizable fan base at the time, but they were certainly alternative.

"Everybody must think we're over here plotting something," Ioni thought as she looked at her three companions. *"Nothing could be further from the truth."* She smiled as she listened to the conversation going on.

"Oh, come on!" Nathan Newell said. "This group is every bit as attention-getting as any other group of obnoxious teens! I have every reason to believe that I can land a Marlon Brando look-alike in this crowd. I stand out!"

"Nath," Arlie Swiger said, smiling. "I'll never understand this weird infatuation with Marlon Brando. Did you ever see him in his later years?"

"Girl, my god!" Nathan squeaked. "Don't try to crap up my mental image like that! I'm talking a young Brando here! Young!"

"Look how you're dressed," Adam Burnside interjected. "Aren't you supposed to lust after dark brooding types who understand darkness the way you do?"

This was an inside joke among the group. They weren't dark, nor were they brooding. They liked art, music, and movies and while Nine Inch Nails and Orgy were CDs frequently listened to by the group, most of them would shame-facedly admit to liking Britney Spears and The Backstreet Boys as well. They weren't much different from their peers, but their aesthetic set them on the outskirts as the strange ones. It bothered them from time to time because the teen years are full of doubt and the need for acceptance, but it also thrilled them because they felt a little bit of pride in daring to be different. That something as trivial as their clothes could upset people emboldened them to take it further, to push ridiculous boundaries.

"Listen here, Mister Adam," Nathan said tartly. "Just because I choose the lifestyle of the dark and malevolent, doesn't mean that I don't enjoy a good ol' American boy every now and then. I know you and Arlie make the perfect picture of goth love, but I really couldn't bear not being the pretty one in my relationship. What can I say, I just want a manly man to sweep me off my feet."

"Whoa, whoa," Adam said, waving his hands. "Are you trying to say my lady ain't pretty?"

"Arlie is breathtaking," Nathan said, smiling. "Only half of her head has hair, and the hair that she does have is purple. She's the only person I've ever met who can actually wear a size zero pant and she has fantastic taste in body ink. I think what I was saying was that it's you who aren't the pretty one." Nathan gestured to Adam. "I mean, come on. Platinum hair, pale skin, shaved eyebrows and like six holes in each ear? Striking? Sure? But Jared Leto you ain't, my friend."

"Piercings, pale skin, eyebrows plucked to near oblivion, and I'm pretty sure your hair was dyed platinum just a couple of weeks ago," Ioni said, smiling.

"I learned from my wannabe ways," Nathan said, gesturing to his pink mohawk with his black painted fingernails and smiling with his black-lined lips. "It's also precisely why I need a manly man in order to be the pretty one."

The group snickered. Nathan was the clown of the group. Ioni became friends with him in the sixth grade. He was the first openly gay peer she'd met up to that point. Their town typically saw the gay kids move far away before coming out of the closet, but Nathan was comfortable with who he was and equally comfortable with letting people who thought him laughable or worse know that they could go straight to hell. Since Ioni had a rather rough time with puberty and identity, it helped her to know someone who was comfortable in their own skin when she felt anything but. As a teenaged girl who carried more weight than others her age and who developed breasts about two years before anyone else, feeling normal was nearly impossible for Ioni Davis.

Arlie and her boyfriend Adam came to the group by way of high school art class. They were a strange couple. Adam's family was famously wealthy for the area and Arlie lived with a single mother in HUD housing. Arlie joked that the only reason they had come together was "when you're the only two goth kids in school, nobody else wants you," because they'd gone to a different middle school than Ioni and Nathan and actually were the only two kids with that aesthetic there. But Ioni knew better. There were real feelings seated in the foundation of their relationship and while it was possible that weird attracted weird, it was deeper than a similar taste in black eyeliner.

Ioni, herself, came from a well-to-do family. With a CPA for a father and a caterer for a mother, money wasn't tight for her family like it was for so many other families in their town. She was the middle of three sisters. Her older sister, Rose, still lived at home with her baby and her younger sister, Amanda, was a shining beacon of perfection and athleticism next to her large, awkward sisters.

Ioni *was* very awkward, she had to admit. She had made it to her final year of high school without ever having a boyfriend, the epitome of the teenaged experience as she saw it. At five feet eleven inches tall, she towered over most other girls, and her curvy figure seemed grotesque to her when compared to the more fashionable bony figures she saw all around her. Her friends did their best to combat her self-loathing, always assuring her of her beauty and winning personality, but she couldn't internalize their words. All she saw when she looked in the mirror was a towering bulk who wore loud clothes to cover up the endless faults reflected back at her.

Nathan let out a long high-pitched whistle. The group looked in the direction of his pointing finger.

"What the...?" Adam said.

"Oh no," Arlie said, laughing.

"Another goth?" Ioni asked, smiling.

"Another goth," Nathan confirmed.

The tall, pale, heavyset, and bald kid was wearing a long black trench coat over black pants, something only the edgiest of personalities dared to do after Columbine. His eyes were lined heavily with black liner and his ears were laden with silver earrings of all shapes and sizes. He was standing alone, staring at their little group. Ioni felt a rush of heat run up her neck when his eyes grazed over her, returned, and settled on her face. His stare was even and intense.

"Let's be hospitable and welcome the new school freak," Nathan said, waving to the new stranger.

Ioni drummed her fingers on the table nervously as he approached them. For such a large guy, he moved lightly. His gaze stayed on the group as he approached them, and Ioni noticed that he refused to push his body up against the wall to avoid the other students passing by him, and he never lowered his eyes to stare at the floor as she often did.

"Greetings!" Nathan said, standing and shaking the stranger's hand. "We were shocked to see another goth in this place, man. Hi! My name's Nathan!"

A warm smile spread across the stranger's full lips and he put a large hand on Nathan's slender shoulder.

"My name is Raber Belliveau." He looked around the cafeteria, at the other tables and then again at the group. There was a note of desperate hope in his voice when he spoke again. "Please tell me you're all seniors," he said.

"Thankfully, yes," Nathan said. "All four of us are Class of 2002, on a glorious countdown until our tenure in the public school system is at an end."

"I'm glad we agree on that sentiment," Raber said, eying Ioni. He turned fully to her and held out his hand. "I saw you from across the room. I'm sorry if I look like a creep, but I just couldn't stop staring at you. Hi, I'm Raber, and you are?"

It felt like gallons of hot blood rushed into Ioni's face all at once as she blushed heavily. Nobody, *nobody* had ever talked to her like that before. Raber looked down at her with amusement in his eyes, waiting for her to gather herself enough to respond. She looked at the trusted faces of her friends and nearly bust out laughing when she saw them all wearing a uniform look of gape-mouthed shock. She looked back at Raber, into his lovely, green eyes. They were wreathed with luxurious, long eyelashes. She blushed when she realized that she had been quiet for too long. She swallowed hard and took his large, cool hand.

"I'm Ioni," she said, relieved that her voice sounded calm and even. "I, uh, I don't think you're being a creep. I didn't really notice you staring at us."

"You," Raber corrected. "I was staring at you. At first I did notice the group. I can't tell you how relieved I was to see a group of similarly-fashioned folks at this podunk school, but once I got a good look at you and your amazing face and that gorgeous hair of yours, I think I almost crossed the creepy line." He leaned ever so slightly closer to her and seemed to almost breathe her in.

Ioni choked on her own saliva and started coughing.

Nathan, Arlie, and Adam burst out laughing at that. Ioni felt a cloud of tension dissipate from the group and she smiled down at her lap. Raber straightened to his full height and joined in on the giggles, still looking down at her.

"You never talk to me that way, you jerk!" Arlie said, playfully swatting Adam on the arm.

"I've seen you at your worst, woman!" Adam said, smiling. "Let's see him talk to her like that after he's seen her with a raging case of the puking flu!"

"And you two are?" Raber asked, still smiling.

"I'm Arlie and this is my long-time love monkey, Adam."

"These two have been a couple since before puberty," Nathan interjected. "The whole school has a sort of long-running bet about how long they'll be together. They just keep beating the odds."

"I like that," Raber said. "This is my fourth school since I started kindergarten and this is the first time that I've met a long-term couple that lasted more than a year or two. Maybe you guys are the real deal."

"Don't get them talking about it," Nathan said, putting his hands over his ears. "They don't believe in soul mates or true love but then again, these assholes have the luxury to say that while the rest of us losers keep looking for the next short-term heartburn."

"But enough about us," Adam said, throwing a wad of paper at Nathan with a smile.

"Yes, enough about you," Nathan said, dodging the paper. "Raber, I'm sitting here and I'm thinking that maybe you should answer us some questions about your intentions toward our beloved Ioni here. She's gorgeous, for sure, but are you some creepy predator hoping for a swim in her cleavage or are you really just some poor schmo that got gobsmacked by her? I'm not bringing the claws out, yet, but I've been this girl's bestie for a while and I'm not gonna be okay with someone who just wants to use her as a grope-fest. I know I'm scrappy and your size, frankly, scares the sparkles right out of my eyeliner, but I will not allow you to make an easy meal out of my girl here."

Raber looked Ioni in the eyes and spoke to Nathan, never pulling his penetrating gaze from her.

"I'm not a predator," he said. "Gobsmacked is a good way to describe my reaction to seeing this beautiful creature. Honestly, I hadn't noticed her splendid womanliness until you pointed it out." Ioni frowned and crossed her arms over her chest. She was uncomfortable being talked about like she wasn't there. Raber went on.

"I was brought in by her beautiful, shiny, black hair and her magnificent lips." Raber laughed and ran a hand over his shining head. "I'm making her uncomfortable. I'll stop. I have no real plans for Ioni as of now, except to just let her know that when I first saw her, I was so taken with her that my lungs could not draw air. I hope to be friends with all of you and that includes Ioni. That's all."

"Well, *damn*," Arlie said, fanning herself, laughing.

"No shit, my friend," Nathan said. "Why can't I find a silver-tongued guy like that?"

"Okay, that's enough of me making an ass out of myself," Raber said. "How about we all compare schedules so I can hope to run into some of you during the day?"

Schedule cards were produced and there were pleased mumbles when Adam noticed that Raber was in a lot of the advanced and college-level classes with him. Then Nathan burst out laughing, pointing at the cards.

"Oh man, we *all* went the predictable route with art class? Could we be any more cliché?" Nathan said.

"It's not cliché! It's the easy class!" Ioni laughed. Art was great because Ms. Mimm, the art teacher, was an old hippie who let the students mess around as long as they took time to admire her work from time to time. They weren't really expected to produce much themselves. They told Raber as much.

"Why are high school art teacher always hippies?" Raber asked, laughing. "I mean, it's that way everywhere I go! Does Ms. Mimm have a little studio somewhere in town? Like a cheap little mission-style house that is just covered with her weird paintings and clay sculptures?"

"Jesus, dude. You describe it perfectly," Adam said.

"Well I have no reason to feel displaced here, then," Raber said.

"Look, Raber," Adam began. "We've got a few classes together and obviously we shop at the same stores so how about we exchange our personal information and just go ahead and call this initiation done?"

"That's a good idea," Nathan said. "Newest member of the weirdo club, welcome!"

Pieces of notebook paper were produced while phone numbers, and ICQ and AIM handles were written down. When Ioni passed her paper to Raber, he looked it over carefully and tucked it into his coat. He put the papers from everybody else into his 5-Star binder. It was a deliberate act that she was meant to see, but her friends' smirking faces showed that they'd seen it too.

The bell rang and the group disbanded, everyone heading to their respective homerooms. Ioni smiled to herself when she noticed a slight bounce to her step. That year, things were going to be much different for her. She just knew it.

CHAPTER TWO

School had been in session for two weeks. A comfortable routine had been established and the group of outsiders had gained a sense of comfort and trust with their new addition. Raber proved to be easy to laugh with and extremely likable, if not a bit hard to understand. He had a way with words that baffled the group at times. He spoke in a formal manner, like someone from a different era. But that didn't make Raber as unique as one might assume. Every generation of teenagers will try to find a way to not only set themselves apart from their parents, but also from their own peers. Language was Raber's form of expression of individuality so that his looks set him apart from the masses, but the way he spoke set him apart from his friends.

Although Raber was ultimately accepted, there were some initial misgivings. Nathan, the truly accepting one of the bunch, was quick to like Raber while Arlie had a few mild gripes about him.

"He's weird, isn't he? I mean, that's not just me talking. The guy is weird," she said.

"He's a little strange, yeah, but I like him. He's nice enough," Adam answered.

"It's the way he talks, I guess," Arlie said. "Who in high school talks that way? Nobody. And I thought Nathan was the limit of crazy-talking."

"Now listen here, lady-bits," Nathan interjected. "How dare you try to proclaim who is and is not 'weird.' How the hell can you be weird among the weird? That's not right, and you know it."

They were all sprawled out on the enormous sectional sofa in Adam's family room watching trash TV. Ioni was cuddled into the inside corner while Nathan was sprawled out with his head resting on one of the arms, his feet on her lap. Adam was propped against the other arm and Arlie was leaning on him. Ioni noticed how Adam's hand rested comfortably between Arlie's thighs. She envied that comfortable familiarity that wasn't necessarily sexual.

"I'm not condemning the guy, I'm just still trying to get used to him is all. I like him, he's totally nice, but I mean, did you hear how he talked to Ioni that first day? I didn't know whether to be happy or terrified for her," Arlie said.

"I actually had a similar moment, there," Ioni said. "I've never had a guy really notice me before, not like that at least. He scared the hell out of me. But it really seems like he's just a normal guy like the rest of us. Sure, he's super smart like Adam and he dresses weird but he's not murdering neighborhood cats or anything. I'm flattered that he has a crush on me, and I'm *really* happy that he isn't acting like a crazy stalker. Aside from a bunch of compliments, he's never really cornered me or tried to ask me out or anything. I like that he made his feelings known, but backed off right after, like he knew he came on a little too strong."

"That's beautifully put," Nathan said. "Really. That's like the perfect way to describe what he's done. It's like he planted a seed and now he's waiting to see what comes of it. I don't care what you guys think, I like that giant bald dude."

"He is big, isn't he?" Adam said. "He might be intimidating if he weren't so soft-spoken and so....so...what's the word I want? Genteel. That's it. Like he was born into aristocracy or something."

"And nobody else finds that sort of scary?" Arlie asked.

"Honestly, and I know this is so girl-with-a-crush stupid of me, but I kind of like it. He really expresses himself. It's beautiful." Ioni said.

"Well since I'm in the minority, I guess I'll just eat it," Arlie laughed. "I trust you guys and if you say he's cool, then he's cool."

And that was the end of it. Raber was one of them.

They were in art class one day painting small plaster of Paris trinkets. Their workstation was little more than a long table and they sat on simple wooden stools. The room was on a corner of the building, so it had windows on two of its walls. Rough outlines of Ms. Mimm's future works of art were hung over the neglected chalkboard.

Ioni was daydreaming as she smeared a creamy-orange color over her seashell-shaped trinket box when Raber's voice startled her back to reality.

"I think we've got an easy repartee, the four of us, so maybe it's time that I reveal something about myself to you, my friends," he said.

They all looked at him, their hands paused above their work.

"I'm not just into the goth clothing line, you know. I feel the need to explain this because I get the idea that you guys are only into the look. No judgment," Raber said, looking down at his tiny half-painted turtle.

"What's up, dude?" Adam asked.

"Well, I want to tell you something about myself, but I really don't want to scare any of you off. You see, I'm not trying to recruit or anything, this is just something you really should know about me if we're going to be friends. I've had an interest in the occult since I was thirteen. I've read a lot about it and I'm on a path right now. I found a blog written by a witch and her writings are helping me a lot in my decision to become a Wiccan. I know maybe this might be a bit much, especially in a town like this. It might become a burden on you guys to associate with me."

The original three glanced at each other before breaking out into quiet, breathy giggles. For a moment, a dark look passed over Raber's face. It was obvious that he was on the defensive because he thought that they were making fun of him.

"My friend, there isn't a one of us sitting here with you now who hasn't dabbled in the occult at one time or another," Nathan said, seeing the look on Raber's face. "Just because we chose as individuals not to go down that path, that doesn't mean that we're going to judge you. And umm, by the way, being friends with you will *not* be a burden on any of us. Have you met *me*? If the hayseed redneck fag-beaters in this school can accept me at least on a formal basis, I'm sure they'll be cool with you. And if they're not, who the hell cares? We're out of here in less than a year."

"There's no judgment from people like us," Arlie said. "That's the last thing you need to worry about."

"I took an interest in becoming a cyberwitch for a while. I found an online coven and everything," Adam said. "If you wanna know some sites, I can get that for you, no problem."

"Oh, thanks, but no. I'm old fashioned. I really feel the need to have physical ritual and motions. I'm going to try to find a coven that practices in-person, not online. But thank you," Raber said, obviously relieved.

Talk settled into the usual chit-chat about classes and gossip before the bell rang. There was one more period after art class, and Ioni was happy for it. She had some thinking to do.

Later that night, alone in her room, Ioni messaged Raber on the messenger client preferred by the group which had a green flower for a logo.

"I have a question."

His reply came back almost immediately.

"Sure."

"You said you weren't looking to recruit anybody in this interest you have in becoming Wiccan. Does that mean you don't want anybody to join you?"

This time there was more of a pause.

"I didn't want anybody to feel pressured, but I'm not adverse to someone going down this path with me if that's what they want," he said.

Ioni became annoyed that he was leaving it so open. He was being careful and not inviting her, which was what she wanted.

"Well, what would you think if I said that I've been looking into Wicca for a while too and that until you said something today, I hadn't decided if I wanted to try it or not?"

"I'm not sure what to say unless I know what you decided."

Ioni cursed at her computer screen and she screamed into a pillow. She gathered her thoughts and her courage and sent a reply.

"I think I was scared about going into it alone, but now that you're doing it, I think I might want to give it a serious go."

"With me?" he replied.

This time Ioni giggled. She was anxious and nervous.

"Yes, with you. Would it be okay if we did this together?"

"Ioni, you've just made my day."

She sighed heavily, her nervous energy mellowing. That was the first real conversation that she and Raber had had since that first day of school. She had fantasized about different conversations and how they would work out, but this was better than anything her mind had made.

"So what happens now?" she messaged. There was a long wait before her computer chimed at her with his reply and when she saw his reply, she knew that he had needed to gather his courage to send it.

"Can I come over?"

Ioni stared at her screen, a smile cemented on her lips. She was frozen in surprise. She knew that by starting this that she and Raber would be spending a lot of alone time together, but she hadn't imagined that it would be this soon. She knew him to be forward, but that last message surprised her.

She must have been staring at her screen for longer than she thought because it startled her by chirping again with another message from him.

"...or we can meet somewhere neutral. I didn't mean to push myself on you, it just might be easier if we could get this hashed out in person."

She sighed in relief. A neutral place would be much better.

"We could go to Eat N' Park and talk. It's never really busy this time of night. Do you want to meet there or carpool?" she replied.

Both of them had their own cars and while it would have been perfectly easy for them to just meet at the restaurant, Ioni was curious about what the tone of the dinner would be. They could take her car since she was closer, but it would make more sense if Raber picked her up since she was on his way. She laughed at herself when she noticed that she was drumming her fingers on her desk waiting for his reply.

"I can come pick you up. I'll be there in fifteen."

That was it. In Ioni's mind at least, it was a date. It would be the first date that she had been on since she was fixed up by Nathan the previous year with a boy from a neighboring school. That had consisted of a few phone calls, sitting next to each other at a basketball game, and then nothing. The most exciting thing to come out of that sad mess was the soft pretzel he'd bought for her at the game.

Ioni jumped up and examined herself in the mirror. She was still such a novice at dating that she didn't know the etiquette on whether or not it was acceptable to wear the same clothes she'd worm at school that day. But did Raber know that they were going on a date? She knew she'd look strange getting all blown out for just a friendly dinner. Strapped for time, Ioni opted to just refresh her perfume and apply some lip gloss.

She grabbed her purse and sprinted down the stairs and out the front door. She was far too anxious to worry about how it would look for her to be waiting for Raber. She sat on the cool concrete step leading up to the porch and folded her hands in her lap.

The sky was a mixture of orange and purple as dusk settled over the world. It was still warm at that time of the year and the crickets were chirping in the bushes surrounding her home. She could hear young children playing down the road as well as somebody's television blasting through an open window. Ioni closed her eyes and let the warm air kiss her face and neck.

She heard a car approaching and opened her eyes just in time to see it cruise by. It wasn't the car she was waiting for. She hated waiting.

Again she closed her eyes and tried to focus on the warm night air on her skin. As she tilted her head slightly to the side, she felt her soft hair brush along the side of her neck as it fell forward onto her chest. She inhaled deeply and pictured Raber kneeling before her. She imagined his big hands reaching out to her. At first his hands and strong fingers ran up her forearms. As he leaned closer, he touched either side of her neck and stroked outwards and down her shoulders. Ioni pictured his shocking green eyes half-lidded and watching his seduction. In her mind, his hands reached up and brushed her hair back to expose the nape of her neck. With the skin now exposed, Raber leaned forward and softly brushed his warm dry lips along her neck and down her shoulder. Ioni felt a barrage of shivers shoot down her spine. She exhaled deeply.

"Wherever you are right now, it sure looks like fun," a voice said right in front of her.

Her eyes snapped open and there stood the object of her fantasy. When her eyes met his, his full lips stretched over his nearly perfect teeth in an amused smile.

Ioni stammered like an idiot before giving up and burying her head in her hands.

At this Raber laughed.

"I was listening to my neighbor's TV, actually," she said.

Raber, still smiling, shook his head.

Thankfully the awkward moment passed and Ioni stood to follow Raber to his car, a yellow Pontiac Sunfire.

He surprised Ioni by holding her hand all the way to the passenger side and opening the door for her. She got into the seat as carefully as she could, praying that she didn't look like a clumsy clod.

"Do you want to tell me why you didn't say anything in front of the others about this interest of yours? I doubt seriously that this embarrasses you. You all seem more than tolerant," he said, starting the engine.

"To be honest, I am a little embarrassed about it. I'm not embarrassed to tell them about it, they're cool, but I was embarrassed to do this by myself. I was scared I'd get caught up in something weird or sketchy. You see, for a while Adam was really interested in it and because of that, Arlie was interested. By extension, Nathan and I started looking into it. Nathan was the first to announce that it wasn't his thing, which I found weird. I thought he'd be all over it, but he said that he just couldn't really connect to people who respected nature that much because he'd have to give up some of his favorite makeup."

"That's totally understandable once you get to know Nathan," he said, laughing. "What happened with Adam and Arlie?"

"Arlie lost interest. She said there were too many gods and goddesses to keep track of. She's agnostic, but she's also really non-committal and I think actually having to pick any sort of religion is more than she wants to do. She didn't ever try to discourage Adam from looking into it, but I think once he realized that it was something that he'd be doing alone he sort of dropped off. He was the one who did the most serious research with it, though. He actually contacted Wiccans online and asked them a bunch of questions. Adam's big on research and being totally prepared for stuff. But I think once Arlie lost interest and he learned all he could, it wasn't new and cool anymore."

As she was talking, Raber had parked and opened her car door for her, taking her hand and leading her into the restaurant. She was mildly distracted from her story because it took a long moment for her to realize that she was walking hand-in-hand with a guy and that they looked like a couple. She was impressed with Raber's smooth execution.

They were seated quickly and had ordered drinks and food. The little restaurant had only a few patrons that night so there was no need to censor their talk. She had worried about people overhearing them, but the relative public privacy was a comfort.

"What about you?" Raber asked. "Did you ever abandon the pursuit or did you just let it go because your friends all lost interest?"

"I mostly let it go because of my friends, but I did always keep this secret desire to look deeper into it. It's not something that you can really just walk out and find in a town like this, and I really didn't feel cool about doing it by myself. If I'd had the group aspect of my friends, I would've probably gone whole hog with it."

Their drinks were brought to them and Ioni thanked the waitress. She looked across the table at Raber and he was smiling at her. She smiled back in a questioning way.

"You're really polite," he said. "It took that waitress way too long to bring us drinks. I mean look at this place, it's empty, and she took at least five full minutes to do a task that is basically dumping ice into cups and sticking them under a spout. Don't think I'm an asshole or anything, I wasn't going to chew her out, but she definitely didn't deserve that sweet smile and thank you, either."

Ioni frowned. That little outburst of annoyance surprised her.

"I guess I was busy talking and didn't notice that she took a long time," she said. "But even if I had noticed, jobs like these suck and I have to try to give these people a little patience. Also, I don't want them spitting in anything I'm going to eat or drink."

"Fair enough," Raber said, laughing.

"The food and drinks aren't really all that important, are they?" she asked. "I mean, I thought we were here to talk and have a conversation about this new venture."

"Of course, you're right," Raber said. "I'm easily annoyed, but you'll learn that about me quickly enough. I'm sorry. I was just charmed by your sweetness is all."

Ioni looked down at her lap and smiled. He was so smooth and knew exactly what to say. She could more easily see the green of his eyes in the harsh light and just how long his eyelashes were. She liked the way he looked just then. There was still a dark look to him with the shaved head, ear metal, and hint of eye-makeup, but she could see more of *him*. There was something strangely intimate about seeing a goth kid slightly stripped down like that. He had noticed her studying him and was smiling again.

"Are you waiting for horns to sprout?" he asked.

"No," she laughed. "I was just admiring your face." She felt herself blushing. "You have the prettiest eyes. I was shocked when I noticed how green they are."

"I'm flattered that you noticed. I'm used to people only seeing the metal and clothes and makeup on me. I didn't know that you were looking that closely," he said.

"I actually noticed your eyes the first day of school when you made it a point to introduce yourself to me. When you leaned down I could see the pretty green color and your super long lashes," Ioni said. She realized she was being forward and flattering, but she couldn't seem to stop herself.

Raber's eyebrows shot up in surprise. He sat back and looked at Ioni in a strange way. He didn't say anything for the longest time.

"You noticed things like that the first few minutes of meeting me?" he asked.

"Well, yeah."

"Really," he said, frowning now.

"Really. What's up?"

"I don't know. People don't usually notice anything about me other than the facade I create. Truthfully, I'm completely bowled over that a *girl,* and a *pretty* girl at that, noticed something like that about me. I've always just been a weirdo sitting alone in a corner, not getting any sort of female attention. For you of all people to notice and admire something physical about me is surprising."

"Me of all people? What does that mean?" she asked.

"Well," Raber began. "I made it pretty clear from the start that I'm completely taken by you. You're probably the most beautiful person that I've ever physically been around. When I saw you from across the cafeteria that first day, I was dumbfounded by how you affected me. You're an ideal to me; something I could never dream of having. So when you pay me a compliment like that, it's surreal."

"You're talking about me like I'm some sort of cheerleader or movie star. I'm just an average person...well below average if you ask me. I mean, I'm a weirdo, too. I've never had anybody compliment me or show any sort of interest in me beyond staring at my chest. Well, besides you. You surprised me by coming on the way you did that first day. I'm totally not used to that," she said, staring at her lap.

"I find it surprising that you aren't constantly complimented. You are unbelievably beautiful. Your hair is the first thing I noticed. You have such lovely hair. And then I saw your face, and I was just floored. Those luscious lips, those blue eyes, that perfect skin. You're amazing. And you're tall which is great. I'm tall and a lot of girls just seem tiny to me. I like being close to you. You don't make me feel freakishly proportioned."

"I don't think you're freakishly proportioned," Ioni said. "I like your size. I like pretty much everything about you. If I'm being honest here, that first day you scared me, but these past couple of weeks and getting to know you, I've come to realize that I'm really attracted to you. I'm not sure what to do about it, but I know that I like you. I like being near you and I like knowing that I'm gonna see you. I just like you."

Ioni had a moment of panic after realizing that she had just made herself extremely vulnerable by expressing her feelings so freely. If he laughed at her, she would walk home and quit school. Raber could hurt her or take advantage of those feelings she'd just expressed. Sorry for her self-perceived folly, she looked into the green eyes across the table.

"What to do about it?" he asked. "At this point, we've admitted to each other a mutual attraction and interest for further exploration of that. I think the only rational next step is to start dating, don't you think? Don't let me be presumptuous. Is this something that interests you?"

Ioni blinked. What had he just proposed? Was this how a guy asked you to be his girlfriend?

"Uhhh, what?" she asked, shaking her head. "I'm sorry, but what's going on here? I get the mutual attraction thing, but are you proposing that we become an item? Is that what's going on?"

"Did I go too far?" Raber asked, putting his hands up in a defensive gesture.

"No! No, I was just confused. This conversation took a weird turn and I'm lost."

Raber smiled and sighed. He put his hands down and reached across the table, inviting her to place her hand in his.

"What I'm proposing, Ioni, is that we further explore this mutual interest by becoming an item. I'm proposing that I call you my girlfriend and you call me your boyfriend. I'm proposing that we pair off and get to know each other on several different levels of intimacy. Is this something that you would find agreeable?"

Smiling, she could feel herself blushing profusely. She didn't want to answer immediately, but found herself speaking, almost as if against her own will.

"I've never had a boyfriend before. I'm not sure of how to do this."

"I've never had a girlfriend before. I'm also not sure of what to do. But I am sure that I want to get to know you better. I want to be close to you and be able to have you for my own. I've desired this since the first moment I laid eyes on you."

"Well," she said. "Since you put it that way, I accept your proposal."

They were holding hands and looking at each other, a newly minted couple. Luckily, their waitress arrived with their food before anything could get awkward.

"I'm not sure what to do now. I feel weird." She laughed. "I'm almost eighteen years old! I'm almost old enough to vote, but I'm totally lost on what to do right now!"

"Eat your food," Raber said with a smile. "That's a good start."

Ioni started on her hamburger. She watched her newly proclaimed boyfriend. His eating was meticulous. There were no smudges of ketchup on his face and not a splatter of grease on his plate. Meanwhile, her hamburger was falling apart on her and she had to finish it with a fork. He caught her watching him and smiled.

"Let's continue our discussion about Wicca, that's why we came on this date after all," he said.

"Okay," Ioni said, relieved to be rid of the uncomfortable silence.

"How about we start by you telling me what you know and what interests you about Wicca. We can go from there." Raber said.

"Well, I wasn't really raised in a religious home. Both of my parents are intellectuals, and for some reason, religion doesn't fit their worldview. They don't judge, it's just not important to them. Officially, I'm agnostic. I believe there's *something* out there, I just don't know the details. When we were all considering Wicca or Paganism as an interest, I was really drawn to the notion of a nurturing goddess. I liked the idea that all of our energies are in sync with the energies of the earth and that the earth was our source. It was something that just made sense to me."

Raber was nodding, chewing his food. He wiped his hands on a napkin even though they were clearly clean, pushed his empty plate away, and sat back in the green and maroon vinyl booth.

"That's probably the best reason I could have expected to hear. You don't sound like you're in love with the fashion of what it would mean to be a 'witch', you sound like you really appreciate the core values of the craft. See, me? I'm in love with an organization that has all of this old, antiquated ritual attached to it. I'm also really interested in the fact that I'm in charge and responsible for what happens in my life. If I do bad, it comes back to me threefold. If I do good, it comes back to me threefold. I don't have to wait until I'm dead to either be rewarded or punished for the choices that I make in my life. I like that I get to be in control. Maybe my reasons come from a place of my being a major control freak, but that's why it appeals to me."

"I think that if you decide to choose a religion, that it should be a personal thing. I think everybody has different reasons," Ioni said, shrugging.

"Exactly," Raber said, smiling at her. "I suppose that our next course of action is to discuss whether or not we want to be solitary witches or if we want to join a coven."

"Well, what do you prefer?"

"Are you not sure or are you afraid to speak your desire?"

"I...uhhh...I'm not sure what to say. I don't want to say something that would make you change your mind on what you want," she said.

"I assure you, that won't happen. I will *always* make my side known. So please, what is it that you were hoping to happen in this?"

"I'm really nervous about joining a coven. I'm not sure how I could be able to fit in. But I also think that I won't get the full experience unless I join one. I like the idea of having a mentor and being able to witness rituals firsthand. What about you?" she asked, unsure. She hated how obvious her lack of confidence was in that moment. She sounded like an idiot.

"I really want to join a coven. I agree with you that the richness of the experience would be much more potent if we were part of a group," he said. "Are we agreed that we would like to join a coven? Just so I'm certain."

"Yes," Ioni said. "I agree that we should join a coven."

"Then I'll start looking into it," Raber said. "Now that we have some of these incidentals worked out on our venture into a new religion, shall we perhaps discuss the scheduling of a date? Or maybe just an alone meeting somewhere so that we can get better acquainted?"

Ioni smiled and eyed him. He was her boyfriend. How was that supposed to work? Would they have to always start with public dates to avoid things getting weird or, heaven forbid, messy? She looked into his face and realized that she was, for all intents and purposes, an adult, and that there was no need for her to play hard-to-get or to be shy about certain aspects of life. She had been curious about sex and sexual experiences, and she was old enough that most people expected that she was at least partially sexually experienced. That was far from the truth, and Ioni was finished with that being the state of her life.

"Aren't we having a date right now?" she asked coyly. "You picked me up, drove me here, we've been holding hands and we've established that we are now an exclusive couple. This sounds a lot like a date to me."

Raber pulled her knuckles up to his mouth and kissed them.

"You have me there," he said. "Well, since this is a date, shall we adjourn to another destination after this or shall I drop you off at your doorstep as fresh and virginal as I found you?

Ioni smiled.

"Maybe not quite as fresh as you found me," she said.

CHAPTER THREE

It was briefly awkward when Ioni told the rest of the friend group that she and Raber were a couple, but they warmed to the idea quickly. They had to admit that they were all curious as to when it was going to happen anyway and Ioni found herself wondering if her friends were hiding a betting pool concerning when she and Raber would get together.

On that first night, it turned out that she was an awkward chicken-shit. Raber had driven her home and walked her to her door where they stared at their feet for a few minutes before he placed a hand under her chin and lifted her eyes to his. He placed a soft, closed-mouthed kiss on her lips and whispered a goodbye into her ear before taking his leave. Ioni watched his retreating back, confused and disappointed. She stupidly assumed that he would know how to move things forward, but she realized her mistake and was angry with herself for leaving everything up to him. She was only sporadically and momentarily empowered by her imminent adulthood, and she needed to find a way to hold on to that mindset and make things happen for herself.

She hadn't quite given Raber enough credit, though. He was still learning and trying to be careful in his navigation of a physical relationship with her. She was quickly put at ease being physical with him because of that cautious attitude. He always made sure to ask her to tell him when she felt things were going too fast or too far.

Nearly a month had passed since that first night at the Eat N' Park, and Ioni was surprised at how free she was with Raber. She rarely told him to stop or slow down. Sex had not yet happened, but there was a fast and heated progression with their explorations. The first time that they were alone and in private, they had approached each other gingerly, but their shy kisses soon escalated to wandering hands and mouths. Ioni's own appetite surprised her. While she expected Raber to be the first to make the transition to the next step, she found herself making the first move more often than not.

They didn't overly prioritize their physical explorations of each other, however. As it turned out, exploring Wicca was becoming very important to the both of them. They had even found a coven, in a strange, but not entirely surprising place.

It happened in Art class. The group was quiet that day because Nathan was absent and Arlie and Adam were working together on a drawing. Because of that, Raber and Ioni were mumbling to each other about what they'd found in their research.

"When you join a coven, you can choose what they call a magical name," Raber was telling her. "It would be a name that you would keep secret from most people except for those extremely close to you."

"Why keep it secret?" Ioni asked.

"In Wicca, some believe that knowing someone or something's name, their *true* name, gives you power over them. So you would keep this name to yourself and only share it with people who you know wouldn't use it in order to have power over you," he answered.

"You two," Ms. Mimm interrupted.

Raber and Ioni jumped and looked up at her. Her graying dark blond hair was a halo of soft frizz. Her long, thin nose was turned slightly upwards and it gave the rest of her face a very dainty look.

"Stay after class for a few minutes, okay?" Ms. Mimm said.

"Okay," Raber said. He looked at Ioni with confusion on his face.

Ioni noticed that Arlie and Adam were gaping at them with questioning looks. Raber and Ioni both shrugged in answer.

"Were you two jerking each other off under the table or something? She sounded kind of mad," Adam whispered

"No, nothing like that," Raber answered. "We were just talking. Is she offended by Wicca? Maybe we shouldn't discuss things like that in school."

"I don't see why she'd get mad over us talking about that when Nathan sits here sometimes and talks about giving blowjobs to the guy that works the drive-thru window at KFC. Hell, she laughs about it sometimes when she thinks we're not looking, doesn't she Arlie?" Ioni laughed.

"Yes, she totally does," Arlie answered.

When the bell rang, Raber and Ioni gathered their belongings and walked to the front of the room where Ms. Mimm had a table set up as a desk. It was covered in small potted plants and sketches from both herself and her students. She was standing behind it looking at them.

"I can't talk about things like this during school hours. The PTA would have a fit, but here," she handed Raber a piece of paper. "That's the address to my studio in case you didn't already know where it is and there are times to come see me. I think I can be of some help to you two," she said. She smiled and gestured for them to be on their way. Raber and Ioni exchanged confused looks and then looked back to Ms. Mimm. She gestured again for them to go.

"What the hell," Raber said to Ioni when they got to the hallway.

"I don't know, what the hell," Ioni answered, taking Raber's arm. They walked side-by-side down the hall until they reached Raber's class. He leaned down and kissed her neck, making her giggle.

Later that night, Raber picked up Ioni so they could visit Ms. Mimm at her studio. In the note she had given Raber, she had stated that after seven p.m. would be the best time to visit.

They piled into his car and made their way to downtown Stearnsville.

Ms. Mimm's studio was a small but immaculately kept home. It wasn't quite the mission-style home that Raber had theorized. It was just a little house with white clapboard siding and large picture windows.

They approached the honey-colored front door hand-in-hand. The sign next to the door read, "Studio Adare."

Upon entering, a small electronic "DING DONG" made Ioni jump. They could hear rustling coming from one of the back rooms. Ioni looked around at the warmly lit studio. She had always assumed art studios tended to have harsher lighting and would be painted white in order to showcase the art. But Ms. Mimm's studio had richly decorated area rugs on the wooden floor and the walls were painted a sage-green color. The whole place smelled of a warmly spiced incense that was extremely pleasant.

"I'm coming! Just a sec!" Ms. Mimm's voice called from the back. A moment later she walked into the large room and smiled at them.

"I'm very glad that you came," she said, a smile on her face. "Let's sit down over here and have us a little chit-chat, okay?"

Raber and Ioni sat on the large, buttery, leather sofa at the end of the room and Ms. Mimm sat next to them in the matching armchair. She seemed to be struggling to organize her thoughts. They sat quietly and stared at her, wide-eyed and curious.

"Um...let's see. How do I begin here? Umm..." Ms. Mimm laughed. She tossed her head, whipping her long frizzy hair off her face, and sighed heavily. "Okay, here it is. I am a witch."

"*You?*" Raber asked, a crooked smile on his face. "A witch? Really?"

"Really," Ms. Mimm nodded. "I am a Wiccan witch and I have been for twenty-three years."

The pair stared at her. It shouldn't have come as the surprise that it was. In their mostly conservative Christian town, one just never expected to have someone confess to being a Wiccan. The two of them thought that they would have to go to a larger town in order to find other Wiccans, but it appeared that their small town had a larger underbelly than they had originally thought.

"So you overheard us talking today and, what? You want to help us, you said?" Raber asked.

"Yes," Ms. Mimm replied. "You see, I was a solitary witch for years and years and I had to do a lot of learning on my own, and it was actually really difficult trying to figure a lot of this out just from books. This was before the internet, you see, and our local library wasn't at all helpful. I was able to order what were called "occult books" through the mail and while they helped with a basic idea of the craft, I found that I still felt a little lost. I had no idea how to go about finding other witches, especially in this area, but a chance meeting with a man at the Apple Butter Festival broke the wall down for me. He was a traveling vendor selling jewelry, daggers, and other little things. I was looking at some homemade jewelry that he was selling and noticed a beautiful necklace with a Lapis Lazuli piece. I picked it up and was examining it when he came over to me. He said, 'Lapis Lazuli is a lovely color on you,' and I said 'I'm actually interested in using it for meditation.' I didn't feel nervous about talking about meditation with this man since he wasn't a local. I remember he gave me the strangest smile and took the necklace from my hands. 'This is a chip. If you want something bigger that will help with your brow chakra, come to this store and look around. My friend Bedelia owns it and she can help you,' and he handed me a card. The card was very simple. All that was on it was the word "Bedelia's" and a street address. I was bowled over when I saw that the store was in North View."

Ioni was engrossed in Ms. Mimm's story. North View was a tiny extension of Stearnsville that was mostly residential. Her grandparents lived there. How many times could she have driven past this Bedelia's in her life?

"I went to the store the very next day. It's just a normal looking 1960s split-level house. There's a small sign in the front yard that says 'Bedelia's,' and nothing else. It's extremely low-key and if you didn't have any clues pointed out to you, you could assume anything about what kind of place it is. Instead of a normal front door like you'd see on any normal house, it had a shop door, like glass and a sign saying they're open, so I assumed it would be all right if I just walked in. You know how with split-level houses when you walk in you are on a landing and you can either go up or down stairs? Well I went up first because it was illuminated better. What I saw was gonzo! There were hundreds of books, thousands of candles, and a bunch of small glittering things hanging from the ceiling. It looked and smelled exactly how you would expect a witch's store to look and smell. There was a large bar-looking area and there was a middle-aged woman standing behind it looking at me. I was actually scared to approach her, but she talked first which helped. She asked me what I was looking for, so I told her about my little exchange with the vendor at the festival. She smiled and nodded to herself and then she asked me if I was a curious person or was I actually a practicing Pagan or Wiccan. I told her that I considered myself a self-taught Wiccan but that I was also a little lost. She told me then that she was a Wiccan priestess and that if I wanted, she would mentor me and initiate me into her coven. I was so overwhelmed with the kindness of her offer, she'd just met me, but I was also bowled over that there was a coven of witches in our area. They'd managed to keep their presence completely secret." Ms. Mimm ran her hand over her frizzy hair and leaned back into the large armchair. "Our coven is very traditional in that you have to learn and train for a year and day before you can be initiated. I mentored under the lady, whose name is not Bedelia, by the way. Bedelia was the magical name of her mother, also a Wiccan priestess. My mentor's name is Karen, but her magical name is still unknown to her. She says that the goddess has yet to whisper it to her, even though she's practiced the craft for over forty years at this point.

"You see, not everybody picks a magical name at the time of initiation. It has to be a name that has importance and the initiate must have a significant amount of reverence for that name. It isn't something that's picked all willy-nilly because it sounds neat. It's a very big deal to have a magical name, so not all of us have one. And also, out of us that have a magical name, not all of us believe in keeping it secret. Some choose to have their name legally changed to their magical name. I didn't go that far, but I display my magical name at the front of this studio."

"Adare?" Raber asked. Raber pronounced the word as it looked, *ah-DAH-ray*. At that, Ms. Mimm smiled a large and warm smile.

"The name is Gaelic. It means 'oak grove' and it's pronounced *arth-dara*. That's the name the goddess whispered to me when I was initiated. The oak tree is symbolic to me because it represents strength, endurance, and wisdom. These are all qualities that I hoped to gain in my place in my coven."

There was a thoughtful silence then. So much to absorb in such a little amount of time. Ioni had a moment to wonder at the various strange and fast-moving turns her life had taken recently.

"That was a lot of information, Ms. Mimm," Ioni said.

"Look, I think since I just opened up about probably the most intimate detail of my life, outside of school you can go ahead and call me Sarah. It feels weird you being so formal with me now. Just don't do it in school."

"Okay, that's appropriate," Raber said. "Well now that the cat's out of the bag, what do we do about it? Can we meet Karen? Can we go to Bedelia's? Do we need a letter of recommendation to get her to talk to us? What kinds of supplies do we need to start learning? Are you offering to be our mentor?"

Ms. Mimm held up her hands and started laughing.

"Whoa, slow down, okay? What I'm doing is offering to be your mentor on the condition that Karen approves of it. She's my superior in the coven and must agree to new initiates. Of course she's gonna want to meet you and I should be with you when this happens. If she accepts you as initiates, you will then train with me for a year and a day before going through your initiations into the coven. But before we can go and meet Karen, I have a few questions for you two. There are some prerequisites to being able to become an initiate."

"Okay," Raber said.

"I'm ready," Ioni answered.

"Okay, then," Sarah said. "Are both of you eighteen years old at this point? I know you're both seniors, but I have to be sure. This might not be a thing in other covens, but it protects us from angry parents who don't approve of the lifestyle and I happen to agree with it. We're teaching, not indoctrinating or brainwashing. You have to be legal adults."

"Yeah, I turned eighteen on the first of September," Ioni answered.

"I turn eighteen in December," Raber answered.

"Okay," Sarah said. "That's good. We should be all right then. Okay, how is it that the two of you came to the decision to pursue a Wiccan lifestyle? I see that you both tend to like the goth or punk sort of fashion and I'm wondering if wanting to be a Wiccan is just another facet of your styling."

"Our choices to dress a certain way have a lot to do with our personalities and our personalities are what drive us to pursue certain interests. I'm not going to speak for anybody but myself, but I choose to dress goth and wear makeup because the romantic side of this look appeals to a nature in me that's buried most of the time. Dressing in all black and wearing crosses and getting tattooed and pierced is an expression of a desire to be creative and just more expressive than men are usually permitted to be. And since I am still young and allowed to express myself as outwardly as this, I'm going to do it while I can. I'm not looking to become Wiccan as a means to remain on the fringe of society. My personality and superior intellect are going to keep me on the fringe no matter what," Raber answered.

"I've always had an interest in religion," he continued. "I was never raised in a religious home. Both of my parents are atheists and seeing how I've always been groomed to be a skeptical intellectual, it would make sense to assume any religion would just be laughable to me. But that's not the case. I've always felt that there is some great power out there and that I am somehow a part of it all. I'm also interested in ritual and a sense of formality to a religion. Because of this, I did some research and Wicca seemed to really stick to me. I relate to it."

Sarah nodded, a smile on her face. She looked at Ioni.

"And you?" she asked.

Ioni looked down at her lap. She thought about how to make her feelings known without giving Sarah the idea that she was just in it to be with Raber. That wasn't the case at all. Being in it together with Raber was just a bonus.

"My parents are intellectuals, too," she began. "We're kind of, like, agnostic at my house. My parents don't think religion is something to make fun of, you know, but they aren't really interested in being part of a religion either. My older sister, Rose, found religion after she had her baby. She's not pushy about it or anything, but she said that it made her feel better knowing that there was someone looking out for her and her baby. That kind of got me thinking. She calmed down a lot after she joined that church and became a part of that whole thing, and she was really wild before."

"I started considering Wicca for myself when the whole group started looking into it together a while back," she continued. "But they all lost interest in it and I got self-conscious about trying to go into it by myself. I never really let go of the possibility of Wicca being something that might be for me. I honestly thought that it would be something that I could pursue in college maybe. It could be more anonymous that way. But then Raber came along and told us that he was going Wiccan and I let him know I've always been interested. But I didn't want to do this because of Raber, I just feel better having someone with me."

"I think we're okay," Sarah said, after a moment. "I just wanted to make sure that this wasn't going to be a passing fad. It would make me look bad in the eyes of my superior to bring two initiates before her only to have them decide that a year and a day of training was too much commitment. Now, you two do graduate high school in just a few months and then I assume it's on to college with you. Will that be a local thing? Will you be going to WVU or will you be going to one of the smaller local colleges? If you have intellectual parents, not going to college must be out of the question for the both of you."

"I'm gonna do the Stearnsville branch of Fairmont State. I'm gonna live at home to cut costs. My dad says that with tuition costs being what they are, I need to try to save money where I can with my education so that I'm not crippled by loans and bills when I graduate," Ioni answered.

"I'm going to WVU," Raber said. "But the campus is only a half hour, forty-five minutes away. I don't think it will interfere with my training."

Ioni's heart sank. That was the first time she heard of him moving to Morgantown. True, it was only a half hour away but there would be so many hours in between where they wouldn't see each other. He smiled at her and that smile told her what she wanted. *Everything is going to be fine*, the smile said. Ioni thanked the universe for Raber.

"This all sounds great," Sarah said. "I think we can go ahead and move forward with this. Are you both free on Saturday?"

"I'm free," Ioni said.

"I have no plans," Raber said.

"You guys come back here at noon on Saturday and we'll go to Bedelia's together and you can have your audience with Karen. She's going to ask you some questions, but I'm going to talk to her tonight and fill her in and give my opinion on you. This is very informal, so don't feel pressured, okay?"

Sarah smiled and stood up.

"I think that's all that I need from you two for now. Just remember, we're normal at school and won't talk of this, okay?"

"Okay," the pair said in unison.

"Then I'll see you tomorrow," Sarah said, leading them to the door.

Raber and Ioni filed out of the door and walked down the short walkway to the street where Raber had parked his car. By this time it was fully dark outside. Raber opened Ioni's door, as he always did and closed it for her once she was seated. He got in from his side and leaned over and kissed her long and deep, his tongue inside of her mouth, sending shivers both down her spine and up her thighs. She put one hand on the back of his head and the other over his heart. She loved feeling his chest rise and fall as his breathing got deeper and faster. Raber's hands found her breasts and massaged them. His thumb found her erect nipple through her shirt and rubbed it.

Ioni remembered that they were in a parked car on a fairly busy street. She pulled away from Raber and pushed his hand down to his own lap.

"We're in the street," she said, smiling.

"Okay," he said his voice low and husky. "My house is empty right now, let's go have some alone time and then I'll treat you to some Eat N' Park." His hand had wandered back up to her breast. She pushed it away with a smile.

"Okay. I have to be home by eleven, but we've got lots of time. It's what, 8:30?"

"Yes, about that," Raber said, pawing at her breasts again.

"So get moving, big guy, quit wasting time here!" she said, smiling.

Raber sighed heavily and started the car. Perhaps he drove faster than he should have, but Ioni was glad because she was just as anxious as he was. His hand kept going up her thigh as he drove and she kept pushing away before it went too high. Her hand would sometimes reach over to his lap where she would stroke the hard bulge in his pants. She loved how he would lift his hips into her hand and moan when she touched his hardness.

When Raber pulled into his driveway, he jumped out and ran to open her door. They ran to the side of the house, to the basement door, and Raber hurriedly unlocked it and dragged Ioni in behind him. As soon as he had shut the door behind him, he pinned her to the wall and began kissing her hungrily. Ioni returned his ferocious kisses and clumsily but eagerly took his coat off and threw it on the floor.

"How long do we have?" she asked, out of breath.

"They won't be back until after midnight. They always stay late at these lodge dinners. We've got lots of time," he answered, his face buried in her neck and then in her cleavage.

"Let's go somewhere where we can lay down," she said.

Without a word, Raber had her wrapped around him. Her legs were around his waist and he had his hand locked under her butt for support. He walked, still kissing her, to his bedroom. It wasn't the first time he'd picked her up like that and Ioni loved it. It made her feel like a "normal" small and skinny girl. He carried her effortlessly, never noticing what she thought of as flaws and seemed only to enjoy her.

He slammed the door behind them with his foot and they both fell onto his bed. He started tugging at her black stockings. As they started coming down and her thighs were exposed, he kissed the bare skin, licking every now and then. Ioni closed her eyes and moaned lightly. After her stockings were off, Raber slid her skirt down and flung it across the room. He started unbuttoning her red shirt and he was pleased to find a matching red lace bra. He buried his face in it and kissed her breasts, nipping lightly at them with his teeth. In response, Ioni wrapped her legs around him and thrust her hips up to him. He growled in a way that made Ioni's body ache for him.

Ioni slid his shirt up over his head and he tossed it away. She relished the feeling of his bare chest on her skin. He was warm and smooth and felt amazingly good. Raber was reaching behind her and messing with the clasp for her bra. He had proven to be a quick learner when it came to the science of unhooking a bra.

He slid it off, slowly revealing her naked breasts, and threw the bra across the room to the pile of already discarded garments and attached his mouth to her left nipple. His warm wet mouth made Ioni moan and wriggle beneath him. She started unbuttoning his pants when he pushed himself up and looked into her face.

"You tell me when to stop," he said to her.

"I won't be saying that tonight," she breathed. "I don't want to stop. Keep going."

He looked at her for a moment, weighing the situation before getting up on his knees and undoing his own pants and pulling them off. He then slid Ioni's panties off. He knelt down, looking at her before taking a large rough finger and stroking up and down her wetness. Ioni wriggled and bucked her hips, wanting him to insert the finger. When he did, she let out a loud moan and said his name.

"I need to get a condom," he said, his voice rough.

Ioni watched him as he crossed the room, naked and fully erect. He glanced at her lying on his bed.

"You are the most beautiful creature in this whole world," he said to her. "I can't believe how lucky I am."

"Show me how lucky you think you are," she said. "Stop talking."

He grinned and pulled a condom from his desk drawer and handed it to her.

"I want you to put it on me," he said, grinning.

Ioni giggled and slid the circle down over him. He made a couple short, funny noises as she did so. When the condom was on, she laid back and held her arms out to him. He came down to her and positioned himself.

"This is the beginning of a great love," he said as he pushed into her.

Ioni hissed through her teeth. She was so excited and aching for him, that she had forgotten that the first time was supposed to hurt. Raber stopped and didn't move. He was looking down at her, concern on his face.

"No," Ioni said. "Keep going."

Raber moved slowly, but kept stopping. Ioni assumed he was trying to give her breaks from the discomfort.

"You're really not hurting me that bad," Ioni said into his ear, as his head was buried in her shoulder. "You don't have to keep stopping."

"I keep stopping because you feel so amazing," he whispered to her. "I want to explode right now."

Ioni closed her eyes and tried to move past the pain. She felt his thick hardness twitch inside of her. He moved again, in and out. His breathing was extremely fast. This time he didn't stop. He kept going, still slow, but not stopping. He moaned and Ioni felt the twitching again, this time a little stronger. Raber let out a sigh and relaxed on top of her.

"I'm so sorry, I really didn't expect you to feel so good," he said.

"Don't be sorry for anything," she said, stroking his face. "That was wonderful. You're wonderful."

"I think I love you," he said to her. "I'm not just saying that because of what just happened. I'm saying that because I feel so close to you. I feel like I would dry up and blow away if you weren't in my life. I can't imagine my first time being any better than this." He kissed her softly and moved out and off of her.

They didn't linger in bed. In no time they were dressing in silence. Ioni was deep in thought. Before Raber came along, she had reached a point of acceptance that she probably wouldn't lose her virginity until at least college. Now, here she was, officially a sexually active young woman. She wanted to jump around the room. Seeing the look on Raber's face if she'd done that would have been hysterical, but she decided to play it cool.

When she was dressed, she started to head for Raber's bedroom door but he blocked her way and put his arms around her. He put his forehead on hers and looked into her eyes.

"This wasn't a one-time thing, you know," he said to her. "This was only the beginning of what I expect will be a love story worthy of centuries of poetry and musings. I have no intention of having this be casual, you know." She smiled at his corny line. His Raber-isms were sometimes hard not to laugh at, but it was undeniably sweet, especially in that moment.

"I'm glad," Ioni replied. "I'd hate to feel cheap on my first time."

Raber smiled and kissed her.

"Come on, let's go get some food," he said.

CHAPTER FOUR

"NO FUCKING WAY!"

Nathan's reply message that Ioni received after confiding in him that she and Raber had had sex was no less than she expected. After Raber had dropped her off at home that night, she couldn't sit on that bit of information for long, so she logged on to her computer and messaged Nathan, her most trusted friend.

"I'm serious. It just happened. I'm not a prudish virgin anymore!"

"Ur a slut!" Nathan replied.

"LOL I am not! But I'm not the only virgin in school anymore!"

"Log off, I want to call…" Nathan messaged. Her house had two phone lines, one for the phone and one for the internet, but Ioni had hooked her bedroom phone to the internet line so that she could have more private phone calls. Her sisters were both in bed by ten p.m. so it had never been a problem.

Before she could get any sort of greeting out, Nathan was squealing.

"I'M SO PROUD OF YOU!" He screamed in her ear. "Oh my God, I was so worried that you were going to stay a tight-thighed cherry forever! I'm so glad that now we can talk about sex together! Tell me everything!"

"We were at Ms. Mimm's studio and when we left he attacked me in the car and we got all hot and heavy in there, then we went to his house because his parents were at some sort of dinner function thingy. And once things got moving there, I told him that I wanted to go all the way and it just happened," she said, breathless in her excitement.

"What the fuck were you doing at Ms. Mimm's stinky hippie studio?" Nathan asked.

"That's right, you weren't in school today. Where were you?"

"I was out late with Chris last night and I faked barfing this morning to catch up on sleep. That man is energetic!"

"Who is Chris again?" Ioni asked.

"I haven't told you guys about him, but I really like him. He's out of the closet, unlike some of my other conquests, and he's a little bit older. He's not exactly the manly man I've been yearning for, but he's pretty great. I met him at the freaking grocery store of all places. I was picking up some vegetables for my mom and he came up to me and was like 'I dig your look.' I expected him to be a creep, but he's like a normal guy. I knew he was flirting with me by the way he was smiling, so I put on my best smile and thanked him. It just went from there. I see him a few times a week. He works at that U.S Cellular store at the mall." Nathan said.

"So you're in a relationship? For real?" Ioni asked.

"I guess I am," Nathan said. "He's not trying to hide me or anything. We go out in public like a normal couple and he's introduced me to a couple of his friends. They looked at me weird at first, but they're all really cool like you guys are."

"Nath, that is so great!" Ioni said.

"Okay, that's enough about me. What the hell is up with you guys going to Ms. Mimm's studio?"

Ioni related to him the strange occurrences that had brought them to their art teacher's studio.

"That's totally crazy," Nathan said. "I had no idea that there were any witches' covens around in this hick town. That's crazy good luck that she overheard you. I didn't think she eavesdropped on anybody but me, but that's because I'm the only person that ever has any good stories to tell!"

"Your stories are yucky! I can't go through a drive-thru anymore without wondering what's going on under the window!" Ioni said, laughing.

"All right," Nathan said, laughing too. "I'm going to hit the hay so I can be at school tomorrow. I don't want to get held back in my last year. Congratulations on getting boned!"

"Thanks," Ioni said. "'Night."

"'Night," Nathan said and hung up.

Ioni stared at herself in the mirror, smiling. She was thinking again on her recent maturation, one of the last steps she had to take in becoming an adult. Life and further experience tends to teach people that there's too much ritual and importance placed on becoming sexual, but as an eighteen year-old girl, Ioni was acting and thinking like most other girls her age. She touched herself and winced at the ache. She wondered how long she would be sore and how long until she and Raber could have sex again. She was anxious to get past the newness of it and on to the pleasure of it.

The next morning Ioni made her way to the usual table in the cafeteria and sat down, all alone and wondering why she was the first to arrive at school. She pulled a paperback from her oversized purse and started reading. When she felt a tap on her shoulder, she looked up from her book and a girl, a junior she thought, was standing over her with an overly excited smile on her face.

"Hi," the girl said. "I'm with the Homecoming committee and I was just taking an informal survey about what theme we should use for the Homecoming dance this year." The girl looked down at a clipboard she was carrying. "Our choices are a heaven-like theme, a superhero and damsel-in-distress theme, or an underwater theme. What do you think?"

"Well...uhhh...I won't be going to the dance. I never do, so I don't really have an opinion either way," Ioni answered, feeling very awkward.

"How can you not go to the dance?" The pretty girl asked, completely shocked. "You get to dress up and get your hair done and have a really nice time! Oh, come on, don't you want to go even a little bit?"

"In the four years I've been here, I've never once gone to the Homecoming dance or the Homecoming game or anything else like that. I'm just really not into it," Ioni answered, trying to be patient.

The pretty girl gave her a look that Ioni had become accustomed to in her time as a student. The look implied that this girl found her to be bizarre and completely unnatural. It no longer bothered Ioni the way that it used to.

"Sorry," Ioni said, looking back down at her book.

"Oh, well, that's okay," the pretty girl said as she moved to the next table.

"All in black today," Nathan said sitting across from her. "Mourning the death of your hymen?"

Ioni burst out laughing and swatted at Nathan.

"I always wear black!" she said.

"Yes, yes," Nathan said, waving his hand dismissively. "Lady of the Night!" Ioni noticed that he had changed his pink mohawk yet again. His entire look was toned down. His head was shaved and he was wearing only a scant amount of eye makeup. She raised her eyebrows and mentioned his creeping conventionalism.

"Well, Chris is kind of a low-maintenance guy and when I spend a lot of time with him, there's no time for me to be high maintenance. I'm no less magnificent like this, I can just go from 'post-sex mess' to 'ready to go out' faster," he said, blushing a little. Blushing was not something Nathan Newell did. Ioni would have sworn that he was incapable of it before.

"You're changing for a guy?" Ioni asked, smiling sarcastically.

"Not changing," Nathan said. "Just toning down a little. The guy likes me the way I am and the way I've always looked. He'd never ask me to change. Honestly, I did this so I don't have to keep the guy waiting while I re-style the mohawk and re-apply a ton of makeup after sex. The sex is crazy with him, you know. I'm always covered in a variety of wet sticky stuff after and it's just easier this way. It's easier for *me*."

"Oh God, I don't want to know details on this one," Ioni said laughing and waving her hands. Nathan had always loved teasing her. She suspected that his sex was as vanilla as anyone's, but he found it hilarious to make her uncomfortable.

"Let me put it to you this way, Miss Innocence," Nathan said. "Before Chris, I thought I had seen and done everything. I was very, very wrong."

"Hey," Arlie said as she sat down. "What are you guys talking about?"

Ioni glanced at Nathan. She wasn't sure if his relationship with Chris was something he was ready to talk about openly yet.

"We're just talking about my new look," Nathan said companionably, pulling a folder out of Arlie's bag.

Of the whole group, Arlie was the only truly artistically talented member. She did drawings and took pictures. Her stuff was colorful and beautiful. Ioni had a painting that Arlie had done for her hanging in her bedroom. It was one of her favorite things to look at when she was alone. The painting depicted a multitude of lidded eyes that were different sizes and different colors. Some had long eyelashes and some were closed. It made Ioni feel strangely comfortable having all of those eyes on her as she slept.

"Toned it down, I see," Arlie said. "Trying something new or is it a some*one* new kind of thing?"

Nathan smiled. Arlie had a way of always hitting the nail on the head.

"I'm seeing someone," Nathan said. "And it might be getting serious."

"That's cool, Nath. I'm glad you found someone you're that nuts over," Arlie said. "How long have you been seeing him?"

"About a month," Nathan answered. "I was thinking about bringing him to Adam's for Halloween so you guys could all meet him. I've met some of his friends already, so you all need to meet him."

"We're doing the Halloween bash at my place this year?" Adam asked, sitting down.

"It's your turn!" Ioni said. Their freshman year, Nathan had been the host, sophomore year, Ioni had hosted, and junior year they had a very cold patio party at Arlie's house. Adam was the only friend who hadn't hosted yet and he was saved for last because his parents were cool with letting them drink and do other unmentionable things at their house as long as nobody tried to drive. The group had figured that they might as well make their last Halloween bash as dependent kids one to remember.

"Hey guys!" The pretty girl was back. "I'm with the Homecoming committee and we're doing an informal survey..."

"NO." Arlie said before the pretty girl could finish her spiel.

"You don't even know what..." the pretty girl started to say. Her nose was crinkled and her tone had gotten snarky.

"It doesn't matter what you were going to say," Arlie interjected again. "WE. DO. NOT. CARE." The pretty girl stared at Arlie and then looked at all the rest of the misfits sitting at the table.

"Might be best if you just take your goody-goody clipboard elsewhere, cutie." Nathan said.

The pretty girl whirled around and stomped off. Arlie glared after her and Adam and Nathan grinned at each other.

"She came over here before you guys showed up and was asking me the same thing," Ioni said.

"I'm surprised she lowered her prissy ass to our level to even speak to us," Arlie said.

"Now, now Arlie. She's a goody-goody doing a goody-goody chore as best as she can. It's not her fault that she's too self-absorbed to realize that us freaks never make appearances at those cheap dances," Nathan said, looking through Arlie's folder again. "Ooooo," he said, pulling a rough sketch out. "When you've filled this one in, I want it. Will you take twenty for it?"

Arlie looked at what Nathan was holding and nodded.

"Yeah, twenty is a fair price," she said.

Unless Arlie actually gifted a piece of her art to them, they had to buy pieces from her. They didn't mind. They were spoiled kids who still received allowances and didn't have to work for money yet. Arlie had to work for her money. She was the only member of the group with a job. She worked as a cook at a cheap and oily fast food restaurant in the food court at the mall. Because of her half-shaved head and piercings, she couldn't work a job that put her in contact with customers. She was just happy to be earning her own money.

"So, Ioni," Arlie began. "You never clued me in on what Ms. Mimm was so grouchy about yesterday."

"It's an interesting story," Ioni said. "Really interesting."

Ioni told them the happenings of the previous evening, ending at when she and Raber got into Raber's car in front of the studio. It wasn't the right time to make her new sex life sensationalist news.

"Weird," Adam said shaking his head.

"Yeah," Arlie said. "I never knew there was a Wiccan population anywhere near here."

"I know, right?" Ioni said. "This will help a lot, having a mentor and not having to feel around in the dark."

"Her night went on to be even *more* interesting, though," Nathan said.

"Oh?" Arlie said, leaning forward and smiling.

"Well, I'm gonna have to tell you about it later because the main subject just walked in," Nathan said.

Ioni turned and saw Raber walking to the table. The pretty girl and her clipboard started to approach him, reconsidered, and moved on. Raber smiled at Ioni in a way that made her fidget in her seat.

They waited nearly eighteen hours before having sex again, and Ioni was crestfallen over the pain still being ever-present. They were lying together on his downstairs sofa, naked and legs tangled. She was close to sleep when he spoke, startling her awake.

"Oh, I'm sorry," Raber said, laughing. "I didn't know you were snoozing, gorgeous."

"I was just drifting," Ioni smiled. "I got too comfortable. What did you say?"

"I asked if you were excited for Saturday," Raber said. Ioni liked the way his deep voice sounded when he spoke softly. She snuggled into him.

"I guess so," she said. "What day is it today?"

Raber laughed.

"It's Wednesday, baby," he said. Ioni smiled at the endearing term. She was going to answer his question when something from the night before came into her mind.

"Hey, something's been kind of bothering me," she said, sitting up suddenly.

"What's that?" he asked.

"Okay, so last night while we were talking to Ms. Mimm, I mean Sarah, you mentioned that you were going to be moving to Morgantown to go to school. You know, I have to wonder if maybe we shouldn't have a lot of high expectations for this relationship." Raber bolted upright and moved so that his face was inches away from hers.

"Why would you say that?" he asked.

"Well let's be honest here," Ioni began. "I'm going to still be living with my parents, you're going to be living in a dorm a half hour away. There's really no room for serious growth. I mean, I love you, Raber, I really do, but maybe we should just enjoy each other now and leave the future up in the air. I don't want to be this obligation back home to you or keep you from really enjoying college. It's supposed to be the greatest time of your life, college. You're on your own more than ever before. There's a lot of parties to go to, a lot of social gatherings to go to." Ioni swallowed hard. "A lot of casual sex to have." At that moment, Raber grabbed her upper arms hard enough to make her yelp.

"You listen to me," he said in a low voice. "You are not an obligation. You are not a chore. You are far too important for me to feel that way towards you. What is a half hour drive anyhow? I can come home on weekends, and you can come stay in my dorm with me on weekends when my roommate is out. It's not like I'm going to another state for fuck's sake. I don't want you to hold back with me out of fear of being a bother or in the way. I *want* this and I want it to be serious and intense and extremely committed." He stared into her face, his nostrils flaring. His fingers were digging into her flesh so much that Ioni was sure there were going to be bruises later. "Do you understand?" Raber asked.

"Yes," she whispered. "You're hurting my arms though." Raber's eyes widened as he looked down and saw the way his fingers were digging into her. He jerked his hands away.

"I...I'm so sorry," he said. He lifted her arms to his face one by one and kissed the red places where his fingers had been. "I'm so sorry," he murmured over and over again. Ioni began to relax again.

He put his thumb under her chin and made her look into his face.

"I meant what I said," he said. "Every word of it. Don't give up on this before it's had a chance to even get to its full speed."

Ioni felt tears flood her eyes. She tried to look down, but Raber still held her face level with his. She saw the seriousness.

"Okay," she said, her voice thick with emotion. "I'll try not to be so negative about this. I'll let what happens happen. I trust you."

He kissed her. It started out soft, but the longer their lips connected, the hungrier the act became. Before Ioni's tears had dried, he was in her again moving fast and hard. She realized Raber wasn't wearing a condom and began to feel panicked.

"Wait," she said loudly. He stopped and looked down at her, out of breath. "You need protection!"

"I thought that we had cleared this up," Raber smiled and began moving again, slowly. "We are committed to each other now. If I want to come in you, I'll come in you."

"No," Ioni said. "No, I don't want this!" She squeezed her thighs as hard as she could and scooted away from Raber. "Stop this right now!"

Raber sat with his legs folded beneath him, his hands on his thighs. He was panting.

"I got caught in the moment," he said. "I'm sorry, but I honestly thought it would be okay."

"Why would you think that I'd be okay with unprotected sex?" Ioni nearly shrieked. She started grabbing throw pillows and covering herself.

"I'm sorry!" He shouted. "I guess I thought that we could get even closer by sharing something truly intimate."

"Sex wasn't intimate enough already?"

"Don't be afraid of it," Raber replied. He had regained his composure and was speaking gently to her. "I just wanted to feel you completely. I'm sorry I took that step without asking. Of course, it's your body and this is a consensual thing. I'm very, very sorry."

Ioni took a deep breath and exhaled. She looked at Raber, who sat there naked and contrite.

"I just don't want to get pregnant," she said. "It's not that I think you're gross or that going bareback would ruin it for me. I just want to be careful. I saw what a teenaged pregnancy did to my sister and I do not want that. I'm terrified of that."

"Of course you are," Raber said. He crawled over to her and laid her back. He was on top of her again, but he didn't push himself into her. "I wouldn't leave you to something like that. Maybe birth control pills are an option we can look into later, okay?" He kissed her softly again.

"Mmmmm, I like you when you apologize," she said. He started kissing her neck. "Is this how we make up from our very first fight? Oh, God," she gasped as he inserted a finger into her.

"You tell me what you want, gorgeous," Raber murmured onto the soft skin of her stomach. His finger was moving faster and faster and Ioni moved her hips into him in response. "If you're curious, I'm happy to comply with your request. Everything feels better without the condom." He began kissing lower until his mouth found her swollen nub. He sucked it lightly and Ioni nearly screamed from the surprise of how amazing it felt. "I want you no matter what, but I'd love it so much if we could be skin-to-skin. It would be so amazing to come inside of you. I think about it all the time."

"I wasn't curious before, but now I am," she said. "I'm scared, though."

"Don't be scared. You said you trust me, so just trust me now. No pushing, but, mmmm," he paused to give her lower area a long and tongue-ful kiss. "If you'd like to try it, I'm game."

"Maybe we should look into birth control pills," Ioni murmured. "I'm dying to know now."

"The chances of you getting pregnant this one time are so small, baby. Let me let you feel how hot I am right now. Let me do this, please. I'm begging. Please," Raber was groaning.

His fingers were still furiously moving in and out of her. "No pressure, though," he said.

"Kiss me," Ioni said. He moved up along her body and kissed her deeply. His kisses were hard and hungry, but he kept himself out of her, waiting for her to make the decision. Ioni's thoughts were red and hot at the moment and she didn't want to make the decision right then. "Maybe do it for a while without a condom?" she suggested.

He needed no further coaxing. He slammed himself into her in the very next instant. Ioni was so wet and swollen from the efforts of his mouth and fingers that the pain wasn't even noticeable. The more he moved, she realized she was forgetting about it. She moved her hips in unison with his movement.

"I can't even describe how amazing you feel right now," he whispered.

Ioni closed her eyes and let the moment take her away. His movements varied between long, slow strokes to smaller, more grinding motions. She was kneading his back and feeling more heated and anxious. She didn't want to stop so that Raber could put on a condom. He was taking a small break and kissing her breasts. He looked up at her.

"Shall I get a condom?" he asked.

"I don't want you to stop," Ioni said. She pulled him back into her and bucked her hips into him before he screamed into the couch cushion and his movements stopped. After a few moments, Raber pushed himself up onto his arms and looked down at her. He had a very big smile on his face.

"God damn, that was fucking amazing!"

Ioni was inclined to agree, but she couldn't help but feel that Raber had just manipulated her into doing that. She brushed it off because in the end, she had wanted it just as badly as he did.

That Saturday morning Raber was sitting on her bed watching her pull her long, black hair into a ponytail. They were supposed to meet Ms. Mimm in an hour.

"You're not your usual neon and black self today," Raber observed. "Why are you muting your look?"

"I'm nervous," Ioni said. "I'm worried about looking like some sort of spectacle. I mean, we want this woman to take us seriously because our interest is serious. I just don't want to be too loud at first glance."

Raber was right, though. Ioni usually loved to pair black and neon colors in her clothes, but that day she was wearing a comparatively somber outfit of blue jeans and a black button-up blouse. Her makeup was applied sparingly and she wasn't wearing any jewelry. She stared at her reflection in the mirror.

"I don't even tone it down like this when I visit my grandparents," she muttered.

"Why are you doing it, then? This woman is going to see you as you are in the future. Own who you are, don't try to mask it to save her some sort of imagined first-impression-shock. I'd like to think that these people aren't into perpetuating stereotypes. I'm sure there are lots of colorful people in this coven. Don't do this."

"Maybe I'll just change tops," Ioni said. She went to her closet and stood back, taking in the neon and black collage of her wardrobe. She pulled an electric blue and black checkered top out. She noticed how Raber's eyes moved over her as she switched shirts.

"You are simply delicious," he muttered. "How about we close that door and screw really fast before we go?"

"My parents are like two rooms away!" Ioni said, laughing. "I don't want you to muss me, anyhow."

"You get on top," he said, flopping down on his back and smiling at her. Ioni looked at him, considering his proposal. They hadn't yet worked their way up to her being on top.

"No," she said with finality and turning back to the mirror. "I don't want to meet this important lady with FFL."

"FFL?" Raber asked, an eyebrow cocked at her.

"Freshly Fucked Look," Ioni said, grinning at him through the mirror. Raber burst out laughing.

"I assume that one came from Nathan?"

"Who else?" Ioni said, giggling. She turned to him and held her arms out to the sides. "Well, am I looking more like myself now?"

"Yes," Raber said, getting up from her bed. "I like you either way, baby, you need to know that. I just don't want you to compromise yourself for this one meeting. If, on the off chance this woman decides not to allow us to study within her coven, we can always find another coven or just go about it alone. This isn't a job interview at a country club or anything. If you're going to be anything, you should be yourself. Fuck them if they have a problem with it."

That helped, and she was surprised at how empowered she felt at his words. Of course he was right. If she really wanted to impress this Karen lady, she would do better to show up as herself and own that personality.

CHAPTER FIVE

"It looks like my grandma's house," Ioni said as they pulled into the large driveway of Bedelia's. Sarah's small car pulled in ahead of them.

"What did you think it would look like?" Raber asked, smiling. "Were you expecting to see a giant pentagram painted onto the side of the house or something?"

"No, but I mean look at the shrubbery and the wreath on the front door. This place looks like an old-lady-house," Ioni said, peering out from the windshield of her car.

"Oh wow," Raber said. "You're absolutely right. Now I can't wait to see what the inside looks like."

The split-level home had yellow siding and tidy windows with white shutters. The yard was well maintained with a lot of flowering bushes, but along the front of the house were square boxwoods. They were so immaculately trimmed that lines of the "box" shape almost looked sharp. The curtains were sheer off-white Austrian shades that were very popular in the seventies and eighties, giving the exterior of the house that noted "old lady" look.

Ioni parked behind Sarah and they all got out of their cars. Sarah's wild hair was barely contained by a butterfly clip attempting to keep it barely contained in a messy up-do. She nodded at Raber and Ioni and indicated that they follow her to the front door. Ioni smiled at the handmade wooden sign that read "Please Wipe Your Paws!" in big pink letters surrounded by tiny pink paw prints.

Sarah opened the glass door that looked just as a small shop door should, save for the wreath made of pink flowers and bows, and walked up the stairs from the landing. Upstairs they saw a scene that was exactly as Sarah had described. There were candles and books and glinting jewels and silver-looking trinkets everywhere. The smell of warming oils or incense hung heavy in the air, making the atmosphere thick. To the left was what appeared to be a converted living room that was now full of shelving and metal trees weighed down with trinkets. To the right was a doorway into another room and a hallway lined with honey-colored doors, all closed. A fat, orange cat trotted by them, tail high in the air.

"A witch and her cats, eh?" Raber said.

"Don't get caught up in stereotypes," Sarah said seriously. "Karen just happens to be a cat person, it has nothing to do with her religion."

"I'll be with you in just a moment!" a strong voice called from the hallway.

"Let's go into the kitchen and sit down until she's ready to see us," Sarah said, leading them through the doorway to the right of the stairs.

The "kitchen" still vaguely resembled a domestic kitchen. The cabinets were a warmly colored wood with retro looking panels. The counter tops were a yellow laminate and the floors were a shiny terracotta tile. There was a yellow cooking range that had large pots sitting on all four metal coil burners. The window above the sink was completely crammed with plants. Ioni saw blocks of what appeared to be wax stacked all over the countertops as well as hundreds of gleaming empty bottles with cork stoppers. In the corner of the room were black cauldrons stacked upon each other in many different sizes. Some were quite small while others were the enormous cauldrons one would expect to see in the kitchen of a witch. To the far left was a completely domestic looking kitchen table with 6 chairs sitting around it. The table was another retro looking piece. It was brass with a smoked glass top with brass chairs sporting cream-colored upholstery.

Raber and Ioni looked around them, their curiosity obvious. Sarah sat across from them, watching their faces.

"Don't be nervous about meeting Karen," Sarah said. "I talked to her earlier this week and she seemed very open to meeting the two of you. She's a very nice person"

"I'm a little thrown off by this house," Raber said, smiling in awe. "Wow. Ioni and I were talking about how much it looks like a little old lady's home." Sarah laughed at this.

"Well," she said quietly, leaning closer to them. "Karen *is* an old lady and this *is* her home." Ioni giggled and looked down at her lap, embarrassed at having been caught making assumptions. "Were you expecting black walls and heavy velvet curtains and lit red candles all over the place?" Sarah asked, smiling.

"Maybe not as dramatic as that," Raber said smiling. "I feel like an ass. I came here with this stiff upper lip mentality thinking Ioni and I might be judged by Karen by how we look, and here I am making idiotic assumptions myself."

"It's really only normal," Sarah said, sitting back in her chair. "You're going to have a lot of surprises in the beginning. Just remember that there is always more beneath. Think of people like a deep, dark lake. You see the surface and maybe it's reflecting its surroundings and you assume that because it is a lake with a clear and still surface you know it's only water, but that's not at all true, is it? No. Beneath that calm exterior things are swimming and there's movement and darkness and life. Beneath that quaint reflection is a lot more that you can't see. Every now and then a ripple from underneath disturbs that calm surface, but it's usually no more than a ripple that you get to see. We're all deep lakes. We're all hiding things beneath the surface."

Ioni was nodding, thinking how brilliant that analogy was when she heard a door close in the hallway. Sarah sat straighter in her chair and got a look of anticipation on her face. Since her back was to the opening to the kitchen, Ioni turned around in her chair and watched the doorway. She tried not to let her jaw hit the floor when Karen walked in.

She was obviously an older woman, but she was not what one would expect to see in a witch or head priestess. She was not a withered old lady wearing a long flowing gown and her hair was not hanging in her face in ratty gray tendrils. No, Karen was a perky looking woman who had a smile that looked like it belonged on The Shopping Channel. She was average height, and her frame was slim. She was wearing well-worn blue jeans and a soft looking pink sweater. Her bare feet showed off glossy red-painted toenails. Her shoulder-length hair was dyed a soft blonde color that had gray and dark brown at the roots. Ioni could picture her happily bouncing from Macy's to Bloomingdales for shoes and purses.

Her well-lined but attractive face was smiling at them, showing straight white teeth. Her blue eyes were twinkling, looking all of them over.

"Hello," she said in a rich voice. "I am Karen McKinney and you must be the possible initiates?"

Sarah jumped out of her chair and the teenagers followed suit.

"Karen, this is Raber Belliveau and Ioni Davis" Sarah said, placing her hands on their shoulders.

"My, my," Karen laughed. "Those are some very distinctive names."

Ioni and Raber both gave nervous, breathy laughs.

"Yeah, our names do stick out," Ioni added.

Karen laughed. "I'd say so. I mean, my name is *Karen*, and our mutual friend here was named *Sarah*. Tell me, how do you come by names like Raber and Ioni?" Karen gestured for everybody to retake their seats. She joined them and folded her hands on the table, looking at the two of them with interest.

"My grandfather's best friend was a man named Arthur Raber. It was a name that my father always thought was interesting. I like it. It's not too often, as a man, when you can have a unique name that isn't just crazy. I'm glad that my name is both unique and still somehow masculine." Raber was sitting in his seat, with perfect posture as always, and he was meeting Karen's gaze steadily. Karen smiled and gave Raber a brief nod before leveling her gaze on Ioni.

"And what about you?" Karen asked her.

"It's funny, actually. My mom is a really super-smart intellectual. She can discuss just about any topic in depth and she reads everything she can get her hands on, but she seems happiest to watch a sappy movie on television." Ioni noticed that all eyes were on her and she fidgeted under the attention. "Well you know that eighties movie *Say Anything*? The girl who starred in that movie was named Ione, but with an 'e' at the end. My name ends in an 'i'. I guess my mom just thought it was a great name. I used to not like having a unique name. People would mispronounce it all the time and it always seemed like all of the dainty pretty girls had really ordinary names like Ashley or something like that. It took a while for my name to really grow on me."

"Hmmm," Karen said in agreement. "There's a lot in a name and it's not always easy letting one stick to you," she said. She adjusted herself in her seat and patted her hair in an oddly business-like way. "Now, I know that Sarah has already asked you your intentions and she informed me that she found your answers to be satisfactory, but I'd like to ask you again."

They answered her questions very much like they answered Sarah in her studio. Karen nodded and grinned in a way that put the two teenagers at ease in her presence.

"I think that's all I need to hear, my dears. I'm gonna give my blessing to the two of you to start your training for a year and a day under Sarah here. She'll fill you in on everything. Now, as initiates, you are not yet full members of our coven. This isn't a bad thing, though, seeing how you both are so young. When you have completed your year and a day, you can either do a full initiation into the coven or you can go off as you please, perhaps to join another coven or to practice in solitude. I want to be able to train anybody seeking it with honesty in their hearts for the craft. I believe your intentions are true and pure and I will allow you to learn from my coven. As initiates, you will be permitted to attend certain rituals and celebrations so that you can get a feel for the way this goes."

"Thank you so much!" Ioni said, surprised at her own outburst. She was becoming accustomed to letting Raber do most of the talking, but she was so relieved that their honesty had shone through to Karen and that she was granting them her blessing to train.

"Yes, thank you very much," Raber said, beaming. Ioni smiled at him and he leaned over and kissed her lightly on the forehead.

"Oh, are you two an item?" Karen asked.

"Yes," Raber said, hesitation obvious in his tone.

"It's not a problem, honey, I was just wondering." Karen said warmly. "I guess I should have seen it before. My age is making my gift of observation a bit flubbery."

They all laughed.

"So, what happens now?" Raber asked.

"Now we need to have some discussions about a training schedule and things that you two will need eventually," Sarah answered.

"Members of our coven get a discount!" Karen said, a Cheshire cat smile on her face. "Initiates to the coven and those training under members of the coven are also eligible for the discount, in case you were wondering. You'll have all the help you need, that's for certain."

"Okay, so I guess that we're done here?" Raber asked. Karen looked at him for a moment, but Ioni couldn't quite place the look she was giving him. The look only lasted a moment before her face lit back up in her warm smile.

"Would you like to see something first?" Karen asked. Raber and Ioni nodded and followed Karen out of the kitchen and down the hallway. Karen opened the second door on the right and it was obvious then that the heavy smell was coming from this room. From the ceiling, bundles of drying flowers and plants were hanging upside down. The one window in the room had regular vinyl blinds pulled up to let the light in. In the center of the room sat a low table with a black cloth draped over it. To Ioni's eyes, the table just had a bunch of strange knick-knacks sitting on it. There were two candles and some bowls and a knife.

"This is your altar," Raber said, looking about him in fascination.

"Very good," Karen said. "This is the room where I commune with my divine influences. This is where I make myself one with the spiritual energies of this world. You will need your own altars, or at least some of the basic necessities to set up an altar so that you, too, might commune with the goddess."

"I live with my parents, and probably will for a few more years," Ioni said, imagining her sisters or parents asking questions about the altar in her bedroom.

"You don't have to keep it set up at all times if you're worried about nibby people," Sarah said, laughing. "You can keep all of your things stashed away and then just do a quick setup."

"Oh," Ioni said, smiling. "Okay. That'll work really well for me. I have two sisters and a nephew in my house as well as my parents. They aren't particularly nosey people, but I just don't want to have to answer a lot of questions just yet."

"That's completely understandable," Karen said, putting a hand on Ioni's shoulder. "Many of us choose secrecy. There's no shame in being a Wiccan, but questions can be very annoying. We all relate to that feeling."

Ioni felt welcomed, comforted, and excited. She'd found her people who put her at ease, and that was a rarity for her.

Goodbyes were said and Karen shook hands with Raber politely, but when she held Ioni's hand, she put her other hand around Ioni's wrist.

"Lovely to meet the both of you," Karen said to her, looking her straight in the eyes. "I have a feeling I'll be getting to know *you* very well." Ioni knew that that last part was directed only to her, and she felt a moment of panic at Raber being clued in, but when she looked to him, he was already walking to her car.

Raber seemed annoyed in the car. At first, Ioni was worried that maybe he'd heard what Karen had said to her. She was very anxious about being showed that bit of favoritism. As she drove them back to her house, she tried to keep her concentration on the road and not breach the subject.

"I'm beginning to wonder if Sarah will actually be a good mentor for us after all," he finally said. Ioni chanced a quick, surprised glance at him.

"Huh? Why do you say that?" she asked.

"All that blathering on that she did about 'more beneath'. That was the most soulless, generic, and self-indulgent speech I think I've ever heard. She obviously thinks way too highly of herself." Raber spat.

Ioni quickly suppressed her knee-jerk reaction which was to inform him that in that moment he was the one who seemed to be thinking a bit too highly of himself. She didn't want to fight with Raber, but she didn't really want him making this experience hard on her because of a superiority complex either. She chose her words carefully.

"I actually found that little speech really helpful," she said. She ignored Raber's disgusted scoff and continued. "Well, look at us. Look at our friends. Aren't we more than what our appearance says we are? Shouldn't we be allowed to have more to us than just what you first see?" She paused, swallowed hard, and added, "I think you're being a little too harsh."

Raber was quiet, sitting next to her. Ioni could see his jaw muscles clenching and unclenching as he stared hard at her windshield. The longer the silence went on, the more nervous she got. They pulled into the driveway in front of her house, and Ioni half expected Raber to storm out of her car and screech away in his own. Instead, he stayed seated, looking thoughtful for a change. She reached out and put a hand on his thigh and he immediately smiled.

"Of course, you're right" he said. He reached out and stroked her hair. "I'm tense because I was nervous, and because I was nervous, all of her talking just annoyed me." He laughed. "If she'd revealed that she knew the secret to immortality I probably would have still been annoyed by her talking. I didn't mean anything by it, baby. Thank you for setting me straight."

A couple of hours later they were cuddled up on Ioni's bed watching television. Raber was propped up on her pillows and Ioni was between his legs resting on his chest. His large hands were buried in her hair, stroking. She snuggled against him and took in his warm smell. He wore a cologne or aftershave, she wasn't sure of the brand, but he always smelled clean and spicy. There was no sex that day because Ioni had started her period not long after they'd gotten back from Bedelia's. The relief that she felt was immeasurable. She didn't share her worry with Raber, or anyone else for that matter, but she relaxed a bit when she saw that red blood. She didn't want to have the life that her sister Rose had. The sex hadn't been that good.

"You didn't fall asleep on me did you?" Raber asked.

"No, I'm still awake," Ioni answered.

"You got quiet. Everything okay?"

"Sure," Ioni replied. "I was just chilling out. After the first half of the day being as stressful as it was, it's just really nice to be with you and have quiet time, you know?"

"It is nice," Raber said.

She started relaxing again, sinking back into his chest and listening to his breathing. She wasn't really watching what was on the television, she was just letting herself get lost in the quiet. Just as she was perfectly settled, he spoke again.

"I was a bit worried that maybe you were mad at me," he said. Ioni sat up and turned to face him.

"Why would I be mad at you? I'm not mad at all," she said.

"Well, that little tantrum I threw in the car and some...some other stuff."

"The thing in the car got resolved," Ioni said. "It's not even a thing anymore. It's done and behind us. And what other stuff are you talking about?"

"I've been thinking about the other day," Raber said, looking down. Ioni found it weird to see him acting sheepish. He was usually the kind of guy that had a direct gaze when he spoke to someone.

"I've been thinking that maybe I forced you to do something that you weren't ready to do. I didn't want to say anything, but I was so relieved when you mentioned that you'd gotten your period. I was trying so hard not to be worried, but it was always in the back of my mind."

Ioni smiled. In a way, it was good to know that Raber was worried about what he'd done.

"You didn't *force* me to do anything," she said. "You may have manipulated me a little bit, but there was no forcing it. I didn't want to do it at first, that's true, but you made me curious. In the end, I agreed to what happened. I'm not mad at you, though, baby. I couldn't stay mad at that sweet face." She reached out and laid a hand on his cheek. He put his large hand over hers and turned his face and buried it in her palm.

"I love you so much," he whispered. "You make me feel so good. You make me feel whole, and I didn't realize that I wasn't whole until you were in my life. I love you," he kissed her palm. "I love you, I love you, I love you."

Ioni kissed him softly. She was relieved when the kiss ended on an affectionate and un-expectant tone.

"I love you too," she said softly. "I'm so glad that we've found each other."

"You'll never need to be lonely again," Raber said, pulling her to him.

CHAPTER SIX

She fidgeted on the large couch in the basement of Adam's parents' house. The wings that came with her costume made it nearly impossible to sit comfortably. She felt Raber's hand touch her back and stroke her shoulder blade lightly. She smiled at him happily. She always looked forward to their annual Halloween parties.

Ioni was dressed as a dark fairy. The costume was actually called "Seductress of the Woods". Raber was dressed as a mad scientist, wearing a long white lab coat and fake glasses. Arlie and Adam were dressed as Raggedy Anne and Raggedy Andy. It was weird to see them looking so traditional. Nathan, usually needing to be the shocker of the group, had gone mild that year and showed up as a pregnant nun. The year before he wore nothing but a G-string made to look like an alien bursting from his pelvis while the rest of his naked body was painted black and covered with orange glitter. It was very festive. Arlie's patio still had orange glitter embedded in the old, warped wood, but she said it was an improvement.

Nathan had brought Chris, his new boyfriend, and there was a slight unease among the assembled group. Everybody was being on their best behavior for the sake of the new person and for their friend. Nobody wanted to make a bad first impression.

Chris seemed to be a really great guy, if a bit unremarkable. He was very average, in every way imaginable. He wore faded blue jeans and a PAC-Man T-shirt. His face was not at all unattractive, but there were really no distinguishing features either. He was just a very middle-of-the-road type of guy.

Ioni was surprised at Nathan's change of tastes. He usually went for ravers and flamboyant types. Ioni knew that if Nathan liked him, there had to be something great to the guy. She could tell by the way Nathan smiled every time Chris spoke, the way he put his hand on Chris's knee, the way he would lay his head on Chris's shoulder, that Nathan had fallen hard.

Chris was feeling the unease. The small talk and 'tell us about you' banter was getting to be a bit too much for everybody.

"Not to be rude or anything," Chris began, "but aren't we supposed to do some drinking and partying up in this place, or what?"

"We've got some Boone's Farm and Zimas because we're all underage and that's all that my parents agreed to get for us. I've got a Playstation and a really sweet karaoke machine, though." Adam said.

Nathan smiled at Chris and Chris bust out laughing.

"You guys do realize that I'm twenty-one, right?" he asked. "Let's pool together some money and I'll make sure this is a truly proper party."

The assembled group eagerly dug deep and produced a pile of cash that had Chris smiling from ear to ear. Nathan pulled out his ATM card and whispered his pin number in Chris' ear before licking it. Arlie offered to go to the store with Chris since she needed cigarettes.

After they left, Nathan looked at the remaining friends questioningly.

"Well?" he asked. "What do you guys think?"

"I really like him, Nath," Ioni said. "He's a really nice guy. But what I like the most is how you light up around him."

"That's true," Raber said. "You've never been a subtle personality, but he obviously moves you. He's a cool guy."

"How's the wiener measure up?" Adam asked, causing everybody to laugh. Nathan hit him in the face with a throw pillow. "I like him. He fits with you in a really weird way."

"Yeah," Nathan said. "I know. He's so different from any other guy I've been with. He's blue collar, likes his beer and his sports, and he's completely happy living in this shithole of a town. But, somehow, he makes me swoon."

"That sounds a little like love," Ioni said, smiling.

"Maybe," Nathan said. "Maybe I lucked out early. Wouldn't it be great to find that one special person early and I won't have to date any more jerks and guys who are only experimenting?"

"We're still really young, dude," Adam said. "We all still live at home with our parents. You can't be wanting to settle down already. Doesn't the thought of all that casual and crazy sex as an independent adult appeal to you at all?"

"I've had plenty of casual kinky sex," Nathan said, looking at Adam through narrowed eyes. "I've had enough sex and rejection to last me quite a long time, thank you."

Adam fidgeted uncomfortably and looked down into his lap. Ioni saw Nathan was staring hard at Adam.

"You're going to dump Arlie, aren't you?" Nathan asked Adam. "You're going off to Morgantown in a year and she's staying behind to start her career. You're just going to dump her so you can cut loose with a bunch of drunk skanks, guilt free."

"That's not how it is." Adam said quietly. "This is something that she and I have talked about for a long time. I love her. She loves me. But our formative years were spent stifling each other. This was mutual. If anything, it was more her idea than mine."

Ioni's hand was at her chest. The shock of Adam's admission was too much for a stoic reaction. Adam and Arlie were the perfect couple. They'd been together since they both hit puberty. She couldn't imagine them as separate entities.

"How am I supposed to believe that this was her idea when you were just throwing a fit at me about casual sex as an independent adult?" Nathan said. "Don't make her the villain in this simply because she has that sharp resolve."

"It's true," Adam said. "Maybe her motives were geared towards making me happy, but she is the one who brought it up. What do you want me to do? Lie? You want me to say that I only want to be with one person forever and never experience other girls? I've never even kissed another girl. It's *my* life, you know. I just feel that I would have a lot of regret if I stayed with Arlie."

Silence settled on the group, but the tension remained. Ioni leaned onto Raber and buried her face into his shoulder. She wondered at her sadness. If Arlie was as at peace with their splitting up as Adam was, then there was no great loss, but Ioni found that she placed some hope on their relationship. She looked up at Raber and wondered again. If Arlie and Adam, the most relaxed and amiable couple she'd ever known, couldn't stay together, what did that say about her and Raber? She shook her head, silently chastising herself for being self-centered. She was worried about Arlie, her friend. Arlie, who had come from a home with a single mother who cared little for her daughter. Arlie, who was, by nature, a strong person, had nevertheless leaned on Adam as her rock in a lot of situations.

Nathan was looking down into his lap. Adam was staring at the wall.

"Well, you know, do what makes you happy, I guess." Nathan said. He laughed after hearing his own sullen tone. "I guess I'm more invested in your relationship than you guys are."

At that, Adam laughed, too. Ioni smiled. Hearing her own thoughts coming out of Nathan's mouth made her feel better. She nuzzled Raber and his arm around her tightened and he kissed her temple, breathing in her scent. She turned her head and met his lips with her own. When she turned her head back and opened her eyes, she saw that Adam and Nathan were looking at her and smiling.

"All this talk about couples and we have yet to address how disgustingly adorable you two are." Nathan said.

"I should thank you," Nathan said to Raber. "She's one of the best people I know, and it killed me to see her lonely. We tried fixing her up with acquaintances, but it never worked out. Until you showed up, we just never thought this tittiful beauty would ever have any sort of meaningful experiences. But really, big guy," Nathan said. "Thank you for loving this girl. Thank you for making her know how awesome she is."

"There's no need to thank me," Raber said. "I'm the lucky one, here. She's flattered and humbled me by being with me."

"See that?" Nathan said sitting up and pointing at Raber. "That's just amazing. You're so complimenting and sweet to her and that's totally what she needed." He sat back and flashed a shark's smile at Ioni. "And, I must add that I am so glad that you defrosted our little ice queen. I was beginning to worry that she was never gonna relax her thighs long enough to let someone in there."

Ioni stiffened, worried at how Raber would take that she had confided in Nathan certain details of their relationship. To her relief, she felt Raber's chest rumble in laughter.

"I know you two are close and I assumed you knew more about our relationship than you let on," Raber said. "I'm just gonna go back to being ignorant of what you know so I can bear to show my face around, okay?"

"I'm not sure that I can contain myself," Nathan began, still smiling mischievously. "I know all the good and squishy details."

Nathan and Adam both laughed at that. Ioni felt her face growing hot and she turned to look at Raber and saw that his face and his entire head had gone beet red. She worried that he was angry, but when she saw the look on his face, that sheepish downcast look of his, she knew that Nathan had managed to embarrass her boyfriend.

She burst into near-hysterical laughter.

"And what has you so tickled, my sweet?" Raber asked.

"I'm sorry," Ioni choked out between giggle-gasps. "I've just never seen you blush before. It's cute!"

"Cute?!?" Raber blurted.

"Cute as the Dickens, you giant god of a man, you!" Nathan said.

"Cute as a fluffy little puppy dog!" Adam said, pointing at Raber.

"I think you guys are a bunch of creeps!" Raber said in mock anger before busting up in laughter.

When Chris and Arlie returned weighed down by brown paper bags, Ioni saw Nathan trap Arlie in a corner and whisper to her. Arlie was looking into Nathan's face in shock and then she leveled an angry glare at Adam. Adam, who couldn't pretend not to see that look busied himself with helping Chris unload the bags and laying out the beer and the one bottle of cheap bourbon. Ioni kissed Raber on the cheek before joining Nathan and Arlie.

"I'm really sorry," Arlie was saying. "I wasn't going to talk about it, we were just going to tell you guys that we decided on a break after graduation."

"He said it was your idea," Nathan said. "I don't believe that for a minute, you know."

"Well, it was my idea," Arlie said.

Nathan and Ioni stared at Arlie in shock.

"Don't look at me like that!" Arlie said, looking at her feet. "I love Adam so much and I really want him to be happy. But you know what? I'm not ready for that type of adult commitment."

"Arlie," Nathan said, frustration in his tone. "He pretty much admitted to us all that he wants this so that he can have a bunch of casual sex in college. I love Adam, but that bastard

71

wants to be single so that he can be a free agent in the land of easy pussy."

"Thank you, Captain Obvious. Do you really think that I couldn't guess that?" Arlie said, smiling. "I know Adam extremely well. I know that he's curious about being with someone else. I know that he's anxious to go away to college. Who am I to tie him down? And if I'm being totally honest here, I think that I might like to try being with someone else too. Someone I have more in common with. Someone I can talk to about things that bore Adam."

"That's it," Nathan said, throwing his hands in the air. "My faith in love has just been pulverized."

"Stop being so serious," Arlie said, poking Nathan in the chest. "Where's my nonchalant Nath? I don't want this to affect our evening. Hell, I'm sure Adam and I will end up having sex tonight and being a completely normal couple. And you know what? Since we decided to break up, the sex with him has been really...interesting." Now it was Arlie's turn to wear a mischievous smile. She cocked an eyebrow at Nathan.

"All right, damn it, you have my attention." Nathan said, smiling. "You can't say something like that without giving me the details as to what the hell 'interesting' means! Come on! Spill it!"

"I think he's using me as a kind of test subject," Arlie said. "He wants to seem sexually proficient in college so he's been wanting to try all kinds of new things."

"Oh, this is too good. Go on!" Nathan said.

"Oh, just different positions. He got a bunch of toys from an online store and we've been playing with those. And let me tell you, Adam is a fan of ass-play." Arlie said.

Ioni gasped.

"You let him in the back door?" Ioni whispered.

"Not *my* back door," Arlie said.

At that Nathan bust out laughing and squatted on the floor, trying to stifle his loud braying. Ioni needed a moment to process what Arlie meant, and when the concept registered in her mind, her eyes got wide and her mouth nearly hit the floor.

"Ewww!" she whispered.

"Oh, don't be a prude! I'm sure Arlie makes him soap up that brown eye before she probes it." Nathan said.

"We have a little silicon sleeve that goes over my finger. It's knobby! So I'm not actually touching anything, but yes. He makes sure he's very clean before we go there!" she said, laughing.

Ioni couldn't help but join her friends in laughter.

"Well now that that's out of the way and I know more about our dear Adam than I needed to," Nathan said, "let's get some partying done!"

It was a good night. They all got fairly drunk and sang horrible karaoke. Luckily, nobody got sick. Chris was good about rationing out the drinks and offering a soda in place of beer if someone seemed a bit too tipsy.

As promised, Arlie and Adam disappeared together at one point, returning with smeared makeup and disheveled red yarn wigs. Nathan caught Arlie's eye and held up his left index finger and wiggled it teasingly. Arlie laughed and waved her hands.

There were two bedrooms in the downstairs of Adam's house and the huge sectional sofa had a fold-away bed. At about 2 a.m. Nathan and Chris retired to one of the bedrooms and Adam offered the other to Raber and Ioni.

As soon as the door was shut behind them, Ioni, overcome with the effects of the alcohol, attacked Raber. She was kissing him hungrily and slipping the fairy wings off when Raber slowly pushed her back.

"Not like this, sweetness," he said, kissing the tip of her nose.

Undeterred, Ioni stood back from Raber and slipped out of her fairy gown, letting it fall to the floor to reveal the lacy red bra and panty set she wore underneath. Raber exhaled roughly as his eyes took her in. She stepped back into him and began kissing him and fiddling with the zipper of his pants. She could feel the hardness beneath the zipper, and knew that he wanted her.

"Not like what?" She murmured into his ear as she nibbled on the lobe. Raber moaned softly, his hands running all over her body.

"We're drunk," he said, slipping his hand beneath her bra. "We shouldn't be having sloppy drunk sex." Ioni giggled as she freed Raber from his pants and grasped him hard in her hand. He tilted his head back and made a pained face.

"This is part of the fun of being drunk," she said. "Our inhibitions are lowered, we want to cut loose. Don't make me beg."

He pushed her away again and looked into her face. A smile spread across his full lips and he looked her over.

"If you had to beg," he began. "How would you go about it?"

Her head swimming from the alcohol and her entire body hot, she threw the bra off of herself and threw it across the room. She then knelt before Raber and took him into her mouth. He gasped loudly. Unsure of what to do, she tentatively kissed the tip and began bobbing her open mouth onto and then off of Raber. Her hands gripped his thighs. Before long, Raber stopped her.

He pulled her up to a standing position and kissed her. She couldn't seem to wrap herself around him tightly enough. She started to back up, but when her thighs met with the side of the bed, she fell over clumsily, hitting the floor with a thump. She giggled and threw herself onto the bed. She slipped her panties off and threw them in Raber's smiling face.

The next morning Ioni awoke feeling heavy and gross. She had never slept in the nude before and found that it was not as sexy as the movies made it to be. Her thighs were wet and sticky and there were parts of her sticking to themselves that she would have rather not thought about.

She started dressing in the soft pants and t-shirt that she'd packed and caught a glimpse of herself in the mirror. Her hair was a rat nest and her makeup was a mess. She turned and looked at the lump of covers that was her sleeping boyfriend and did her best to set herself to rights. When she felt that she no longer looked awful, she climbed back onto the bed and pulled the covers off Raber's head. She playfully stuck her finger in his ear and he jerked awake and sat up with such force that she tumbled backwards off the bed.

"Ow," Ioni said, looking up at the still surprised Raber.

"What the hell?" Raber said, feeling in his ear and looking at her angrily.

"I'm sorry," Ioni said, standing up. "I was just playing."

"You can't wake me up like that," Raber said, still scowling. "You're lucky I didn't hit you."

Ioni frowned and put her hands on her hips. She took a step back from the bed and glared at him.

"Lucky?" she asked. "I'm lucky that you didn't completely overreact, more than you are now, to my playfully waking you up after what I thought was a great night? That makes me lucky?"

"You don't know what I'm like when I'm sleeping," Raber said, making his tone less harsh. "I startle easily is what I meant. I'd never hit you on purpose."

"Well thanks for that non-apology," Ioni said angrily. "This morning has already been ruined."

She turned and stomped out of the room.

CHAPTER SEVEN

Life went on for a few weeks in a comfortably normal way. School strolled along at a relaxed pace. Home lives were quiet and uneventful.

Thanksgiving break came and went. Raber and Ioni split the day between their two homes. Raber's family typically liked to have their holiday meal early in the day while Ioni's family preferred to eat at a more regular dinner time, so it worked out nicely for them to be able to be together the whole day. Over the months the two had become comfortable in the company of each other's families. While Raber's family tended to be a bit icy in nature, they seemed to like Ioni and were always kind to her and Raber got along with Ioni's parents.

The pair had visited Bedelia's on a couple of occasions in order to procure some supplies for Wiccan beginners. Ioni enjoyed Karen's company and looked forward to being a part of her social circle. They'd been formally invited to the coven's Yule ritual and celebration on the winter solstice as outsiders of the coven. Ioni understood what an honor that invitation was. The Yule ritual would mark the first day of their training under Sarah. After a year and a day, it would work out nicely to be done with their training around the holidays.

Ioni found herself, for the first time in her life, making serious decisions for her future. She was planning her college education, her future career, her future lifestyle, and possibly even the future of her love life. She and Raber spent more time together than apart. She realized that it was not atypical in a teenage romance, but she felt such a strong bond with Raber that it scared her into a pause from time to time.

YOU'RE MINE

The first time they'd had a serious talk about their future and the possibility of marriage was discussed, she felt a surreal numbness. She loved Raber and she was committed to him, but she also felt that the commitment was temporary. Maybe it was because her sister and her friends had had her ear on the subject of settling down too early in life or maybe it was because sometimes Raber frightened her. He'd never threatened her or caused her any sort of real harm, but every now and then he would say something or react to something in a way that made Ioni look at him and think it wouldn't be smart to have him as a permanent fixture in her life. Those moments were fleeting and she would berate herself for being too harsh on a guy who loved her as honestly as Raber did.

For the most part it was turning out to be the best year of Ioni's life. School was going well, her friends all seemed to be happy, and she had someone with whom to spend the long hours. For the first time since hitting puberty, Ioni felt as if she were finally getting a clue as to the type of person she wanted to be. After years of emulating others and hiding behind her loud exterior, Ioni felt that there was finally something beneath all of that. The makeup and clothing wasn't going to stop being a part of her or her identity, but it was also no longer the defining thing about her. Her future was secure and planned, and her path was laid out clearly before her. All she had to do was move forward.

CHAPTER EIGHT

"Do I have to worry about how I dress?" Ioni asked Raber, looking at herself in the mirror. "I mean, I don't want to show up to this thing in jeans if it's a formal affair."

"I don't think you have to worry about something like that," Raber said, smiling and putting an arm around her waist. "We're there as outsiders anyhow, I assume people will say hello to us and then get to their business. We're just shadows tonight."

He kissed Ioni on her neck and cupped a breast in his hand. Ioni smiled and put a hand behind her onto his crotch.

"You'd better watch what you start tonight, Ms. Davis," Raber said into her ear.

She giggled and moved away from him and reexamined her reflection. She was wearing a pair of old and well-worn jeans with a thick black sweater, and lots of silver jewelry. Her eyes were heavily lined with black liner and her lips were pale with only a simple lip balm. She turned and looked at Raber, examining him. His shaved head gleamed in the late afternoon light. He wore black slacks and a dark green formal T-shirt. He was looking at her thoughtfully.

"What are you looking at?" she asked, smiling.

He just smiled and shook his head. He came close to Ioni again and kissed her cheek.

"We'd better go meet Sarah now," he said. "We're supposed to be at this ritual place at dark."

They bundled up in their winter gear and got into Raber's car and headed for Studio Adare. When they entered the warm interior, they were greeted with the sweet smells of cinnamon and berry.

"I swear she's burning a Walmart Christmas candle in here," Ioni said, smiling. "Like what my Nana has this time of year!"

Raber frowned down at Ioni, obviously annoyed with what he must have thought was an idiot observation.

"The holiday that we now call Christmas takes a lot from Yule," he said, looking away from her. "It's only common sense to know that you'll see some things that you recognize."

Ioni rolled her eyes and stepped away from him.

"Hello?" she called out, eager to have someone else to talk to for a moment.

"Hi, you guys," Sarah said coming out from the back. "Are you ready?"

"I'm really excited," Ioni said.

"Should you brief us on what we're about to see, so that we can learn from it?" Raber asked. Ioni stared at her shoes, her cheeks getting red.

"No," Sarah said, smiling. "I'm not gonna prepare you for a thing tonight. I want you to watch this with new eyes. This will be the last time you can view a ritual like this with a cowan perspective and I don't want to rob you of that wonder. If you have questions after, of course you can ask any of the coven about it. But going in, I'm not saying a thing, okay?"

Ioni looked up at Raber and saw that he was looking thoughtful and clenching his jaw. Fearing one of his scenes, she spoke up.

"I like that," Ioni said. "We won't be looking *for* things but *at* things."

"I understand why you're wanting us to go into this blind," Raber said. "I see why it would be important. I should tell you, though, that I did some research on Yule rituals and what to expect. I know the rituals differ greatly, but I couldn't go into this totally ignorant."

"Naturally," Sarah said, waving her hand in a matter-of-fact way while retrieving her coat from a hook on the wall. "I anticipated that you would do some reading on it. That's okay."

Sarah got into her car and Raber and Ioni settled into his. They followed Sarah to their destination. Ioni sat in a moody silence, looking at the bare trees and soft mountains in the distance. She leaned her head on the cold glass of her passenger-side door and sighed loudly.

"May as well tell me what you're sighing about before we get there so we can enjoy this evening," Raber said.

"Why do you have to be such a know-it-all?" Ioni demanded, whipping her head around so that she was facing him. "Why can't we just be new to this and not know anything?"

Raber looked over at her. To her surprise, he burst out laughing.

"Well, I'm sorry!" Raber said, still laughing. "That's just how I am, in case you didn't notice, dearest. I have tools at my disposal and I use them. I don't like being the dumb guy in the room. Maybe it's ego, maybe I've got a case of little man syndrome, I don't know. I just didn't want to go in without at least an idea of what was happening." He reached out and put his hand on her thigh.

"You were being a rude ass about it," Ioni said, grumpily. "Especially that comment you made to me about common sense. You may be smarter than me, or at least you love to think you're smarter than me, but I don't like you talking to me that way."

Raber looked back over to her. The smile was gone and he frowned.

"That was a bit of an asshole thing to say, wasn't it?" he said, squeezing her thigh.

"Yes," she said, placing her hand over top of his. "You're no better than me, Raber Belliveau and you just need to remember that."

"I will, sweetie. I will. I'm sorry." he said, sounding cowed.

Having that out of the way, the rest of the trip was pleasant. It was a long drive, and eventually they left the paved road behind them and started driving down what looked more like twin trenches in the dirt, more path than road. Ioni was pleasantly surprised at how close truly rural settings were to her hometown.

Nearly forty-five minutes later they followed Sarah's car down a horrifyingly steep hill to a large flat area, where several cars were already parked. It was dark outside, so they were unable to see much, but the car lights illuminated a large and well-maintained old barn right off of the gravel driveway.

"This is a fully functioning farm. A lot of us get our eggs and seasonal vegetables here. Those of us that eat meat can sometimes get some from here as well when an animal is slaughtered." Sarah said, meeting them in the darkness.

"Ritual slaughter?" Ioni said, her eyes wide. Raber laughed.

"No," Sarah said, laughing as well. "We don't use blood. That's a no-no. But you'll learn, don't worry."

They fell in behind Sarah and followed her through the dark. Ioni elbowed Raber in the ribs. He laughed again and held her close to him. She was good enough to realize that maybe her question was a bit naive, so she snuggled into her guy as they walked.

Sarah rang the doorbell and Karen answered the door. She embraced Sarah and kissed each of her cheeks. She then greeted Raber and Ioni in the same way.

"Welcome, brother and sisters!" Karen said, stepping to the side so that they could enter, revealing several people gathered within. "Happy Solstice! Happy Yule! Hail the rebirth of the Oak King!"

"HAIL!" all of the assembled called in response.

"This is going to be the second stupid thing I say tonight, but what the heck. Umm, why aren't you all wearing robes?" Ioni asked, her confusion overpowering any self-conscious thoughts that would have surely kept her from asking such a question.

Good-natured laughter answered her and she was embarrassed until Raber whispered in her ear, "I was wondering that too."

"Something you're going to learn as you become more acquainted with this is that nobody, but nobody practices the same. There are more variations of Wicca than just about any other religion out there. There are, I'm sure, some covens out there that wouldn't even consider having a ritual without ceremonial garb, especially on an important night like tonight. But we're a bit more laid-back about all of that. I have robes for sale at Bedelia's, and some of the members of this coven use them for personal use when communing. When we gather, we just like to show our respects and have our ceremonies and then kick back together. I'm sure there are a few things about tonight that are going to surprise you." Karen said.

Karen led them from the entrance of the house into a large living room. The room was warm and glowed with candlelight. Boughs of evergreen were draped over nearly everything that wouldn't run away and there were tall glasses filled with different red berries. It looked like a Victorian Christmas celebration. The air was filled with the rich and spicy scents very similar to the way Adare smelled earlier. Beneath that smell, the enticing smell of food greeted Ioni and her stomach grumbled.

"Everybody, your attention, please!" Karen said in a loud and authoritative voice. The assembled coven all turned their attention to the elder of their group and listened intently.

"Brothers and sisters, these two young people with our sister Adare are cowans here to witness our Yule ritual. They are to begin their year and a day training tomorrow with Adare. My friends, these two young people are initiates into our resplendent way of life. Raber Belliveau and Ioni Davis, these lovely people are my coven."

There was a loud boom of voices as the assembled coven wished their greetings to the couple. All wore smiles on their faces and seemed genuinely interested in meeting them. Ioni was thrilled to see sincerity rather than a feigned interest done in the guise of politeness.

"Um, excuse me," Raber said quietly so only Sarah and Karen could hear. "This is a weird thing to make a point of contention, but *why* don't you use ceremonial garb? Laziness can't be the only reason."

Ioni noticed that most of the people present were in blue jeans. She saw one lady wearing a filmy black dress, but most had opted for a casual type of clothing. Karen was wearing khaki slacks and Sarah was in her usual flowy hippie skirt.

"Karen," Sarah began. "Raber's intentions are clean and good, but he is a person who's really in love with the showmanship of a Pagan or Wiccan lifestyle. I think maybe we've put him off by being low-key."

"I'm sorry, I don't mean any offense by that," Raber began.

"No, honey, it's okay." Karen said. "You aren't even close to being the first person who was annoyed by our laid-back tendencies. The real reason why I've always shied away from demanding that this coven wear ceremonial garb is because of our area. We live in a part of the country where quite a lot of our residents are living below the poverty line. See, in my mother's day, you wouldn't have a hard time at all finding a person who could sew robes for the whole coven as a favor. But in this day and age, that skill isn't really all that important to learn anymore and it's quite costly to buy your own robe. It's merely a consideration. Every now and then, for certain rituals, a few members of this coven choose to perform in the nude. And when we have a Wiccan wedding, sometimes the couple choose to be skyclad when they make their vows."

"Skyclad?" Raber asked.

"Just another way of saying butt nekkid, honey," Karen said, smiling.

"Okay, why do you keep calling us cowans?" Ioni asked. Before Karen could answer, Raber turned to Ioni, smiling.

"It means that we're outsiders. We are neither members of this coven nor are we practitioners of Wicca." he said.

"Very good," Sarah said. "I knew you'd done some homework already."

"These two are going to be easy for you," Karen said, putting a hand on Sarah's shoulder.

Not long after, the group was called to assemble. Ioni and Raber stood by the front of the room, near the entryway. All but two people sat on the floor and seemed to be in a deep meditation. Karen stayed seated on the floor, eyes closed, and deep in her thoughts. The two people who did not sit were a man and a woman. Both were very tall and had dark skin. They held hands as they walked from the room. Many minutes passed before the woman returned alone.

"Let us cast the circle now and call the corners," she said.

The assembled coven rose up and followed her. Sarah waved for Raber and Ioni to follow, but they made sure to keep their distance. They all went into an upstairs room that was dark and cold. In the center of the room was a low table that Ioni knew to be an altar. The man and woman were standing on either side of the altar watching as people walked in. The coven assembled around them in a circle and clasped hands.

"I'm going to be nice to our visitors tonight and narrate some of the more basic things that we do. You two are welcome here and I hope you learn much in your journey," the woman said.

"This is how you cast a circle," the man said.

There was a lot of talking and motions made with a double-bladed ritual knife, incense, a chalice and a bowl of what looked to be salt. At first they walked around the coven members in a counter-clockwise circle and banished bad energy from the circle. They called it "widdershins." Then they walked around the coven, who stood perfectly still through the process, always making sure to go in a clockwise motion, what they called "deosil." There were candles lit and deities called and welcomed. Ioni found it all very overwhelming. She wondered how she would ever be able to memorize it all.

Once the circle was cast and the corners had been called (Ioni was completely confused as to what was going on), the ceremony started. The man brought out a chalice and held it out before him. The coven held their arms up above them, still clasped, and repeated what he said.

> *Darkness of winter's night*
> *Be overtaken now by light.*
> *We are thankful for your gifts bestowed*
> *Appreciation to the darkness owed.*

The chalice was passed around and every member took a drink. The woman refilled the chalice and Ioni almost fell over when she saw that the chalice was being filled with orange juice from a paper carton, common in any grocery store.

The woman held the chalice before her, and the coven, arms still above them, repeated after her.

> *Holly King, we humbly thank you for all you've wrought*
> *Your reign is done and another before us is brought.*
> *Oak King reborn, be strong above us in the sky*
> *Warm us with your blessings, bright from up high.*

Again, the chalice was passed around. When the last member drained the cup, the woman placed it on the altar. Then there was a lot more talking and the dispelling of the circle. Ioni was not at all confident that a year and a day was long enough for her to learn everything she'd just witnessed.

"Okay everyone, let's light the Yule log and then we'll feast!" Karen said, leading the way back to the warm light of the living room.

The man brought out a charred slab of wood and placed it inside of the fireplace on top of a lonely log sitting on the iron grate. The black shard went up in flames rather easily, and the fresh log started to burn in no time.

"We use a piece of last year's Yule log to light the one for this year. A piece of that one will be saved for next year," Sarah said behind them, making Ioni jump. Sarah laughed and hugged them. "Okay, I'm open for some questions now, as long as we can eat, too."

In the humble kitchen, the countertops were completely filled with trays of food. There was a huge turkey on a platter and Karen was busying herself by carving it and filling plates. There were more vegetable dishes than Ioni could count and five dessert dishes. The smell was pure heaven.

After their plates had been filled and they were seated on folding chairs in the living room, Raber and Ioni began asking Sarah about the ritual.

"Was that actually orange juice you guys drank the second time around?" Ioni asked.

"Yes, it was."

"Call me crazy, but I sort of expected you guys to be drinking wine." Ioni said.

"Some covens do," Sarah said. "But we have some people who aren't comfortable drinking alcohol when doing rituals. They feel it fogs them and they can't really commune with the higher powers. Also, one of us is a recovering alcoholic. It's a consideration. Alcohol isn't necessarily universally taboo, we just use juice in this coven to make sure no one feels excluded. The first chalice had apple cider in it."

"There was an awful lot of talking," Ioni said. "I don't know how I'm ever going to memorize all of that."

"Me too," Raber said, surprising Ioni.

"I think all beginners worry about that," the dark man who led the ritual said. They hadn't noticed he and the woman making their way over to them.

"I had all of that stuff written on a piece of notebook paper and I had to read off of it for a long time until I had it all memorized," the woman said.

Sarah smiled up at the two and waved Karen over to them. Karen walked over and put her arms around the man and woman's waists.

"Raber, Ioni, this is Tristan and Freya," Karen said. "They're my kids."

"Kids?" Raber asked, shocked.

Karen, Tristan, and Freya all laughed.

"I know it's not obvious on first glance of these two that they're mine, but I assure you, they are. They are my heirs and the future head priest and priestess of this coven. Tonight's ritual is one that works best with a priest and priestess so they've been heading it for us for the past three years now." Karen looked at Tristan and Freya, beaming with pride.

"It's so nice to meet you," Raber said, standing and shaking their hands. Ioni followed suit. Both Tristan and Freya were taller than Raber by at least two inches so Ioni had to angle her head back to look them in the face.

"I hope you don't find what happened here too intimidating," Tristan said. "We all had to start somewhere. It comes with practice and it really does get easier."

"It really does," Freya said, nodding.

"Tristan and Freya," Raber said, frowning. "I hope this isn't a faux pas to ask this, but are those your birth names or are they your Wiccan names?"

"In most cases, one's magical name is usually a very private matter and it would be kept either totally secret or shared only with one's coven." Tristan said. He put a hand on Sarah's shoulder and squeezed affectionately. "Our girl Adare here, well she's not greedy with her name and I'm sure you already knew it."

Raber and Ioni both nodded.

"The point my brother is making," Freya began, "is that if we had magical names that differed from our birth names we would not have shared them with outsiders. As it is, our mother gifted us with these names and the goddess knows us by these names. They are our names."

"I didn't mean to offend," Raber said. Ioni smiled to herself because Raber seemed to be saying that a lot that night. It wasn't a phrase he was accustomed to saying, she knew.

"Absolutely no offense taken," Tristan said, smiling widely, revealing imperfect but white teeth.

"You need to learn these things," Freya said, matching her brother's brilliant grin. "As we said before, we've all been in your place as beginners. There's no shame in curiosity."

Tristan put a hand on each of the newcomer's shoulders and leaned down so that he was looking into their faces.

"Welcome to you both. My sister and I look forward to seeing you again and communing with the goddess with you." At that, the siblings turned away in unison and began talking with the other people in the assembled group.

Both Raber and Ioni were left with no words and instead turned to Karen and Sarah, confusion plain on their faces.

"Twins," Karen said, gazing after her children. "They've finished each other's sentences and moved in tandem like that since the beginning."

"Um, well, it's hard to see a family resemblance," Raber said. Ioni jerked upright, offended by his unnecessarily nosey remark.

"My dear, they are my own flesh and blood. Their father was a witch too. We were briefly involved but ultimately decided to go our own ways. He's a big part of their lives nonetheless. A good man." Karen said, unperturbed.

"Okay, but if their father was a Wiccan and you're a Wiccan, weren't they brought up to be Wiccan? How is it that they were ever beginners at this?" Raber said.

Ioni smiled and rolled her eyes at Sarah and Sarah returned a knowing smile. Raber described himself as a glutton for information. Ioni was more inclined to describe him as a nibshit.

Luckily, Karen was a pillar of patience and it seemed like it was almost impossible to offend her.

"It's true that some people will raise their children in the Wiccan religion the same way Christians raise little Christians and Hindus raise little Hindus and so on. Their father and I, though, we thought it would be best to let the goddess call to our twins. We wanted them to choose this on their own. They were, I think, about fourteen years old when they asked to start their training and they did it in the very same way you're about to do it."

They didn't stay much longer. Sarah told them that it was fine for them to leave as soon or as late as they wanted. Ioni was relieved when Raber wanted to leave almost immediately after that. She was nervous being around all of those strangers and she was feeling a little wiped out from information overload.

CHAPTER NINE

The next day Raber and Ioni met with Sarah at her studio. Thanks to Raber's constant pursuit of information, they worked out that they would call her Sarah instead of Adare. Ioni was relieved to have that simplified because she was completely confused on the name-protocol thing. She understood that she was at the beginning of her education, but there were so many small details that she felt decidedly stupid when she thought on them for too long.

Learning was slow at first, but Sarah was trying to impart the philosophy of Wicca on them before the actual practice. Ioni was almost horrified by the complexities of words like intent, desire, will, and belief. Those were words that were larger and more intricate than she'd ever considered them to be.

It was complex and a bit daunting, Sarah made it a smooth journey. Even though Sarah was employed as an art teacher, she had never really come across as an impressive educator to Ioni before. As a mentor, Sarah proved to be extremely competent. Even Raber seemed satisfied with Sarah's knowledge and patience.

A comfortable routine was established. Twice a week Raber and Ioni met with Sarah at Adare and had lessons. Before long, they each had their own personal altars and were tentatively beginning communing rituals and meditations.

The pair continued steadily as a couple. Ioni was able to have an adult conversation with her mother about acquiring birth control pills and Raber was more than happy, as she knew he would be. They spent every spare minute with each other either in person or talking on the phone. Ioni loved Raber and she knew he felt the same. Of course, there were fights, but there were also resolutions. By the time spring rolled around, Ioni was wearing a simple silver ring that Raber had given her as a promise for a future together.

Graduation day came and went. Ioni was immeasurably relieved to be free of high school and the near-crippling awkwardness that she'd suffered as a result of labeling. She was happy to leave her more vulnerable years behind her. Thanks to a perfect storm of circumstances and coming of age, Ioni was finally starting to feel more firmly seated in her personal identity.

As promised, Arlie and Adam parted ways right after graduation. Ioni cried and had to be comforted by Arlie who laughed at her and called her a sentimental dummy.

Adam prepared for his departure to WVU and life in Morgantown. He went shopping at Abercromie and Fitch and Old Navy and bought all new clothes. He grew his hair out and stopped wearing makeup. Nathan called him a conformist fake, not trying all that hard to hide his disgust.

"I think that maybe he was only a member of your group because of Arlie," Raber had said. "I think he was trying to fit in with his girlfriend more than anything."

At first, Ioni was offended by Raber's claims, but as summer went on and they saw less and less of Adam, she knew that he was right. She'd heard that friends come and go, but she never really thought that any of *her* friends were capable of drifting off.

Arlie took a job at a photography studio and moved out of her mother's house. She rented a small trailer that was already on a lot in a trailer park in town. She was extremely proud of her first place and happy to have a steady paying job. She had dreams of someday being a full-time artist that were partially realized when Sarah told her about a starving artist's sale put on by the art students of WVU. Arlie took some of her works and was able to make a couple of sales. She was elated.

Nathan continued seeing Chris and they became serious fast. Nathan had no interest in higher education, so he took a full-time job at his father's store. He'd given up on being arm candy for a rough Hollywood-type man and said that working an honest job made him happy. Ioni and Arlie knew that Nathan's feelings for Chris played a large part in the new mindset, but there was nothing to be done except smile and be happy for their friend.

By the time August rolled around, Ioni started becoming anxious about Raber moving to live in the dorms in Morgantown. She had become accustomed to seeing Raber almost every day. While she was looking forward to her own first day of college, she was dreading having nobody in her day-to-day life besides her parents and sisters.

Ioni loved her family, but there was a distance between all of them, a lack of closeness or confidential relationships. She and her sisters were all so very, very different from each other and it was difficult for them to find any sort of common ground on which to bond. Rose and her deeply Christian religious views made it impossible for Ioni to feel that she could talk to her about anything personal. Amanda, although a sweet girl, was working hard on making sure that she was nothing like either of her sisters, who always flouted conventions. If conventional were a person, Amanda would be it.

As for her parents, Ioni knew that they loved and supported her. The fact that they were willing to let her live with them while she went to college showed that they cared for her and wanted to help her. They were good parents, but as a whole they could tend to be distant. They had their own lives, their own friends and their own careers. They viewed their daughters as more or less grown and independent and felt no need to be around them all that often. While that may seem like a dream to a teenager, it made Ioni feel abandoned. The love that she felt for her parents was sometimes seated in the shadow of the resentment that she felt for them for not being around in her times of hurt and teenaged vulnerability.

CHAPTER TEN

Ioni started having more alone time with her friends, without Raber, beginning in August as a sort of preparation for his departure. She was thankful that Arlie and Nathan were staying in town so that she wouldn't feel so alone. Of course, her friends were wise to her reasons for wanting happy friend time.

"He's only gonna be forty-five minutes away, you know," Nathan had said.

"Won't he be coming home on the weekends anyway?" Arlie asked.

They were right, all of that was true and it was what kept Ioni from having a complete meltdown over his leaving. She knew that if she needed him, it was completely reasonable for her to get in her car and go to him or vice versa. However, she and Raber had already discussed his not being able to come home every weekend. She understood that with his future hanging so heavily on this phase of his education, he had to make his schoolwork a priority. Logically, she knew that she couldn't come first in his life, not at that time at least. But her logical mind wasn't always driving the Ioni-bus and she had to grapple with the fact that she was going to miss him terribly, logical reasoning be damned.

"You guys can chat and talk on the phone, like every day," Nathan told her. "It's not like you won't have any contact with him at all. I've had entire relationships with closeted men and we would go weeks at a time without any sort of communication at all! You're lucky that we live in a time where communication can be quick and easy, like it is now."

"And he'll still have breaks," Arlie had added. "Christmas break is really long and he'll still have summers off."

"Unless he decides to take summer classes in order to shave a semester off of his time there," Ioni added glumly. "He hasn't decided yet if he's gonna go that route or not."

Nathan and Arlie were seated on a futon in Arlie's small living room and Ioni was sitting on a wooden chair across from them. They were both leaning forward and looking at her. She smiled at the concern on their faces.

"I know you guys are trying to help," she said. "I'm just determined to be in a shitty mood right now."

"We're perfect company for that kind of mindset," Arlie said, smiling. "We were never ones for sunshine and rainbows, were we, Nath?"

"Speak for yourself!" Nathan said. "My kind are all about the rainbows!" Arlie laughed and pushed Nathan over.

"Maybe change the subject?" Ioni offered.

"Sure," Arlie said.

"Tell us about how your witchy stuff is going," Nathan said. "That's not offensive, is it?"

"Nah," Ioni said, waving her hand dismissively. "I mean, once this is all over, I'll identify as a witch, so that word isn't hurtful or anything. Besides, I know you don't mean anything by it."

"And what about when Raber is done? Do we call him, like, The Great Exalted Warlock?" Arlie asked, snickering.

Ioni wasn't hurt by their playful teasing. She'd certainly done her fair share of lovingly teasing them.

"Well, actually, Sarah says that calling male Wiccans by a name different than what you would call a female Wiccan is divisive and sexist. According to her coven, all practitioners are witches. By calling the men warlocks, it gives an implied power to the men over the women." Ioni said.

"Hmm," Arlie said, giving a sideways smile to Nathan. "I think I like this view."

"It's good for you to be in something that empowers you, either way," Nathan said. "You get to own your femininity without having to step out of your comfort zone. I know what a delicate and non-confrontational little flower you can be," he said. "You're not outspoken like me or militant like Arlie."

"I'm not militant!" Arlie said, fake-punching Nathan in the arm. "I'm just short on tolerance for non-tolerance."

"I actually feel a lot better about myself than I have in forever," Ioni said. Hearing herself talk sometimes, she wished she were as eloquent as Raber.

"Because of Wicca?" Nathan asked.

"I think that's a big part of it," Ioni said. "I mean, I have Raber and he really makes me feel good about parts of myself that used to really disgust me. And then there's the getting older thing. I don't know, I feel really good about my life. I'm not a high school kid anymore. My best friends are independent and productive members of society. It's weird, but it's liberating. And with Wicca, I feel like I have something in my future that has nothing to do with school or a job or anything like that."

"Does it help that you share that with Raber?" Nathan asked.

"It's something else that we have in common, but it's more personal to me than even sharing it with Raber. I have no plans to break up with Raber, but if something were to happen and I were alone again, I take comfort in knowing that I would still have Wicca in my life. Does that make sense?" Ioni said.

Nathan and Arlie were both leaning forward on the futon looking at her hard again. Arlie was wearing a thoughtful frown while Nathan had a sideways smile.

"What?" she finally asked.

Arlie and Nathan gave each other knowing looks that said that Ioni had been a topic of private conversations between the two of them.

"*What*?" She asked again, annoyance plain in her tone.

"Don't get mad at us," Arlie began.

"We just love the hell out of you, you know," Nathan added.

"Well, what?" she said, throwing her hands up in frustration.

"There have been some very mild concerns over you maybe being a bit too attached to Raber. I mean, we almost haven't seen you at all this summer until this week and we know it's because you know Raber is going away. Don't get us wrong, we understand that you two are bonding and enjoying a good thing. We get that and I swear to God that we really do like Raber. We are so so so happy that you finally found someone and we can see how much you guys love each other..." Nathan trailed off and looked at Arlie helplessly.

"But..." Ioni said.

"It's not really a 'but', it's just we were wondering if maybe Raber was leading you to the Wiccan thing. We know you approached him about it but you've really taken to it and really made it your own. And that's a good thing! It's great!" Arlie said, looking at Nathan. "Nath and I are just really happy and relieved that you're doing it for yourself and not to make him happy."

Ioni sat back in the chair and looked at them. She could feel her face tighten into a frown. Arlie and Nathan were nervously glancing at each other.

"Is that how our relationship looks from the outside? I'm just the lovesick puppy doing whatever I can to make my master happy?" Ioni asked quietly.

"No!" Nathan said. "That's not it at all!" He looked back at Arlie and Arlie shrugged at him. "It's just that we know you and your sweet temperament. We've had a while to get to know Raber too and we see that he is a person who knows his own mind and nothing is gonna stop him. It's not a critique on you or your relationship, I swear, babe."

"We see that you guys really love each other," Arlie said. "We know that the feelings are mutual and that Raber really puts effort into making you happy. It was just us speculating is all. We're happy. That's what we're trying to say. We're happy for you. All of this, all that you've told us, is good."

Ioni stared at them for a moment longer trying to decide whether she wanted to be mad or not. Ultimately, she knew that their concerns were out of love for her and she let out a long sigh before giggling to herself. Nathan and Arlie relaxed and slumped back onto the futon.

"I know what he's like," Ioni began, smiling at her friends. "He's difficult and sometimes he's a know-it-all arrogant ass. He's got a temper, but I'm still my own person. I know we moved really fast, I saw your faces when I showed you my promise ring. I just figured that I was old enough for it to be okay for me to move a little faster. I mean, I've got a driver's license, I can vote, and I am a legal adult. It's not really such a big deal for Raber and I to at least daydream about our future together."

She was fiddling with the shoestring on her shoe to keep from looking at her friends. "I'm not completely stupid, you know. I know we may split up because we just aren't good together, or maybe he cheats or I cheat or a whole bunch of other possible reasons."

She was quiet for a while and kept her eyes lowered, concentrating on her shoelaces. Arlie and Nathan didn't so much as move. She couldn't even hear them breathing.

"I'm still my own person." She said finally.

"We're sorry," Arlie began. Ioni looked up at them and smiled at the way both of their mouths were turned down and their hands tightly clasped in their laps. They looked like two contrite little children.

"You guys are just too cute," Ioni said. "I know you're just concerned about me. I know that, so I am choosing to forgive and forget. There's nothing to be sorry about, okay?"

Arlie and Nathan eagerly nodded.

"Do you guys not really see Raber as a member of our little group?" Ioni asked suddenly.

Arlie and Nathan stiffened again and looked at each other.

"Well," Nathan began.

"No, not really." Arlie finished. Both of them looked sorry for having to admit that.

"Again, it's not that we don't like the dude," Nathan said. "But if we had to choose between the two of you, it would be a no-brainer. We love you and he could fuck right off."

Ioni couldn't help but laugh at that.

"He has a stand-offish way about him," Arlie said. "It's not necessarily bad and you have to remember, we haven't really known the guy all that long and for most of that time he's been 'Ioni's boyfriend.' It might be us being too protective of our inner circle. It probably has nothing to do with him at all."

"I'm not offended," Ioni said. "It just never occurred to me before that he might not work on you guys like he does with me. You don't have to love him or have him present at every birthday party. All I can ask of you guys is that you're nice to him, and you do that. I never once considered that you guys didn't feel as comfortable around him as me, but how could you? You don't see him nearly as much as I do and most of what you know about him you've learned from me."

Arlie and Nathan kept quiet and seemed to be waiting for her to finish her train of thought.

"That's all I had to say," Ioni said, smiling self-consciously.

"That's good, then," Arlie said. "We see that he makes you happy, so he's good in our books."

"And we know that he gives it to you good," Nathan said, smiling. "You can't ask for much more at this point."

Ioni felt her cheeks burn and she lowered her gaze. She was eager to change the subject.

"So, Arlie," she began. "How's the single life treating you?"

Arlie inhaled sharply and immediately looked over at Nathan.

"Don't look at me! I haven't been servicing you and your icky bits!" he said.

Arlie laughed and looked down at her hands.

"I'm just enjoying some quiet time right now, getting to know myself as a singular entity. I needed to really get in touch with my inner femininity without having a masculine presence around to cloud that discovery."

"Ugh," Nathan said. "I swear you quote feminist propaganda just to annoy me."

Arlie laughed.

"I'm just being honest. Adam wanted to be free to be a walking boner, and now I've got all of this alone time. I might as well make myself a creature of substance instead of a guy-crazy…thing."

Ioni listened, thinking. Arlie had a point and Ioni found herself grateful that there was something in her life that could benefit her with or without a man in her life. She had school and Wicca, and they could be her things of substance. Raber, as much as she loved him, was just a bonus, not her entire life experience.

CHAPTER ELEVEN

Ioni stood with her back to Raber, looking out of the window of his dorm. She had driven her own car to Morgantown to help him unpack his belongings and was now dreading having to leave without him.

His dorm was small, as most dorms tend to be. There were two unfortunately narrow beds on either side of the room. Raber, arriving before his roommate, took the bed that was closest to the window. He'd finished unpacking all of his clothes and hooking up his computer and printer, and was now sitting on his bed looking around him.

"I'm really going to miss you, baby," he said quietly. Ioni squeezed her eyes shut, trying to control the tsunami of emotions barreling through her head.

"I'm really gonna miss you too," she said quickly, trying to mask the thickness in her voice.

"Will you come see me next weekend?"

The topic of "next weekend" had been a tense subject between the two of them for nearly a month. Raber wanted to be able to stay in Morgantown the weekend after classes began to become more accustomed to the area and possibly make some friends. Ioni wanted to be able to have a quiet weekend at home after the first week of classes. To him, she should come to Morgantown and party with him. To her, he should come home and spend the weekend with her. He was asking about it then because they had yet to resolve the issue.

"I'm gonna stay in town," she said, keeping her back to Raber. "I'm gonna go to Bedelia's on Saturday and then on Sunday I am gonna have dinner at Arlie's with her and Nath."

"That means we won't be seeing each other for a while," Raber said gently. She was grateful that he wasn't angry with her. She turned to him finally. He was looking at her, his eyes wide and his mouth pursed tightly the way it tended to when he was unhappy. She smiled and sat down next to him and put her head on his shoulder. She felt him kiss the top of her head.

"We're supposed to be adults now, babe," she said to him. "Or at least adults in training. I think we can manage to not be all up in each other's butts for a while." He chuckled deeply against her.

"We've still got phone calls and messaging," he said.

After hugs and kisses and Ioni embarrassing herself by crying, they finally parted ways. She drove half of the way back home sniffling and hiccupping before she pulled into a gas station and got herself an Icee to make herself feel better. She sat in her car sipping the super sweet drink, but still couldn't shake her emotional state.

She called Nathan from the payphone next to the bathrooms.

"I take it the goodbye wasn't as easy as you said it would be," Nathan said, upon hearing her voice.

"I'll be okay," Ioni said. "Eventually."

"Meet me at Eat N' Park. I'm leaving now." Nathan said.

She knew she was lucky to have such good friends. Nathan would have been within his rights to simply say a few generic comforting words and then go on with his life. Instead, he decided to drop everything to be there for her when she sounded like she needed it.

Ioni sat in her car a moment longer, staring down the straw of her Icee, wondering if she was a damsel in distress always in need of rescuing. She thought of Arlie who had just ended a years-long relationship with relative ease. Arlie was a low-maintenance and independent person and Ioni envied her friend her easygoing and confident nature. She knew that she'd been a handful to Raber in their time together, and she knew, thanks to her friends, that perhaps she relied too heavily on him, but she hoped that being conscious of that was the first step toward fixing it, toward growing the hell up.

She thought of Nathan, who had been used in disgusting ways and still believed in the good in people. He was a tireless optimist and when he loved a person there was no limit to what he would do for them. There was a lot of good in her friends and she wished she could match them. She knew she fell short of the standard that they represented, that her low self-esteem could tend to make her self-involved and she knew that of her friends, she was the weak one, the one always needing help and uplifting. Sitting in that gas station parking lot, guzzling frozen syrup, Ioni was disgusted with herself.

She met Nathan at the Eat N' Park and they ate bad food and talked about nothing for two hours. When the checks were paid and they were standing under the awning getting ready to go to their own vehicles, Nathan turned to Ioni.

"You're going to be just fine, you know," he said to her. "Don't be a Negative Nancy and keep that chin up and you're gonna be great." He turned, got into his car, and left Ioni staring after him.

"I'm not a Negative Nancy," she muttered to herself.

The next week was hectic. Ioni was trying to get used to the pace of college on top of looking for a part-time job. She met with Sarah at Adare for some lessons and basic companionship on Wednesday as had become their routine. She and Raber were able to maintain near-constant contact thanks to ICQ and phone calls. She surprisingly didn't miss his presence as much as she feared when she left him in his dorm.

CHAPTER TWELVE

That Saturday, Ioni and Sarah spent the afternoon at Bedelia's eating lunch with Karen and her son, Tristan. She felt a little uncomfortable around Tristan because she had only seen him once or twice since the Yule celebration, and that was mostly in passing. She kept quiet and listened to the others talk until Sarah nudged her and asked quietly if everything was okay.

"*I guess as much as I'd like to think that I'm a grownup, I'm still a stupid, shy little girl,*" she thought to herself before answering that she was fine, just totally fine. Sarah saw through it.

"If you join this coven, you're going to be seeing a lot of Tristan," Sarah said quietly. Then a wide smile cracked her face and she chuckled. "Quite a lot."

Ioni cocked an eyebrow at Sarah in a questioning manner and Sarah leaned in closer to Ioni.

"He's rather fond of being naked and will sometimes strip down and dance during some rituals."

Ioni's eyes widened and she turned her head to look at Tristan's back. He was standing next to Karen, helping her dry the lunch dishes. Without thinking, her eyes moved over his long, lean body and her mind flashed a mental image of what he might look like naked. She felt the corners of her mouth starting to pull into a small smile, but when she looked back at Sarah and saw her mischievously smiling back at her, Ioni blushed and looked down into her lap.

"It's not an odd thing," Sarah said, keeping her voice low. "It's common for some Wiccans to choose to be skyclad during certain rituals and ceremonies. Not too many in this coven opt in on that, but it does happen."

"It's nothing to be scandalized about," Tristan said, sitting himself across from Ioni. His wide smile lit up his face and the corners of his eyes wrinkled in a pleasant way. "I am as I was made and sometimes I think it's only fair that the goddess gets to see her good work."

Ioni blushed even deeper and looked into her lap while Tristan, Sarah, and Karen laughed. Sarah reached out and put a hand on Ioni's shoulder and smiled at her sympathetically.

"Oh, honey," Karen said, still smiling. "You'll learn soon enough to let go of these learned prudish ideas. There's nothing at all perverted or sexual about a bit of nudity and dancing. Not in this context, at least. But...well," she looked at Tristan and then to Sarah. "I guess we ought to be entirely open about what you can expect if you choose to be in a coven, though. If you're uncomfortable with a bit of nudity..."

"Oh god, you're not gonna tell me you all do orgies, are you?" Ioni asked. She was beginning to feel cornered and uncomfortable.

Again, the other three burst into laughter.

"No, no!" Tristan said, waving his hands in front of him. "We get together to practice our religion and sometimes we are moved to remove our clothing and worship like that. But we do not all collapse onto the floor afterward! Despite the nudity, it's actually very pure."

Ioni's heated blush just wouldn't quit. She was embarrassed at her presumption.

"I'm waiting for the 'but' of this," Ioni said. The others continued to grin.

"Well, sex between coven members isn't taboo," Sarah said. "It's, of course, completely consensual, and we aren't doing it in the middle of the room or anything but certain ceremonies and rituals *can* tend to bring out an amorous mood. We don't consider it dirty or promiscuous and we absolutely respect our members who choose to be monogamous." Sarah frowned a little when she saw that Ioni still looked aghast.

"It happens sometimes, is all," Karen added calmly. "There's no such thing as a slut in Wicca. If the mood overtakes you and you aren't hurting anybody, there's nothing wrong with some healthy sex."

"There are members of this coven who have never so much as kissed any other member. We aren't a sex group," Tristan said, pulling at his lower lip, obviously trying to calm his smile.

"I'm so sorry," Ioni said after a moment. "I really misunderstood that and I didn't mean to sound like an old lady."

The other three laughed again.

"I was a little worried your head was going to start steaming, you were blushing so hard," Karen said.

"I'm still kind of new to...err...well...sex." Ioni said, fidgeting.

"You'll grow out of it, honey," Karen said. "Just give it time. You'd be surprised at how much comfort with oneself comes with age. Our bodies start to sag and go wonky on us, but by the time that starts happening, we've had the chance to really get used to and bond with them. You have to remember, you've only been an adult and physically mature woman for a short time. It does take a while."

Ioni nodded and tried to avoid making eye contact. She heard Tristan chuckle.

"I don't have nearly enough contact with these green ones," he said. "This is just damned adorable."

"She's a sweet one," Sarah said.

"You two are making it worse on this poor girl!" Karen said. "How about we change the subject before her face stays red forever?"

"Please," Ioni said.

"Oh, all right then," Tristan said, feigning disappointment. "What should the new subject be? Do you have any questions?"

"Actually, I do have a question," Ioni said, sitting up straight.

"Let's hear it," Tristan said.

"It's about the power hand," she began. "Well, there are a couple of questions about hands, actually. But let's start with the power hand. Okay, so, is my power hand my dominant hand? Like, I'm right-handed in every other aspect of life, so does that mean that my power hand is my right hand? I've tried using both hands and to be honest, I'm not that sure. Maybe I'm overthinking it?"

Sarah eased back into her kitchen chair. Karen began to say something, but Tristan put a hand on her arm and stopped her. He leaned forward over the smoked glass of the kitchen table and looked Ioni in the eyes.

"Hold both of your hands up before you," he said. "Palms out and in front of your face so that all you can see is the backs of your hands."

Ioni did as he said. She sat, tense, waiting for Tristan to throw something at her or anything else to startle a defensive reaction. Instead, she felt a hand slide onto her knee and start to creep up her thigh. Ioni jerked her leg away, and flung her chair back from the table. Furious, she stood up and pointed at Tristan.

"That was unwanted, and uninvited!" she said, furious. "I thought you guys were all about consensual issues and you know that I'm with Raber! Why would you trick me like that?" Huffing, she looked at Karen and Sarah and was stopped by what they were doing.

Both women were smiling and looking at Tristan, shaking their heads slowly. Tristan, too, was wearing a grin. He was pushed back in his chair and his arms were crossed over his chest, his smirk confusing Ioni.

"Okay, see that hand there?" Tristan said, pointing to the finger that she had thrust into his face. "That is your power hand. That hand is your instrument of power and persuasion. And I see that it is, indeed, your right hand, so that'll make things easy to remember."

Ioni stood there a moment longer, her finger still jabbed accusingly at Tristan, looking from face to face. Finally she puffed out a large breath and sat down again, resuming her position across from Tristan.

"What else about hands had you curious?" he asked.

She sat for a moment, trying to gather her thoughts and remember her other questions. She felt Sarah put a hand on her shoulder and give her a comforting squeeze.

"Oh, Tristan," Karen said. "You insensitive idiot, you frazzled the poor girl."

He opened his hands, inviting Ioni to place her hands inside of his. After a moment of hesitation, she did as he wanted and he gently closed his long fingers over her hands.

"I'm sorry," he said kindly. "I just wanted to shock a reaction out of you. Your body knows which hand is your power hand more than your mind. I know you're in a relationship and I'm not trying to be inappropriate." He chuckled and smiled wider. "Okay, not *that* inappropriate. You're safe around me, okay?"

Ioni nodded and swallowed hard. Tristan let go of her hands and sat back in his chair, folding his arms over his chest again.

"Umm, I was reading this thing online," she began. She picked up her glass and took a long sip of water. "Okay, I'm okay." Tristan made a motion with his hands that bid her to continue.

"Okay," she began. "Right hand versus left hand. When you refer to paths and stuff, what does that all mean? I'm asking because I'm actually worried about how you guys might view Raber. See, I seemed to get the impression that left-handed people are seen as bad, and Raber is a lefty, but he's not bad."

"That's a bit of old thought," Karen said. "All right, let's see how to make this easy. Okay, in this instance, right and left refers to paths. Say you come to a fork in the road and you can either go left or right. In this case, if you go right, the right-hand path, you are taking a path of someone who wishes to *serve* the divine. In Wicca, we like to be servants of the higher power, not the possessors of power. Now, if you take the left fork, the left-hand path, you are taking the path of someone who believes that they have the divine within themselves. You see how Wiccans wouldn't see that as a good thing? This is typically where people turn to black magic.

"Now, in the old days," she continued. "Old days meaning before even I was born, left-handed people were generally shunned by covens that practiced white magic because it was believed that they would tend to take a left-hand path regarding magic. We don't really believe that anymore. Hell, I don't even pay attention to who uses what hand. We're all good people."

Sarah and Tristan were nodding in agreement.

"Is black magic something that we would normally worry about?" Ioni asked.

"We're wary of it," Sarah answered simply.

"We don't even associate with practitioners of black magic," Karen said. "It's a dangerous game that is made all the more slippery by how seductive that kind of power can be to a person. Even the most well-intentioned Wiccan can be enticed and lured into that kind of thinking. Sometimes the reasons for trying to gain that kind of control start out noble and unselfish, but they warp and become self-serving all too quickly. The thing that makes dark practitioners most dangerous to us and our beliefs is that they sometimes don't even identify as white or black. They like to say things like 'it is what it is, there is no white magic or dark magic,' but they couldn't be more wrong."

"So, it's like Satan worshipers are to the Christians?" Ioni asked.

"No, not really." Tristan answered.

"It's not quite like that," Karen said, a smile tickling the corners of her mouth. "Maybe a little bit, though."

"Is it?" Sarah asked, a frown knitting her brows together.

"Well, in some ways, yes." Karen answered. "You see, the Church of Satan was set up to be purely adversarial to the organized powerhouse of the Christian church system. It was a way to throw mud in the face of power. At first, they wanted to be known as the anti-religion religion. That changed of course, over time and with the changing of the people who run it, and it's now a way of life that has practitioners and rituals and gatherings the same as pretty much any religion. The thing about the Church of Satan, though, is that despite the name, they seem to take a lot of power and control into their own hands. They don't put any faith or trust in the all-knowing power of a higher being. That aspect of it is pretty similar. Do I believe members of the Church of Satan are all evil? No, not at all. I even know a few members. Lovely, kind people, all of them. As for black magic, there is something very seductive about not being in the mainstream of things, especially where the mainstream can sometimes seem like it is populated with brainless followers with no thoughts or will of their own."

"But isn't that kind of thinking dangerous? Isn't that kind of control what we seek to avoid?" Sarah asked.

"I'm gonna be honest, I am not really an expert in the Church of Satan. I was around when Anton LaVey founded the church and wrote the Satanic Bible. I saw all of the horror ramped up by the media and the general public. I was always taught to have an open and accepting mind, so I didn't really see anything too terribly shocking about it. I mean, I've been a practicing Wiccan all of my life. Rituals and costumes are just that in my eyes. I didn't see a group of evil people trying to harm others unless there were cameras around, then they acted the shit out of it, especially in Anton's day. But mostly I saw a group of people trying something new. True black magic, thank the goddess, is rare to come by. The worst thing about it, is that it almost makes sense. It sounds rational. But you always have to remember, no matter how good the intentions start out, it always becomes self-centered and destructive in the end."

"Okay," Ioni said. "I'm not making a case against you or anything, but if we're taught to be accepting and tolerant of other lifestyles and beliefs, why go to so much trouble to stay away from black magic? Why is there such an urgency to keep that away from you?"

"Great question," Tristan said, smiling.

"We're the most susceptible to the lure of that kind of life," Karen said. "We're also the people who have the most at stake if we lose ourselves in that. Take your average Baptist on Main Street, Stearnsville. They're not going to be at all seduced by the call of black magic. Their faith holds them steady for the most part. But seeing how we're just one side of the same coin, we're very easily led astray. We hear the beat of that drum more acutely than others might and it is an intoxicating beat that we all secretly want to dance to. Does that make sense?"

"I think so," Ioni said. "So, it's a danger to our faith?"

"Black magic is a danger to everything that we believe and everything we are. We're better off staying as far away from it as possible. Where we're usually eager to learn about new and strange things, that is not one of them. It's just too dangerous, and we need to know that we can't trust ourselves around it." Karen said.

"We're a danger to ourselves..." Ioni said thoughtfully. "Yeah, that makes sense. Like maybe you want to save someone who is dying and instead of relying on a higher power who is more or less usually absent, you want to take that power into yourself. It would start out as noble and selfless, but then it would be like a domino effect and where one thing didn't seem like an abuse of power. It would keep one-upping."

"Exactly," Karen said. "You get it now."

"So is this just a sort of unwritten rule or am I obligated to not have any sort of contact with people who practice black magic?" Ioni asked.

"Are you thinking about exploring it?" Sarah asked.

"No! No, I'm just asking. Isn't it okay to be curious?" Ioni asked.

"Of course it's okay. We even encourage it," Tristan said. "For now."

"When you are initiated into this coven, you are expected to adhere to this rule. It's something that we believe in strongly enough to dismiss you from the coven should you disobey." Karen answered.

"Oh," Ioni said. "Wow."

"We can't let you endanger the rest of us if you get sucked in," Sarah said.

"So this is really serious business, then?" Ioni asked. "I mean, for the most part, Christians don't really seem to spend too much time or energy worrying about the Satan worshippers. I don't think your Main Street Baptist would be friends with a Satan worshipper or anything, but there isn't a really stringent no tolerance policy either. It seems like the only time Satan worshippers get any real attention is when some sort of weird murder happens and it looks like a cult thing. Otherwise, people seem to think that Satan worshippers are reserved for horror movies."

"Yup," Tristan said.

"Our horror comes from knowing that black magic is very real and is a very real threat to us and our way of life," Karen said. "It's scary because we, us, ourselves, would be the instruments of our own demise."

"Okay," Ioni said. "I think I understand."

"You are a very astute young woman and I have nothing but the highest hopes for you." Karen said, a warmth and appreciation coming from her that Ioni wished she could have had at home from her own mother.

Ioni felt herself blushing again and wished dearly that she could stop herself from going red every time someone complimented her. She decided to start popping off whatever came out of her mouth in order to change the subject. It didn't go as planned.

"Really?" she said. "I mean, you really think I'm promising, or whatever? I'm not fishing for compliments, oh my God, I'm really not. I mean goddess. Or god. There are both. But oh geez, stop it, girl. No, what I mean, is...damn it. Okay, let me regroup. Okay, I mean, do you really think I'm cut out for this because Raber isn't really all that dedicated to it anymore and my family doesn't know about it and my friends are really supportive but they don't really understand and I'm just really insecure that I'm just being a sort of wet rag and just going along with the motions."

There was a silence as the three elders stared at Ioni, their eyebrows all raised in confusion and amused shock at her outburst. Tristan's cheeks puffed out as he was trying to hold in laughter, and when Karen got a load of his face, she lost it and laughed loud and heartily. Sarah patted Ioni on the shoulder as she laughed too. Ioni was embarrassed at having shown her desperate, awkward side, but she wasn't afraid of being laughed at by the kind people sitting with her. Perhaps that was progress.

"That was quite a rant," Karen said, wiping tears away from her eyes.

"I'm not sure where that came from," Ioni mumbled to her lap.

"Honey," Karen said, reaching across the table and offering an open hand for Ioni to take. "I think Sarah and I know you well enough at this point to say that you are obviously very committed to Wicca and to service to our higher powers. There isn't anything about your unwavering dedication to learn that has ever indicated otherwise to us. You don't need to feel self-conscious around us. Not any of us. Those of us who have met you just think the world of you."

"And as for Raber's dedication," Sarah began, "I've already gathered as much. I don't think he thought much of me and my knowledge, but that's okay. I'm okay with that. At least we're getting you out of this, and you're wonderful."

"Okay, I'm blushing way too much here," Ioni said, covering her face with her hands. "I'm sorry to act like such a stupid kid."

"You're sweet and innocent," Karen said. "There's nothing wrong with that. It's one of the things that endears you to me."

"To all of us," Tristan said.

Ioni and Sarah left soon after, hugging Karen at the door. Ioni extended a hand to Tristan to shake, but he instead stepped his tall figure into her personal bubble and hugged her. Ioni stood there, rigid and freaked out, with Tristan's long arms wrapped around her. She lifted her arms and politely patted him on the back before pulling away. Tristan was smiling down at her.

"May the goddess rain her blessings down on you," he said.

"Oh, umm, thanks." Ioni said. "You, too."

Tristan smiled at her and walked back into Bedelia's. Karen watched him go and turned to Ioni and smiled warmly at her.

"He's friendly with everyone like that," she said. "Don't let it upset you."

In Sarah's car, Ioni watched the scenery from the passenger window. She wanted to ask Sarah about Tristan's seemingly over-attentiveness to her, but was afraid of sounding full of herself. Finally, the curiosity got the better of her.

"Can I ask you something?" Ioni asked.

Sarah chuckled softly and looked over at Ioni.

"I was wondering when you would," she said. "Let me guess, Tristan?"

Ioni nodded, embarrassed.

"He *isn't* normally that friendly with people. Yeah, he's an affectionate guy, but I think that he was pretty focused on you today."

"Oh God," Ioni said. "What do I do?"

Again, Sarah chuckled. When she saw that Ioni was actually very serious, she frowned.

"Do you feel that maybe he was being inappropriate or aggressive? Because if so, you tell me and I promise it will never happen again."

"NO! Nothing like that! I don't feel victimized or anything, but I'm dating Raber. I've been dating Raber for nearly a year now! How could he do that?" Ioni said. Her stomach was in knots.

"Oh. Oh, Ioni. I forget sometimes what a shy girl you are," Sarah said, pity in her voice. Ioni became both embarrassed and annoyed.

"I'm dating the first and only guy to ever really flirt with me, so excuse me if I'm not sure how to handle this." she said grumpily.

To her surprise, Sarah laughed.

"That's okay," Sarah said. "Look, it's like this. Some people are just flirts. You'll run into a lot of them in your life. It makes them feel good about themselves and it entertains them to flirt with people. It's not some nefarious plan to make you their love slave or anything. More often than not, it's just innocent fun. I mean, it does mean that Tristan likes you, but he knows you're with Raber and he'll respect that. And I don't think anyone would think less of you if you found yourself flattered. But again, if you feel it crosses a line, let me know and I'll put a stop to it, no judgement, no questions. Okay?"

Ioni took a moment to process that and finally nodded.

"Okay," she said. "I think once I stop being weirded out about this, I might be able to feel good about that."

She sat in silence, looking out of the car window, but not really seeing the familiar landscape rushing by. She was thinking hard, wondering if she was bothered by Tristan. Something about him made her uncomfortable, and upon thinking about it, she realized that it was her own attraction to him that made her nervous. Her devotion to Raber made her afraid of even an innocent appreciation for another guy. She sighed and slumped down in the seat, feeling hopeless with herself. But then she smiled.

"A good-looking man flirted with me today," she said softly. "I could never tell Raber about this."

CHAPTER THIRTEEN

It was the first weekend of October before Raber and Ioni finally had a physical reunion after more than a month. It was a Friday and Raber had come immediately after his last class of the day. Ioni had never been happier to see anybody.

"I'm so happy to be sitting here with you right now," he said to her as they sat waiting for their food to arrive. "I'd forgotten how good your skin feels and how intoxicating you smell."

Ioni smiled and reached for his hand across the table. She noticed that he looked slightly haggard but chalked it up to either the harsh lighting of the restaurant or his hectic schedule.

"I'm just so glad you're here," she said to him.

She leaned across the table so that her face was inches from his and whispered, "I think that was the best sex we've had yet." Raber chuckled, reached out and stroked her hair.

"I love how you end that with the word 'yet'," he said. "There's a lot more of those in store for you, Ms. Davis. Wait until I've gotten sustenance from this greasy food. Just you wait."

Later that night, Raber made good on his promise in the back seat of Ioni's car. They had not taken the time to fully strip, so recomposing themselves was a quick affair. They cuddled, relaxed. Ioni was glad that their closeness had not been damaged by physical distance.

"I love you," she said softly.

Raber stroked her hair and kissed her temple. They settled into a comfortable quiet, and Ioni felt herself getting drowsy.

117

"Hey, baby," Raber said.

"Hey, what?" she said, sitting up.

"I'm really sorry I missed your birthday."

It had been a heated argument between the two of them. Ioni's birthday was a week after classes started. She understood that Raber couldn't come in to help her celebrate, so she offered to drive to Morgantown so that they could be together. Raber had said that he had a lab on that evening and then a study session with a classmate. Pride got the better of both of them where each took an opposing position and they argued how the other was not being considerate. Eventually, seeing that they were at an impasse, Ioni had shut down the conversation by ignoring any other messages or phone calls from Raber for two days. She realized that was not the most mature reaction, but she was hurt that even when she offered to make the drive to see him, he still shot her down. Until that moment, the subject had been avoided.

"Don't worry about it," she said, trying not to sound bitter. "Arlie, Nath, Chris, and me all had a nice dinner and a movie thing. It was fine. And mom and dad gave me two hundred dollars and I'm thinking about getting a tattoo."

"I feel bad, though. I hate the fact that you got so upset with me that you wouldn't even communicate for days on end." he said.

"It was two days, and don't worry about it. I don't really want to get into this again because it's still an exposed nerve so just drop it, okay?" Ioni started to feel herself going tense and hoped Raber would drop it.

"Okay," he said after a minute. "I'll drop it. Just know I feel bad about it, okay?"

"Okay," Ioni said.

"And are you sorry that you refused to talk to me for two days?" he prodded.

Ioni bolted up to a straight-backed position and stared at Raber in disbelief.

"Are you fucking kidding me?" she asked quietly. Raber looked shocked at her reaction and his mouth started trying to form words that didn't come out at first.

"Uhh, what?" he asked finally. "Was that offsides? I thought since we were apologizing to each other, you might want to apologize for your reaction..."

"Just change the subject, Raber." Ioni said, still quietly.

"You're not sorry?" he asked, sounding genuinely hurt.

"Change. The. Subject." she said, her voice almost a low growl.

"Oh. O-okay," he said, looking confused. "Well, uhh, what movie did you guys go and see?"

"It doesn't really matter," Ioni said, knowing that the mood was ruined. "My friends took care of me and wouldn't let me be alone on my own birthday. That's what matters."

There was a long silence. Ioni had moved away from Raber and was looking out of the window, her back to him. After a few minutes, she felt his hand on her back. She almost pulled away from him, but he started talking.

"Oh, baby," he said. "Shit, I'm really sorry. Goddamn it, I wasn't even thinking about that. I'm so sorry. I'm sorry I wanted you to apologize when you had a perfectly good reason to be furious with me. Baby. Hey, look at me."

He reached around and gently moved her face so that she was looking at him.

"I'm sorry, Ioni. I really am. I wasn't thinking like that. I love you," he said, kissing the tip of her nose. "I love you and I don't deserve you. I'm so sorry."

Ioni felt the heat of anger leave and the lump in her throat loosen. She relaxed and leaned back onto Raber. She realized that she was being a brat, but it still felt good to get an honest apology.

The next day, Saturday, Raber showed up at Ioni's parent's house before noon and told her that he wanted to go to the nearest Rail Trail for a walk.

It was in the low seventies that day. The sun was warm and the breeze was cool and pleasant, and the leaves were just starting to turn. It was a wonderful day to be out with a loved one. As they walked hand in hand, they chit-chatted about nothing.

"Have I told you about Andrew yet?" Raber asked.

"He's your lab partner?" Ioni asked.

"Oh, so I didn't tell you everything. Okay, well Andrew lives in my building and we know each other from this class. We've started hanging out on our off time. He's not a goth or anything, but he practices magic."

"Really?" Ioni asked, suddenly interested. "Is he Wiccan or just a witch?"

"I don't think he's Wiccan," he said. "But he's been practicing magic for about five years, or so I gather. He seems to know a lot."

"That's really awesome," she said. "How crazy to find someone with something as big as that in common with you, huh?"

"I know. I'd really like for you to meet him," Raber said. "I've told him all about you and he wants to meet you. He says he could teach us things. Things Sarah might not know."

"Sarah knows a lot, though," Ioni said, tired of how Raber was always underestimating their mentor.

"She does," Raber agreed. "But there are so many different sects of Wicca and magic that Andrew might know some things that you and I might find useful. Will you meet him?"

"Sure," she replied, deciding to relax and enjoy his company. "When?"

"You want to come back to Morgantown with me tomorrow afternoon and meet him there? I won't keep you too late."

"I can do that," Ioni said. Raber kissed her and they walked on.

The rest of the day and night were spent in constant physical contact with each other. Ioni felt happy and completely satisfied. She hoped it would be like that every time they got to be together. She was certain of it, in fact, and was already looking forward to the long winter break she and Raber would get from school in just a couple of months.

CHAPTER FOURTEEN

After one last toss in the sheets of Raber's bed, they were off in their own respective cars to Morgantown. Ioni felt extremely upbeat and happy after such a great weekend and sang loudly along with the radio for the whole drive.

She and Raber pulled into a public parking area where she left her car and got into his car so he could drive her to his dorm. He had his own parking pass that his father had been able to finagle thanks to some well-connected friends. She slid into the passenger seat and put her hand on Raber's thigh. When he didn't really react, she started to slide her hand further up. When she got to his zipper he smiled and moved her hand away.

"Aren't you satisfied yet, you lusty woman?" he asked, laughing.

"We could always pull over and have a quickie," Ioni said, a mischievous smile on her face. "Come on, you stay right where you are, just move your seat back and I'll get on top."

"Ioni!" Raber laughed. "Andrew is expecting us. Now behave yourself!"

Laughing, Ioni left his personal space and sat quietly until he parked. As usual, she waited for him to come around and open the door for her. When her door opened and a hand appeared for her to take, she took it without really looking. When she stood, she was face-to-face with someone who was not her Raber. She jumped and jerked her hand out of his grasp and looked around for her boyfriend, only to spot him standing directly behind the stranger.

Ioni quickly gathered herself and held her hand out again for a shake.

"I'm guessing you're Andrew?" she said as he slowly raised her hand to his lips and kissed the knuckle.

"That's right," he said, smiling at her.

He was about her height, thin as a rail, and wore a head of shaggy, sandy blond hair. His nose was long and thin and his eyes were close together. His lips were almost nonexistent, but there was a jolly upturn to the line of his mouth. His neck was long and scrawny, his Adam's apple protruding in an almost obscene way. Ioni looked down at his thin, knobby hand holding hers. She slowly withdrew it and discretely wiped it on her pants.

"Beautiful," Andrew said to Raber. "I didn't realize guys who wear as much makeup as you could get such breathtaking creatures."

Raber laughed heartily and clapped Andrew on the back. Andrew's whole body rocked forward.

"Oh, I'm sorry," Raber said. "Don't know my own strength, I guess."

"I guess that's something I need to remember! Geez, you horse!" Andrew said, grinning.

"Well now that you two have been introduced, what do you want to do?" Raber asked.

"Let's go to my room," Andrew said, starting to walk away. "Ben won't be back until late tonight. He's got a piece at home too, so he'll be rolling in that for as long as he can."

Raber laughed and Ioni smiled uncomfortably. Raber put his hand on the small of her back and let her walk behind Andrew. They got to the bank of elevators and Andrew hit the UP button. He stood back and studied Ioni, making her fidget and wonder if it would be rude to hide behind Raber.

"You're a little fleshy," Andrew said, his eyes still moving over her. "But it's a nice look on you. You look like you'd be squishy in just the right places."

Ioni flashed a look at Raber and saw that he was grinning as if someone had just paid him a compliment. Ioni looked back at Andrew and saw his eyes focused on her breasts. She crossed her arms over her chest.

"I don't like to be talked to that way," she muttered. "I just met you, please don't talk to me in a familiar way like that. I'm not here for your pleasure so quit examining me like I'm some faceless pair of breasts."

"Baby!" Raber said, sounding shocked and embarrassed. "That's not at all what he was doing. Andrew is just really forward. He's not one to talk around corners. He speaks his mind."

"Yeah, sorry about that," Andrew said, looking at his shoes. "Sort of a bad reaction to being on Adderall since I was twelve."

Ioni looked at Raber to gauge how to react and saw that he looked calm and serene. So Ioni puffed out some air and nodded at Andrew.

"Well, that's okay," she said. "Goodness knows I get foot-in-mouth disease from time to time."

The elevator doors opened and the three of them got inside. Ioni was thankful that the elevator was large so that she wouldn't have to be too close to the decidedly creepy third wheel. She turned and nuzzled her face into Raber, trying to ignore the sniggering that she heard. She felt slightly comforted when she felt Raber's hands stroking her hair in that familiar way.

When the doors opened, Ioni was greeted with the stink of the dorms. The smell of cigarette smoke, vomit, and smelly unwashed bodies made her nose crinkle. Raber noticed this and chuckled.

"It is a smell, isn't it?" he said, smiling down at her. Ioni couldn't help but smile back.

"Yeah, you give some people freedom from mommy and daddy and they forget how to wash themselves," Andrew muttered. "Fucking dirty apes."

"There are some disgusting mouth-breathers on your floor," Raber said.

"Well, here we are," Andrew said, unlocking and opening a door with a flourish. "My humble room that I am lucky enough to share with a guy who has a mom who buys him soap on a regular basis."

Andrew's room was very tidy. While neither bed was made, there was no clutter on the floor. Both desks were mostly free of garbage and the room smelled faintly of the cool scent of men's deodorant.

Andrew seated himself on the floor and Raber and Ioni followed suit. Ioni made sure to sit as close to Raber and as far away from Andrew as she could.

Andrew pulled out a bong and held it out in an offering way.

"Shall we spark?" he asked. "Or perhaps we should break out the groovy stuff."

"Uhh, maybe not right now," Raber said.

"What's the groovy stuff?" Ioni asked.

"Oh, are you down?" Andrew asked, pulling a wooden box out from under his bed.

"No," Ioni said, forcing a smile to keep from appearing rude. "Just curious."

"I've got all the good hallucinogens," Andrew began. "I also keep a bit of coke and extra Adderall."

Ioni looked at Raber and saw that he was staring at his lap.

"Okay," Andrew said, seeing that the moment had gotten tense, "Raber says you guys might want to know a thing or two about magic."

"Okay," Ioni said. Her stomach was starting to hurt and if she could get this over with faster, that would be best.

"Well, I understand you're almost done with your Wiccan 'training', so what comes after that?" Andrew asked.

"I'm going to join the local coven and practice with them," Ioni began, noticing that her tone had gone haughty. She softened. "I've gotten to know most of them and I feel really comfortable around them."

"Yeah, yeah, community, religion, blah blah blah," Andrew said, waving his hand in a dismissive gesture. "What about magic? I'm not talking about religion or empty rituals, I'm talking about real power, real results. I'm talking about using a force of will to make your desires reality."

Ioni frowned at him. She needed a moment of quiet to make sure that her initial reaction of panic at what he just said was deserved.

"Can I ask you a question?" she asked Andrew.

"Shoot," he said, popping a pill into his mouth.

"Are...are you a practitioner of black magic?" she asked, almost in a whisper.

"And there's the religion part coming out," Andrew scoffed. "There is no white magic or black magic. There are idiotic misguided super nerds who like to reenact rituals that they believe predate Christ and then there are those who think for themselves and understand the real meaning behind the ritual. Those of us with our own working minds don't rely on a whole goddamned coven. We know how to make the world move to our will. *That* is magic. It isn't fucking color-coded."

At that, Ioni stood up and walked out of the room. She closed the door behind her and practically ran to the elevators. When the elevator door didn't open as soon as she pushed the button, she turned, hoping the stairwell door was close by. She spotted a lighted exit sign around the corner and found the stairwell there.

By the time she was on the ground floor, she was breathing heavily both from physical exertion and from her racing emotions. Raber was involved with someone that both Sarah and Karen had sternly warned her to avoid. She was well aware of her future coven's feelings on people who practiced black magic. The people of her coven were very loving and open-minded people, but they made it a point to not even so much as speak to people like Andrew. She trusted her future coven members, especially Sarah and Karen. She also trusted Raber, but Andrew had rubbed her the wrong way from the very first second she saw him. It wasn't the wisdom of the people in her life speaking to her in that moment, it was her very own instincts and at that moment, her instincts were screaming that Andrew was bad news.

She entered the lobby and headed for the front doors, intent on walking the almost three miles to her car. She would talk to Raber later, but at that moment she just wanted to be around people she trusted. As she reached the doors, she heard Raber bellow her name. She turned and saw him walking quickly toward her, his entire head a bright red. Ioni almost winced when he came close to her.

"Come on," he said in a low tone. "I'll drive you to your car."

She almost declined his offer, but he had his arm around her waist and was pushing her out of the doors before she could. She braced for a full-on fight once they were in his car. She sat, staring ahead at the glove compartment as he situated himself behind the wheel. When he didn't say anything, she looked over at him.

"You embarrassed me in there," he said. "But I understand why. I know he's a bit harsh and I realize that I can't expect you to like everybody that I like. He wanted to meet you, so I made it happen, but you won't need to be around him like that again, okay?"

Ioni frowned and caught herself blinking rapidly in her confusion. Raber looked over at her and smiled his sweet comforting smile.

"Raber," she began.

"Don't." he said sternly. "Just don't. If you don't want a part of it, that's fine. But I'm going to at least listen to what he has to say, and learn what he has to teach."

"So, what? You're suddenly done with what is almost a year's work over this one guy?" Ioni asked, angry.

"I'm not sure yet, baby." he answered. "I just don't know anymore."

"Okay, well we can revisit this. I have another bone to pick," Ioni said. "The drugs."

Raber huffed and made like he was going to start yelling but Ioni threw a hand in front of his face to stop him.

"Now listen to me!" she said. "I'm not above a bit of pot, you know that. I smoke up sometimes and that's fine. But this is hard stuff. Don't you ever watch the news? How can you mess with stuff like that?"

"We don't do stuff like that very often," he said sullenly.

"Are you still going to classes?" Ioni asked.

"Of course I'm still going!" Raber yelled. "This is important to me, I've told you that before!"

"Look, I'm allowed to be worried about you, damn it!" Ioni yelled back. "I can't tell you what to do, but I can say that doing drugs like that is extraordinarily stupid, especially for a smart guy like you! But that's all I *can* do, isn't it? All I can do now is hope that you're as careful and in control as you think you are. I have no choice but to trust you."

"That's right," Raber said. "You have to trust me! And why should that be such a leap? We've been together for a year! Haven't I earned at least that yet?"

Ioni closed her eyes and tried to let go of her panic and anger. She breathed deeply and tried to calm down.

"Of course you've earned my trust," she said, taking his hand. "I'm just worried. And I'm a little miffed at you for considering not joining the coven with me. But hey, I'm an adult and so are you. We don't always have to be in the same clubs, right?"

Raber squeezed her hand and kissed her. They sat in silence for a bit. Raber went to start the car, but stopped and looked over at Ioni. She smiled at him.

"Just out of curiosity," he began. "If I were to choose to be more like Andrew and less like that coven, would you be okay with that?"

"My elders have warned me that I am to not even acknowledge practitioners of black magic, let alone sleep with them." Ioni said. "You mean a lot to me, but so does that coven. Please don't make me choose between the two of you, because I will never want to be like Andrew."

"Well, on that cheery note," Raber said, and started the engine.

CHAPTER FIFTEEN

As life went on as it usually did, Ioni was aware of, but trying to ignore, a rift between her and Raber. They still talked on the phone each night, but there was a noticeable coldness. She wasn't sure if it was her or Raber causing the chill, but she was worried about their relationship.

They didn't see each other again until Thanksgiving. The reunion that time wasn't quite as passionate, and she was stunned at his appearance. He looked ill and had lost a considerable amount of weight, but he assured her that he was just tired from the pace set by his classes. Ioni, of course, suspected otherwise but she tried not to bring up the name "Andrew" and his bag of illegal goodies in any of their conversations.

She'd been able to land a part-time job as a waitress at a local chain restaurant. One of the coven members, a woman named Barbara, had helped her get the position. Ioni liked the job just fine once she got used to it and understood that even though she was a waitress, certain attire aside from the required uniform was important if she was to make money from tips.

Ioni had noticed at first how her tips were really low, so much so that she wasn't making any money after taxes on her paychecks. At first, she thought that maybe it was because she was still getting used to everything and wasn't a very good server, but as time went on and she became adept to the job, she knew something else was up. She asked Barbara what she was doing wrong.

"Oh, sweetheart," Barbara had said. "I hate to have to do this to you, but you need to remember where we live and who our customers are. Conservative people are eating here and they aren't noticing how sweet you are and what a great and polite server you are, I'm afraid." Barbara seemed uncomfortable and embarrassed to continue, but Ioni understood.

"It's the makeup and jewelry, isn't it?" Ioni had asked.

"It's shitty, I know," Barbara had answered.

Ioni had been indignant about it at first, but had come to a quiet acceptance that she needed to be more vanilla while on the job. Immediately, her tips grew and well-meaning people had fallen over themselves to tell her how much prettier she looked when she wasn't wearing so much makeup.

Because of her job, she wasn't able to spend much time with Raber while he was in. It made her sad that she couldn't be with him very much, and Raber had indicated that he felt the same.

"I miss you," he had told her one night that they were actually together. They were cuddled up on the large cushy couch in Raber's parents' house. "I feel like I've hardly seen you at all since school started."

"That's because you haven't," she replied. "I miss you too, babe. I wish we were better at time management, you know? We'd be better at making time for each other."

"Life got in the way of us, didn't it?" he asked, stroking her hair. "I'm sorry that it did. I'm sorry that it's gotten messy like this." He paused and she looked into his face and smiled. He didn't smile back.

"Maybe if you didn't hate the one friend I have, you'd be more willing to come to Morgantown to see me on your free nights," he said, his jaw tight.

Ioni reacted instantly with silent anger, but chose to stay cuddled into Raber and be careful with her words instead of shooting off at the mouth. Trying to ignore the heat in her face and that the sound of her own heart beating was suddenly deafening, she calmly replied.

"Maybe if you chose friends who weren't drug addicts who opposed a belief system that I hold dear, you might be more moved to get in your own fucking car and come see me sometimes."

"I'm supposed to weed friends out based on your belief system now?" Raber asked, his voice going shrill with anger. Ioni saw no point in staying calm and she pulled away from him to look into his face.

"Never once have I ever tried to control you or even influence your decisions," she said. "You wanted me to meet Andrew and I did and he did nothing but make me uncomfortable and shit all over my beliefs! And you know what? You sat there and did nothing! I don't care who you choose to be friends with, but when you're choosing someone who is so obviously cruel and rude, all other things aside, and those are big things, Raber! Big things! Those things I'm putting aside mean a lot to me. But excluding those, Andrew is not someone that I can be around and he's not someone I trust around you, seeing as you're being so devoted about everything he says. And because of all of that, well, you have no reason to say things to me like I'm not doing enough to keep this relationship working!"

"Andrew really gets me," Raber said. "He understands that I want more than just philosophy and, and…" he stopped, trying to think.

"And?" Ioni asked.

"Servitude! I want more than servitude out of life!" Raber finished, sounding angry again. Ioni slumped back against the couch and stared at him with her mouth open. Her heart sank.

"Look," Raber began in a more gentle tone. "One of the things that seduced me about Wicca was the power to control my own life. I thought I didn't have to answer to anybody or anything. I wanted the ceremony and I wanted the control. I can't tell you how frustrating I've found Sarah and her bullshit teachings to be."

"So you're telling me," Ioni began, "that you don't want that path."

"No, I don't," Raber answered.

"You're not going to train under Sarah anymore? You're not going to join the coven in December?" she asked. "Like we planned? Together?"

Raber lowered his head.

"No," he answered softly.

"Raber!" Ioni shouted, throwing her hands in the air. "Why didn't you tell me this ages ago? I love you and I want more than anything to be with you, but thanks to you, Wicca now means a hell of a lot to me! This is a terrible position you've put me in!"

"I love you so, so much," he said after a tense pause. "I don't want to lose you. In fact, I'm not willing to let this split us up. If that means that I practice my way away from you and in secret, that's what I'll do. I'll do that for you. And as far as Andrew goes, you won't have to be around him ever again. He's my friend and I'm not going to get rid of him just because you were uncomfortable. But you were being very judgmental of him, Ioni. I mean, look at your friends."

"What about them? And why are they suddenly only *my* friends? Aren't they your friends too?"

"No they're not my friends!" he shouted. "And you know they're not my friends! I was happy to commiserate and be friendly with them, but I've always known that you were a package deal and they were the sides. I haven't seen or talked to Arlie or Nathan since I started school and I've only seen Adam maybe twice."

"Okay, I accept that point," she said. "But what's wrong with my friends that you're throwing them in my face? Just so you can defend Andrew?"

"Andrew isn't a bad guy," Raber said. "He's a little off, I can admit that. You just have to get used to him. But you were completely revolted by him after just a few seconds. Your friends aren't exactly something to be uppity about, you know. Nathan is crude and over-sharing and Arlie is the perfect picture of the poor, dirty artist."

"What's the matter with you, you snob?" she asked, aghast. "No, never mind. I don't care what your issue is. I can see from looking at you that you're getting a bit more involved with drugs than you want me to realize and I can also see that we have a serious problem of conflicting ideologies. You've only been gone for a couple of months and it's like I don't even know you anymore."

"Don't do this," Raber said, catching her by the wrist. "Don't. We had a good year, Ioni. A damned good year. Don't do this."

"I'm not doing anything," Ioni said, wrenching her wrist from his grip. "I need to talk to some people and I need to think." She started to get up and leave but Raber grabbed her upper arm and squeezed it.

"I'm not willing to end this relationship. I love you," he said, his voice low and fierce.

"Raber, let go. You don't get to make that decision on your own. I'll call you later."

She jerked out of his grasp and stalked out of his house and got into her car. Noticing her hands shaking and the tightness in her throat, she drove to Nathan's house. He wasn't home, so she tried Arlie's next. Even if Arlie wasn't at home, she had a spare key and knew that she was welcome inside.

At Arlie's tidy little trailer Ioni walked in without knocking. Arlie greeted her with a look of concern.

"What's up?" she asked Ioni.

Wanting to keep her composure, Ioni smiled her bravest smile and took in a deep breath. She plopped on the couch and began sobbing. Arlie sat next to her and put an arm around her.

"I...if we could," Ioni said between sobs, "it would be b...better to call N...Nath so I o...only have to explain it once."

"Okay," Arlie said. She made a few phone calls and tracked Nathan down and ordered him to drop everything and get to her place. When Nathan stepped in a little while later, he was immediately frowning in concern.

He rushed to the couch, knelt down in front of Ioni, and took her hands in his. He glanced at Arlie, who shrugged, and they both put their attention on their sobbing mess of a friend.

"I hate to push," Nathan began, "but I'm not so sure I can take seeing you like this much longer. What's the matter?"

Ioni took a few minutes to calm herself enough to start talking, but when she did get started, the words poured out of her so fast that Nathan and Arlie didn't even have time to nod their heads in understanding. They just looked at her intently as she told the story of Andrew (which she had withheld from them) and his views, Raber's drug use, and the things that he'd said. She told them about the stern warnings that Sarah and Karen had given about people who practiced dark magic and how she was worried that Raber was going to negatively impact her initiation into the coven.

As the last word left her mouth, she collapsed back and closed her eyes, suddenly exhausted.

"You're sure," Nathan said, "that he's doing drugs and getting into dark shit?"

Without opening her eyes, Ioni nodded.

"You should see him," she said. "He's lost probably fifteen pounds and he looks really pale and sick. He tries to say it's because of his hectic schedule, but he's taking as many course hours as I am and I've got a damned job on top of that. And about the black magic, yeah, I'm pretty sure. He told me today that he's not going to learn from Sarah anymore and that he doesn't have any interest in joining this coven. He said their version doesn't give him enough power."

"What a fucked up, egotistical mess," Arlie said.

"Have you talked to Sarah and Karen about this?" Nathan asked.

"No, I needed to talk to you guys first." Ioni grinned. "You guys are the lucky ones I unload on."

"That ain't no problem," Nathan smiled, stroking her forearms.

"I think Nathan had a point though," Arlie said. "I think it's good that you're getting the emotional part of this out of the way with us, but you should probably talk to your...what do you call them? Bosses?"

"Elders," Ioni answered.

"Elders," Arlie repeated. "If this coven means as much to you as you've told us more than once, you should make sure that they know about this mess and let them counsel you on what to do."

"What do you guys think I should do?" Ioni asked. "You're my best friends and I consider you family. Tell me what you think."

There was a long silence. Ioni looked at both of their faces and saw that they were struggling with how to reply.

"Don't hold back, guys." she said. "I really need some input. Lay it on me."

"I just don't know how to answer this," Arlie said.

"Yeah, this isn't easy," Nathan answered. "You guys have been together for over a year now and it's really obvious that you love each other. Aside from some weird stuff on his end and the fact that he's a bit of a weirdo, it's been a good year. If he fucked someone else or was, I dunno, traditionally terrible..." he faltered.

"Yeah," Arlie finished. "It's obvious that he's taking a path that will eventually lead to you guys splitting up, but..."

"Maybe he can be turned back?" Nathan finished.

"Turned back?" Ioni asked, stunned.

"Well, yeah." Arlie said.

"Yeah, maybe a come to Jesus talk could work on him. I'd just hate to see you sad and miserable because he's being an idiot college freshman. I mean, aren't all college freshmen idiots?" Nathan asked.

"Again, you also need advice from your fellow Wiccans," Arlie said. "We can't fully understand how bad that side of this is. But I do agree with Nathan. After a full good year, maybe he deserves a little leniency."

"And if he isn't open to at least being sympathetic to the really shitty situation he's made for you, then toss him. You're wonderful and you've found something for yourself that makes you shine. If he wants to take a position that is totally opposite to that, then he can fuck right off." Nathan said.

Ioni nodded, seeing that they had made some very good points. She smiled at the concerned faces of her friends.

"Okay," she said. "Thanks. Now, do you guys mind if we get something to eat? I'm starving."

"Yeah, Chris and I had, like, the best sex ever earlier and I'm crazy hungry too."

"Geez," Arlie laughed. "Ioni, did you at least get to bang Raber before he started being a tool?"

"Yeah, but it was just okay," Ioni answered. "Whatever drugs he's on, they're not the sexy kind."

"Well, that means that all three of us have had busy mornings," Arlie said.

"You start talking and I'll order a pizza!" Nathan screeched, running for the phone. His enthusiasm was infectious and they were soon gushing and laughing as Arlie filled them in on a guy she'd started seeing casually.

Ioni was able to relax for most of that afternoon with her friends and she almost forgot about her drama. But after the pizza was gone and they had to return to their own little corners of life, Ioni felt flooded with stress again. She knew that she would have to talk with Sarah and Karen first thing the next day.

CHAPTER SIXTEEN

Early the next morning Ioni sat in one of the kitchen chairs at Bedelia's and talked to Sarah and Karen about Raber and her fears.

"Please understand that I worry about him and him first," she said. "I care about him and I don't want anything bad to happen to him. But I'm also really worried that his stupid decisions might affect me and my standing in this coven. I'm not even a member yet, but I'm really committed to being a member and I've really tried my best to learn."

"Ioni," Karen said, frowning. "Honey, we know you're committed. You've been an exemplary student. I'm glad that you care for Raber and I think it's very responsible of you to be worried. I'm also glad that you took our warning about black magic seriously. It is a serious thing. You can love and interact with whoever you want and ultimately the choice is always yours. You are and will forever be your own woman."

"But what do I do about this?" Ioni asked, pleading with them.

"We can't tell you what to do, sweetheart," Karen said.

"My friends think I should try to give him a come to Jesus talk. They think we've had a really good run as a couple and that he deserves at least to hear me beg him."

"What do you want?" Sarah asked.

"I want to give him a chance. I want to talk to him and plead with him. But I also want this life with you guys. I'm hurt by him and I'm confused. If I choose to stay with him, and

138

I know that he's maybe practicing black magic, I'll get expelled from the coven, and I can't have that."

"If you love Raber and see something in him as a person and in your relationship worth trying to save, then maybe you should do that. We're here for advice and to talk if you need it. And you're blessed with close friends who are happy to be there for you, too. You're not alone. You've always been faithful in your studies and we absolutely believe in your commitment to Wicca. We're here for you." Karen said.

At those kind words, Ioni felt tears start to streak her cheeks. She looked down at her lap and tried to stop the waterworks. She had spent a lot of the previous night crying and curled up with stomach cramps brought on by the stress of the situation.

"Thank you so much," she whispered.

Karen and Sarah both reached out and laid their hands on her.

"You may not be formally initiated," Karen said, "but you're one of us and we're here for you."

"And you should know that I look on you as a friend at this point," Sarah said. "We spend enough time together and we talk about more than just your studies. I hope that you look on me the same way."

"I didn't know that was allowed," Ioni laughed, wiping at her nose.

Karen and Sarah laughed too and they petted and patted Ioni while telling her that everything will work out fine. Ioni felt much better, but was still dubious about her next task, which was talking to Raber. She was uncomfortable with what she thought was telling Raber what he could or couldn't do. She didn't want to be the type of person that gave ultimatums. But standing firm in her resolve, and not letting him manipulate her into moving her lines in the sand to accommodate his whims, was something important to her as well.

Later that night she called Raber and asked him to meet her at a secluded place so they could talk.

Stearnsville was technically a city, but it was surrounded by many country roads and hollows. If a couple of teenagers were wanting for a place to make out in the backseat of a car, they only needed to take a short drive to an old dirt road and park. Ioni had chosen a place in an intersection of sorts. There was a clearing off to the side and a large oak tree in the middle. She and Raber had come to that place to have picnics under the tree and have sex out in the open with no fear of being seen. It was a special place to them as a couple but it was also special to Ioni. She didn't normally consider herself to be a person with any sort of extrasensory capabilities, but she'd always felt something inside of her stir at the sight of that great tree. A sort of familial tug. She needed its comforting presence to be near as she prepared to make her feelings clear to Raber.

She sat in her car enjoying the heat and the radio when she saw lights approach. She knew it was Raber. He parked behind her and got in the passenger side of her car. Once he was settled, Ioni reached down and turned off the radio.

"Hi," she said, trying to break the ice.

"Hello," he said back, not looking at her.

"Raber," she began.

"Please tell me that you didn't ask me to meet you here in this place that is so special to us to break up with me," Raber said. His voice was thick with emotion. He was close to tears.

"Stop it and let me talk," Ioni said, a calmness coming over her.

Raber looked down at his large hands as they gripped the slack in his pants and stayed silent.

"I asked you here to talk," Ioni began. "How you react to this talk will decide how we walk away from this. Will we walk away still together or will we go our separate ways? I don't know, so be quiet and let me talk, okay?"

"Okay," Raber said.

"Okay, look. I know that you're out on your own there in Morgantown and I know that you've bonded with Andrew. I get that. But Raber, I'm still here for you. We talk on the phone all day and night and when you come in, I devote every spare second that I get to being with you. You're important to me. I love you. But you know what? You haven't been totally honest with me. I can see that you're doing some crazy drugs up there and I can tell by making love with you that you're not really taking care of yourself. And yes, I'm going to blame a lot of this on your friendship with Andrew.

"I've never asked you to do anything big for me in this whole year we've been together and I've never given you any ultimatums," she continued, "but I need you to choose. Is it me and our relationship, or is it Andrew and this weird power trip?"

"Power trip?" Raber said, his voice going high-pitched. "Is that what you think I'm doing?"

"Explain it to me again, then," Ioni said, calmly. "Explain it to me in a way that doesn't sound like how you explained it yesterday where you said you needed control and power. Please, do that so I know that I've spent the last day and a half getting advice from people and freaking out for no reason."

Raber was quiet for a long time after that. He kept watching his hands wring at his too-large pants, working his mouth as if he were talking to himself.

"My friendship with Andrew will really cost me what I have with you?" he asked finally.

Ioni felt her stomach sink. She was flooded with guilt over making him choose and she felt out of line in her demand. A passive person by nature, she usually let him have his way because he was the more vocal one about what was and wasn't his wish. But she found herself unwilling to make concessions with him just then, and despite the guilt, she also felt good, like she was channeling Arlie and her strength.

"Yes," she answered. "Wicca is important to me partly because of that little push from you, baby. Andrew is a person who opposes a lot of the beliefs that have come to mean a lot to me and shape my way of thinking."

When Raber failed to reply, she continued.

"I want you to know," she said, "that I feel really guilty about putting this on you. I want you to have friends and I want you to enjoy your time in Morgantown, but if I'm a big part of your life, I need you to know that you being close with Andrew and buying into the stuff that he says is a deal breaker."

"I don't want to join that coven," Raber said.

"I know," she replied. "I never said that you had to do that to be with me, though. If you don't want to join, that's okay with me. But I want to join, and I'm going to be initiated in December. The thing that's important to me is that you're still a good guy, Raber. You used to be my good guy. You weren't losing scary amounts of weight really fast because you're off at college doing drugs. You weren't screaming at me about power and control and how what I believe is too weak for you. You're taking a stance that basically makes you my villain. I can't have that."

"It's the same thing as if you were Protestant and I were Catholic, Ioni!" Raber shouted. "The same core of beliefs are there, but there are small differences! If that were the case and I were Catholic, would you still be calling me your villain?"

"That's not a good comparison and you'd know that if you gave Sarah half a chance to explain this stuff to you!" Ioni shouted back.

Raber huffed and slammed his fist into the passenger door. Ioni flinched and stared at her steering wheel, waiting for his next move.

"This is stupid," Raber said at last, his voice soft. "I think maybe I've gotten a little carried away with things. I'm sorry. This whole argument is dumb. Considering what you and I have? Baby, that's the closest to any sort of god that I've ever been. Of course I'm going to choose you and us. I'll start avoiding Andrew. He's probably going to flunk out after this term anyhow, so you won't have to worry about me seeing him."

Ioni was stunned by the quick turn the conversation had taken and needed a moment to process.

"Flunk out?" she asked, finally.

"Yeah. Maybe we were going a little overboard with the drugs. I have a hard time getting to my classes sometimes, but I always go because I have plans for after college. Andrew, though, he's there because his parents gave him no other choice. He misses class all the time and he's always messed up on something. I don't think he can hack it."

"Where's he from?" Ioni asked, still stunned.

"He's from New Jersey, so if he flunks out, he'll have to go back there. There won't be any further contact between us." Raber said.

"Raber," Ioni began. She was finally soaking in the weight of what Raber had said to her and she burst into tears.

He reached over and buried his hands in her hair, pulling them close together. He kissed the nape of her neck and nuzzled her throat, whispering to her.

"I love you," he whispered. "I'll never let you go. You're mine."

Ioni, still in tears turned her face so that their mouths met. They kissed hard and deep, their tongues roughly tangling about each other. Raber's hands moved from her hair to her breasts. She started undoing his pants. She knew her desperation was easily matched by Raber and she quickly led the way to the backseat.

When he climbed over the console and joined her, she pushed him into a seated position, opened his pants and let loose his excitement in the form of an upright and eager member. Ioni lifted her skirt and pushed her panties off to one

143

side and lowered herself onto him. They both groaned low in their throats as she settled and began to grind on him.

Raber's hands couldn't settle on one place, they were all over her body, gripping one place and then massaging another as she moved. Their breathing was heavy and in time with the other as they reached their climaxes. Ioni screamed and bit down on the soft flesh of Raber's neck, causing him to scream and thrust himself deeper into her as he had his orgasm.

Panting and sweating, Ioni moved herself to the side so that she was sitting next to him. She laid her head on his shoulder and felt the tension melt away with the quivering of her thighs.

"The bigger the fight, the better the makeup sex," Raber said between gasps.

"No joke," Ioni said. She lifted her head and kissed him on his cheek and snuggled him as hard as she could.

"I love you so much," she said. "Thank you for choosing me."

"As if there was ever any real competition," Raber said, stroking her hair. "I love you more than I've ever loved anything."

CHAPTER SEVENTEEN

Ioni was working a late Saturday shift. It was the weekend before finals week at school and Raber had opted to stay in Morgantown to get some last minute studying in, but had assured her that his last exam was on Thursday and he was coming home immediately after.

She hoped that Christmas break was going to be long and fruitful. Things still weren't completely back to normal between the two of them. She found that the total trust that she had once had in Raber had taken a hit. She silently questioned things he told her, like where he'd been and what he'd done that weekend. Everything was suspect.

She also discovered that she wasn't comfortable talking with him about her studies with Sarah. She was having to compartmentalize her life, and she didn't like shutting the person she loved most in the world into his own little cubby away from other dominating parts. After he'd shown such disgust and disdain for Sarah and Karen, however, Ioni felt that it was best to not talk about it, mostly out of fear that Raber might say something condescending and start a fight. It ended up being an empty spot in her life, the place between Raber and the coven and that they couldn't meet or touch left Ioni feeling oddly empty.

She set a tray loaded with meals down onto the little folding stand and gave her customers their plates, smiling and making sure everybody was satisfied before gathering her tray and turning around. To her surprise, seated at the booth across the aisle from the table she had just served sat Tristan, his signature kilowatt smile beaming at her.

"Hi," she said. "You here for some dinner?"

"And more," Tristan said. He frowned and looked her up and down. "You look very..."

Ioni fidgeted self-consciously. Her long hair was pulled into a ponytail high on her head, looking desperately perky. Her white polo shirt that bore the logo of the restaurant and her khaki pants all worked together to make her look almost as if she were a towel girl at a country club.

"Normal," Ioni finished for Tristan.

"No, no that's not it," he said. "Your normal is much more theatrical than this. This is just weird!"

Ioni laughed and reached up to grab her hair before forgetting that it was pulled back. She went to quickly put her hand back at her side, but ended up dropping her enormous tray and it went rolling across the restaurant. Ioni clumsily chased after it, stooped over with her arms outstretched. When she finally caught the tray, she stood to see if she were being watched. To her horror, many smiling faces were watching her in good-natured amusement. Blushing furiously, she walked back to Tristan's table.

"So what can I get you?" she asked, pulling out her order pad, angry with herself.

"Maybe sit down with me for a second?" Tristan said, extending one of his large hands to the seat across from him.

"I already took my break and I'm kind of busy," she replied.

"Just for a second," Tristan said. "I'm here on business."

Looking around for management or diners in need of refills, Ioni slid into the booth across from Tristan.

"Now," Tristan said, leaning back. "I'm here to make sure that you're prepared for your first Yule and also for your initiation ceremony. Have Mom and Adare...errr...Sarah told you everything you need to know?"

"I think so," Ioni said. "Sarah told me about what goes on at the Yule ceremony and I guess she told me all I need to know about my initiation ceremony."

"Did anybody tell you that I'm the one initiating you?" Tristan asked. Still smiling, he leaned forward, stretching his hands out so that his fingertips were almost touching hers.

"I thought Karen would be doing that," Ioni said, never taking her eyes off of Tristan's fingers. She was being torn between warring emotions. Desire and fear. Curiosity and guilt.

"See, I knew you needed me to help you," Tristan said, the tips of his fingers lightly grazing hers. "In our coven, we do initiations in the Kingstone tradition. A man initiates a woman and a woman initiates a man. On this occasion, I'm your man."

"Oh," Ioni said, still staring at their fingertips. "Well okay. Is that everything?"

"We seal your initiation with a kiss," Tristan said.

"I knew that," she replied. "I thought I was going to be kissing Karen, though."

"Is that a problem?" Tristan asked.

Ioni kept staring at their fingers, wanting something she couldn't articulate, but knowing enough to feel bad about it, but Tristan withdrew his hand and took it off the table. She looked into his face and saw that he was studying her.

"Why would you be okay with kissing my mom and not me? I'm just another senior member of the group," he said. His smile had diminished to a small half-smirk that held even more amusement. "Surely I don't make you uncomfortable, do I?" he asked.

"No," Ioni said. "No. It's not that. But you're, you know. A man. And I'm in a committed monogamous relationship. You know." Ioni said.

Tristan laughed loudly and Ioni noticed a few patrons looking their way.

"You sweet, innocent thing," Tristan said. "This is not a sexual kiss! This is a quick smackeroo on the lips and then we get to have food and punch!"

Ioni laughed and stood up with her order pad.

"Okay, you've had your fun at my expense, now what can I get you?"

Tristan ordered a large meal and a drink from the bar. She scribbled the order onto her pad and put the order into the computer. Her fingers smacked at the screen clumsily and her heart was beating fast. Why had he come to her place of work to tease her like that? Was it flirting again or was he really just having fun? She decided not to worry about it and get on with her job.

Tristan's drink from the bar came first, and Ioni delivered it expertly, placing the tiny napkin onto the table before gracefully placing the glass on top of it.

"Let me know if you need anything else, okay? A refill, anything." Ioni said, brightly, perky in the way that got her better tips.

"Yes, ma'am," he replied.

It was almost fifteen minutes before his food was ready to serve, and Ioni had done her best to avoid his table during that wait, sweeping floors in other areas and refilling napkin holders at the bar, ignoring the annoyed look of the bartender. When Tristan's food came up, she placed it on her large round try, balanced it on her right arm and glided to his table. She tried to avoid his gaze and sparkling smile as she placed the two plates and bottle of steak sauce before him.

"Can I get you another drink?" she asked, out of duty. "A glass of water? Or another drink from the bar?"

"I'd love a glass of water," he said. "I'll be here a while, but I shouldn't drink too much anyhow."

"Okay, I'll be right back with that for you!"

She rushed to the drink station and filled a plastic cup with ice and water. She placed a lemon wedge on the edge of the cup, making sure it was perched perfectly before heading back. She put the drink before him and deftly produced a paper-wrapped straw from a pocket in her apron. As she turned to walk away she heard him speak.

"So," he began, and she stopped and turned back. "When do you get off tonight? Do you close?"

"Oh, uhh, no I don't close tonight. I get off at eight." she answered.

"Any plans after?" He asked.

Ioni quietly began to panic.

"No..." she answered. "Not really."

"Well my sister, Freya, is having a movie night at her place tonight. We like to watch really bad B-rated movies, a bunch of us from the coven. I was wondering if you'd like to drop by and watch a crappy movie with all of us?"

"Oh! Well sure, I'd love to!" Ioni answered, trying to hide her relief at not being inappropriately propositioned. "But when does it start? And I don't know where Freya lives."

"Don't worry about that," Tristan said. "We always wait for everybody to show up before we start, and I'll hang around here for you and you can follow me there, if that's okay."

"That sounds great!" Ioni said excitedly. She really didn't have any plans after work and was glad to not have to go right home to her parents' crowded house.

"Fantastic," Tristan said coolly. "Then, Ms. Davis, I will wait here until dear lady is ready to depart."

Ioni smiled bashfully despite herself and walked away. She had always loved it when Raber called her 'Ms. Davis' and she felt a physical rush from Tristan calling her the same. She brushed off her excitement and powered through the rest of her shift.

When she had clocked out, she approached Tristan's table. She slid into the booth across from him and looked at him expectantly. She'd already given him his check and taken his payment before clocking out, so all that was left was for him to finish the giant ice cream covered brownie that he had ordered for dessert. She watched how he would put the food into his mouth, close his eyes, and then slowly pull the fork from his mouth with a look of pleasure on his face. He did this with every bite and when he finally looked at her, he laughed suddenly, startling her.

"Am I making a spectacle of myself?" he asked.

"Huh?" Ioni asked.

"You're looking at me like you're studying something bizarre." he said.

"Oh," Ioni giggled. "I'm sorry. I was just watching you eat, and I don't think I've ever seen anybody...I don't know...make love to their dessert like that before."

Tristan laughed again and wiped his mouth heartily with his napkin before plopping it on top of his dessert plate. Ioni noticed that he was quick and hard where Raber was usually dainty. He sucked loudly on his thumb, devouring a last bit of chocolate left behind.

"I have a terrible sweet tooth," he said, looking longingly at the streaks of chocolate on his plate. "I have to really watch myself or I'll eat sweets all day long. And when I do allow myself a treat, I try to take it slow and really savor every bite, every chew, every taste. Maybe I'm a little weird about it, but I don't care! I love a good brownie!" He was patting his flat stomach, looking jolly and satisfied. Ioni couldn't help but laugh.

"I like sweets," Ioni confessed, "but salty snacks are really my downfall. If it's a pack of cookies, I can hold off at eating only one or two. But if you put a bag of good chips in front of me, I'll eat the whole thing if I don't pay attention."

"Well," Tristan said, putting on his coat and standing up. "There's enough sweetness to you already. You can't possibly hold any more."

Ioni playfully rolled her eyes. He held his hand out to her and she took it and stood, looking up into his face.

"I'm losing my touch already?" he asked. "I usually don't start coming off as corny and insufferable until you've known me for a couple of years."

"You guys have been telling me I'm a fast learner," she said, sticking her tongue out and leading the way out to the parking lot.

"I'm over here," Tristan said, pointing to a pickup truck. Ioni shook her head, amused at her misconception. She'd have never thought that a man like Tristan would have a muddy pickup, but there it was.

"It'll take about ten minutes to get there, okay? I'll be watching you in the rearview so you don't lose me," he said.

"Okay, I'll keep up."

Freya's house was on a small, quiet street. The house was tiny but the outside was, like Bedelia's, neat and manicured. Tristan waited on the sidewalk for Ioni and put his hand on her back when she caught up with him. She tensed and looked up into his face, but he wasn't even looking at her. He was looking up at his sister's porch light. Realizing she was merely being herded, Ioni relaxed and let him push her up the concrete steps and onto the porch.

Freya was warm and personable, as Ioni had remembered her. She was someone who instantly put everyone at ease. Ioni blushed when Freya called her "sister" and Tristan laughed and kissed Freya's cheek, telling his sister that Ioni was a shy one.

"There's no need for that among your Wiccan family, darling," Freya said, her smooth voice holding the attention of everyone near.

The night went nicely. Freya produced an enormous bowl of popcorn and a bucket of ice with bottles of water and soda tucked inside. Ioni sat on a loveseat and was relieved when Tristan chose to sit on a bean bag chair in front of the television. A young woman, maybe five years older than Ioni, named Tasha, sat on the other available space of the love seat.

The movie was a low-grade sci-fi movie and it was terrible, but that ended up being what made the night so much fun. The group yelled at the television, criticizing characters and trying to will the plot into a more functional situation. They laughed and talked through the whole thing.

At the end of the night, as Ioni was gathering her coat and purse and preparing to leave, Freya kissed her on the cheek and thanked her for coming.

"Oh, no," Ioni said, waving her hands. "Thank you. This was so much fun. I hope I'll get another invitation."

"Your invitation is always open, sister," Freya smiled. "Let's exchange phone numbers and I'll call you when we plan these from now on. You fit right in!"

Ioni exchanged numbers with Freya and then said her goodbyes to Tasha and the other coven member, whose name she couldn't remember, and started for her car. Tristan was right behind her before she knew it. Nervous, she unlocked her car and threw her purse into the passenger seat. Tristan situated himself so that she would have to brush past him to get into the driver's seat. A broad, bright smile was on his face.

"Thanks for coming!" he said happily. "You really did fit right in. I hope you'll do this with us again. It was fun to have a new person."

"Thank you for bringing me here," Ioni said. "I had a great time. I exchanged numbers with Freya and she said she'll let me know when you all do this again."

"Very good," Tristan said. "Do you know your way home from here? I could lead you back to your house if you like."

"No, I know where I am," Ioni grinned.

"Okay," Tristan said.

"Okay," she replied.

An uncomfortable silence followed. At first, Ioni thought that she was the only uncomfortable one, but when she looked into Tristan's face, she saw the same indecision.

"Is there something you want to say to me?" She was grinning like a fool and she knew it, but she was dying to know what had him all tongue-tied.

"Well," he said. "Yeah, there is. You see, I know you're in this serious committed relationship. I know this because you tell me every time I smile at you, you know."

Ioni blushed and playfully pushed Tristan. He chuckled and continued.

"Well, the thing is, I like you," he said. "I don't wanna make waves or anything and I'm not throwing any sort of responsibility your way, but I think that you should know that. I think about you a lot, and when I do I can't help but smile."

Ioni was quiet, trying to contain the sheer panic that was causing her heart to nearly beat out of her chest. She looked away from his dark shimmering eyes and at her car, contemplating jumping in and driving away as fast as she could.

"There's no action necessary on your part," Tristan said, putting a hand on her shoulder. "If this is the most intimate you and I ever get, I'm okay with that as long as you know that I think you're spectacular."

"But…" Ioni began, but he stopped her.

"I also want you to know that if the situation of you not being in this big important monogamous relationship ever came up, I'd really like to be in the line of possible alternatives."

She was frozen, unable to respond. She wanted this, she had to admit that to herself, but she didn't have to admit it to him. It would be wrong of her to do so, to let him see that his words thrilled her. But she was also annoyed at his pushiness. Couldn't they just be friends without the feelings and hormones? Were there no other single women in Stearnsville who met his type who he could get all smiley and charming with? Annoyance and anxious titillation beat inside of her head and she ended up just staring into his face.

"That's all I wanted to say," he said, pulling back from her. "I'll see you on Yule."

Tristan spun on his heel and waltzed back to his sister's house, leaving Ioni stunned and staring after him. After a moment, Ioni got into her car and started the engine.

She was smiling from ear to ear.

CHAPTER EIGHTEEN

Because of his refusal to join the coven, Raber was not invited to participate in the Yule celebration. Ioni was worried that he would be angry, but he seemed so tired and withered that he only nodded and grunted when she told him.

"Will I be allowed to come to your initiation ceremony?" he asked after a moment.

"Yeah," she answered. "You're my special guest. My parents wouldn't be interested in that and Arlie and Nathan both have to work that day. Anyhow, this is an important day for me and I want my important man there with me." She leaned across Raber's parents' couch and nuzzled his neck, nipping at his ear, hoping for a reaction. He wasn't looking any healthier than he did at Thanksgiving. In fact, he looked worse. He was paler, thinner, and there was a dull look to his eyes that worried Ioni.

Raber buried his hands in her hair, almost as a reflex to her come-on. She kissed him softly. His lips were dry and warm, and the kiss that he returned was closed-mouthed and without feeling. Upset, she sat up straight and looked at him. He was slouched down, which was unlike his prim, perfect-posture self and he was reading something on his laptop, completely distracted. Ioni reached down and used her hand to cover the screen. His red-rimmed eyes slowly raised to meet her own. She smiled at him, hoping for something. Anything.

"Can I treat you out to dinner?" she asked at last. "I'm really hungry and you look like you could eat a horse."

"Uhh," Raber said slowly, moving her hand to look at his laptop again.

"Are we going to be together today or what?" she asked, the irritation plain in her voice.

"Yeah, yeah, we are," he said, still engrossed in his screen. "I'm just, uhh..." he trailed off.

Disgusted, Ioni jumped off of the couch and stood before Raber. He didn't react. She snatched the laptop off of his lap and looked at the screen. He was in a chat and the name at the top of the window said 'Andrew.' Raber stood and glared at her.

"Give it the fuck back," he said, his voice low.

Stunned, Ioni placed the laptop into his waiting hands and turned and walked out the door without another word. She got into her car and sat in the driver's seat staring at his house, waiting for him to come after her. He did appear a moment later, stomping out to her, his arms swinging angrily. He opened the passenger door and flopped his body down into the seat and stared ahead.

"Well, let's hear it," he said, sounding indignant. "Tell me how betrayed you feel. Tell me how I'm an affront to a belief system that you didn't give a fuck about until I came along. Come on, let's hear it."

Ioni was surprised by how calm she was. Before he sat down next to her in her car, she was furious. She could almost feel her blood boiling. But listening to him and his attitude somehow put a calm resolve into her. She looked at her steering wheel and gathered her thoughts before speaking.

"Let me take you out to that dinner, okay?" she said quietly. "We have some talking to do, you and I."

"Okay," he replied, sounding confused.

She drove in silence to Eat N' Park, a place that was special to them as a couple. She parked and they walked apart from each other through the front doors to the hostess station. As they stood there waiting for someone to come seat them, Raber lightly took her hand into his. She didn't smile at him as he raised her hand to his lips and kissed it.

When they were seated in a brightly colored vinyl booth, Ioni reached across the table and held her hands out to Raber. He took them obligingly and looked into her face.

"You need help, baby," she said quietly. "You're losing control of your hobby and you're slipping. Do you think I can't see how pale and thin you are?"

Raber looked down at the table and nodded slowly. When he didn't say anything, Ioni continued.

"You need to get help. I'm not going to yell at you or talk about me right now. I wanna talk about you. I wanna talk about you seeing that you're in a dangerous place, health-wise."

"Don't you want to yell at me for lying to you about Andrew?" he asked suddenly.

"No," she said. "I don't want to talk about Andrew."

She paused and stared at her hands nestled comfortably in his. Their hands had always fit together so well. She felt her throat going tight and tears starting to well up in her eyes. She looked into his face. It was a face that she once saw as sweet and loving, but all that she saw then was the sunken cheeks, red eyes and glassy gaze.

"I love you," she said, emotion making her voice crack.

"I love you, too, baby," he replied, a thread of desperation starting to make itself known.

"But I can't do this with you," she said. "Things have been so strained between us lately and you're unhealthy and I really need for you to concentrate on taking care of yourself. I don't want to be this overly dramatic couple that prolongs a breakup just because there's guilt or we don't know how to end it."

"What?" Raber asked, his eyes wide and his brow furrowed in a deep frown.

"Raber," Ioni said. "I'm telling you that I love you. First and foremost, I love you. But I'm also telling you that I don't want this mess in my life. This drug use and drama between us is more than I can handle on top of school and my job."

"You're breaking up with me," he said flatly, pulling his hands away from hers.

"Yes," Ioni said, matching his flat tone.

"And this," Raber said, waving his hands around his head, "is what, our last supper or something?"

"I guess I feel that I owe it to you, to this relationship, to be civil," Ioni said. "And you look like you could use some food. Let's order, okay? Let's not fight here."

Ioni slid the plain silver band off of her ring finger and placed it lightly in front of him. He picked it up like it was a sacred artifact and slid it onto his pinky finger. She cleared her throat to stifle a sob.

"I've said what I needed to say and that's it. Let's get some food, then I'll take you home."

"I feel like a child being pacified," he said, rage bubbling beneath his words.

"Things are happening this way because I don't know what else to do," she said calmly. "Now please order some food."

He grabbed a plastic-covered menu and opened it, shaking his head dramatically. She relaxed and looked at her own menu, but she was startled by Raber slamming his fists onto the table top and laughing hysterically.

"Did you really just dump me in the same fucking place where we began as a couple?" he asked.

Ioni looked around self-consciously and then leveled a glare at Raber that made him stop laughing.

"You brought this on yourself," she said through gritted teeth. "I was very vocal with you and you really are making yourself look like a dumb shit by being surprised right now."

"I'm not letting you go this easily," he said.

"Raber, you get clean and get your priorities straight and I'll be happy to discuss a reconciliation. Until then, please order some food and know that I'm happy to be here for you as a friend."

"That is so fucking cold, Ioni," he said.

"Maybe it is," she said. "But I'm done talking about it right now." She pointed to his menu which was lying closed on the table and buried her nose in her own menu.

Raber was sullen, but he ate a large meal. She watched his dainty, meticulous manners and longed for the days when he was himself. There were several moments when she almost lost her composure, but she managed not to burst into tears. They ate in silence, and after Ioni had settled the bill, they walked separately back to her car.

The drive back to Raber's parents' house was quiet and tense. She was unwilling to break the silence for fear of what he might resort to in order to get his way. When she pulled to a stop in front of the house, he opened the passenger door and started to get out. He stopped and turned back to her. Ioni held her breath in anticipation.

"Would it be all right if I still came to your initiation?" he asked.

That surprised her. She was unsure of how to answer him, partly because she was unsure if she even wanted him there.

"It's important to you," he said. "And I want to be there to support you."

"Oh, okay," she said. "Well I mean, I said you could come, so yeah. Do you want me to come get you?"

"I'll just show up as a guest on my own, okay?"

"Okay." she answered.

He leaned in and kissed the corner of her mouth and put his hands in her hair.

"I love you," he said before turning quickly and exiting the car.

She drove away and parked on the next street over. Her hands were gripping and wringing the steering wheel as she stared straight ahead. The pressure building behind her eyes was becoming intense, but they were surprisingly dry.

"I can't believe I just did that," she said to herself.

Her head aching, she drove around until she came to the only payphone in the streets of their little town. She tried calling Nathan, but there was no answer. She called Sarah next.

"I just had kind of a dramatic evening and I need to talk to someone," she said. "Mind if I drop by?"

"Come on over," Sarah replied.

Ioni drove to Adare's and walked through the front door without ringing the bell, as she had become accustomed to doing. Sarah wasn't in the front room, so Ioni went to the back and saw Sarah in a painting smock working on a piece of canvas.

"You don't have to stop," Ioni said, sitting on a stool. "I'll stay out of your way."

"Did you and Raber have another fight?" Sarah asked, turning back to her painting. "I know you were going to be seeing him today."

"We broke up," Ioni said. Her voice was flat and void of emotion.

Sarah spun around looking bug-eyed at her apprentice and friend.

"What happened?"

"He's still talking to Andrew and doing drugs." Ioni answered. "He's been lying to me and he's putting himself into a hole that I want no part of."

"Ioni," Sarah said, stepping closer and looking into her face. "Are you okay? I'm really sorry that this has happened, but you're kind of worrying me."

Ioni focused her gaze onto her friend's face and managed a small smile.

"Not really, actually," she answered. "I didn't realize until I did it how long I've been entertaining the idea of breaking up with him. I'm so fucking angry with him right now, I'm not sure what to do. I can't seem to cry and I don't really want to scream. I'm just sort of numb right now. Is that weird?"

"No, not really. The strong emotions will come on when you can handle them," Sarah answered.

She was right. Later that night, alone in her bed, Ioni felt herself break through some sort of wall and the tears came. They were tears of loss and sadness, but also of anger. Betrayal was the dominant feeling, but there was a sadness for Ioni as she realized that she and Raber had been growing apart ever since the school year had started.

"A forty-five-minute distance shouldn't have torn us apart like it did," she whispered, hugging a pillow to herself. "His bullshit bad taste and stupid decisions did this."

It wasn't until the next day, as she was getting ready for work, trying to ignore the red eyes that looked back at her from her mirror that Nathan finally got back to her.

"What's up?" he said. "I just checked my machine and you sounded weird."

"Oh nothing much, just getting ready for work and trying to not cry because I broke up with Raber yesterday," she replied.

"How long until your shift starts?" Nathan asked, his all-business tone taking over.

"Half hour," she replied.

"What time do you get off?"

"Four," she replied.

"You take your ass to Arlie's right after," he said. "No arguments, lady. Be there."

The shift at work was busy, but a nice distraction. She made a good haul on tips and had been able to relax enough somewhere in the middle to have a genuine smile. When she'd clocked out and gotten into her car, she went to start her engine but she heard a loud bang. Startled, she jumped and saw that Raber was banging on the passenger door, looking in at her. When he saw her staring and not moving, he yelled in at her.

"Let me in!" he yelled. "I want to talk to you!"

Ioni hesitated. She was nervous and thinking fast. She started the engine and rolled the passenger window down a couple of inches.

"Why are you sneaking up on me like this?" she asked, sounding angry to hide the fact that she was afraid.

"I said I want to talk to you! Now let me in!" Raber bellowed.

"No." she said, flatly. "You're acting like you're high or something and I don't want to deal with you when you're like this."

"I'm not fucking high!" he screamed

"Raber, look at yourself! Look how you're behaving! You're being scary right now, do you realize that? Now get the hell away from my car!"

He straightened his back and stepped away from her car, breathing heavily. Ioni quickly rolled up the window and put her car into drive, but before she could inch out of the parking space, she heard a lighter knock on the passenger window. Raber waved at her.

"I love you," he said.

Ioni was still really shaken up when she pulled into Arlie's small trailer park. She sat in the car a moment, trying to stop herself from trembling. When she felt that she was slightly more composed, she walked into Arlie's trailer and sat with her dear, trusted friends.

She told them everything, including the scene in the parking lot just minutes before. When she finished, her throat was dry because she had been talking so fast. She looked into their stunned and concerned faces and waited for them to respond.

"Well..." Nathan began. "Fuck that bald behemoth. If the moron can't see far enough past his own nose to see that he's doing you a major wrong, then he can just go sit and spin."

"Do you think you should be afraid of him?" Arlie asked. "You said you were scared of him in the parking lot, do you think you should worry?"

"You know, it's weird," Ioni began. "He's always been a forceful person. It's just part of his personality. And yeah, he can be really manipulative too, but never before today have I ever really been afraid of him hurting me. Never. And six months ago, I would have never believed that I *could* feel threatened by him in that way. But here we are."

"You think it's the drugs?" Arlie asked.

"Yeah, I do." Ioni answered.

"What a fucking idiot," Nathan said quietly. "I know he's still fairly new to the area, but surely he looked around enough to see all the freaking drug addicts in this town. The pills alone are enough to keep me straight. Well, not like *that*." Nathan smiled and winked. Arlie and Ioni laughed.

"You smoke pot!" Arlie said, pointing at Nathan.

"Like that counts," he replied.

"So Nath," Ioni said, breathing out heavily. She suddenly wanted a change of subject. "How are you and Chris doing? I guess that's where you were last night when I called?"

Nathan glanced at Arlie and she shook her head, willing Nathan not to answer.

"What?" Ioni asked. "You guys didn't break up too, did you?"

Again there was a pause and Nathan looked down at his lap trying to hide a smile. Arlie was staring hard at him.

"Oh come one, guys!" Ioni said. "What's the good news?"

"We moved in together," Nathan said. "That's what I was doing last night. I was moving all of my stuff into his place." His smiled faded a bit as he looked into her face. "Sorry, babe. I didn't want to suck up the attention you rightfully need right now because of Druggy McBaldhead."

CHAPTER NINETEEN

Ioni talked to her father about getting her own place the next day, and he had strong objections, logical ones, she had to admit. He felt that it was better for her if she stayed at home and continued to save her money and not worry about massive student loans. Ioni's counter to this was that the house was becoming crowded. There were too many adults living under one roof. Her father begrudgingly agreed with that, making sure to state that he was happy to help his daughters so that they could work to make their situations better.

In the end, he agreed to help Ioni at least look for an affordable place and if she could cover the rent and basic utilities, he would cover the rest. The big stipulation was that the rent had to be affordable, and on a part-time waitressing job, that was going to be tricky. Arlie was able to afford her own place because she worked full-time and supplemented that income with money made from selling her art. Nathan was living with his boyfriend and they both worked full-time as well.

Ioni understood that the odds were against her, but at least it was something to look forward to, to plan for herself. She was finding that keeping her mind busy was helping her with her breakup from Raber. She missed him in quiet moments. She missed him with such ferocity that she had to immediately busy herself with some task to keep from calling him.

It was lucky that Yule came about not long after their breakup. She had something to occupy her mind and she hated to admit it even to herself, she was looking forward to seeing Tristan. She felt a twang of guilt when she thought of Raber and how he was clueless of how she and Tristan had been, as she had seen it, inappropriate with each other.

When Ioni followed Sarah into the home of the coven member that hosted Yule every year, a sweet man named Mike Post, she was happily greeted with hugs and warmth. By that time she had met all of the coven members at least once and had working friendships with a couple of them. As opposed to the previous year when she was just an observer, Ioni felt much less like an outsider. After the initial crowd had said their hellos and parted, she saw Tristan smiling at her from across the room. Unable to stop herself from smiling too, she walked over and accepted the kiss to her cheek.

"Let me just get this out of the way," he said, pulling her away from the others. He leaned down so that he was looking straight into her face and he lowered his voice.

"Gossip travels fast, even in the biggest social circles," he said.

"Oh, geez," Ioni said, angry and embarrassed.

"No," Tristan said, holding his hand up. "I want you to know that I'm sincerely really sorry that things played out like that. I know how much you loved him. I'm sure you still love him, actually. All I'm saying is that I feel for you and I'm here if you need anything."

She huffed loudly, trying to let go of her anger. She looked into Tristan's sparkling eyes and felt a smile pulling at the corners of her mouth. He smiled back.

"I'm doing okay," she said. "I do love him, but you know, that relationship was starting to die a slow death. It was depressing because I don't think my feelings were being returned."

"That's not fair to you," Tristan said, shaking his head.

"I think so too!" she replied excitedly, thrilled that he could see her point of view. "I mean, don't go thinking that I didn't get any sort of good out of that relationship, because I really, really did, but you know, he started getting distracted and hiding things from me and, you know, when you start hiding things then that means that trust is gone and when trust is gone, what else is there besides sex?"

He burst into laughter and put his hands on her shoulders.

"What?" She asked him.

"You're the innocent one, remember?" He said, still chuckling. "You just surprised me by yelling the word 'sex' at me just now."

"Oh geez, was I yelling?" Ioni said, looking around. Nobody was looking at them.

"Don't worry about it. That was a nice little outburst. I'm sure you needed it."

"I did, actually. Thanks for listening." Ioni said, shyly stepping back.

"I said I was here for you," he said, folding his hands in front of him. "If you need to yell, then you can yell at me."

Freya approached them then and kissed Ioni on her cheek.

"Are you ready to begin?" she asked.

"Yeah, I'm really looking forward to it. Maybe I'll know what's going on this time!" Ioni said.

And she did. In a year, Ioni had been able to familiarize herself with a lot of the acts of such rituals. She understood that casting a circle deosil meant circling clockwise, and that the ceremonial dagger that Freya held was called an athame, and that the ritual was a way of saying goodbye to winter's dark and welcoming the coming light as the days started to get longer.

Ioni was pleased that the ritual moved her. She didn't feel like an onlooker nor did she feel like she was performing in a hollow theatrical farce. She felt the movement of the coven members around her and she felt the words spoken settle into her in a strangely comforting way. When Tristan brought the charred shard of the previous year's Yule log to the fireplace and used it to set the new log ablaze, she felt herself loudly saying, "Blessed be!" before anyone else. But instead of

166

making her feel weird, the other members echoed her exclamation and laughed in kind fraternity.

The feast was amazing, and Ioni wondered if it was the lack of self-consciousness that made the food more delicious. Karen and Sarah sat on either side of her on folding chairs, plates overflowing with food balanced on their laps. Tristan and Freya sat across from her, shoveling food into their mouths.

"I really have no idea how they learned their eating habits," Karen said, smiling indulgently at her children.

"We're enjoying ourselves!" Freya said, her cheeks puffed out with food.

Again, Ioni was reminded of the difference between Raber and Tristan. She felt such a stab of longing for Raber at that moment that she excused herself to the bathroom. She sat on the edge of the bathtub and put her head in her hands. Just a year ago everything was fine between them. They were in love, they were beginning an interesting journey together, and he was still hers. Just at that minute, her cell phone, which was in her pocket, chirped, alerting her that she'd received a text message. The piece of new tech was an early Christmas gift from her father. He'd gotten each daughter one and they were on a family plan. She checked the time to see if it was late enough for unlimited texts yet or she was going to be charged for every message that came through. It was after nine, so she was in the clear.

"Was the Yule ceremony better for you this year?" The text read. It was from Raber.

"Oh gosh," Ioni said to herself. She stared at the screen of her phone, not knowing whether to respond or not. She wanted to talk to him. It was surreal that he had texted her at the same moment she was missing him so deeply. Then again, she didn't want to talk to him. She was still very much wounded and hesitant because of how threatened she felt on their last meeting. And how the hell did he know that she had a cell phone? Who gave him her number?

"I understand if you don't respond," he texted.

"I wanted to apologize for being a crazy person the other day, and I have had a really hard time gathering enough courage to be able to contact you. I'm embarrassed and I'm so sorry. I love you so much, I hope you know that. And I also hope that you've had a fruitful evening." This came through in four different messages.

"Now tell me some excuse as to why you acted crazy," Ioni spoke aloud to her phone, waiting to see if he would text again. She considered replying, but found she had nothing to say. Her phone chirped.

"I was high, you were right about that. I'm sure you didn't need confirmation on that, but I needed to come clean to you about it. There's no excuse beyond that. Just know I'm sorry and I love you." He wrote in three separate messages. Her phone was being very noisy.

"Okay," Ioni said aloud. "I guess that at least deserves a reply."

"Thanks for asking," she wrote. "Tonight went great. I understood it a lot better this time around. I wish U had been here. U might have liked it..."

She stopped and erased her message before hitting send. She huffed and fidgeted, thinking of the right thing to say.

"Thanks for that," she wrote. "I appreciate the apology and the honesty. Tonight was fun. Take care."

She stared at the message before hitting "send" and wondered if it was too cold. Raber hadn't always been a scary drug addict. Maybe he deserved a little bit of tenderness from her. And then, as if it were an act of providence, there was a soft knock at the bathroom door.

"Ioni?" Sarah's voice called. "You okay in there?"

Ioni hit the "send" button and shoved the phone back into her pants pocket.

"I'm fine," she called. "I just needed a second of quiet. I'm coming."

The next day was Ioni's initiation into the coven. She and Sarah had prayed for a fair day so that her ceremony could take place outside.

"It's so much more profound a ceremony out in the elements," Sarah had told her.

To their utter relief, the day was mild and clear. It was still West Virginia winter and it was hovering at just below freezing, but it was as good a day as any to stand in the hallowed realm of nature and become a sister and confidant to a group of Wiccans.

In order to carry out the ceremony, the coven reconvened at Mike Post's home. Mike owned quite a lot of land that surrounded his house and it was common for important ceremonies to go on there because of the access to nature and the privacy.

The first half of the ceremony involved only the current members of the coven, so Ioni and Sarah were waiting inside of a small shed on Mike's property. They were both wearing virginal white robes, and Ioni had a wrapped bundle in her arms that contained all of her magical tools so that Freya could cleanse and bless them ritually.

"I keep meaning to ask this, but what do I call you once I'm in?" Ioni asked Sarah. "I'm so used to calling you Sarah."

"Call me Sarah, then," she answered, smiling. "Adare is the name the goddess knows me by. Just use Adare as my formal Wiccan name. Only use it if we should be practicing together, okay?"

"Okay," Ioni said. "That's a relief, I was still confused on that part."

"Are you nervous?" Sarah asked her. They had been sitting in a meditative silence before, but Ioni was glad to be talking.

"Not really nervous, but I'm anxious." Ioni answered.

"You're gonna be just fine. I'm glad that you're joining because I really feel like we've connected this past year. You know you've really blossomed. When I first met you as your art teacher, you were such a shy and insecure girl. Most high schoolers are insecure, but you seemed really withdrawn. But this last year you've really come into a much stronger personality."

"Thanks," Ioni said, feeling herself blushing. "I feel much more sure of myself now. I hate to use him as a reason, but Raber had a lot to do with that. I don't like to think that I'm the type of girl that *needs* someone to love her, but it really helped my view of myself when he came along. He was complimenting and his feelings were always very strong and out front. And he's a strong-willed person. Seeing him and how he would just go for things that he wanted without letting anyone or anything hinder him, well, that was an example that I wanted to follow to a lighter extent."

"You think you learned that?" Sarah asked. "Girl, that's not a learned trait. I think that it was in you all along, but it was simply awakened in you when you felt that you were good enough to have it your way. Having someone love you made you realize that you were good enough. Don't think that it was all on him. It was you all along."

Ioni smiled at Sarah and returned to her quiet meditation, finding herself missing Raber again. She lowered her head and tried to blink away the tears welling in her eyes. Luckily, the door opened not long after and Mike walked in.

"Mentor, you are to bring your initiate before the coven now," he said, addressing Sarah.

They stood and followed Mike out of the shed and along a path that lead to a small clearing where a large tree had been cut down and the wide stump was being used as an altar. All of the coven members watched her as she brought up the rear on the quaint three-person succession, all of their smiling faces shining at her. Tristan was standing next to the stump/altar, taller than everybody else, looking like a deity himself in his white robe.

"Mentor," he began, his deep, rich voice clear in the open atmosphere. "Bring your initiate into the circle."

Sarah slipped behind Ioni and gently pushed her into the circle. She then knelt down beside Ioni and curled the bottom of Ioni's robe up around her knees, revealing her blue jeans underneath.

"Kneel within the circle," Tristan commanded.

Ioni placed her knees on the provided towel that was laid out, another consideration so that her costume wouldn't get dirty.

"Mentor," Tristan said. "Who is this you bring before us, your coven, for initiation?"

"I, Adare, daughter of the goddess, bring before you Ioni, daughter of the goddess."

"Has Ioni completed a training period of a year and a day?" Tristan asked.

"She has, with much dedication and fervor," Sarah answered.

"Coven," Tristan said loudly. "What say you? Are you in agreement that Ioni shall continue with her initiation ceremony? Your silence speaks in the affirmative."

The air was thick with silence as Ioni strained to hear anybody objecting. She didn't expect that anyone would, but she was glad when Tristan smiled down at her and continued.

"Ioni, this coven gives its blessing that you be initiated and accepted to us. We shall continue. Have you your tools of magic for cleansing and blessing?"

Ioni silently extended her white bundle to Tristan. He handed the bundle to Freya who took them to the altar and began cleansing them in warm salt water and whispering blessings over them.

"Ioni, are you ready to be purified so that the initiation can begin?" Tristan asked.

"I am ready," she answered.

Tristan went to the stump/altar and took up a silver bowl of salt and sprinkled a tiny amount on her shoulders. Then he lit a stick of incense and circled it around her head, leaving a light halo of white smoke. Next, he took a lit white candle and circled it around her. Last was a light sprinkling of consecrated water from a silver bowl. Tristan mumbled blessings all during the purification process. When it was done and Ioni was deemed 'purified', Tristan extended his arms and spoke loudly.

"Hail to the gods and goddesses served by this coven. Hail to those of blood and spirit we name as family who have gone before us. I, your humble servant, Tristan, present to you Ioni, daughter of the goddess who has sought initiation into our spiritual family."

Tristan then looked into Ioni's face.

"Ioni, you are to understand that this initiation is a death and rebirth. Who you were before entering this circle dies today and you will be reborn a daughter of the goddess and a sister to this convened circle. You are to pursue a life of service to the goddess and gods we serve. The mysteries of these higher beings are many and you are to spend your days pursuing a greater understanding and knowledge of those mysteries, though we dare not assume we might know them all. You serve the light and should wish to obtain nothing more than enlightenment and love. Do you agree to this, Ioni?"

"I agree," Ioni answered.

Freya approached and handed the re-wrapped bundle of tools to Tristan.

"These tools of our faith and practice have been cleansed and blessed in accordance with our beliefs and traditions. Use them well and do not taint them with dark intentions."

He put a hand on her head and spoke again.

"As an elder member of this coven, Ioni, I bring you into this circle. I, Tristan, who was brought in by Karen who was brought in by Thorn who was brought in by Eupraxia. We honor those who came before us and respectfully carry on their traditions. From Eupraxia, from Thorn, from Karen and from I, Tristan, we bestow our acceptance of you, Ioni, into our most trusted circle. Now, rise."

Tristan helped Ioni to a standing position. When she looked up into his face, he smiled and winked at her. Her cheeks grew hot and her pulse quickened.

"Brothers and sisters," Tristan boomed. "We are now one person stronger and it is my belief that the goddess has smiled on us this day. Ioni is now one of us! Welcome, Ioni and blessed be!"

He leaned down and kissed her. She knew it was coming, but she was still shocked. She had expected a dry, formal brush of the lips, but Tristan opened his mouth slightly, wetting her lower lip. When he pulled away, the assembled coven shouted "Blessed be!," then whooped and cheered.

Tristan handed Ioni her bundle of freshly cleansed tools and brushed her cheek with another kiss before making room for the other members of the coven to welcome her. She was hugged and kissed and welcomed as warmly as she could have hoped. When the last coven member had hugged her and they began the trek back to Mike's house for a celebratory potluck feast, she found herself alone among the trees. In the silence, she took a moment to take the ceremony in. She was still standing by the tree stump/altar, looking down at her robed self when she heard a voice.

"That was not quite as theatrical as I expected it would be, aside from the fetching costumes."

Raber was standing by a tree, away from the path that led to Mike's house. He started walking toward her. Ioni narrowed her eyes, looking at him hard, trying to gauge whether or not he was a threat to her. Thankfully, his eyes looked clear, and there was a red color to his cheeks. He stopped right in front of her and put a hand on the arm that she was using to hold her bundle to her chest.

"I guess congratulations are in order?" he asked, not meeting her eyes. When she didn't say anything he stopped touching her.

"You said I could come. This is an important day for you," he whispered.

"I did say that," Ioni answered.

"I didn't want to miss this. I made it a habit of missing too many of your big days."

"Okay." Ioni said.

"Well I'm here. And I saw it. I saw everything. That kiss at the end, well maybe it explains a few things." he said, meeting her eyes.

"Raber, do not come here and try to start a fight or accuse me of anything." Ioni said, stepping back from him. "We managed not to end our relationship in a big ugly fight, and let me tell you, pal, I've got material for a big fight. I've got plenty. How dare you come here acting like you're earning big brownie points with me and then start making hints that maybe I've been up to something. Fuck you, Raber! Just fuck you!"

He stepped closer to her and grabbed her arm above the elbow, squeezing painfully. He brought his face close to hers so that she could feel his breath puffing in her face.

"Don't talk to me that way," he said in a low, growling voice. "I didn't agree to end a goddamned thing with you, you know. I could make you come back. I know you miss me. Unless you're fucking that other guy, I know you don't have any other prospects. I'm under your skin, now. I'll always be in you somehow."

Ioni quickly and violently twisted her arm out of his grip and stepped away.

"You keep your fucking hands off of me, Raber Belliveau," she said. "You don't get to treat me like a belonging. That was never what our relationship was about, so don't go doing some pathetic power play like that on me, do you understand?"

"It's not a power play, you moron," Raber answered, keeping his distance. "It's the truth. I can make you do what I want, even now when you can look at me like you hate me."

"Don't flatter yourself," Ioni answered.

"I still love you. I still want you." he said.

"You've got a nice abusive way of showing it," Ioni said. "I can't wait for you to make me do whatever the hell it is you think you can so you can stoop to beating me too."

He looked down at his hands and exhaled heavily.

"I wouldn't beat you, baby," he said. "I'm just so fucking lost without you. I go back to school in about a week and I can't bear being up there knowing that I have no reason to come home anymore. You know how my parents are. They've got their own lives going on and I don't fit into their itinerary. I'm always alone in that big fucking house and I miss you so much it hurts. Don't you know that? Don't you know that your absence is physically painful to me?"

"So now we come to the guilt trip part of the discussion?" Ioni asked. "Raber, you made your decisions and chose your sides with open eyes. I drew the line in the sand, and you stepped over it without any hesitation."

"I know," he said. "I made mistakes. I didn't put you first, I made bad decisions, I handle conflict really badly. I know. And I know that if I want you back, we have to deal with the Andrew situation. I know. It's on me, I know."

"You say one thing and do another, Raber," Ioni said. "You made so many empty promises to me that I can't even bring myself to believe you anymore."

"Well I can see that you're not too heartbroken over what a dishonest, lying asshole I am, what with your new man and all." Raber said.

"Don't start," Ioni warned. "You have no right to question anything that I do. I never cheated on you. Tristan is my friend and so are a lot of these coven members. Now that we're not together anymore, if I feel inclined to have sex with someone, that's not something you get to know about. It's none of your business."

"Well I guess everything's been said," Raber said quietly.

"I guess it has," Ioni snapped back.

Without another word, Raber turned and walked away, this time taking the path. Ioni stayed behind, still clutching her bundle to her chest. When Raber was out of sight, she started the walk back. She got to the house just in time to see Raber's car leaving. She exhaled her relief and joined her coven for food and talk. The tenseness that she acquired from her meeting with Raber eventually melted among the kind, smiling faces of her new family.

CHAPTER TWENTY

January came and went and so, too went Ioni's dream of getting her own place. She'd looked high and low and had to admit that she simply couldn't afford it. But she was working hard, focusing where she needed to and her grades from her first semester of college were good enough for her to make it onto the Dean's List. Her father made it a point to tell her how impressed he was with her for carrying a job and making good grades at the same time. She floated on that compliment for a solid week.

With her newfound focus, she decided finally to major in Accounting, which also pleased her father in part because she was following in his footsteps and in part because he could relax, knowing that her job prospects post-graduation would be much better than the Liberal Arts degree he was worried she might choose.

Life moved smoothly for Ioni, despite a few rocky weeks following that last fight with Raber. After that day, she set her jaw and determined that their relationship was finished, whether he agreed or not. She didn't hear from him after that. No texts, no calls, no surprise visits and she was thankful. Arlie and Nathan were wholly supportive of her decision not to take him back.

"You're single, gorgeous, and mostly independent. Life is your buffet, baby! Eat 'til you're puking!" Nathan told her.

To some extent, she took Nathan's advice to heart. She wanted to have fun and enjoy her life, but she still felt unsure of herself, mostly due to lack of experience. She saw Tristan at least once a week, but it was mostly social or pertaining to coven matters. They hadn't been alone, but she thought about it. In fact, her fantasies about Tristan were becoming more frequent and detailed. He was in her mind and imagination to the point of distraction. She was inching closer and closer to a resolve to make the first move since Tristan, despite his frequent professions of 'like', had yet to make a real move.

Her chance came in mid-February. She had the day off and was sitting alone in her room reading when her cellphone rang. It was Sarah asking if she'd like to go out to lunch with her and a few other people. Eager to get out of the crowded and noisy house, Ioni agreed.

They met at a small, locally-owned Italian restaurant famous for bland food. Ioni was pleased to see that Sarah was accompanied by Karen, Freya, and Tristan. The lunch talk came easily and there was a comfort among everybody that she had grown to appreciate. There was a definite intimacy that went along with practicing a religion with those people. Because of that, Ioni didn't feel a self-conscious need to order a small plate of food and pick at it, embarrassed of her size and worried that people might find her displeasing. No, around her coven she could order a large plate of spaghetti (bland though it may be) and eat every last noodle along with a breadstick or two and know that nobody was watching her too closely or thinking her an unpleasant glutton.

After they had all finished their food, they walked together to the parking lot. Karen kissed her son and daughter, hugged Sarah and Ioni and made her way off in her own car. Freya kissed everybody that was left and she and Sarah left in her car, leaving Tristan and Ioni alone.

"Hey," Ioni said, gathering all of her courage and trying to look calm and collected.

"Hm?" Tristan responded, smiling easily.

"I was wondering if I could treat you to dinner tomorrow night. I work the lunch shift, so I'm free in the evening and I thought maybe it would be nice if just you and I tried a bit of mutual eating."

Without his smile fading even a bit, Tristan frowned and blinked. Blushing, Ioni raised her eyebrows, waiting for Tristan to answer.

"You know," he began, "I've been trying not to be a predator. I wanted to make sure that you had adequate healing time before I made my move on you. Did I wait too long?"

She laughed and looked away. Sometimes questions are too direct for any answer to prove satisfactory.

"I'm sorry if I did!" Tristan said, laughing, too. "I guess I should be the one doing the asking here."

"Oh, it's too late now," Ioni said, playfully. "So is five o'clock okay with you? I'll pick you up, make sure you're home at a reasonable hour?"

Tristan laughed heartily and hugged Ioni to him amicably. She had come to understand over time that Tristan and Freya both were touchy-feely people. Some of those early encounters that had left her panicked were easily explained away by that realization, and it made her feel more at ease around Tristan.

"That sounds great to me. Maybe we can go back to my place after and rent a movie or something?" Tristan said.

"That will work. So I'll see you tomorrow. Umm, where do you live?"

"Oh, ha! Yeah, you've never been to my place," Tristan said.

He gave her directions that were easy to follow. Thankfully, Stearnsville was a small enough town and most houses could be associated with gas stations or fast food joints. Saying, "I live about a block away from the GoMart next to the VA Park," was always almost all of the directions needed aside from the house number.

They parted ways, both of them smiling themselves to sore cheeks, and Ioni sat in her car and watched Tristan's truck pull out before excitedly pulling out her cell phone and sending a text to Arlie and Nathan.

"You guys are not going to believe how fucking awesome I am," it read.

After everybody was caught up on Ioni's exciting news, Nathan gave Ioni a piece of advice.

"Live in the moment, ok?" His text read. Ioni stared at it for a moment before her phone chirped again.

"Don't hold back on something you want out of fear of how it will look," he texted.

"Don't think about words like 'slut' or 'whore'. Those words are pretend words," Arlie joined in.

"If you want it, and the mood is right, scratch that motherfuckin' itch. OK?" Nathan texted.

"OK," Ioni replied.

"U GONNA GET SOME!" Nathan texted.

"Get some!" Arlie texted.

"I might not, you guys!" Ioni texted. "We might just end the night with a handshake. Maybe a kiss. I dunno."

"Just do what you want, that's all we're saying," Arlie replied.

"GET SOME!" Nathan replied.

Ioni finished her shift at three o'clock the next day and rushed home to get ready. She was able to pin down one of the bathrooms long enough to get in a shower and shave her legs. When she was done, she rushed to her room, applied lotion all over and stood staring into her closet. It seemed that every time she would pull something out, she found that it had a memory of Raber attached to it. Cursing herself for not getting a new outfit before work, she pulled on a pair of black jeans and a fuzzy neon pink sweater. She obsessed over her every angle in the mirror, mildly annoyed that the fuzz of the sweater seemed to add bulk to her, but the deep V-neck made her breasts look amazing. Waving her arms in frustration, she decided the outfit would work.

She blow-dried her hair and let it fall about her shoulders in soft, shining cascades. She reached up and stroked it and, for the millionth time since December, missed how Raber had always touched her hair.

"I'm not thinking of you tonight," she said to the mirror, pulling out her bag of dark makeup. "It could have been you with me tonight, but you'd rather be a waste."

She applied her makeup in her usual manner and put on an enormous pair of hoop earrings. When everything was applied and placed perfectly, she stared at her reflection and smiled.

"I'm moving up in the world," she said to her reflection. "And I look damned cute."

She found Tristan's house easily. Like his mother's and sister's houses, the exterior was neat as a pin. It was a tiny white house with its own small carport at the side and a tiny yard. She rang the doorbell and heard Tristan from inside.

"It's open, come on in!" he said.

Meekly, she opened the door and peered inside. To her surprise and delight, she was greeted by the most colorful house she had ever seen. The front door opened immediately into the living room, which was painted a fire engine red. A dark leather sofa sat against the wall and two white, shining, plastic chairs sat on either side of it. Off to the left, there was a hallway the color of hotdog mustard. Ioni smiled at the condiment colors of Tristan's house and wondered if he was a ballpark fan.

"Hi!" Tristan said, striding in, his height dwarfing the already small room. He came to her and kissed her on the cheek.

"Hey," Ioni said, flashing her best smile. "Are you ready to go?"

"I am!" Tristan said, brightly. "Let me get my coat, I'll be right back!"

"You sure are a fan of bright colors!" Ioni called out to him a moment later.

"I lived with my father in Brazil on and off as a kid. I go and stay with him for a couple months out of the year, or I try to. These bright colors always remind me of him."

Ioni smiled. He held his hand out to her. She took it and led him out of the house. The drive to the restaurant was steeped in a strange, but not uncomfortable silence. When she pulled into the parking lot of the town's only Mexican restaurant, Tristan smiled widely.

"I love this place," he said happily.

"I do, too," she said, relieved that her choice was a good one. "I don't get to come here often, so I thought this would be fun."

They walked into the restaurant looking like a couple on a date. Tristan had stopped and offered Ioni his arm, and Ioni draped her arm through his. She had a small tug of doubt, but tamped it down. Nathan and Arlie would never forgive her timidity.

As they sat waiting for their food to arrive, munching happily on tortilla chips and salsa, Ioni was making basic conversation with Tristan and he happily listened and asked her relevant questions. She mentioned to him how she had looked for her own place, but found she couldn't afford rent on her own. Tristan became very quiet and she looked up at him questioningly.

"I might be able to help you there," he said thoughtfully. "Do you remember my telling you that I visit my father for months at a time every year?" Ioni nodded.

"I'm leaving the second week of March until September to be with my dad. Normally, I have my mom come and check on my house while I'm gone, but I know it gets tedious for her. How about this, how about you house-sit for me while I'm gone. It's not permanent by any means and it's also not really your own place, but you can get out of your parents' crowded house and have your own space for six months. I own the place so there's no rent, and I pay the utilities myself. Just keep the place clean, the yard needs tending in the summer, and keep me updated on whether everything's working."

Ioni chewed on a chip and thought about it.

"That's so nice of you to offer," she said.

"You're doing me a favor if you do it," he said.

Ioni chewed some more, looking into his open face. Slowly, she started smiling and Tristan mirrored the act.

"I'll do it," she said at last.

"Oh, good!" Tristan said. "The ways in which this evening could have gone great have grown! I'll have to give you a tour of the place when dinner is over and then we'll settle in for a movie…if you're still okay with that."

"That sounds great," Ioni said.

"I don't have any pets, and since I go on these long trips, I don't have any plants either, so that part will be easy," Tristan was telling her later, walking her through his house.

"There's one bedroom and one bathroom. The kitchen is pretty compact and there's a washer and dryer down in the basement," he said, opening a door in the hallway and flicking on a light.

She followed him down an old, bare wood staircase into a dark basement. In the very front, the floor was cement and that's where the washer, dryer, water heater, and furnace sat. But near the back the floor was simple packed dirt. It was clean and free of cobwebs and surprisingly dry and pleasant.

"Gee, you and your mom and sister are such tidy people," Ioni said, looking around her.

"I guess," Tristan said with a surprised chuckle. "So do you think you'll be okay with all of this?" He led the way back up the stairs and closed the door.

"Oh yeah, I have a couple of unrelated questions, actually."

"Go for it," Tristan said, sitting on the couch, smiling. She sat next to him, fighting her awkward urge to sit on one of the chairs away from him.

"Okay, the first question is, what do you do for a living? I have no idea how you make money."

"I'm an independent contractor," he answered.

"What's that?" Ioni asked, smiling and interested.

"Well, I help build and repair stuff. I'm my own boss, but my time and skills are hired out to clients who need a bit of help with work. I can set my own hours usually and I don't have to work in an office. As long as I keep clients coming it's a pretty cozy living. I can do it here or in Brazil with my dad."

"Wow," Ioni said. "So are you educated? Did you go to college?"

"I did," Tristan began, absently taking her hand. "But I studied Astronomy, if you can believe it. I got into construction with a friend of mine back in the day. It started out as fun, but when we saw that the money was good, it became full-time. I work on a skill set, not a degree, although I do need to be certified to do my job. I had to pass a test to get it."

"Okay, second question. How old are you?" she asked, enjoying the feel of his warm hand around hers.

He reached out and touched her fuzzy sweater.

"I'm twenty-six," he said. "Is that okay?"

Ioni was quiet while she thought.

"Is that yucky?" she asked him. "I mean, I'm still technically a teenager."

"Are you put off by my age?" he asked, his face serious.

"No, not really. Honestly, I thought you were younger. But, well," Ioni faltered.

"What?" he asked.

"I like you. I really like you and your age really doesn't change that. I guess I'm just wondering how other people might view this."

"Who cares," Tristan said, resuming his stroking of her sweater.

"That's what my friends would say," Ioni said, smiling. "They'd tell me that I'm a consenting legal adult and that the rest of the world can take their twisted ideals and make sour grapes casserole out of them."

"Your friends sound kind of great," Tristan said, laughing. "Was that all you wanted to know?"

"Yeah, that's about it."

"Then, I was wondering if I could kiss you." he said, smiling.

Ioni felt hot all over. All she could manage was a nod. Tristan leaned in and kissed her softly, much like he had kissed her at her initiation, sucking on her lower lip. Ioni put her hands up on his long neck. He scooted closer to her and put his arms around her, bringing her close into him and kissed her more deeply. He hooked a hand under her knee and brought her leg up on the couch while gently pushing her back. She allowed herself to lie back and wrapped her legs around him, still enjoying the newness of kissing him.

"Is this okay?" he asked her. "Not moving too fast?"

Still unable to make herself speak, Ioni only shook her head before grabbing Tristan's face and bringing it back down to her own, pushing her tongue into his mouth. He grunted and put his arms around her.

Ioni let herself relax. She let herself stop thinking about the what-ifs of what she was doing. Tristan felt good, and she could tell that the feeling was mutual. His hand was inside of her shirt, stroking her breasts and grazing over nipples. Still without thinking, she started pulling his shirt off of him, revealing a deliciously flat stomach and unblemished, smooth skin.

"My turn," Tristan grinned down at her. Allowing herself to feel more than think, she permitted Tristan to slide the pink fuzzy sweater over her head, revealing the white lacey bra she wore underneath. It clasped in the front and Ioni reached down and unclasped the bra, spilling her breasts into the open air, causing Tristan to whistle and bite his lip.

"You're gorgeous," he said, looking down at her.

"Then come here," she said, finally finding her ability to speak.

He was happy to comply. He lowered himself back down to her and kissed her neck, returning momentarily to her mouth before moving down to her breasts. He sucked lightly on her nipples, making Ioni arch her back and gasp. When he came back up, she forced herself not to rush, but instead enjoyed him kissing her and the way his long fingers stroked her skin.

He was noisy. He moaned happily and stopped to giggle when she nibbled on his ear. He was a man who savored his joys, and Ioni found herself smiling as they explored each other. He smelled clean and his shaved head was nothing new to her. She would have been shocked to touch hair on a man's head. His kisses were deep and his touch was gentle.

When the ache in Ioni's loins became too much to ignore, she found herself unbuttoning his blue jeans. He sat up on his knees and allowed this, watching her hands work. He helped her to move them over his slender hips and his boxer briefs came off next, revealing his excitement.

Tristan did not rid his body of its hair, but he kept it closely cropped. It made for an attractive presentation that Ioni could not resist stroking. When her hand found the intense heat of his manhood, she gripped it lightly and stroked. He looked up at the ceiling and laughed.

"If your hand feels that amazing, how must the rest of you feel?"

Taking that as an invitation, Ioni sat up and took him into her mouth. He moaned loudly and laughed again. She took it slow, not wanting to spend his vigor before she had gotten all that she wanted. Luckily, he took her face in his hands and tilted it up so she was looking in his face.

"It's my turn again," he said.

He lowered himself back down to her and kissed her mouth, then moved down to her throat, her breasts, her stomach. He deftly unbuttoned her blue jeans and she arched her hips so that he could slide them off. He stroked her over her panties, looking up into her face.

"Are we still okay? Not moving too fast?"

"Not fast enough," Ioni answered.

Laughing heartily, Tristan slid her panties off of her. Again, he took a moment to look at her and admire her before going into action.

He was good at what he did. His messy eating habits at the dinner table translated to enthusiastic, yet skillful oral artistry. When Ioni, out of breath and beginning to sweat, grabbed him gently by the ears and pulled him back up to face her, her desire for him was so great that she almost forgot about protection. Luckily, Tristan was still in control of his faculties enough to think for the both of them. He stood up and held a hand out to her. Ioni smiled and took a moment to admire his long, lean body.

"Come with me," he said, after giving her a moment to enjoy the view.

Without any hesitation or shame in her nudity, Ioni took his hand and let him lead her to his bedroom. She had been in the room earlier when he was giving her the tour and she was still impressed. The room was painted a bright green color and the furniture was minimalist, but everything was clean and gleaming. Even his bed was made. The all-white bedding, smoothed and tidy, made for a welcoming site.

Tristan leaned down and pulled back the covers. He smiled at Ioni and patted the spot, inviting her. She sprawled out and looked up at him. He knelt at the side of the bed and kissed her gently.

"I'm on the pill," she said.

"That's encouraging, and I may take advantage of that someday," he said to her, still smiling. "For right now, let's be cautious and safe, okay?"

She nodded in agreement, happy at his caution and watched as he pulled open a bedside drawer and removed a condom. He smiled mischievously and handed it to her.

"Would you like to do the honors, I wonder?"

She took the small square from his hands and looked at it.

"In a minute maybe," she said. "Now come here."

They kissed and touched and explored until they were both panting in desperation. Tristan sat up on his knees and looked down at Ioni.

"I can't wait," he said to her. "I want you so badly right now."

Without saying anything, Ioni opened the small envelope and removed the condom and rolled it onto him. In one smooth movement, he lowered himself back onto her and immediately pushed himself into her. Surprised, but pleasantly so, Ioni arched her hips and moaned her pleasure, her hands kneading the muscles in his shoulders as he began to slowly move.

Despite his eagerness, Tristan was a tender lover who took his time. She could tell that he was waiting for her to climax before he allowed himself to finish. When her moment finally came, she told him, causing him to go over the edge of his own orgasm.

After, they held on to each other, panting and quivering. She stroked Tristan's long neck and he came out of his post-orgasmic trance and kissed her gently. Ioni returned this kiss with gratitude and found herself giggling.

"What?" Tristan said, smiling and looking down at her.

"Oh, I'm sorry," she said. "It's just that I couldn't help but have myself a little self-celebration for no longer being someone who's only ever had sex with one person. You're my plural lover."

Tristan laughed heartily and rolled off of her to the side. They sat in silence staring at the ceiling when Ioni again became aware of her nakedness and tried to grab some blankets to put over herself. Tristan snapped back into the moment and looked at her. He smiled and playfully pulled the blankets off of her body.

"Let me loan you a T-shirt and we go watch a movie. Then...maybe after it's over...we can do that again? Then I'll make you breakfast tomorrow?"

"You want me to spend the night?" Ioni asked, clearly shocked.

"Well, yeah," Tristan said.

"Hmm," Ioni said, relaxing and looking back up to the ceiling. "You better make sure it's a *really* big T-shirt to cover these puppies," she said gesturing to her breasts. Tristan laughed and rolled over and put one of her nipples into his mouth.

"Mmmm," he said, pulling away. "I'd better save some of that for later."

Before Ioni knew it, nearly a month had passed and she had spent many a night falling asleep next to Tristan. He'd insisted that she become comfortable in the house. Ioni's parents had no real reaction when she told them she'd be house-sitting for six months, but she sensed a bit of relief from Rose and Amanda.

Her family had asked her where she'd been spending her nights, and Ioni lied to them and said that she had been crashing at Arlie's trailer. Tristan had offered to let Ioni move her stuff into his house early, but she didn't want to have to answer questions about their relationship to her family just yet. As far as they knew, he was a friend and she was doing him a favor. If things continued to go well, she knew that she would have to eventually introduce him into her family life, but for the time being, they were just having a good time with no real commitments. She wasn't hiding Tristan. They were together in public all the time, but she didn't want to do the sit-down family thing just yet, both for her own comfort and to keep her father from grilling Tristan.

"So when's moving day?" Arlie asked her over breakfast one morning.

Ioni had stumbled out of Tristan's house, sore and happy, and walked into Arlie's place and busied herself in the kitchen making pancakes and scrambled eggs. Arlie, hearing the commotion, waddled into the kitchen, her blue hair sticking out in all directions, and expressed her gratitude at having breakfast served to her.

"He leaves in two days," Ioni answered her, stuffing a large piece of syrup-soaked pancake into her mouth with glee. "He'll leave early and after I see him off, I'll just load up my car and move my stuff in."

"Yeah, since it's mostly just, what, clothes, jewelry, toiletries, and your computer, it won't take long at all." Arlie said, shaking so much black pepper onto her scrambled eggs that they were gray when she tossed them about.

"Isn't it crazy how lucky this all worked out?" Ioni asked, happily.

Arlie looked up from her plate and smiled.

"You sure have lit up since you've started messing around with this guy," she observed. "It's nice to see you cut loose."

Ioni smiled, wiggled her eyebrows, and continued to eat with glee.

"Have...have you heard from Raber?" Arlie asked cautiously.

"Nope," Ioni said, unfazed. "Hopefully he's getting his shit together, but I'm not gonna wait around for him or anything. I really hope he doesn't come looking for me over summer break or anything. Him and his damned jealousy issues, he would go nuclear if he saw me living in another man's house!"

"Oh my god, yes he would," Arlie agreed, laughing.

"I feel like I haven't seen you guys in a long time," Ioni said, in reference to Nathan as well. "I miss you two. That's why I broke in this morning. I was hoping that you and Nath would maybe want to come have a dinner and a movie thing at Tristan's house on my first night alone there. Nothing big, just a mini-celebration of me getting out of my parents' house for a while."

"Oh, that will be fun," Arlie said. "I know Nath will love that. We miss you too, but you know, we totally understand that we can't see each other all that often anymore. We've got jobs, you've got school and Wicca, I've got art, we've all got adult stuff going on. But you know, that's something that's great about us as friends. We don't *need* constant contact in order to stay close. We just sort of pick up where we left off like there was no break. I love that about you guys."

"Hm, I've never really seen it like that before, but you're right. You think we'll be gross middle-aged people who are still friends? Like, this will be a thing that endures?" Ioni asked.

"I do," Arlie answered. "I trust you and Nath more than I've trusted anybody in my whole life. I trust you guys more than I ever trusted even Adam."

They finished their breakfast and Ioni stayed just long enough to help clean up and put away the dishes, then she went to her parent's house and took a nap.

When Tristan left, he carried his bags out to his truck and kissed Ioni passionately, lamenting not being able to take her on the floor one last time. But he had a plane to catch, so he was on his way, leaving Ioni standing on his porch wearing one of his shirts and waving at him.

It took one trip and about two hours to get all of her stuff moved and settled in to Tristan's house. She walked a few laps around the place, breathing in deeply and smiling widely. Knowing that she had guests coming in a few hours, she went to the grocery store and bought some of her favorite staples, stuff for hamburgers and hot dogs, potato salad and baked beans from the deli, as well as potato chips and soda. She nearly skipped through the front door as she carried the groceries into the house.

The party was a lot of fun. Nathan and Chris showed up first. Nathan squealed and ran from room to room making observations about what he called "the crayon house," while Chris was kind enough to fire up the grill and cook the meat. Arlie had smiled and said the house was very interesting. Ioni made a mental note to introduce Tristan to her friends as soon as he got back.

They ate food and danced to obnoxious music and watched whatever lunacy was on MTV. Ioni had a moment where they were all piled into the tiny living room where she looked around her, at the faces of her two closest and dearest friends, and she said a silent prayer, thanking the powers that be for the sweet fortune of having people in her life who loved her so effortlessly and with no demand. She knew that as long as she had them, everything would eventually be good in her life. They were her constant, even more so than her own family.

CHAPTER TWENTY-ONE

In mid-June, Raber came in to her place of work and was unluckily seated in her section. He was alone and had a fuzzy growth of hair on his head, a small mustache, and had obviously put on weight. His usual eyeliner (Nathan called it guyliner) was present, something he'd stopped wearing towards the end of their relationship, but he was wearing khaki pants and a green polo shirt, which was bizarre compared to what she thought of as his usual attire. As she was looking at him from her waitress station, taking in the oddness of the combination of JCPenney and goth, she noticed her promise ring on a chain around his neck. Fully expecting a scene, Ioni braced herself and went to his table.

"Hi," she said in her perky waitress voice. "Can I get you a drink?"

"Can I at least get a real greeting?" Raber asked, smiling up at her.

"Hi, Raber. You're looking well. Now, can I get you a drink?" she said with a little less perk.

"I am doing well. I'm healthier than I was the last time you saw me. I miss you, but I'm taking care of myself like you told me to," he said.

"That's good," she said. "Can I get you a drink?"

"I'm not here to start anything. I wanted to see you, but I'm not here to bother you, okay? I have a new girlfriend in Morgantown and I'm only here for a couple of days anyhow. I just wanted to see you, that's all. I'll have a glass of tea, please."

"Raspberry, sweetened, or unsweetened?" she fired back, flatly.

"Don't you know the answer to that, beautiful?" he asked, reaching up and stroking the back of her hand with his fingertips.

"Okay," she said, jerking out of his reach and going to the drink station to get his usual preference, sweet tea.

When she returned with his drink, she immediately went to talk to another table as soon as she set his cup down. When she could no longer avoid him, she walked back over and took out her order pad.

"Are you ready to order food?" she asked, smiling her polite smile.

"What time do you get off?" he asked, looking at the menu.

"What's that matter?" Ioni asked, lowering her voice.

"It's an innocent question, Ioni."

"Would your girlfriend approve?" She snapped back.

"She's not a jealous type," he said dismissively. "And anyway, we're not serious or anything. If I want to catch up with you and have a talk about how I treated you, that's none of her business."

Ioni stood looking down at him, debating whether or not to give in. She wanted real closure to their relationship, to hear him confess to some things and say to her how he realized what a huge mistake he made in losing her. But she also knew Raber enough to know that he could begin by saying what she wanted to hear only to try to weasel in his own agenda.

"I know about you and that guy from your coven. I know you're staying at his house," he said, still staring hard at his menu.

"How?" she asked, fury building in her. They didn't have friends in common and she didn't believe that her official story of house-sitting would be hot town gossip. That only left something creepy from Raber. Had he followed her? Spied on her?

He looked at her and smiled his sweet, full-lipped smile that she had loved so much, seemingly so long ago.

"Ioni, baby, it's a small town. Aside from that, it is a redneck town. Did you really think that it wouldn't get around that a young white girl is sleeping with an older black guy? It got to my parents and they told me."

"I don't believe you," she shot back, her voice, quivering with rage, was almost too low to hear. "Your parents don't associate with anybody who would notice me going about and living my life. The lodge and country club aren't exactly interested in non-paying members. I think you've been spying on me, you damned creep."

She leaned down to deliver the last word through gritted teeth, and Raber serenely studied his menu, disengaging from her wrath.

"It is what it is," Raber said calmly. "My point in bringing it up is that I'm aware that you're in a relationship with another person. Now can I ask again when you get off work? I'd like to talk to you, get some closure."

"Damn it," Ioni said, slamming her notepad onto the table. "How is it that you can always read my mind like that?"

"I told you," he answered simply. "I'm in you. I'll always be in you, like it or not."

She knew he'd get his way sooner or later. His calm resolve was maddening, but Ioni decided that it would be best to just get it over with and hopefully finally be finished with him once and for all.

"I get off at nine," she said.

"I'll meet you at Tristan's place at ten," he said. "That will give you time to get cleaned up. I'll wait in my car, I won't invade your space."

"Are we going to sit in front of the house in your car?" she asked.

"Well, no. I wanted this to be an occasion. I wanted to drive somewhere that was special to us," he answered.

"I'm not really comfortable with that, Raber." she said sternly.

"Please, just trust me." he said. There was no anger in his voice. He was pleading.

"I'm going to make sure that someone knows I'm with you," she said at last.

"If that makes you feel better."

"Okay, that's settled. So are you going to order, or what?" Ioni asked, tapping her pen on her order pad.

Thankfully he ordered and Ioni was able to get along with her shift. He didn't bother to try to talk to her after that. He ate his food, accepted his check silently, and left cash on the table. He even tipped generously.

She finished her shift and drove to Tristan's house. Raber's car was nowhere to be seen so she parked inside the carport and walked into the house, making sure to lock the door behind her. She showered and put on a pair of blue jeans and one of Tristan's T-shirts as a way to keep him close. Thinking of ways to keep Raber from getting familiar with her, she decided to braid her hair. He'd always loved touching her hair and the braid would thwart that compulsion. At ten o'clock, she looked out of the living room window to see if Raber had shown up.

He was there, parked, engine running, watching her. The sooner it was done, the sooner she could curl up in Tristan's bed and dream of the people in her life who made her happy. Ioni braced herself.

Locking the door behind her, she walked to Raber's car and opened the door. She stopped short of getting in and instead peered into the car at him.

"You know, I'm wondering," she began. "How is it that you knew where this place is?"

Raber blushed and stammered for a moment.

"Okay, well I followed you home from work one night," he said. "But before you overreact, I was there to try to talk to you, but I chickened out. I have enough sense to be embarrassed by how I acted the last couple of times we spoke and I didn't know how to approach you, so I sat in my car and argued with myself when I saw you get into your car. I followed you thinking I would catch you here, but then I thought that that would seem creepy so I went back home."

Suspicions confirmed, Ioni got into the car. While they drove through town, they were quiet. Raber seemed tense. Ioni assumed that he was nervous about having to admit that he had been such an ass to her. When they turned off onto a road that would lead them out to the more rural roads, Ioni knew where they were going.

"The tree?" she asked.

"Our tree," he answered.

"Why a secluded place? I mean, Eat N' Park is a special place to us, too." Ioni said, nervous about the prospect of being so totally alone with Raber. He'd frightened her, her trust and sense of safety around him no longer existed.

"You've been in a restaurant all day and, well, Eat N' Park is kind of a sad place, you know? I'm trying here, okay?" Raber said.

Ioni nodded and stared ahead. The drive to the big oak was going to take almost twenty minutes so she settled in and tried to calm her nerves by breathing deeply.

"There's a thermos in the backseat with your favorite lemonade. I bought it special," Raber said. "Why don't you get some, try to relax?"

Ioni turned and got the blue thermos from the back, noticing the picnic basket and blanket as well. Rolling her eyes, she poured herself a cup of lemonade and started to sip. It was good and sweet. She refilled her cup and looked at Raber. He was sweating.

"We can roll down the windows and drive slower if you're so hot. Maybe some fresh air would be nice?"

"Yes," he said. "There's no rush to get there. I'll do that, thank you."

Ioni watched in wonder as Raber fumbled to get the windows rolled down. They were still in town, so his speed was only about thirty-five. She noticed the way he was gripping the steering wheel and suddenly she felt sorry for him. Surprising herself, she reached out and put one of her hands on top of his. He looked at her, shocked.

"Please don't be nervous on my account," she said. "It's only me."

Raber laughed nervously and nodded, looking back to the road. Ioni had never seen him in such a state before. In the restaurant he'd been so calm, so sure of himself. What changed, she wondered?

"Is that lemonade good?"

"Mmm, it is," she answered. "Nice and sweet."

"Drink as much as you like, gorgeous. I made it just for you."

Ioni frowned and sipped her drink in silence, enjoying the fresh air blowing in her face. She decided to ignore Raber for the time being, since he was acting so out of character. She knew he would make his agenda known soon enough.

She gave herself a mental pat on the back when Raber's car came to a stop. She was no longer anxious or nervous and she credited that to her breathing and meditation. Looking around, she remembered that she hadn't been there since the last time she was there with Raber. Months ago.

"We're at a crossroads," she said, her voice sounding dreamy. "Why is it I never really noticed that before?"

"Your perception changes. I bet your coven members know about this place. Crossroads are special places, yes?" He made no move to get out of the car.

Ioni was jolted into a slight panic when she realized that she had failed to text anybody to tell them that she was with Raber. She fumbled with her purse and pulled out her phone, but realized that there was no reception. She tried to play it cool and put her phone back into her purse, annoyed with her carelessness. Raber either pretended not to notice or was too absorbed in his thoughts to see.

"Well, we're here, so what now?" Ioni asked.

"How are you feeling?" he asked her.

"I'm fine," she answered, frowning at him, trying to shake the weird, watery feeling out of her brain. "What about you? Are you okay? You seem kind of tense."

"I guess I just wasn't really looking forward to this. I mean, you remember the last time we were here. We talked and worked out our problems. We were so in love. I don't want to give you some sort of generic, bullshit speech about regret and remorse. You mean more to me than that and I know that I've probably used up my Hallmark excuses with you at this point."

He turned to her suddenly. Ioni flinched, thinking he was going to try to touch her, but he made no move toward her.

"I still love you, so very much," he said. "I intend to get you back, if it's the last thing I do. I've worked very hard these last months on myself and I'm going to do it."

"Raber," Ioni said, crestfallen that the twist had happened right off the bat. "You've got a girlfriend, I'm seeing somebody. Okay, so you're not serious with your girlfriend, and Tristan and I are still pretty casual. Aside from that, you messed up so bad. The bottom line is that I don't trust you anymore. You turned scary and I didn't feel safe around you, you lied to me, you sectioned me off from other parts of your life. I have no desire at all to do that again. None at all. You just turned into a problem for me."

Raber looked down into his lap and nodded. He still looked anxious and tense. Ioni waited for his response. Before he reacted, though, she started feeling very hot and constricted.

"I need to get out of this car, Raber," she said, before immediately stumbling out. She rounded the car and instead of going through the field to get to the tree, she went to the middle of the intersection. She closed her eyes, suddenly completely uninterested in Raber and felt the power of the crossroads going in and through her.

"I could make flowers right now," she said to nobody. "They would be yellow and white. I would do it because the Goddess is here in this place and she'll favor my flowers."

Raber was beside her, smiling at her. She stepped away from him. He stepped closer. She bent to pick up dust from the road and threw it in his face. Surprised, he spat and coughed and wiped at his face maniacally.

"Keep your distance," she said fiercely.

Raber put his hands up in surrender and stayed back. Ioni relaxed. As she stood looking at his dirt-streaked face, she started hearing something.

"Are there wild dogs out this way?" she asked.

"Probably," he answered. "But I think we'll be okay. The car lights are on. They'll avoid us."

"I hear them barking," Ioni said. "A lot of them. All barking. It's really loud. Don't you hear it?"

"Come with me to the tree," Raber said. "Here, take my hand and I'll lead you. The ground is bumpy. I won't touch anything but your hand, okay?"

Ioni looked down on the ground as she let Raber lead her. It *was* bumpy ground, but it was also moving. It was a tectonic shift of dry, dusty earth, a dizzying wave of dandelions and overgrown weeds, lapping at the edges of dirt spots like an ocean. She was amazed how her steps were so steady on the moving earth.

"You're keeping me steady," she said. "The ground would slide me over, but you're keeping me steady."

Raber didn't say anything. He just kept gently leading her toward the tree. When they were close enough, Ioni gasped. The tree was bending to the left and groaning. It was a deep and echoing groan that sounded all around her. She thought she could see a mouth on the trunk, looking as if it were in pain.

"It hurts," Ioni said. "Something's wrong with it. In this powerful place, where the Goddess lives, this beautiful tree is in pain. How can I help it?"

"I know it's in pain. I've known about this tree's pain for a long time," Raber said. "I set up this ladder so that you can climb up to that really thick branch up there. It needs the touch of someone more pure than me. I can't do anything about it because I lost my way. But you're still pure. The Goddess favors you."

"I don't know what to do." Ioni said to him.

"Maybe you will when you get up there," he said, leading her to the ladder.

She was usually afraid of heights, but she climbed the ladder and balanced herself on the very top.

"Get away from the ladder," she called down to Raber. "I don't want you kicking it out from under me."

He did as she requested, taking two large steps away. She focused her eyes on the large trunk and saw the yellow snake. She screamed and nearly lost her balance. She could hear Raber screaming at her down below, but she was trying to get down the ladder, away from the snake.

"IONI!" She finally heard Raber. "What's the matter? STOP CLIMBING DOWN GODDAMN IT!"

Ioni stopped and looked down at him. She looked back up, but realized that it wasn't a yellow snake at all. She could have sworn she saw it uncurling to come at her, but she must have been wrong.

"What is it?" she asked Raber. "I thought it was a snake."

"That's part of the tree! It's a piece of itself that it brought out so that it can make contact with us."

Ioni looked at him a moment and then back up at the yellow cord.

"What the hell are you talking about?" she asked.

"Ioni, this tree is dying! You have to get back up there and try to help it!" he screamed.

She balanced herself again and climbed. This time, she reached out and grabbed the yellow cord and noticed it had a loop at the end. For the briefest of moments, she was certain that it was a yellow vinyl rope fashioned into a noose, but then that wasn't what it was at all. Suddenly she was holding a veiny, pulsating umbilical cord in her hand.

"It's lost its baby!" she called down to Raber. "I think it's sad! Its baby is gone!"

"Take the place of it, then!" he screamed up at her.

"I'm not a tree!" she screamed back. But suddenly, she heard the tree. It was talking to her and she couldn't help but laugh, thinking that it was a slow talker, like an old man.

When it was done talking, she looked down at the umbilical cord and slipped it over her head.

"Are you comforting her?" she screamed down.

"Come back down to me! Now!" Raber screamed.

"I've got to stay with the tree! It wants me!"

"Don't detach from it! Just jump! The tree will protect you!"

"Jump? No, come get me! I'm scared!" she said.

"Ioni," he screamed again, angry. "You have to do this. It has to be done by *you*, do you understand me? It's a leap of faith."

"Will it help the tree?" she asked. "To have faith that it will protect me?"

"I think that's exactly what it needs!" Raber shouted. "Now jump! Come to me!"

"I trust you, tree. I trust you because I trust the Goddess. I hope this helps."

And she jumped.

PART TWO

CHAPTER TWENTY-TWO

Raber stood beneath the branches of the tree, panting. *She did it.* He tried to catch his breath as he watched her swing lifelessly, her eyes bulging and her broken neck making her head sit at an unnatural angle.

He had very little time and had to work quickly. First, he had to make sure that she was truly dead. He climbed halfway up the ladder, reached out for the yellow vinyl rope and pulled her to him. He put his fingers to her lips, feeling for breath. When he discovered all was still, he felt her throat for a pulse. She was definitely dead.

"How lucky for us, baby, that it happened fast," he said, releasing her body and trying not to watch it swing. The rope made a groan as it twisted and pulled.

He ran to his car, popped the trunk and pulled out his flashlight as well as a pair of lopping shears that he had taken from his parents' gardening shed. He ran back across the field and climbed the ladder again, using the lopping shears to cut the rope near the top. She fell and hit the ground in a dull thud that made him wince. He avoided looking down as he retrieved the last piece of rope from the tree, a consideration for if things went wrong. He climbed down the ladder, folded it up, ran it back to his car, and piled everything into his trunk, trying to be fast and thorough. When he made it back to her crumpled form lying on the ground, he was out of breath and sweating profusely.

He knelt down next to her, rolled her onto her back, and removed the noose from around her neck, marveling at how her head moved fluidly in all directions thanks to the broken neck. Gently, he picked her up and carried her back to the road. Stopping to listen and look for lights, he crossed the road when he was satisfied he was alone.

He was thankful that he'd dug the hole earlier. It takes a long time to dig even a shallow grave for a full-grown adult, and doing so in a rush and under duress didn't suit his plans. He removed the tarp that he had thrown over the hole and placed her inside, curling her up. Brushing the small baby hairs hair off her face, he resisted the urge to kiss her cheek.

"It's a good thing you didn't see this hole," he said to her as if she could hear him. "A million small things could have gone wrong, but you made it all so easy."

He ran back to the tree and retrieved the rest of his things, including the rope. When he returned he knelt down by the hole, opened the backpack, and removed a double-edged blade.

"Powers of the crossroads, I call on you to grant me the power to do my work tonight," he said, holding the blade above him.

"Rebirth cannot happen without death. Ioni, your curse for taking your own life is your loss of free will. I, Raber, grant you rebirth with the power of the crossroads and it is I who shall be your ruling will. You will stay with me and serve me. You will not abandon me and you will require only my company. Tonight you sleep in the cool earth, severing yourself from the life you had. When you wake, you will be mine and mine only."

He sliced the pad of his left thumb with the blade and watched the blood start to ooze from the gash.

"An offering of blood ties you to me. I am in you, as I always said."

He parted her lips and opened her jaw. He put his thumb in her mouth and smeared the blood on her tongue, making sure to coat it. He slammed his blade into the earth just outside of the hole, covering the blade in dirt, and then removed it and wiped the dirt on his sliced thumb. He replaced the blade in the bag, brought out a small bundle, and placed it in her right hand. It was one of his shirts wrapped around a series of roots and leaves as well as an egg and a dead chickadee, all things meant to facilitate her rebirth.

"I'll be here when you wake up, my Ioni," he said quietly.

He packed up all of his belongings and filled the hole with dirt, thankful that it had been dry enough lately that the ground was patchy, not lush and grassy. The hole wouldn't look suspicious to the few people who traveled that road.

He got into his car and drove to Tristan's house, using the key he found in Ioni's small purse to open the door. The smell of Ioni filled the place even though he wrinkled his nose at the loud colors and cheap furniture. He felt that because she was comfortable there, he could be, too.

He made himself comfortable in the bedroom and called Andrew who answered after two rings, sounding hoarse and hyper.

"Hey," Andrew said, knowing it was him. "Well?"

"I did it," Raber said calmly.

"Are you fucking jerking me right now? Because I don't think I can handle that, man." Andrew said.

"I'm serious," Raber answered. "The lemonade worked great and she was actually really easy to manipulate."

"Did you do the ritual like I told you? I mean, you memorized it, right? You can be a dense motherfucker sometimes."

"I did it," Raber answered, distracted by looking through Ioni's phone to see who she contacted as her safeguard against being alone with him that night.

"You cut on your left thumb and put the bundle in her right hand? Damn it, if you messed up even something small like that, you're going to have your dumpy ass in prison serving blowjobs to the wife beaters," Andrew said. "She'll stay dead and then your ass is grass, my friend."

Raber laughed out loud and threw her phone onto the bedside table, feeling relaxed and smug.

"What?" Andrew squealed. He sounded like he was tweaking. Raber wondered with longing what he was on.

"I was just making sure that she didn't tell anybody that she was with me. She said she would, but I guess she forgot. She's always been really forgetful and flakey," he said.

"I just don't get it, man," Andrew said. "There are a million dumb bitches in the world. Some of them are pretty nice looking and aren't all high opinionated of themselves like her."

"Yes, well, she's my bitch and I never consented to a breakup," Raber said.

"Whatever, man." Andrew said. "Tomorrow at sunset you be there to meet her and then fucking call me so I don't have a goddamned coronary from worrying."

"Yeah, okay," Raber said and ended the call.

He took off all his clothes and pulled an old amber colored prescription bottle out of his pants pocket. He dumped the contents onto the bed and sorted through the pills looking for the downers. He popped two into his mouth and tried to swish enough saliva to swallow. When they were on their way down his throat, he put the rest of his stash back in the bottle and got under the covers. The pillow smelled of her and he breathed deeply, waiting for the pills to take him to darkness.

He slept until about two in the afternoon the next day. The muscles in his arms, shoulders, and back ached deeply from the digging and excitement from the day before. He groaned and found his way to the bathroom, thankful that the house was small. He showered and rummaged in the closet for a clean shirt to wear. Among Ioni's colorful clothes, he found a large man's button-down shirt.

"Fuck you, imposter. I'm taking your shirt," he muttered.

He gathered up his own dirty clothes and went in search of the laundry machines, hoping that the house had some. When he went to the basement, he was happy to find what he was looking for. After putting his clothes in the wash, he poked around the area before losing interest and going back upstairs.

He had no interest in food and opted instead for his amber bottle of what Andrew called "candy". Raber chose a Codeine tablet and found a large bottle of Mountain Dew in the refrigerator. He settled onto the couch with his cool beverage and the heat of the Codeine beginning to spread across his face. There was a full menu of cable channels at his disposal, but seeing that there were no movies of interest on the movie channels, he decided to watch a show about UFO hunters.

When the Codeine started to wear off and his clothes were clean and dry, he drove to his parents' house and packed a bag, telling his mother that he was going to be staying with a friend for a few weeks. His mother asked simply that he stay in touch and bid him farewell.

He was at the crossroads before sunset. The day was hot and humid. Even though the sun was low in the sky he was still sweating profusely, standing by the road. An old rusted pickup truck approached and the old man behind the wheel asked if Raber needed help.

"Oh, no thank you," Raber said, smiling. "I called AAA and they're on their way. The damned thing needs a new fuel pump, I think."

The man nodded and drove off. Raber sighed heavily.

Finally, the sun dipped below the horizon and the sky started slowly to turn ever darkening shades of purple. Crickets started chirping and Raber could just make out the silhouettes of bats flying overhead. Anxious, he kept his attention focused on the small mound of dirt by the heart of the crossroads.

He had just grabbed the small yellow flashlight from his car when he noticed that the crickets had stopped. Being in the country, surrounded by woods and knee-high grass, their sound had been pervasive only moments before. Now, the ubiquitous silence unnerved Raber as he turned on the light and walked back to the mound.

She was already halfway out of the hole when he saw her. The only noise was the sound of the dirt moving around as she emerged from the ground. His heart caught in his throat and he felt faint.

"Holy fucking shit, it worked," he whispered.

Hearing him, she whipped her head in his direction. She pulled herself totally from the hole, never taking her eyes off of him. Her hair was matted and filled with dirt, her clothes were dirty and wrinkled, and her head was hanging at the side, rocking as she moved.

She walked to him stiffly and stopped about a foot away from him. He shined the light on her and looked at her face. Her eyes were red. It wasn't a supernatural glowing red, but it was the most severe case of irritated eyes he had ever seen. She was dirty, but she was there.

"Baby," he said, holding a hand out to her. She looked down at his hand and then back into his face. She was showing no emotion, something that was very unlike his Ioni. Raber assumed that she hadn't yet fully recovered and might need more time.

"Come on baby, let's go get you cleaned up and then I'll take you to dinner."

"Eat," she said, her voice high and desperate-sounding.

"Oh baby," he said, reaching out and grabbing her arm gently above the elbow. "I'm sure you're very hungry. Don't worry, I'll take care of you."

"Hungry," she said.

"Come on, sweetie," he said, leading her to his car.

He helped her into her seat and buckled her seatbelt. As he drove through the dark, seeing her unmoving form sitting next to him, he smiled to himself, proud of his accomplishment. He had her now, and nothing was going to keep him from her.

When they got back to Tristan's house, he undressed her right in the living room, and led her to the bathroom. He took his clothes off, too, and got into the shower with her so that he could more easily wash her. Very gently, he cleaned her body and washed her hair. When she was free of mud, he wrapped her in a fluffy yellow towel and led her to the bedroom. He dried her thoroughly and dressed her. She placidly accepted his succor.

He combed her lustrous hair and let it fall loose over her shoulders, just as he liked it. He stroked it, smiling

"Even after all these months apart," he murmured, "this is still so familiar, so comfortable."

She said nothing. She wasn't even looking at him. Her head was sitting normally now. Her eyes were fixed on a point right ahead of her. He touched her face. Her red eyes moved and focused on him.

"Hungry," she said in her weak voice.

"Of course," he said, getting to his feet and taking her by the hand and leading her back out to his car.

He chose the drive-thru of a fast food restaurant that he knew she liked and ordered enough food for the both of them to completely stuff themselves. He parked behind the restaurant, near the dumpsters.

"I forgot to eat today," he said, digging through the bags and stuffing french fries into his mouth. He handed her a vanilla milkshake, knowing that it was one of her favorite treats.

She took the paper cup and slowly, clumsily put the straw to her lips and sucked lightly. She then opened the passenger side door and dropped the cup nonchalantly onto the ground and turned back to Raber.

"Hungry," she said.

"Here," he said, frowning and handing her a burger wrapped in wax paper. "You love these."

She unwrapped the burger and inspected it with indifference before giving it the same treatment as the milkshake.

"What are you doing?" he asked, confused.

"Hungry," she said.

"So, eat!" He said, a knot of apprehension beginning to build in his gut.

Her attention was caught by one of the teenaged employees, a scrawny boy, bringing enormous bags of garbage out to the dumpsters.

"Eat," she whispered.

And then she was on him. The passenger door was still open from where she was discarding her unwanted food, so there was no noise as she sprinted from the car to the kid. Raber sat glued in his seat, both fascinated and horrified by what he saw. In a series of very fast moves she descended on the kid and hit him in the head quietly. She then caught him in her arms and lowered herself and the boy to the ground. Raber sat up so that he could better see as she used her teeth to rip the skin from the boy's throat. As the blood spurted and poured from the wound, Ioni licked it up, and then covered the wound with her mouth and drank.

"Oh shit," Raber gasped, panicked. "What the fuck is she doing?"

He opened his door and slowly approached Ioni and the boy. The sounds of her sucking and grunting were disgusting, but she was oblivious to his presence.

"You need to stop," Raber said in a hissing whisper. "Why are you doing this?"

She lifted her head to look at him. Blood smeared all around her mouth, looking a bit like dark clown makeup. There was no more blood pumping from the raw wound at the kid's throat. His face was pure white and Raber knew that he was dead.

"What the fuck?" He whisper-screamed at her.

She stood and quietly walked back to the car. She got into the passenger seat and closed her door.

Panicked, Raber looked all around to make sure nobody else was around and then looked for security cameras.

214

"For once I'm thankful to live in this shitty backwards town," he said, getting back into his car when he saw none.

He sped out of the parking lot and drove back to Tristan's house. He led Ioni into the house, situated her on the sofa, and frantically called Andrew.

"Well?" Andrew said by way of greeting.

"I need you to get here, like right fucking now," Raber said.

"Fuck!" Andrew screamed. "It didn't work?"

"No, it worked, but something's wrong!" Raber said.

"Man, if she's walking and talking and is allowing you to boss her around, that's a fucking success," Andrew said. "Is she doing those things?"

"Well, yes," Raber said. "But there's more."

"She gave you the best blowjob of your life? She's suddenly a fan of anal?"

"She fucking killed somebody and drank their blood, Andrew!" Raber said through gritted teeth.

"I'm leaving right now, I'll be there in a half hour."

Raber hung up. He didn't need to give Andrew directions. Andrew had been with him as he followed Ioni around after learning of her affair with Tristan. They had driven past Tristan's house dozens of times and even sat in the street and watched the lights go on and off in different rooms of the house as Ioni moved about in the night.

He went to the bathroom and wet a washcloth. He turned on the television and knelt before her, wiping the blood from her face, neck, and hands.

"Do you want to try to eat one of those burgers?" he asked her.

"I ate," she said simply.

He stared up into her face from his crouching position when a funny idea struck him. He reached up and angled her face so that he could see her eyes better. Still red. The edges of the upper and lower eyelids were extremely red and now that he was really looking in a better light, the whites of her eyes looked more than just irritated. There was something unsettling about them, something that would warrant a double take from people, and he felt his stomach cramp in anxiety. Maybe he could play it off by saying she was a big pothead.

Still gnawing on the worry that she wouldn't pass as normal, he parted her lips with his finger and looked at her teeth. They looked as they always had. Straight, perfect and white. Nothing out of the ordinary. Giving up, he sat next to her on the sofa and watched television until the loud, rapid knocking on the door signaled Andrew's arrival.

"I've got to see this," Andrew said, pushing past Raber and standing before the still seated figure on the couch.

"She looks okay," he said, looking at Raber. "I can't fucking believe you did it. I really can't fucking believe this. Hey, you want some heroin? I've got some heroin. You've got a kitchen, we can cook up and shoot up."

"I need you to tell me why she killed a kid and drank his blood," Raber said calmly.

Andrew smiled.

"I told you. It was in the book. THE book," he said, still smiling. Did I ever tell you that my uncle could read it, too? He made the sacrifice and had the mark and he warned me against using that spell. Said that it had a warning or something prefacing it. I don't know, but I do know that this spell in particular hasn't been carried out in this country in more than a hundred years."

"This is a spell to get control over another person's will," Raber said slowly. "I watched her kill herself so that I could have her back."

"Yeah, and you got her." Andrew said, reaching down and touching her hair. Raber looked at the strange brand on the back of Andrew's hand and fought the urge to slap it away from Ioni.

"What aren't you telling me?" Raber asked, his anxiety giving way to anger.

"Look, you know as much as I know. I have a suspicion about what happened, but I told you all I know." Andrew said, sitting down beside her heavily.

"No," Raber said. "I'm not gonna buy that." He knew Andrew's suspicions were the same as his own, but his sanity and his slipping grip on reality wouldn't let him accept them without a fight.

"You already do in some way," Andrew said, tossing a pill into his mouth. "Do you need me to say it out loud for you so that your brain can have a meltdown or are you going to chill the motherfuck out and shoot some sweet, sweet smack with me?"

"Stay on fucking track, damn it! I'm in serious trouble if she has to keep killing people. I mean, fuck, the only words she's said to me are 'eat' and 'hungry'!"

Andrew laughed maniacally, curling up into a ball and holding his concave stomach.

"Is it really that stereotypical?" he asked, finally.

"Yes. She doesn't talk, she doesn't look at me, she just sits there, all quiet. And look at her fucking eyes. We can't pretend to be normal with those things!" He was near hysterics.

Andrew leaned over her and looked into her eyes. He plopped back into his original spot and started rolling a joint.

"You ever read Dracula?" Andrew asked.

"Wha? Yes..." Raber answered.

"That guy had red eyes too." Andrew said.

"Oh fuck, what am I going to fucking do?" Raber asked, close to tears.

"Calm the hell down and puff this baby," Andrew handed Raber the joint. "This will take a little bit of creativity, but ultimately you still got what you wanted. It's just going to be trickier to feed her, that's all."

Raber pulled heavily on the joint and inhaled the hot, acrid smoke. When he puffed it out, he felt a calm settling in. He sat down on one of the distasteful plastic chairs and looked at her.

"I've got her. She's with me. She won't leave me to fuck some other guy. I guess that works in my favor," he said.

"'Atta boy," Andrew said, smiling. "It's all about perspective. And you know what? I'm of the opinion that you're actually a fucking hero here. I mean, really. You wanted something and you went for it. You love this girl so you drug this overly sweetened lemonade with a shit ton of acid and give it to her and then trick her tripped out brain into committing suicide so that you can lay some chaos on her to control her. I mean, that's a level of dedication that has to be admired, my friend."

Raber took another long drag off of the joint and handed it to Andrew. Andrew waved it away and instead produced a syringe and a small bag of heroin.

"Aside from that sort of fucked up-ness, you are the first person in a century or more to use witchcraft to make an honest-to-fucking-god vampire. Kudos to you." Andrew said, saluting Raber with the syringe.

CHAPTER TWENTY-THREE

They stayed up all that night doing drugs and talking about Ioni. At one point in the early morning hours, Ioni pinned Andrew to the floor and started digging at his throat with her short fingernails. Raber ordered her to stop and she calmly resumed her quiet, unmoving position on the sofa.

"I forgot about that part," Andrew said, sitting up and rubbing the raw spot on his neck.

"What part?" Raber asked, shaken.

"You're safe from her," Andrew answered. "You made her. But I'm not safe, not yet. Did you keep the hanging rope, like I told you to?"

"Yeah," Raber answered.

"Go get it," Andrew ordered, resuming his seat next to Ioni, keeping a wary eye on her.

Raber ran out to his car and pulled the rope pieces from the trunk, doing as he was told, without hesitation.

"Good, now cut off a piece for me. About five inches." Andrew commanded when Raber returned.

Raber eyeballed the five inches and handed the cut piece of bright yellow rope to Andrew. Andrew wrapped it around his wrist and tied it with his free hand and teeth. He then thrust the rope into Ioni's face. She flinched away from it, whimpering.

"You see this, bitch? Yeah, that means you don't get to fucking eat me." Andrew said.

Raber stepped in and cradled her face in his hands, shushing her whimpering, tending to the immediate need of her crying and not really seeing the problem that was his companion. Andrew watched with a blank face.

"Have you thought about where she'll sleep?" Andrew asked.

"Well I can't put her in a bed, now can I?" Raber said. "Do I need to protect her from the sun?"

"I have no idea, man," Andrew answered. "I think for now, playing it safe is the best idea. We can test lore on her later. Is there a dark place where she can be during the day? And what about her job? Or her friends and family? Have you thought that shit out yet?"

"I didn't really plan for that. I wanted to make sure this worked. But I've got her cell phone, I can hold a lot of them off through text messages for now. Obviously, she's going to need to quit her job. I'll come up with something more permanent later." Raber answered, stroking Ioni's hair.

"As for where she'll sleep, this place has a packed dirt basement with no windows. I think that'll work great."

"Great. I'll sleep on the couch and we'll talk this out tomorrow while Princess Bloodsucker slumbers her sleep of the undead," Andrew said before bursting into frantic laughter.

When dawn was near, Raber led Ioni down the narrow stairs into the basement and showed her the dirt-floor part of the basement. He had his arms full of blankets and a fluffy pillow. He laid them out on the floor, trying to make it as comfortable as he could. Ioni watched him, disinterested. When he was done, she walked past her "bed" and instead curled up in a corner. Raber, in his drug-fueled mania, noticed with horror that she curled up in exactly the same position that he had placed her in her shallow grave the night before.

"Will you be okay down here?" he asked her. She made no reply, she just stayed curled up, her eyes closed.

"Well that's fucking creepy," Andrew said from behind him.

They slept until early afternoon, Raber in Tristan's bed and Andrew on the couch. When Raber woke up, he shuffled into the living room and saw that Andrew was gone. A glance out of the front window showed that his car was also gone. Shrugging, Raber went to the bathroom and showered. When he came out, he grabbed a Mountain Dew to wash down his Codeine tablet.

When Andrew returned, his arms were loaded down with bags from Walmart.

"Hey, honey, I'm home and I've been to the market!" he declared brightly.

Andrew had been busy as Raber slept. As he plopped his bags down in the kitchen, Raber searched through them. Inside he found a large plastic cross, a crucifix complete with crucified man, a produce bag full of fresh garlic, a hand mirror, a steak, and some actual groceries. Raber looked at the smiling Andrew and opened his hands in a questioning gesture.

"We have to find out what's what, Frankenstein." Andrew answered simply. "And this place didn't have any good food, so, you know, you're welcome."

Raber looked down again at the bags and smiled.

"Most of these can wait until she's awake, but there's one that we need to try while the sun is still up," Andrew said seriously.

They went to the basement, flipping on only the light in the front. Raber could see that the blankets sat empty on the floor, untouched from the night before. He had to walk into the back to see the curled-up figure, unmoving, on the floor. He reached down and felt her cold skin.

"This is a corpse," he said to himself.

"We have to move her into some sun. Here, I'll go open the basement door and let some sunlight in, then we'll carry her over so that only a little bit touches her. If that's a truth, hopefully she won't get totally destroyed."

Raber nodded and Andrew sprinted up the stairs, propped the door open, then came back down to help Raber lift her. They dropped her in shock.

"She's stiff!" Andrew exclaimed more in disgust than surprise.

"Rigor mortis in a vampire?" Raber asked.

"Here let's keep going. I'm freaking out down here, man," Andrew said, lifting her again.

She was easy to move with her stiff, curled-up position. It wasn't unlike lugging a piece of furniture across the room. They carried her to the foot of the narrow basement steps where a golden ray of sunshine spilled down. They stopped just short and turned her body so that only a small piece of her exposed foot would come into direct contact with the sun.

"Hold your breath and cross your fingers," Andrew said as he started inching her closer to the ray.

Nothing happened. Andrew scooted more of her into the light. Still nothing. Andrew stood up straight and looked down, frowning. He turned her so that her face was bathed in the warm light. Still nothing.

"I guess we can put that one to bed," Raber said.

They put her back into her corner, perhaps to preserve her own comfort when she woke or perhaps they were acting on instinct, hiding the dead body from sight. They sat in Tristan's house for the rest of the day, eating, smoking pot, and popping various pills.

With Andrew's help, Raber sent a text message to Ioni's sisters and her father, letting them know she was fine but very busy. He decided to let other people initiate texts before answering so it wouldn't look forced or suspicious.

A text from Tristan came just as the sun was setting.

"Hello, beautiful. I've been thinking about you and I just wanted to let you know that I can't wait to get back and make love to you. You'll have to take a vacation from work because I intend to have you for a week straight." The message read.

222

Raber read the message, fury heating his ears and face.

"LOL" was the reply he sent.

"Fucking ape," he muttered through clenched teeth, and turned the phone off.

He stashed the phone in the kitchen and started walking through the small house, turning on lights. Just as he made his way back to the living room, he heard the basement door creak open. He looked at Andrew, who had been sitting on the couch playing on his phone and saw that he was at attention, looking toward the hallway. A moment later, Ioni walked into the room and stood before them.

"Hungry," she whined.

"Get the steak," Andrew said, throwing his phone onto the coffee table.

"You know that a steak s-t-e-a-k and a stake s-t-a-k-e are different things, right?" Raber asked.

"Yes, I fucking know," Andrew said angrily. "Go and get it. You'll see what I wanna try."

Raber obediently retrieved the steak in its styrofoam tray. He handed it to Andrew, who used his index finger to poke a hole into the plastic wrap. He tipped the tray up and red liquid dripped into the palm of his hand. He held his hand out to Ioni, the liquid pooled in the center.

"Will you eat this?" he asked her.

Ioni walked to him and got onto her knees before him. She licked the liquid from his hand and smacked her lips loudly.

"Thin," she whined. "Watery."

Andrew looked down at his hand thoughtfully.

"Yeah, it's not really blood, just sort of a meat juice. What about the raw meat? Will you eat that?" He tore the plastic wrap off of the steak and held it out. Ioni nibbled it and licked it, but ultimately sat back on her haunches and shook her head.

"Not right," she said simply.

"But is animal as good as human?" Andrew asked her.

Ioni looked thoughtful for a moment, and Raber, who was watching all of this, thought that it was the first time that she showed any sort of intelligence or personality since her rebirth.

"Maybe," she said at last.

Andrew smiled and put a hand on her cheek in an affectionate way that made Raber sick to his stomach.

"Good girl," Andrew said to her before standing and heading for the door.

"I'll be back in about an hour with something for her to eat. Just keep her here and don't try anything else on her yet. I want her at full strength in case we do hurt her."

After he was gone, Raber sat in front of the still kneeling Ioni and took her face into his hands.

"Why will you talk to him and not me?" he asked her.

She looked straight ahead in indifference.

"Come on, let's get you showered and fresh," Raber said after a moment. He took her hand and led her to the bathroom. As before, he took her clothes off and stripped himself. With his anxiety levels considerably lower, he took more pleasure in the act of showering with a naked woman. He lingered in the washing of certain parts of her cool body and by the time he turned off the water, his excitement was painful. He took Ioni by the hand and led her to the bedroom. He pushed her back on the bed, got on top of her, and started kissing her neck. When he tried to kiss her mouth, she didn't return his kisses, she just looked straight ahead.

"I want you to kiss me back," he said to her.

Without a moment's hesitation, she started returning his kisses in a cold and uninterested way. His excitement overruled his discomfort and he tried to push himself into her only to find a lack of lubrication. Frustrated, he spit into his hand and spread his saliva onto her. He pushed hard into her and began moving back and forth.

Something was wrong. There was something wrong with how she felt aside from the coolness of her body temperature.

There was a lack of elasticity to her insides that made being inside of her almost disgusting. When she was awake, she could pass as a living, breathing woman. When she was asleep, she was a corpse. In this intimate moment with her, her eyes looking off to the side indifferently, she *felt* like a corpse.

Raber squeezed his eyes shut tightly and quickly finished his endeavor.

He cleaned her up and dressed her. He brushed her hair and then opened her small, zippered bag of cosmetics.

"Do you remember how to do this?" he asked her. She looked down at the bag and pulled out a tube of mascara. She turned it in her pale hand before dropping it back in the bag.

"No," she said without inflection.

"I'm going to show you, but I expect you to be able to do this stuff on your own from now on. Showering, dressing, primping, this should all be done as soon as you wake up." Raber said tersely.

When she was made up like the girl he had once loved, he led her into the living room and instructed her to sit on the couch. He sat on a chair and turned on the television. They sat in silence, she, indifferently staring at the floor, while Raber stewed. He started suddenly and remembered something that he wanted her to do. He walked to the kitchen and retrieved her cell phone, placing it before her.

"You need to call your place of work and quit your job," he said to her. "Do you know how to do that?"

She stared at the phone and then slowly lifted her eyes to his face.

"Hungry," she whined.

"We will get to that, for fuck's sake!" he screamed at her. She didn't flinch, just stared into his face coolly.

"I want you to call this number and tell the person who answers who you are and ask to speak to the manager," he said, finding the number in her directory.

"Who I am," she said quietly.

Raber's eyes shot to her face and he looked at her closely.

"Do you know who you are?" he asked her. She didn't react.

"Do you know who I am?" he asked. She looked at his face.

"Master," she said.

Raber started sweating and his stomach cramped. She didn't remember. All of the memories they had together were lost to her. His significance to her was deteriorated to one of a caretaker. To her, he was a pet owner, and she his naughty cat. He reached up and stroked her thankfully still silken hair.

"Your name is Ioni Davis. I love you and you love me. My name is Raber Belliveau. We are in love, and you will never leave me. I'm the only person you need, okay?"

"Okay," she said.

"Now call this number and do what I told you to do," he said, handing her the phone after pushing 'send'.

He watched her as she mechanically followed his command. When it was over, she handed the phone back to Raber without ending the call, obviously not knowing how to do it. Trying to be patient, he showed her the 'end' button.

Not much later, Andrew came bounding happily through the door, an old cardboard box tucked under one arm.

"I come delivering dinner, sweetheart!" he said, placing the box on the floor before her.

He opened the box and two small kittens popped their round heads out. Andrew gently picked one up and handed it to Ioni. Raber flinched when she twisted the kitten's head off and gulped greedily at the bright blood that shot from the neck. When the tiny body was drained, she handed it back to Andrew. He dropped the dead kitten back into the box and handed her the other, who got the same treatment. As she slurped, Raber noticed that Andrew was playing with one of the severed heads, poking and pushing the small fuzzy thing around.

"Christ," Raber muttered when the other body was dropped into the box. Ioni licked her lips lustily.

"I guess those serve as a good meal?" Andrew asked.

"Okay," Ioni said.

"Where the fuck did you get kittens?" Raber asked.

"Craigslist is a great thing," Andrew said, kicking the box away from him. "I bought them from a fat housewife for $10. She was afraid that I was going to use them to feed a pet snake. Stupid bitch," he finished, laughing.

"Surely you can't keep buying kittens like that," Raber said. "I mean, word might get around."

"Although I highly doubt that, I did have another plan. What if we got a few rats from some big chain pet store or something? Rats reproduce like fucking mad and we could have enough after a while to at least keep her satiated enough to not eat teenagers in parking lots. If she gets really hungry, I'll get her a nice puppy, won't I, bright angel?"

"Did you just quote fucking Shakespeare at her?" Raber asked, unable to mask his annoyance.

Andrew glared at him for a moment before reaching out and stroking her cheek again. Raber started thinking that Andrew was getting entirely too familiar with Ioni and he didn't like it.

"Never was there a tale of more woe than this of Ioni, and Raber Belliveau." Andrew said seriously. "This little girl is amazing and I think that you should recognize how I've gone out of my way to not only help her, but I've helped you a whole fucking lot. If I choose to quote Shakespeare or Marilyn Chambers at her, you maybe need to get off your high horse and fucking be okay with it." Andrew said.

Raber tried to mask his anger, but he knew that his ears were red. He chose to change the subject.

"Well, now that she's been fed, maybe we should start some of the other tests."

"Oh, yeah, okay. Let's see what works and what doesn't," Andrew said.

"Now, Ioni," Andrew began, "We're going to perform a few tests on you. Some of these may hurt you, but I need you to remember that these tests are for educational purposes. If it hurts, tell us and we'll stop. Okay?"

"Okay," Ioni answered.

"Let's start with the ones that we're pretty sure aren't going to work," Andrew said. "Let's try the cross and crucifix."

Raber handed the crucifix to Andrew while he held up the cheap plastic cross. They looked at each other and mouthed a 1-2-3 before pushing their objects into the skin of their vampire. When she didn't react, they tried putting their objects in front of her face. Still nothing.

"I knew it," Andrew said, stuffing his crucifix into the kitten box.

"Well, yeah," Raber said. "What if someone is Jewish or Muslim? Why would a cross or crucifix be a universal vampire deterrent when Christianity isn't the only game in town? That one was easy. What now?"

"Let's try the mirror,' Andrew said.

"She passes in front of a mirror before she showers and sits in front of one when I brush her hair and put her makeup on. She definitely has a reflection," Raber answered.

"Has she actually looked at her reflection before, though?" Andrew asked.

"I taught her how to apply makeup today, but I can't answer that with any real certainty," Raber answered.

"Okey dokey, let's give it a try," Andrew said.

Raber passed the hand mirror to Andrew, who held the reflective surface in Ioni's face.

"Look at yourself," Andrew commanded her.

Raber watched as Ioni's eyes moved down and focused on her reflection. She blinked and looked at Andrew.

"Yeah, nothing to be scared of there, huh?" Andrew said, smiling.

"Andrew," Raber began. He was getting tired of Andrew flirting with her.

"Get the garlic," Andrew said.

Raber brought out an unmolested bulb of garlic and held it under Ioni's nose. Her little nose crinkled slightly and he felt his heart jump.

"Did you see that?" Raber asked Andrew.

"Crack it open and get a single clove out," Andrew said excitedly.

Raber did as he was bid and when he had a naked clove of garlic, he held it up to Ioni's face. She shrank back from the small piece and whimpered.

"That's interesting, but it makes sense too," Andrew said.

"Why's that?"

"You should have done a little bit of studying with that idiot Ioni used as her mentor," Andrew said. "You might have learned a thing or two. Garlic has cleansing properties, both spiritual and physical. This girl here is a cursed being. She's filthy in a metaphysical sense."

Raber frowned and shoved the clove of garlic into a grocery bag, away from Ioni.

"Walmart didn't have any silver, but I know you keep that ring you gave her. Let's see if she can wear it," Andrew said.

"Silver? Oh yeah, okay," Raber said, removing the chain from around his neck and dropping the ring into his open palm.

Raber gently lifted Ioni's left hand and slid the ring onto her finger. To his horror, smoke rose from her skin and she shrieked in pain. He quickly removed the ring and held it away from her, cooing and comforting her.

"Silver has cleansing properties too," Andrew said, petting Ioni.

"That was a violent reaction," Raber said, putting his hand to his chest in a feeble attempt to calm his racing heart.

"Now we know," Andrew shrugged. "I guess she won't be wearing your special ring anymore, but that's okay. She's more faithful than any mortal woman would ever be. Right now, let's take this little girl out on the town and show her off."

"No," Raber said. "I don't want to risk anything by taking her out."

"You seem to think that I was asking for your permission," Andrew said. "I wasn't. I'm telling you that I'm taking her out. If you'd like to come, that's cool. If not, I'll have her home by three."

"She's mine," Raber said, angry now. "She called me 'Master' earlier. She'll do what I tell her to do, not you. Now step the fuck down, Andrew."

Andrew walked up close to Raber. Since he was the shorter of the pair, his face was level with Raber's clavicle. It somehow didn't diminish his ability to intimidate the taller man, especially considering some of the things that he had seen Andrew do in the year that they'd known each other. For the most part, Raber knew to stay on Andrew's good side, but when it came to their current power struggle over Ioni, Raber felt that he needed to stand strong and not back down.

Still, Andrew had proven to have no qualms about going that extra step in order to show his dominance in the past. Raber had to calculate his moves in order to get his way.

"I don't want us fighting over her, man," Raber said, looking down. "You really helped me with this and I still need you and your help, but I'm really paranoid about her going cannibal on someone else."

Andrew looked up into Raber's complacent face for a moment before backing away and resuming his seat next to the vampire.

"Yeah, I wasn't there when she killed that kid. I get how that would freak you out," Andrew said. "But you can't keep her prisoner all the time. Really, you should have a bit of fun with her. I mean, *FUCK*, you've got a fucking vampire here now! Let's go see if she seduces people in order to try to eat them! Let's see if she knows how to dance! Let's see if she can scare the shit out of those goth club kids!"

Raber, seeing that he wasn't going to win, conceded.

"You want to go to Black Veil?" he asked Andrew.

Black Veil was a rave club in Morgantown that catered to goths and people who gravitated toward a more romantic ideal to life and fashion. Raber had been there several times. It was a place to get a hit of ecstasy and go home, sweaty and exhausted, with a random girl. Andrew went with Raber once or twice and ended up serving as a businessman shilling pills, buds, and powders to the club kids. To his knowledge, Raber had never known Andrew to hook up with anybody, male or female.

"It's as good a place as any, Lenny," Andrew said, laughing.

The trio made the trip in total silence. Andrew drove while Raber sat in the backseat with Ioni. She sat still, looking straight ahead, and before long, Raber found his mind wandering.

He was thinking of Andrew calling Ioni "bright angel," and he started repeating the phrase, "speak again, bright angel!" in his head over and over again, feeling his anger starting to simmer toward Andrew. He looked at Andrew's eyes watching the road in the rearview mirror and recalled the time that Andrew had had a run-in with the resident adviser on their dorm floor.

The RA had come to Andrew and accused him of using and selling drugs. Andrew dared him to come up with proof, and the RA informed Andrew that his constant disregard for noise level rules would be enough to get Andrew thrown out of the dorms and put on probation. What Andrew did next solidified Raber's belief that Andrew's version of witchcraft was the type he preferred over the more flower-child type that Ioni had learned to love.

Andrew broke into the RA's room and took one of his socks, and soaked it in some sort of herb/root liquid broth that smelled horribly. He then kindly laundered the sock and returned it to the RA's dorm.

"Just wait until he wears it again. That fucker isn't going to be RA much longer," Andrew had told him.

It took a few days. Raber came back to his dorm one day to see the RA being loaded, screaming, into the back of an ambulance. He ran to Andrew's room only to find his friend sitting at his desk, playing an online game and smiling widely.

"What happened to him?" Raber had asked.

"Oh, nothing too bad. He's just going to lose whatever leg wore that sock," Andrew said calmly. "He'll live. Hell, he might even get a really nice prosthetic and get some sympathy pussy...or dick. Whatever that asshole's preference was."

"Holy shit," Raber said, smiling.

"I told you, this is the way to go. Stay with me, Mister Clean, and I'll teach you what you want to know."

Raber's mind then wandered to later in the school year, not long after Ioni had met Andrew, when they'd encountered a homeless man after visiting a drug den. Andrew had stopped the man and handed him a tiny envelope of heroin.

"This is three hits, my man," Andrew had told the man. "I'll give it to you in exchange for a few of your teeth."

Raber had been completely taken aback at Andrew's business request, but the man, hurting for a hit, agreed instantly. Andrew must have anticipated such a meeting, because he produced a pair of pliers from his jacket pocket. The man groaned and grunted as Andrew extracted the four teeth. When he was done, Andrew gave him the envelope.

"Take the pain away, guy," Andrew said. "I'll be seeing you around."

Andrew had told him that human teeth, ground into a powder, were powerful ingredients to different spells. He called them a "staple." Over the next two months, the pair would go out and find the man and Andrew would provide him with heroin in exchange for a few teeth. Not long before

Christmas break, however, Raber had been walking through that area alone and the man, always in the same spot, was gone. When he asked Andrew about it later, Andrew had shrugged.

"He ran out of teeth," he said simply. "Didn't want him talking about me. But he had other uses at the end, and you'll benefit from those as well. Look," He'd held out his left hand then and brandished a gnarly scar on the back. "I'm marked now and I can finally read my uncle's spell book."

Raber had been panicked at the knowledge that Andrew had killed a man without compunction, but it also thrilled him. It had further emboldened Raber to seek out Andrew's ways, ways that held true power. Raber wanted it desperately.

"We will always be cloaked," Andrew told him. "We're protected by our own will."

Raber believed in those words with a fervency that delighted him. His own will, the most powerful thing he had, was going to be harnessed to live up to a potential that most people couldn't even imagine.

He looked over at the shell of the girl he loved and wondered if he were too easily romanced by the power that Andrew wielded.

"We're here!" Andrew announced suddenly, jerking Raber back into the moment.

"Put on your dancing shoes and prepare for a great fucking time!" Andrew said, opening Ioni's door for her.

CHAPTER TWENTY-FOUR

Because Black Veil was a niche club in a college town, there was never a line to get inside unless it was Halloween. The trio walked to the front door and showed the doorman their IDs. They all received stamps on their hands that indicated that they weren't old enough to purchase alcohol.

The inside of the club looked very similar to any rave club. There were black lights and strobe lights poking through the mass expanse of general darkness. The music was loud, as it was in every other nightclub in existence, but the clientele was decidedly unique.

While black clothes, black hair, and heavy black makeup dominated, every once in a while a gangly youth with a twelve-inch high green mohawk would walk within view or a misplaced young girl in a tight dress would stare about her in confusion. The trio stood near the entrance watching the movement of the club and Andrew and Raber took an interest in watching Ioni. Her red eyes were darting from figure to figure. Once, when a short, round boy walked by her a little too closely, Ioni made a move toward him. Raber shot a hand out and gripped her arm, holding her back.

"You can't have anyone here, baby," Raber said to her when she turned on him and whimpered.

"We're just here to play, okay?" Andrew said to her. "Do you know how to play?"

Ioni turned to Raber and looked in his face.

"What we did earlier?" she asked him.

Immediately, Raber felt a blush rushing to his face and ears. He hadn't wanted Andrew to know.

"What?" Andrew asked, smiling widely. "You didn't wait long to see if those perverted Harlequin novelists had a good idea, did you?"

"No, baby," Raber said to Ioni, trying to ignore Andrew. "This is something else."

"You're not getting out of talking about it," Andrew laughed.

"Not here!" Raber shouted.

Andrew guffawed and put his arm around Ioni's waist, pulling her closer to him.

"All right, princess," Andrew began. "When I say that we're here to play, I mean let's have fun with these people. Let's dance and flirt and watch and be watched. No biting, no scratching, no eating any of these people! Let's see what it really means to be a vampire, okay?"

"You show me," Ioni said to Andrew.

"I'll show you," Raber said, putting his arm over her shoulders and leading her away. He knew he would win that little battle with Andrew because Andrew hated dancing and had very little interest in actually "clubbing."

Raber led Ioni to the mildly crowded dance floor. He stood opposite of her and began moving to the heavy beat of the music. Ioni watched him for a moment and began mimicking him. Raber stopped and laughed, realizing what a bad dancer he was.

"Don't dance like me," Raber said into her ear. "Listen to the music and move to it in a way that gets attention. That's what you want. Attention."

Ioni stood back and watched him again, then she began watching the other club-goers dance. Eventually she started moving to the music and Raber was impressed with how effortlessly she oozed sexuality in her movements. Slowly, he started inching away from her, wanting as much as Andrew to see how she would handle an interaction in that setting.

Never taking his eyes off of Ioni, Raber began dancing with a deliciously curvaceous girl wearing black leggings and a flowing black blouse. As the girl allowed Raber to put his hands on her hips, Raber saw a guy with long, tightly curled hair make his way over to Ioni. He watched as Ioni looked at the guy and swayed her hips in a way that invited him closer. Raber watched in amazement, losing interest in the girl with whom he was dancing, as Ioni reached down and guided her dance partner's hands to explore the entirety of her body. He fought the urge to separate them, but decided to wait.

The idiot started smiling when he realized that Ioni would allow him to feel the soft curve of her breast as he pressed his hips into her while they danced. Ioni kept an intense stare focused on her dance partner, looking into his eyes as she moved and guided his hands.

Raber watched, mouth agape, as his vampire reached up and placed her hands on either side of her dance partner's face. She pulled him down to her and they kissed, the idiot licking her lips lasciviously. Ioni manipulated him so that her mouth was on his neck. Raber felt a stab of panic and shouted to her. Her eyes darted to him instantly and she shoved the guy away from her, turning away. The young man, who had fallen on his ass from the force of Ioni's shove was confused and angry and he went to grab Ioni. Raber knew it was time to step in.

"Hey, leave her alone," Raber said to the dance partner before he could touch Ioni.

"What the fuck is her fucking problem, man?" the dance partner asked, angrily.

"She was done with you, okay? Now get the hell out of here before I make you go," Raber said.

The dance partner flashed his middle finger in Raber's face before stalking off.

Raber turned to Ioni. She was still dancing, apparently off in her own little world. He put his arms around her from behind and moved with her. He breathed in, smelling her soft hair and nuzzled her neck.

"I love you," he whispered into her ear.

She made no reply. She made no move to move closer into his embrace as she had once done. In those days she would try to squeeze so close to him that she might suffocate any atom that stood between them. Now she stared straight ahead, accepting his advances with disinterest as she moved rhythmically to the music.

Raber looked around for Andrew. He found him standing by the bathroom doors, making a sly exchange with a wisp of a girl with pink hair. When Andrew noticed him, Raber motioned with his head toward the door.

"We've been here a half hour," Andrew said, annoyed.

"I know that," Raber said, holding a hand out to Ioni. "But she's performed well. Were you watching?"

"What, the idiot feeling her up on the dance floor?" Andrew asked. "Yeah, I saw. She's quite the little seductress, isn't she?"

Raber frowned and led the way to Andrew's car.

On the drive home, Raber sat in the passenger seat next to Andrew while Ioni sat like a statue in the back seat.

"She doesn't remember me," Raber said as soon as they were back on the highway.

"Hmm?" Andrew said, looking over at him.

"She doesn't remember me. She has no memory of her life."

Andrew was quiet for a while. He drove in silence, chewing on his lower lip.

"It would have to work that way, wouldn't it?" he said at last. "I mean, you can't fully possess someone who has memories of either not knowing you at all or knowing a side of you that was diametrically opposed to their beliefs. Right? This wouldn't have worked if she remembered how she felt about you."

"Wasn't there a spell that I could have worked on her that would have changed her perception or made her forget the bad things?" Raber whined, rubbing his temples.

"This spell did the trick just fine, my friend," Andrew said. "You have her. She's all yours. And from what I've heard, she's the most complacent toy you could ever want."

"Yeah," Raber said, sourly.

"You need to spill it, man. Is she a wildcat in bed now? Does she have superhuman sucking powers?" Andrew asked, excitedly.

"No," Raber said.

"Well?" Andrew asked, nudging Raber in the arm.

"It was weird," Raber began. "I don't want to get too detailed, but let's just say that there was a certain elasticity...a certain firmness of skin, that seems to have been lost. She felt like a corpse from the inside."

Again, Andrew was quiet for a while.

"Well," he said finally. "Shit."

"Yeah," Raber agreed.

"That ruins some of the fun for you, doesn't it?" Andrew asked. "I mean, you have her. She's all yours. It's a fact. But there's this stupid twist that she's completely disgusting to fuck and now you're stuck with it."

"Yeah, I know," Raber said, nodding. "But you know, she seems to have a capacity for learning and adapting. You saw her dancing and seducing that guy back there, and I taught her how to dress and groom herself. Maybe, with some patience, she could learn how to...I don't know...do Kegels or something. Is that what they're called?"

Andrew burst into hysterical laughter and banged on his steering wheel with glee.

"We're actually talking about making a dead girl do pussy-muscle strengthening exercises? Is that what you're proposing?" Andrew asked between gasps.

"That and maybe teaching her how to get into it. I mean, she just laid there." Raber said, annoyed.

Andrew laughed some more and wiped the tears from his eyes.

"It's worth a shot, I guess," he cackled.

Sometime the next morning, Raber was awakened by a knocking on the front door. He waited, hoping the visitor would go away, but the knocking persisted. A familiar voice yelled out.

"Get up, lazy bones! I brought doughnuts!"

Raber rubbed his aching eyes and groaned. He crawled on all fours to the living room where Andrew was crouching beside the sofa away from the door and windows, his eyes wide with panic.

"It's one of her friends," Raber whispered to him. "Just be quiet, I'm gonna go get her phone."

"Hey! Ioni! Are you in there?" Nathan yelled from outside.

Raber crawled to the kitchen and retrieved her cell phone from where it was charging. He turned it on and silenced it as fast as he could. After a few minutes, he heard a car door slam in front of the house and immediately her phone vibrated. A text notification popped up.

"Worried abt u." The text from Nathan read. "At the house banging on the door and ur not answering. R U ok?"

Raber started texting back, sweat pouring down the back of his neck and his pulse pounding behind his eyeballs.

"Sorry!" He texted. He needed to try to channel her sweetness and eagerness to keep the peace. "Not at house right now. Didn't mean to worry you."

"Ur car is here, where R U?" Nathan's reply came quickly.

"Don't get upset, but I'm with Raber."

"WHAT THE FUCK" was Nathan's reply.

"We've been talking and he's changed." Raber replied.

"Kudos to you for not fucking your old boyfriend in your new boyfriend's house." Nathan replied. Raber sneered at the phone screen and began typing a reply when another text from Nathan came through.

"That asshole is violent and I want you to be careful. I'm serious. I'd hate to have to start stalking you so that prick can't hurt you." Nathan texted.

Raber felt the heat rising in his face.

"Fuck you," he spat at the phone. Then, thinking, he chuckled. "You're instincts aren't actually too far off, flamer."

Just then, Andrew, on all fours, poked his head around the corner.

"Who are you talking to?" he asked.

"The guy at the door. He's texting." Raber answered.

"What did you tell him?"

Raber explained the conversation and Andrew chuckled.

"He's astute, isn't he?" Andrew asked. Raber laughed and nodded.

"I'll be fine, I promise. I know what I'm doing," Raber texted to Nathan, hoping to wind the conversation down.

"Call me 2night," Nathan texted back. "And b careful."

"Ok," Raber replied. It occurred to him a moment later that that simple conversation was going to cost a fortune in texting fees and that Ioni's dad was going to be livid at the frivolity of it. He'd have to tie a few loose ends and then lose the phone permanently.

Andrew pulled a baggie out of his pocket and popped a few pills. Raber rubbed his aching head and face.

"Upper?" Andrew asked, holding the baggie up in front of Raber.

"No, I need to sleep some more," Raber said.

"Suit yourself. I need to start planning her dinner tonight anyhow," Andrew said. "We could always take her the park and let her have a homeless person."

"We could probably do that sporadically, but in this small town, that would get a lot of attention," Raber said.

Ioni had complained that she was still hungry when they returned to Tristan's house after Black Veil, and Raber and Andrew knew that she probably would never be satisfied on a diet that was wholly devoid of human blood. They had to adjust their thinking so that it included at least the possibility of human meals for the vampire.

"I've actually got an idea for her dinner," Raber said.

"That's a nice change of pace," Andrew said. "Do tell."

CHAPTER TWENTY-FIVE

Raber slept until nearly four p.m. When he rolled out of bed, he showered, knowing he wouldn't need to do it a second time that night with Ioni. The hope was that she would awaken and immediately shower and groom herself. Any urges that he'd previously had to be naked with her had gone.

He found Andrew pulling a needle out of his arm and laughing loudly at a movie on the television. Raber sat on the couch next to him and began packing a bowl with some nice, sticky pot.

"That phone of hers has been buzzing like crazy," Andrew said, his eyelids closing slowly as the drugs pumped through him.

Raber collected the cell phone and saw that several missed texts, calls and voicemails waited for his attention.

"Damn," Raber murmured as he began to go through the texts.

Some were from her sister, Rose, talking about mundane things. Some were from people whose names he didn't recognize. They must have been members of Ioni's coven. There were some angry, freaked-out texts from Arlie because the news had gotten to her from Nathan that Ioni was back with Raber. And lastly, there was a series of texts from Tristan.

"Hello, beautiful. Are you feeling better? You seemed preoccupied last time I messaged you. I miss you and I wish so badly that I could smell you and touch you right now. Perhaps you could be kind enough to send me a picture to keep me warm at night?"

Raber gritted his teeth and stared at the phone, wishing a painful death on Tristan.

"She'll be very happy to see you when you get back, fucker. You can be her fucking holiday meal," he snarled at the phone.

He threw the phone onto the counter in disgust and grabbed a cool drink from the refrigerator. After a long pull on the bottle, he picked up the phone again. He made mildly interested and polite replies to Rose, deflected committing to any plans with the coven members, and wrote a long text to Arlie that basically asked for understanding and privacy. He needed more time to think on how to properly reply to Tristan.

He slipped the phone into his pants pocket and resumed his place next to Andrew on the couch. He finished packing the bowl and lit the tight bud until it glowed red, inhaling the thick, acrid smoke and letting it burn his throat before letting it out. He took another hit. With each deep exhale, he felt the tension easing out of him. He could see that Andrew was in a beautiful place just then. His eyes were just barely open and his face was flushed. Raber slumped back on the cheap sofa and stared at the television. A woman was frolicking through the woods bare-ass naked. Raber smiled.

As soon as Andrew started showing signs of animation again, Raber suggested that they feed themselves. He got takeout from a local Chinese place. As they ate the unnaturally massive amount of food, Raber told Andrew of the texts that Tristan had sent Ioni.

"You ought to give him what he wants," Andrew said over a mouthful of lo mein.

"Why would I do that?"

"He's not here. That's a good thing. If he thought things weren't normal, he might wanna cut his trip short. We haven't exactly made solid plans for the future yet, you know. This needs to be home base for a while longer." Andrew replied.

"Yeah. You're right, I guess," Raber said.

"It's just the obvious answer," Andrew said. "You hate the guy and want to deny his requests, especially where she's concerned. But in the interest of maintaining what we have right now, I don't think you have any choice. It's tits and ass photography up in this place tonight, Frankenstein!"

"I think I can handle that part alone."

"Whatever," Andrew said. "I'm not going to steal your precious girlfriend, you idiot. Besides, if I want a peek, I'll peek and there isn't a damned thing you can do to stop me."

"Just leave it alone," Raber said.

"She'll be waking up soon," Andrew said. "Do you think she should wait until after your dinner surprise to shower?"

Raber didn't say anything, he just looked at his friend and smiled. Andrew returned his smile and they finished their food in silence.

They were putting their empty takeout containers into a garbage bag when Raber heard the basement door creak open. He shoved the bag into Andrew's arms and dashed to intercept Ioni. He put himself between her and the bathroom door, getting her attention from the front. He had decided that surprising her from the back might be a bad idea.

"I know that I told you to take care of this as soon as you rise in the evening," he began, leading her into the living room. "But tonight you're going to get pretty messy eating your dinner, and you can shower after you've eaten."

Ioni's eyes got wide and Raber entertained the idea that the vampire almost smiled at him.

"Eat?" she whispered.

"Yes, gorgeous," Raber said. "You'll get your fill tonight, I promise."

Andrew had finished bagging up their garbage, and he threw it in the bin outside as they made their way to his car. Raber took the driver's seat as Andrew helped Ioni into the backseat before sliding in next to her.

"You can find this place in the dark?" Andrew asked him after a few minutes of driving.

"Sure," Raber answered. "I've only been there a couple of times, but I know where it is."

They drove deep into a rural area where the road became dirt and gravel and no light came from anything other than the headlights on the car. Raber stopped on a desolate stretch of road. There were only trees and nighttime sounds around them.

"We need to walk from here or we'll be seen," Raber said, opening the back door for Ioni.

The trio travelled down a steep hill. Raber wondered if Ioni might remember the place. When   they reached the driveway, Raber led them left, away from the small house and toward a barn. They passed a chicken coop, but all of the birds must have been asleep because all was quiet. As they got closer to the barn, the smell of warm hay, hot animals and manure hit them.

"It stinks," Andrew whispered. "Why does it always smell like dirty asses and poop?"

Raber chuckled in spite of himself. He was simply giddy about what was about to happen.

"I hope they have one," he said to Andrew. "Otherwise, she's eating chicken."

"They have something big enough for her. Only a barnyard animal makes a stink like that," Andrew said sourly, holding his hand over his nose and mouth.

"It should have a pen by the side of the barn, so it can access a mudhole or something," Raber said. "Let's go to the far side, there should be an open place."

They came to a large, fenced-in area. Raber used a flashlight he'd found in Tristan's house to illuminate the inside. There was only bare mud and a long feeding trough. He looked around and saw a large box with hay sticking out of the sides. They climbed over the fence. Raber shined his light inside the box and they saw four medium-sized pigs cuddled up and sleeping.

"They raise their own animals so that the meat eaters of the coven can eat humanely treated beasts," Raber said, sneering. He looked at Ioni and stroked her face. "Only the best for you. Besides, you used to buy into that ridiculousness."

"Go on," Andrew urged her. "That's your dinner, Countess."

Ioni glanced at Andrew over her shoulder and then back at Raber. Raber nodded approvingly and she descended upon the pen with a preternatural swiftness that startled her spectators. In a series of fast moves that would suggest forethought, she snapped the backs of the pigs, severing their spines and killing them with no mess. Then, one by one, she used her flat but strong teeth to rip a hole in their throats where she would suck the dark, thick blood.

Raber felt a tightness in his throat and a pain in his gut that warned he might vomit. As the metallic smell of the blood mixed in his nostrils with the other barnyard aromas, he felt the greasy Chinese food start to disagree with him. Ioni's slurping and grunting didn't make the spectacle any easier to witness. Andrew grabbed his shoulder and squeezed.

"Keep it in," he said sternly. "Do not vomit here, do you understand? We're dealing with people who are going to be very suspicious of this and not just on a 'holy shit someone killed my pigs' way. Do you understand? Don't leave a part of yourself here. Suck it up."

Raber nodded quickly and started taking deep breaths through his mouth. He didn't need to do it for long. The vampire was a fast eater.

"Well," Andrew began, looking steadier than Raber.

"Better," Ioni said to them, not bothering to wipe the gore from her pale face.

"Let's go," Raber said.

They made their way back to Andrew's car as stealthily as they could. Ioni climbed into the backseat quietly while Andrew decided to sit up front next to Raber. Raber grinned to himself at seeing Andrew actually get grossed out. He drove them back to Tristan's house as fast as he could with all of the windows down. The smell of blood and barnyard hung heavy on the silent vampire in the backseat.

Raber ordered Ioni to shower immediately as soon as they were through the door. She walked off in totally silent obedience while Raber and Andrew kicked off their filthy shoes by the door. They each got something cold to drink and Andrew offered Raber his baggy of pills. Raber accepted.

Raber went to check on Ioni. He poked his head into the shower to see her rinsing thick, white lather off of her smooth skin. She turned to him without shame.

"Are you finished?" he asked her.

"Yes," she answered.

"Okay, then. No need to get dressed yet. Turn off the water, here's your towel. Meet me in the bedroom." He glanced at her nudity one last time as she began toweling the droplets of water from her skin and went into the bedroom.

She walked in a moment later, the towel crumpled in her hand, her body on full display. Raber jumped up and shut the door quickly, making sure Andrew was nowhere near. He turned to her, annoyed, and wrapped her in the towel.

"When it's just you and me, you can walk around naked all you want," he began angrily. "But when other people are around, *including Andrew,* you need to keep your body covered up."

Ioni stared at him coolly, unaffected by his anger. Raber sighed heavily and pointed to the makeup and hairbrush laid out for her.

"Do you remember what to do?" He asked her.

Without speaking, she picked up the hairbrush and started brushing her hair. She used the blow dryer to dry it and smoothed it out so that it was its usual silkiness. She then set about applying her signature heavy eye makeup. When she was finished, she turned to him, serene and awaiting instruction.

"Very good," he said, pleased. "Now we have a special task at hand tonight. We need to take some pictures. You have to be nude for these pictures and I want you to do some posing for these pictures, okay?" He pointed to the webcam on her computer.

Ioni stared back at him.

"Okay, well, umm, why don't you get on the bed. Get on all fours, no on your hands and knees. Yes, that's perfect. Spread your legs a little bit. Okay, now look back at me and smile. Okay, there's one. Now I want you to lie on your back. Okay, now spread your legs. Okay there's two. Now stay just like that, but use your hand to touch yourself. No, touch your vagina, Ioni. No, just prod at it with your index finger. No, Christ, let me show you."

Raber was awkwardly trying to position Ioni's fingers so that it would look as if she were pleasuring herself when he heard Andrew snickering. Raber straightened quickly and glared at Andrew who was standing in the doorway.

"Calm it down," Andrew said. "There's no way in hell that this can be construed as sexual. This is just sad. What are you doing, anyhow?"

"I'm taking the pictures!" Raber replied angrily.

"You need to make it look like *she* took the pictures, idiot!" Andrew said, smiling broadly.

"Oh, shit," Raber said, looking down at Ioni in her awkward pose.

"Yeah. Look, don't over-think it. He just wants to see her tits, you know."

"Okay, okay," Raber said, nodding. "I know what to do. You can go now. Thanks."

"Pssh," Andrew said, waving a hand. "Get over yourself. I'm not moving, this is too funny."

"Andrew," Raber began.

"Look, man, I don't want to stand here all damned night, let's go!" Andrew said, clapping his hands.

Raber glared. Andrew smirked back and crossed his arms over his narrow chest. Raber sighed and looked down at Ioni.

"Sit up, sweetheart," he said to her.

She sat up without being self-conscious in the slightest. She showed no shame. Raber smiled down at her.

"If only you'd been so unafraid before," he said, stroking her hair. "You're perfect."

He knelt before her, fussing with her hair and adjusting her head angle. He put her in front of the computer and stood off to the side, his hand on the mouse, ready to click.

"Look into it and give me a small, sideways smile," Raber said, looking at the camera view on the screen. When her smile was just right, he tapped the mouse and took the picture. Andrew was looking over his shoulder.

"See, that's simple and it looks like she took it herself. That's all he needs. This is just for the spank bank."

Raber nodded and attached the picture to an email that read, "Here you go, handsome :)"

"I feel disgusting for doing this," Raber said.

"Your morals and standards are fucked up," Andrew answered. Raber laughed.

"She needs to call her fucking friends now," Raber said. "She needs to smooth over the mess that they're making over her being with me."

"Wanna go out again?" Andrew said excitedly.

"Fuck, I don't want to," Raber began. "But I think that that's what needs to happen."

"I'll let you guys take care of that. I'm on rat buying duty tonight."

He knelt down before the still-nude vampire and stroked the side of her neck. Raber tensed, waiting to see how far Andrew would go.

"If only to keep you like this a little longer, you tasty thing," Andrew said. "But alas, the work of a monster-keeper is never done!"

And at that, Andrew jumped to his feet and was out of the house before Raber could react. Raber looked at the empty doorway leading from Tristan's bedroom to the hallway, then at the unmoving, naked Ioni sitting on the bed. He sighed heavily, found his amber bottle of pills, and threw one into his mouth.

"Get dressed," he said to Ioni. "We have to go pretend to be normal for some people tonight."

He sent out texts to Arlie and Nathan, asking them to meet at Eat N' Park. Ioni was dressed and standing before him before he received both of their acceptances of his invitation. He drove them to the restaurant in Ioni's car. When he was parked, he turned to her, putting a firm hand on her shoulder.

"Don't attack anybody in here tonight. The people that we are meeting used to be your friends. They are not food, but they are not important to you either. Only I am important. But you have to talk to them and try to act like what they say matters to you. Do you understand?" He was sweating profusely.

"Yes," Ioni said.

"No, I need you to repeat that back to me so that I know you really understand," Raber pushed, annoyed.

"I don't eat anyone in here. Only you are important to me, nobody else. I have to talk and act like I care about these people," Ioni deadpanned.

Raber sighed and reached out to touch her silken hair.

"Good girl," he said. "Let's go get this over with."

Once inside, Raber searched the red and green booths for Nathan and Arlie. When he spotted them, he gently led Ioni to the table. Arlie and Nathan looked tense as they smiled at the duo, but Raber ignored them and helped Ioni slide into her seat before boxing her in. Although he'd told her that she couldn't eat anybody in there, he felt better being a barrier between her and the clueless rabble.

"Well well," Nathan said, trying to sound pleasant. "How on earth did this reunion come about?"

"I came in for the summer and visited her at work and begged her to give me another chance," Raber said, a false smile stretching his face. "She made me work for it, but I think I've shown her that I'm rehabilitated."

Raber caressed Ioni's hair and looked daringly into the faces of her friends as they tried to hide their disgust. He chuckled softly and kissed Ioni on the cheek for good measure.

"Well, Raber, you should know that Ioni was very open and honest with us about how you were before," Arlie began. "Don't be mad at us for not trusting you or for being concerned for her."

"Yeah," Nathan said. "We have to look out for our girl here, right?" Nathan reached out and grasped one of Ioni's hands.

Raber tensed when Ioni had no reaction. She stared placidly ahead of her as usual and didn't even acknowledge that Nathan was touching her. Feeling panic start to rise in his throat, Raber quickly glanced at Nathan and Arlie as they stared at their friend, confusion and concern creasing their young faces.

"Ioni," Arlie said. "Hey, look at me."

Raber watched as Ioni smoothly focused her gaze on Arlie. Her friends continued to study her.

"What's the matter with her eyes?" Nathan said, reaching out to touch her face.

"Why are they so red?" Arlie asked.

They both glared at Raber, silently demanding an answer.

"She lost her job," Raber said softly. "She was crying about it earlier, I guess her eyes haven't cleared up yet."

Nathan and Arlie squinted back at Ioni.

"I sure am sorry, babe," Nathan said, leaning back into the booth.

"You'll get another job. What happened?" Arlie asked.

"The manager said that they were downsizing waitstaff," Raber said.

Arlie looked hard at him and then turned to Ioni.

"Hey, do you want me to help you look around?" Arlie asked Ioni.

Raber nudged Ioni's thigh discreetly under the table and Ioni looked into Arlie's face.

"That's nice," Ioni answered dreamily. "Raber helps me."

"That's good that he does," Nathan said, side-eyeing Raber intensely.

"We're here to help, too, if you need it," Arlie said, frowning.

"You have such wonderful friends," Raber said, smiling. "You're such a lucky girl to be so loved."

Ioni kept her stare straight ahead and said nothing.

"All right," Arlie said, slamming her hands down on the tabletop. "What's she on? What have you done to her, damn it?"

Nathan grasped Arlie's shoulder, but they both stared into Raber's face accusingly. His heart was nearly beating out of his chest as he struggled to stay calm.

"Look, she was upset, so I gave her something to calm her down. I didn't know you guys were going to launch some sort of Raber intervention on her. She had a problem and I tried to solve it. Don't sit there and act superior to me." Raber said, struggling to keep up the façade of innocence.

"You drugged her!" Arlie whisper-screamed at him.

"She took it of her own free will," Raber said through gritted teeth.

"Stop," Ioni said in a firm voice. "You're making Raber angry. Stop."

Raber snapped his head to the side in surprise to look at his vampire. Her red eyes were focused on the two people she had once counted as friends. Raber ventured a glance at them and saw that they had recoiled from Ioni, her glare stopping whatever hot emotions they had been feeling before.

Slowly and cautiously Raber reached out and touched her. She didn't so much as blink.

"Hey," he said softly to her. "It's okay, baby."

Finally, a tension was broken and Ioni took her gaze off of the people sitting across from her and turned her head to look at him. Raber stroked the side of her face. He was becoming impressed with his showmanship techniques.

"They're your friends, baby. They're only concerned for you." he said, stealing a glance at Nathan and Arlie. "They only want what's good for you."

Arlie and Nathan made no move or reply. They both sat back firmly against the booth, pale-faced and wide-eyed.

"They need to stop making you angry," Ioni said simply.

Raber nodded slowly and looked at her friends, still nodding in a 'look what asses you are' way.

"Do you want to go home now, baby?" Raber asked. Ioni looked at him in that blank way that was her new normal and his stomach cramped. "You do, right?" Finally, she nodded slowly.

"All right," Raber said.

He stood up and held his hand out to her. He looked down at Arlie and Nathan.

"I'm in her life. If you want to be in her life, you might want to learn to watch how you throw your asshole opinions out at her."

Without waiting for them to so much as blink at him, Raber turned and guided Ioni out of the restaurant and back into his car. When she was seated quietly in the passenger side, Raber went around to the back and vomited on the black asphalt. He hoped that nobody would walk out and see him emptying his guts in the parking lot. As he hunched over the back of her car and retched, he was livid over his inability to control his emotions. He made his decisions and his moves very carefully and deliberately. There should have been no panic. He resented having to explain anything to anybody. He resented other people feeling that they had any sort of say over Ioni.

He straightened himself, wiped his mouth, and sucked back a glob of mucus into his throat. He looked at the back of the head of the female form sitting in his car and smiled to himself. The girl that they thought they could sway with their opinions broke her stupid pretty neck by hanging herself in a drug-induced hallucination. The one that was sitting in that car waiting for him was a creature that stood as a testament to his power and his indefatigable will. That she took up for him when she thought that he was being attacked was a powerful sign.

"I don't owe anybody a fucking thing," he snarled.

CHAPTER TWENTY-SIX

Andrew came bounding into Tristan's house in a flurry of excited energy. He had a box in his arms that bore the logo of one of the large chain pet stores in the area.

"I've got some nice tasty rats here," he said, carrying the box into the kitchen. "And I've got some very interesting news. Let me ask you something, dude, how long have you lived here? In this town?"

"I lived here for a year before college. Why?" Raber answered, confused.

"Man, I sold some weed to this meth-mouth looking bitch at the pet store and she was telling me about her son and grandkids living in this one part of town that has some serious drug problems. So I pretended like I gave a damn about her stupid family and she spilled to me that this white trash hellhole of a city has quite a few areas where drugs are a serious problem. This is good news for us!" Andrew said, gesturing excitedly.

"I thought your drug connections were all in New Jersey?" Raber asked, not sure where Andrew was going with his tirade.

Andrew laughed in his high frantic way before answering.

"I would never be desperate enough to put any drugs in my body that came from this sister-fucking town!" Andrew said, catching his breath. "If there's a drug problem in a town like this, nobody is gonna miss a druggy or two. Our girl can still have some satisfactory eating time." Andrew said, stuffing an entire Twinkie into his mouth.

"But in a place like this, I think people would notice it, even if it was the most lowly of their community turning up dead and drained of all their blood." Raber answered, wishing he had a Twinkie.

"Ahh, but you see, I've been thinking on that one." Andrew said, wagging a finger at Raber. "There's that crap-filled river that runs past your VA hospital, and it's really close to one of the heroin-addled parts of town. These people who've lost their way to God can just keep getting so high out of their gourds that they fall into that river only to turn up weeks later, mostly decomposed and rotten."

Raber sat for a moment, thinking on that.

"I want a Twinkie," he said.

"Then get the hell up and get one," Andrew said, setting up a large cage that he'd gotten for the rats.

"Did you eat them all?" Raber asked, annoyed.

Andrew stopped what he was doing and turned to glare at Raber.

"And what in the sweet name of fuck is your problem?" Andrew asked.

"I'm sick of you acting like you have any right to be here," Raber said, walking to the kitchen to find an empty Twinkie box. "And you did fucking eat all of them. You're going to go get more!"

Andrew stood up and tried his usual intimidation tactics. He walked up on Raber and got as in-his-face as his short stature would allow. Raber puffed his chest out and smiled into Andrew's angry, upturned face.

"I think you forget a thing or two about me," Andrew said menacingly.

"I know everything I need to know about you," Raber returned. "I know you've killed people, I've seen you steal, and I've seen you perform at least a thousand drug-related offenses. But you know what? I don't fucking need to be afraid of you, you little piece of shit."

Andrew frowned and jerked his head back in a twitch. Raber burst out laughing. He had caught the little twerp completely by surprise.

"Did you really think that I was going to let you take this all away from me because you're on some sort of little-man-syndrome power trip?" Raber asked. "Well, it's not happening. You're here to help, not be the commander-in-chief of these proceedings."

Andrew stepped back, huffing in pure rage. Usually, seeing Andrew, someone who had proven to be a psychopath completely lacking in empathy, in such a froth would make Raber nervous. But not anymore. After seeing how Ioni stood up for him, Raber knew that with or without that length of rope around Andrew's wrist, the vampire formerly known as Ioni Davis was there to do his bidding and his bidding only.

"You had better think long and hard about how you talk to me, Frankenstein," Andrew said, a grin spreading across the entirety of his face. "I know things about you, too."

"Yes, I suppose we both have our history of boo-boos that might upset the more polite side of society. But let me tell you something, you're nothing more than a drug-dealing scumbag from a greasy family of scumbags. I'm an intelligent, upstanding fellow from a very good home. Tell me, Andy, how is it that your family came by their money? You don't look like an Italian, so surely it wasn't a mob thing. Is your mother really that good at sucking dick?"

Raber had a moment to see Andrew's eyes bulge from his head and his nostrils flair. Then, Andrew was screaming and lurching toward Raber with murder in his eyes. The smile never left Raber's mouth.

Andrew was able to take a clumsy swing at Raber's head, landing a soft knock to Raber's jaw, before Ioni, who had been standing behind Andrew during the whole stand-off, wrapped her arms around his slight waist and restrained him from any further movements. Andrew screamed and twisted against her powerful hold, but to no avail.

"She can't hurt you, but she *can* protect me," Raber said, stepping forward and leaning down into Andrew's face. "My ace in the fucking hole."

Andrew, still mostly animal in his rage only snarled at Raber and struggled against the unmoving Ioni. Raber smiled congenially and patted his enraged companion on the head.

"You're going to learn your place, small one," Raber said, soothingly. "You're going to learn that you are the Igor to my Dr. Frankenstein. The Renfield to my Dracula. You are the servant, Andrew. You had better learn to deal with that, or the next time you shoot up heroin, I'm going to relieve you of that bit of rope around your wrist and let my darling Ioni eat you for breakfast."

Andrew spit into Raber's face and screamed. Straightening and wiping his face, he looked down at Andrew and idly wondered what drugs were coursing through that small young man's body.

"What input can you offer, my sweet?" Raber asked Ioni. "Is Andrew better as a gopher or as a delicious treat for you and your gloriousness?"

Ioni placed one of her deceptively delicate-looking hands under Andrew's chin and wrenched his head so that she could look into his face. Andrew grunted in panic.

"He's good," Ioni said simply.

Now it was Raber's turn to laugh maniacally. Ioni released Andrew's greasy face. Raber could see the rage and fear apparent there.

"I'm not so sure that this is a glowing recommendation to your character, old friend," Raber said, clapping Andrew on the shoulder. "My thinking is that this sweet creature is appreciative of the help you have given thus far, but that she would be more than happy to let your still-beating heart pump the hot blood down her throat at my urgings."

Raber watched as Andrew began to relax. Strangely, he was relieved at the way the situation was progressing. Raber smiled and nodded at Ioni, who released Andrew from her powerful grasp.

"Well what the hell's next?" Andrew said, adjusting his clothes. "I *was* trying to set up that rat cage before your meltdown. What should I do instead?"

"I want more goddamned Twinkies," Raber said. "Then do whatever keeps you useful."

That night, Andrew managed to set up a delightful looking rat enclosure (after making a trip out for more Twinkies) while Raber sat slumped on the couch watching television and smoking weed. Ioni sat on the floor, her face blank and her eyes focused on nothing.

Raber awoke on the couch many hours later, the sun making the side of his face feel hot and tight. He saw hide nor hair of Andrew. He knew that Ioni must have retreated to the basement, but he wondered where Andrew had gone. He got up slowly and waddled to the main bedroom. The bed was messy and the room smelled of sweat and body oil, but there was no Andrew. After a visit to the bathroom, Raber located his own cell phone and sent Andrew a text.

"Where are you?" he typed. He put the phone on the dresser and took a short shower, washing the sweat and smoke smells off of him. When he'd brushed his teeth and dressed, he decided to do a bit of laundry, laughing to himself over the coziness of those chores in another man's home. He avoided the back area of the basement, the packed-earth crypt. The sleeping place of his vampire.

Andrew hadn't gotten back to him yet, so he stuffed the phone into his pants pocket, grabbed a cold drink and examined his pill bottle gloomily, noting that it was nearly empty. He popped a pill, walked over to the rat cage, and watched the small furry bodies huddled in a corner sleeping.

His head started swimming. He fell heavily onto the couch and stared at the television which hadn't been turned off in days.

He was shocked out of his hazy state by a sharp knocking at the door. He huffed in frustration before throwing himself to the floor and crawling around so that he could see who was knocking. He gasped and needed a moment to catch his breath when he saw that it was Sarah at the door. The witches were sniffing around. That was not good.

As Raber sat on the floor close to panic, trying to decide what to do, he heard Andrew's voice.

"Hi there!" Andrew said brightly. "Are you looking for Tristan or Ioni?"

"Oh! Um, I'm actually trying to get to Ioni," Sarah said, sounding very confused.

"I'm sorry," Andrew said in his sweet voice. "She's spending the day with her sister. Hi, I'm Andrew! I'm a friend of Ioni's. I'm just here to drop off some groceries and supplies that she asked me to get."

"Oh," Sarah said, still sounding confused. "Well, uh, Andrew, do you know when she'll be back?"

"Not until tonight, I don't think. You should text her and let her know you're looking for her. She's always great about responding to texts."

"Well, she hasn't been. Not lately. Not like her usual," Sarah said.

"Well then you send her a sternly worded text! That always works for me!" Andrew said. "I'm really sorry, but I've got to get these bags in! Excuse me!"

Raber scrambled to the basement and crouched on the steps, barely closing the door over so that he could still hear what was going on without being seen. He heard Andrew open the front door and a soft rustling noise as he brought bags in.

"Oh my, she needs to open some windows in here!" Sarah said.

"She's not much of a housekeeper yet, I guess," Andrew replied, a smile apparent in his voice.

"Well, Andrew, I thank you for talking to me," Sarah began. "I'll make sure to text Ioni and let her know that there are people she needs to see. If you should hear from her first, will you please let her know that I was here? My name is Sarah."

"I sure can!" Andrew said brightly.

"Thanks," Sarah said.

Raber stayed where he was. He could hear that Andrew was being still, waiting for Sarah to leave. After a moment Andrew called out.

"She's gone."

Raber tried his best to look dignified as he came out of the dark basement doorway. He walked back into the living room and sat on the couch. Andrew took an armload of bags into the kitchen and then joined Raber in the living room. He held a bag out to Raber and shook it.

"I noticed that your little happy bottle was running low, so I made a trip to Morgantown and got refills. I've got your usual and I even got some Viagra!"

Raber looked at Andrew uncertainly and then accepted the bag. He opened it and saw that it was indeed the pills that he'd become so intimate with in the past year. He knew them all by sight.

"Thank you," he said softly. "And for getting rid of her," he said, jerking his head toward the door.

"Your time in this house is running short, Frankenstein," Andrew said.

"Yeah, I know." Raber said, dumping pills into his amber bottle.

"Time to start making some more long-term plans," Andrew said.

"Yeah," Raber answered.

"I got us some food," Andrew said.

"Thanks," Raber said.

"Anything I can do? I hear the washer going. Need me to do anything with that?"

Raber looked at Andrew sharply and narrowed his eyes.

"Eager to start touching my clothes, Andrew?" He asked fiercely.

"Nope, not at all," Andrew said brightly, adjusting the rat cage. "Just trying to be a good Igor, that's all."

Andrew walked into the kitchen and started puttering around in there noisily and whistling. Raber rubbed his temples and wished for a visit with a warm woman. Just as he was almost resolved to make a drive to Morgantown himself for a visit with one such body, he realized that he should be expecting a text to Ioni's phone. He searched for it in the living room, but couldn't find it. He stomped into the kitchen and looked on the counter where he usually left it charging.

"Looking for her phone?" Andrew asked amiably.

"Yes," Raber said.

"I've got it. I took it with me in case someone started going apeshit with the texts. I thought it would be nice to let you sleep." He took the phone from his shirt pocket and held it out to Raber.

"Here you go," Andrew said, looking away at a box of Cheez-Its.

Suspicious, Raber plucked the phone out of Andrew's hand and examined it. Andrew continued to ignore him. He was focused on groceries in a way that Raber found curious.

"Are you straight right now?" Raber asked Andrew.

"I was running low on heroin and pills," Andrew said. "I get my personal stuff from Jersey, so that has to wait for a trip home for that. I'm just conserving."

"It's not like you to let your stash run low like that," Raber observed.

"This is true," Andrew answered. "But I've been just a wee bit preoccupied with the kickass fucking vampire over here."

Raber looked at Andrew a moment longer and then tucked Ioni's cellphone into his pocket.

"I'm going to make a run to Morgantown for a few hours," he told Andrew.

"Okey dokey," Andrew said happily from the kitchen.

"Andrew?"

"What?"

"Don't fuck with me."

"I wouldn't dream of it."

Raber got into his car and texted Jordan.

"Got a little time for me today?" He wrote.

"Only a little," was her reply. Raber smiled to himself and sped all the way to Morgantown.

Two hours later he was pulling up to Tristan's house feeling much more relaxed than he had been in days. He didn't need long with Jordan. It took longer to drive to her than screw her, but he was happy that he'd made the trip. Jordan had been his most steady casual girlfriend and her ambivalence toward him made him strangely comfortable around her.

He sat in his car looking at the tiny house. Andrew's car was still where it was when he'd left. Raber idly wondered if Andrew had been up to mischief while he was gone. Oddly, those thoughts didn't linger. He'd known that once Andrew was made aware that he no longer held all of the power that he would back down, and that was exactly what had happened. He was being a bit too eager to help, but Raber assumed that the threat of having Ioni breathing down his neck was enough to completely reform power-hungry Andrew into a faithful sidekick.

Smiling to himself smugly, Raber sauntered into Tristan's house. He breathed in deeply and wrinkled his nose.

"Hell, it *does* smell in here," he said to no one.

"I know," Andrew said, popping his head out of the kitchen. "We're not very good at being Betty Homemaker over here. Maybe we should open some windows?"

"Yes," Raber said, waving his hands in front of his face, trying to dissipate the stale but heavy odors. "That's nasty."

Raber and Andrew opened all of the windows that they could find and Andrew found a box fan in the basement to move the air around a little bit.

"This place did seem to be in okay shape when I first got here," Andrew said, inhaling deeply. "Maybe she's not a sloppy pig like we are. I wonder if that's something that we can teach her."

"What, to clean? Are you serious?" Raber said.

"Well I sure as shit don't enjoy it," Andrew said unhappily.

"That's sexist of you, my friend," Raber said playfully.

"Hey, man, what's between her legs has nothing to do with it. I'm simply pointing out her proclivity to keep a neat dwelling, that's all."

Raber chuckled and stretched out on the couch. He knew Andrew was looking at him, so he popped open one eye and looked sideways at him.

"What?" Raber asked.

"You're in an awfully good mood,' Andrew observed. "I guess that was a booty call you made?"

"Jordan," Raber answered.

"Nice," Andrew said, a smile on his face. Then, after a moment he added, "You don't think *she'll* get jealous, do you?"

Raber thought for a moment.

"I don't think so," he said at last. "I mean, she isn't a sexual creature, not really. I don't see how she'd give a damn about my smelling like someone else."

Andrew was quiet after that, but Raber thought and worried about it enough to shower again. When it came to a dangerous being like Ioni, he couldn't be too cautious.

At around five o'clock, Andrew placed a savory plate of food in front of him. Confused, Raber looked up at his companion.

"My mom is a great cook," Andrew said. "I used to help her when I lived at home."

"You made a chicken?" Raber asked, looking at his plate with satisfaction, saliva nearly spilling from his mouth.

"Yeah. Roasted. And the veggies are roasted too. It's pretty good." Andrew said.

"Are you joining me?" Raber said carefully.

"Yup," Andrew said, revealing a full plate of his own.

Raber waited for Andrew to start eating before digging in himself. Andrew paid him no attention and began shoveling the food into his mouth. When Raber had seen him eat a little bit of everything, he dug in, too. It was delicious and Raber was sure to tell him as much.

Andrew washed the dishes and then the two sat on the couch watching television for the rest of the afternoon. Darkness fell and the two men perked up when they heard the basement door open. The bathroom door closed a moment later and the shower began running.

"She's a good learner," Andrew said.

"That she is," Raber agreed.

"You want anything from the kitchen?" Andrew asked. "I'm going anyway for a drink."

"No thanks," Raber said.

Ioni came out of the bathroom and took Andrew's spot on the couch next to Raber. Raber reached out and stroked her shining hair absentmindedly.

"Hungry," Ioni whined.

"I've got a surprise for you for dinner tonight, baby," Andrew said, coming out of the kitchen. His hands were behind his back and he was smiling broadly.

Raber looked at Andrew inquiringly, but Andrew just smiled.

Raber became nervous.

Andrew produced a large bowl from behind his back and flung its contents all over Raber and Ioni. Raber, shocked, looked down at himself. Stinking herbs and some sort of sticky liquid was all over him. Andrew was chanting something with his eyes closed. Suddenly, he opened his eyes and walloped Raber in the head with the bowl.

"You're free now," Andrew said to Ioni. "You belong to no one, so why not chow down on this big guy here? He's sure to fill you up! I'll take care of you!"

Ioni, also covered in the sticky, stinking liquid sat staring at Andrew with no emotion on her face.

"What the fuck, Andrew?" Raber shouted.

"I broke your bond, you arrogant cunt!" Andrew screamed. "Now you get to be eaten by your girlfriend while knowing that I'll be taking care of her now! She's mine!"

"The hell you say," Raber said, nearly seeing red through his rage. He looked at Ioni.

"Baby?" he said to her. She turned to him. "Are you still with me?"

"I am," she replied dryly.

"What?" Andrew said, shocked. "No. NO! Bullshit! This was supposed to work and I'm never fucking wrong!"

"Ioni, my darling," Raber said, staring at Andrew.

"Yes?" Ioni asked.

"Will you do your master a massive favor and kill that asshole, please?"

"That's not going to work, Frankenstein!" Andrew screamed, near hysterics. "I still have this!"

Andrew held his arm out and revealed that he still had the yellow nylon rope tied around his wrist. Raber, upon seeing the rope, went into a primally violent state and jumped on Andrew. He was amazed at how easy it was to subdue the smaller man. Raber had always assumed that there would be more fight in him than what he got at that moment.

Raber was screaming as he tackled Andrew and slammed his head into the floor repeatedly. Andrew lay dazed as Raber tore at the rope around his wrist. When Raber had it, he flung it across the room.

"Have fun being dinner, you little shit," Raber breathed into Andrew's face.

As soon as he was off of Andrew, Ioni took his place. She pushed her thumbs into his eye sockets and there was a wet, squishing sound before Andrew started screaming in a high-pitched voice.

"Too much noise!" Raber screamed, panicked.

Before he could say another word, Ioni brought her forearm down onto Andrew's throat in a blindingly quick motion. There was a crunch, and Andrew was silent. Raber saw a small smile on Ioni's lips before she bent her head to Andrew's throat and tore a large chunk of skin away. She lapped greedily at the blood that slowly seeped from the wound and when it stopped flowing freely she sucked.

Raber sat heavily on the couch and watched. It didn't take long for Ioni to drain Andrew and when the deed was complete, she calmly joined Raber on the couch and stared ahead of her. Still the messy eater, her entire front was covered in gore.

"You got more of it on you than in you," he said in a stupor. "We need to go shower and change our clothes."

Without a word, Ioni rose and went into the bathroom. Raber stared at the pale, dead Andrew and wondered what to do with him. He pulled out his amber pill bottle and popped a Codeine. He winced as he dry-swallowed the large pill.

"Well, what in the hell am I going to do with you now?" he asked the dead body. Then he smiled, remembering that Andrew had already come up with a plan for disposing of bodies.

When Raber and Ioni were clean and fresh, they loaded Andrew into the backseat of his own car and drove to the river, close to where Andrew had told Raber that the local drug problem lived. Raber found a soft shoulder right after a large bridge and got out of the car. He looked around cautiously, silently thankful that the stretch of road was quiet.

"Okay," he said to Ioni. "Pull him out and throw him in the water, but make sure he goes into the water, not the bank. Okay?"

Ioni pulled Andrew out of the backseat easily. Raber marveled at her strength as she carried him to the edge and threw him into the center of the moving waters. There was a splash and then nothing. It was dark and there were no streetlights to indicate whether or not Andrew was floating, but Raber was sure that Andrew did not sink.

Raber left Andrew's car with his keys still in the ignition. He wasn't worried about his prints being in the car. It was known that he and Andrew were friends so it wouldn't be odd to find a friend's prints in a car. Raber decided to use Andrew's own idea on what could have possibly happened. He was doing a drug deal out that way and either things ran afoul with the dealer or Andrew wandered into the river in a drugged out daze. He'd give it a few days before calling the authorities. His hope was that he and Ioni would be squatting elsewhere when that happened.

It took nearly an hour to walk back to Tristan's house, but Ioni was a refreshingly silent companion. Raber was confused as to why Andrew's ploy to free Ioni hadn't worked. He'd always been successful with his spells before. Ultimately, he decided to believe that Andrew's low level of intelligence had finally caught up to him, that brutality didn't go hand in hand with meticulous workings. He was a sloppy drug addict and that was that.

When they were safely inside, Raber spared a thought for all of the violent noises that had accompanied Andrew's murder, but an authority figure would have already pounded the door down if someone had heard. Since all was quiet, Raber directed Ioni to sit on the couch while he went to her computer to check emails.

There was one that made his heart jump into his throat.

CHAPTER TWENTY-SEVEN

"Nathan and Arlie came to see me and expressed a deep concern for you. It seems that you are back with Raber, but they say that you are not yourself. Your friends both fear that you are either drugged or being abused and I am here to let you know that your coven has been notified of this and we are here at the ready to help you. If this is not Ioni reading these messages and this is Raber instead, you need to know that Tristan has been notified of this as an elder member of our coven and also the owner of the house you seem to be staying in. Ioni told me about Andrew and when he told me his name this morning, I knew that things were fishy. We demand to see our Ioni either today or tomorrow or we are going to call the authorities and explain that we fear you are wrongfully imprisoning her. Present our sister to us. Bring her to Bedelia's. You are not welcome. That is all."

Sarah's message drained all of the giddiness that Andrew's demise had brought Raber. He sat next to the vampire feeling sticky sweat trickle down his back. His eyeballs thumped in time with his racing pulse and he could feel his stomach acid starting to rise. He buried his face in his hands and pushed in on his eyeballs.

"We're in trouble, baby," he said. "Big, big trouble."

He looked at Ioni, hoping to see some sort of concern for his well-being. If the thing sitting next to him had truly been Ioni, her pale hand would have been gripping his shoulder and her soft face and bright eyes would have been gazing at him in distress. As it was, the creature sitting next to him was completely unaffected by his mood.

Acting on an impulse and hoping to quell his rage, he hit her, an open-palm slap to the face. Her head rocked to the side, but she immediately resumed her gaze. He hit her again. And again. She made absolutely no move to retaliate or even acknowledge that she was being abused. Raber doubled over and groaned. Too much had gone on that night. For the briefest moment he wished Andrew was still around with a needle full of life-silencing heroin.

He popped a Viagra and a random pill, not caring if it killed him, and turned to the unblemished vampire.

"Take off your shirt and bra," he commanded.

As she was complying, he unzipped his pants and pulled himself out, stroking to stiffness. When her still beautiful breasts were bared, she returned to her staring.

"Turn to me. Touch me like I'm touching me," he said.

She turned and watched him for a moment before taking him into her hand. At first her grip was too tight, but she loosened up when he told her to. When she seemed to get the hang of it, he reached out and stroked the breast closest to him, laying his head back and closing his eyes. After he came, she resumed staring at the television, his ejaculate on her hand.

"Go wash your hands and bring me a towel," he said. She complied silently.

He fell asleep not long after and awoke with the sun on his face. She was gone, back to her stiff death in the basement.

All alone in the house of another man, Raber had time to start worrying about all that had gone on the night before. Andrew's demise, Ioni's coven finding out about what he had done, it all weighed heavily on him.

"Those idiots wouldn't know a vampire if it bit them in the ass," he said at last, laughing to himself.

He reasoned that Ioni's coven-siblings were so awash in their own self-righteousness that they wouldn't be able to fathom true magic, be it white, black, or chaotic. They would assume, like her stupid friends, that she was on drugs, but there was no proof of that. On the off chance that they happened to suspect the truth, they wouldn't know what to do about it. He laughed to himself again.

How does one report to the authorities the existence of a vampire? How does a group of small town weirdos go about the destruction of a practitioner of the powerful magic and his minion? They wouldn't, that's how. They were supposed to turn their lily-assed backs to black magic, as they called it, and not even acknowledge the practitioner. He relaxed, knowing that he was safe.

Since there was no Andrew to entertain him during the day, Raber nosed around Tristan's home. He found Ioni's wooden chest where she kept her altar. He assembled it and lit the white candle. He performed an ablution with the sea salt that she kept in a small glass bottle and some water.

"Oh great goddess, please watch over me and your stupid cow that I made into my slave," Raber said, his hands over his head.

"She wasn't strong enough or smart enough to resist me, *great goddess*," he continued. "If only you were actually real and actually protected your stupid cows, maybe she would be the girl that I loved instead of a dead thing wearing her beautiful skin. If only she weren't so entrenched in your stupid group, if only she didn't feel so attached to that tree. If only she didn't trust me. Well, great goddess, I took her and she's mine. I don't know if I'll keep her. She's more trouble than she's worth. I wanted her so I could possess her and fuck her, but the fucking isn't all that fun. Aside from that, though, I've got a treasure. I've made a true blue, through and through vampire. You don't throw away a treat like that. I just won't try to fuck her anymore, that's all. And if anybody does try to take her from me, I'll use all that Andrew taught me to punish them. Through Andrew and his knowledge, I found the power and control and self-preservation that I'd always wanted. I am powerful. Nobody can take from me what is mine so long as I wish to keep it."

He then blew out the white candle and flipped the small altar, flinging the ritualistic garbage all over the room. He used his large foot to stomp the table to splinters. Panting, he went to the kitchen for a cold drink. Feeling less tense, he picked up Ioni's phone and sent a text to Sarah.

"Tonight at nine o'clock," was all the text read.

He got into his car and went to his parents' house. His mother was at home, but his father was at work. She greeted him at the door with an air of cold civility.

"Hello, Raber, honey," she said. "I wondered if we'd see you again this summer."

She looked him over coolly, much like Ioni has started doing at the end of their relationship.

"You're awfully pale and thin," she observed. "Can I get you something to eat?"

"No, thank you," Raber said, returning the polite but distant attitude. "I'm just here for all of my belongings. I'll be going after."

"Going?" his mother asked.

"Yes. I won't be returning to school, so don't bother sending a check. I'll be leaving the state tomorrow and I doubt you'll hear from me again."

"Raber," she said, concern actually creeping into her voice. "What on earth are you talking about?"

Raber pulled out his wallet and removed the two credit cards and debit card that his parents had given him. He threw them carelessly on the console table in the entryway of their cold, showpiece home.

"I won't be in touch. Our time together has ended. I won't be around to ignore any more. Goodbye."

"Raber, stop it!" his mother said, her voice shaky. "You're taking drugs! You've gotten into some kind of trouble! Honey, your father has connections! We can help you! We love you, don't you know that?"

Raber laughed.

"It's a bit late for that, Mother," he said. "I never knew love until Ioni came along. You've never been anything to me but a money and food dispensary. Now I'm taking my things and I'm gone."

"You can't just do that," she replied. "You can't just disappear. There are ways to find you. There are ways to restrain you. There are ways to make you clean, get you off of whatever it is you're on. What makes you think that your father and I would allow this?"

"This is boring me, Mother," he said. "And so unlike you. Whenever did I become indispensable to you? I'm very much unafraid of you and Dad doing anything to stop me. It would just be another bother. You can stop with the posturing now. There's nothing to gain from this relationship, so I'm going. If you try to stop me or threaten me again, I will harm you, do you understand?"

She stared at him, her face white with shock and her mouth agape. He smiled, went to his room, and packed everything that meant anything to him. There wasn't much. It took him only an hour to pack and load his car. As he was dragging the last armload out, his mother stood at the door. She spoke softly to him as he walked past her.

"I have always loved you," she whispered, tears making even the air in her words sound thick.

He slammed the door in her face and drove back to Tristan's house.

He showered and dressed in all black. He carefully applied eyeliner and put silver in all of his piercings. He felt powerful and alive.

He'd hooked up his own computer in Tristan's living room and he was fiddling on it when he heard Ioni go into the bathroom. He was looking into cheap motels that rent by the week in North Carolina. He figured that he could get an hourly job for money and let Ioni sleep in the bathtub during the day. By night she could prey on the human garbage while he made himself available in a place that would provide an alibi. When things started getting suspicious, they would move on to the next town. He would learn what he could and try to find a way to make a living from his experience and knowledge in dark magic. He had a couple of Andrew's notebooks that he had taken from his trunk before abandoning the car by the road, although THE book that Andrew always talked of wasn't there, which was a huge disappointment. There was unlimited promise in the book that had contained the spell that made Ioni what she was, but Raber was confident in his own knowledge and abilities.

Raber had also started considering how lucrative some people might find Ioni to be. She was fast, lethal, and one hundred percent compliant. Other practitioners of the dark arts might be willing to pay for her assistance. Hell, some people might even be willing to pay just to meet her.

"Everything's coming up Milhouse," he said, smiling. With Andrew and his incessant buzzing gone, Raber was finally able to think clearly.

He smiled at his beautiful vampire when she emerged from Tristan's bedroom. Her hair was shining and beautiful, her dark, heavy makeup brought out the deepness of her blue eyes, and her luscious lips glimmered from the gloss applied to them.

"You're going to a party tonight, my darling," he said. "We need to accessorize a bit more than that."

He took her cool hand and led her back to the bedroom. He put rings on all of her fingers, slipped long, silver-looking earrings in her ears and clasped her pentagram necklace onto her. It was good that none of her jewelry was real silver.

If she had smiled at him, she would have looked as she had the first time he laid eyes on her. He leaned down and kissed the nape of her neck.

"I love you so much. Now listen to me carefully. I'm taking you to see some people, and I can't come in with you. You're going to answer some questions for them. Be honest and be sweet. Don't hurt anybody and I'll take you out for a special treat after. I'm sure you're hungry."

"Hungry," she whined.

"Yes, sweetheart," he cooed, stroking her hair. "I know. And we're done with that ridiculous animal-eating stuff. I'm not going to smother your instincts or your marvelous essence by trying to tame you. You will eat what comes naturally for you to eat. Just not the people at this party, okay?"

"Okay," she replied.

"There's no need to be afraid of these people. They are weak. Even if they figure out what is really going on, they are powerless to do anything about it, and we'll leave tomorrow and be safe. It might be good for them to know my power. They would know that it's best to forget that either of us ever existed."

She made no reply. He smiled and kissed her cheek.

"Come on then, precious. It's time to make your debut to your coven."

He drove her to Bedelia's. His stomach clenched inside of him when he saw all of the cars. He recognized Nathan's car and he actually gasped when he recognized Ioni's father's car.

"Well, hell," he said, grasping his chest. Her parents were there. That made things a bit more complicated. Like his own parents, hers were the absent type, but they still play-acted that they were a happy, close family. He looked at Ioni and remembered how she had defended him to Nathan and Arlie. She would handle it. She was cunning.

276

"We're okay. This will be okay," he said. He opened her door. Knowing that people were surely watching from inside the house, he turned her to face him.

"Kiss me," he said. Without hesitation, she leaned in and kissed him. It was a quick kiss, but not so quick that it looked forced.

"I'll be right here when it's over," he said, stroking her hair.

"Okay," she said. She walked to the front door and knocked.

Karen opened the door and made a show of glaring at Raber before standing aside so Ioni could enter. She didn't move. Raber frowned before pure panic struck him.

She had to be invited inside.

Karen looked at Ioni crossly. He heard her speak, and Ioni didn't move.

"Ioni, *come in*," Karen said, exasperated, loud enough for Raber to hear.

Ioni complied. Raber sat back and rubbed his temples.

He wiped the sweat from the back of his neck and wondered why she needed to be invited into Bedelia's, but not Tristan's house. It was a good thing, because they would be living out of cars otherwise. Had he invited her into Tristan's house that first night? He was so keyed up he couldn't remember. It wasn't important. Not really.

An hour and a half later Ioni walked out of the house. She walked straight to the car and got in as commanded. Raber started the car and looked back up at Bedelia's. Everybody was standing in the yard staring at them. Karen and Sarah were holding hands. Nathan and Arlie were whispering to each other. Ioni's father was walking toward him. Raber considered driving away before he got there, but decided against it. He had nothing to fear. If she had been honest, they knew that she was committed to him whether they liked it or not.

He rolled down his window and looked up into her father's face.

"You bastard," her father said quietly. "Whatever you've done to her, this will not stand. I know my daughter. She had plans for her future. She was excited about her prospects. Now all she wants is to be with you. No more school, no more work, and no more Wicca. If it's drugs, or you're beating her, this will end."

"I'm not drugging or hitting the one I love," Raber said. "What you are failing to see here is that she is with me because she wants to be with me. The girl you thought you knew had a lot of secrets. How long ago did you learn about her Wiccan playdates? Today? She only showed you the side of herself that would please you the most."

"Oh, so now instead of living to please me, she's moved on to living to please you?" Her father said, rage obvious even in his soft tone.

"Yes," Raber said, smiling.

"Fuck you," her father seethed. "You give my daughter far too little credit. She may have had self-esteem issues, but she knew her own mind and never let anyone else push or pull her too far from her own center. Not even you."

"And yet here we are," Raber said.

Her father turned and walked back to the group on the lawn. Raber drove away.

"They told me to give you a message," Ioni said, before he could start interrogating her.

"The man on the screen said that we need to stay where we are until he comes back so that if we did anything destructive to his property, they wouldn't need to scry for our location to extract payment. The older lady said to tell you that you're not as smart as you think you are." She relayed this quickly and with no inflection. It was the most she had said in a single breath since her rebirth.

"The man on the screen...I guess he used a webcam or something. What did he look like?" He knew the answer.

"He had darker skin. Big ears," she replied.

278

Raber smirked. She didn't remember *him* either.

"What do you see when you look at me?" he asked, suddenly curious how she saw him.

The vampire took a moment to look at him before returning her eyes to the forward position.

"Bald. Tall. Sickly."

He frowned and wondered at her describing him as sickly. The simplistic way she described him as tall and bald would have bothered him alone, but sickly?

"I am not sickly," he said defensively.

"You are not well," she replied.

"I am strong!"

"Not physically," she said.

He clenched his teeth and decided to change the subject.

"What kinds of questions did they ask you?"

"They didn't ask many," she began. "A woman asked me if I was in my right mind and I said yes. They looked at my eyes and I didn't attack anybody. Another woman kept asking me to eat and I said no every time. The man on the screen didn't talk except to give me the message for you. They looked at me more than they talked to me."

Raber bit the inside of his cheek, thinking. Could they suspect? Andrew had said that it had been at least a century since anybody had performed that particular spell. Certainly they were unaware of what Ioni had become. Considering their no-tolerance policy toward practitioners of black magic, he was sure that they had never seen a spell like the one used to make Ioni.

They must have still been chasing after the theory that he was drugging her. Her eerie eyes certainly supported that theory. Her lack of appetite for traditional food did as well.

He drove past the exit that would have taken them back to Tristan's house. He drove past downtown and toward the town's one and only big park. The park was always clean and sightly during the day but at night, even in a small town like that, there were always a handful of homeless people.

He parked on the street and opened Ioni's door for her. He held a hand out to her and she took it obediently. They walked back to the trunk of the car and Raber took out his long black coat and a pack of wet wipes. He draped the coat over one arm and offered the other to Ioni. She slid her hand in the nook and he kissed her cool cheek.

"I promised you dinner, I believe," he said, smiling.

"Hungry," she whined.

"I know, baby," he said soothingly. "Raber's going to take good care of you."

They walked through the always open gate and started strolling around the perimeter of the tidy park. Raber was starting to get annoyed at the lack of other humans when they happened upon a young couple sitting on a blanket. They had heard Raber and Ioni approaching and were sitting up looking disheveled and embarrassed. Raber smiled at them.

"It's okay," he said to them, holding a hand up before him. "We're not the cops or anything. Feel free to resume the hanky-panky."

The young man laughed and waved, looking relieved. He didn't know that he should have been relieved because Raber had an iron grip on Ioni's wrist so that she wouldn't lunge at the lovers. Her entire body was tense and leaning menacingly in their direction, and Raber knew that if she weren't bound to be obedient to him by magic, those two young canoodlers would have been dead before they knew it. He couldn't have citizens of the city dying randomly. A homeless person wouldn't be seen as very valuable in comparison to a couple of clean-cut kids. They walked on.

They found what they were looking for sitting on the grass, her back propped against a trash can. She was much older and there wasn't but a single tooth in her head. Since it was so warm out, she was wearing a strange shift dress and long socks. She was cinching and un-cinching the dress, talking to it. When she saw Raber and Ioni approaching, she blinked at them once and continued with her dress.

"Go eat, darling," Raber whispered into the vampire's ear.

Ioni was gone from his side in a rush of air. The woman began screaming, her nearly toothless mouth open wide. Ioni crammed her hand into the woman's mouth and down her throat. The screaming was replaced with a choking sound and Raber nearly gagged when Ioni's fingers burst out through the woman's throat. She didn't die immediately but instead started choking on her own blood, her eyes bulging from their sockets. Ioni kept a strong grip on her to lessen the struggling. When the sickening, airy, choking sounds stopped and the woman was still, Ioni attached her mouth to the ragged hole in her throat. Raber put a hand over his mouth and closed his eyes when he heard the sound of Ioni's sucking come through the dead woman's open mouth, the air moving from opening to opening. When it seemed that Ioni wasn't getting much from the hole, she repositioned the dirty woman on her lap and used her sharp teeth to bite into the side of her neck. Since the heart was stopped, there was no great rush of blood, but as Ioni sucked noisily, it seemed that she had found a juicy source.

When the woman was dried out, Ioni tossed the body aside and stood, covered in gore and looking nearly happy. Raber took a step toward her, opening the pack of wet wipes, but when he got a good whiff of the blood and the dirty woman, he gagged again. He stepped back and tossed the wet wipes to the ground at Ioni's feet.

"Clean the blood off of you with those and throw them in the trash can," he commanded.

She obeyed silently. Her face was not nearly as messy as her arms. There were strips of meat on her fingers where she had forced them through the woman's throat. Twelve wet wipes later, she was looking mostly clean. Raber handed her his large coat and put an arm around her, his nose wrinkling at the smell of her.

"You'll need to shower when we get back to that man's house," he said, annoyed. "I wonder if you can't learn to be a neater eater. You never were, though. You've always been messy."

She said nothing.

"We'll do what your stupid coven wants. We'll stay at his house until he comes back. It might be for his ego to personally show up and throw us out. He probably wants to break up with you in person as well. *You* get to be dumped this time. That won't be nearly as satisfying for him. You're all mine now and he means less than nothing to you unless you're hungry." He looked at her. She was nearly as tall as he was. He had always liked that about her. Jordan was much shorter and while it made him feel a great power over her, it didn't feel right, like Ioni did. The intimacy came easier with her.

"Do you know what your coven is? Do you know about Wicca or magic?" Raber asked.

"No," she said flatly.

Raber frowned. She wasn't going to be much use in the two-sided conversation department. He decided not to dwell on that. He kept talking so that he wouldn't focus on her smell or remembering the sound of the air sucking into the dead woman's mouth.

"Those people are Wiccans who live a life of servitude to an imaginary deity. You used to pray at that ridiculous altar. But me? I serve only myself. The power that comes from magic, the elements, and pure strength of will is best served in practical purposes like self-preservation, not stupid goddess worship. But even so, those people do possess a power that I would be stupid to not be at least a little worried about. We want to leave this place clean of them so that we can disappear. We don't need them scrying for us or putting the authorities on us. So we'll stay put until that Tristan can throw us out. We've got nothing but time for us, now."

CHAPTER TWENTY-EIGHT

The next two days, Raber laid low and made Ioni stay put in the house. She drained all of the rats that Andrew had bought, but continued to whine about being hungry. Raber lost his temper and hit her. It was unsatisfying because she never reacted, she just kept saying she was hungry.

Raber depleted the contents of his amber pill bottle and barely ate. He thought briefly about cleaning the house so that Tristan wouldn't have much to complain about, but decided against it.

"Fuck him if he thinks I'm going to be his maid," he mumbled to himself.

On the third night, there was a knock at the door. Tristan, Nathan, and Arlie stood on the small stoop looking up at Raber.

"I don't like having to knock on my own door," Tristan said, his voice deep and smooth. Raber swallowed, trying to contain his rage.

Before stepping aside to let them in, he turned quickly to Ioni, who was sitting on the couch and mouthed the words "don't hurt these people" at her. She nodded slightly. Her attention had been pointedly focused on the people at the door. She was very hungry and Raber hoped that his pull on her would hold long enough for them to get out of town before she killed again.

The trio walked into the house. Tristan and Nathan were focused on Ioni but Arlie was glaring at Raber. Raber glared back.

"Problem?" He asked her.

"Not at all," Arlie said to him through clenched teeth.

"Then quit trying to stare holes into my head," he shot back, hotly.

Nathan and Tristan were standing in front of Ioni, looking down at her. She was looking at Raber placidly, ignoring them. He shifted nervously from foot to foot, wishing that he had known they were coming so that he wouldn't have felt so thrown off.

Tristan was shaking his head, looking down at her. Raber was certain he was going to start lecturing Ioni, but instead he turned his head and looked at the wall. Nathan's eyes never left her. He looked tense, ready for a fight.

"Why so many people?" he asked them. "Did you think I would refuse to leave quietly? Most of my stuff is in my car. I'll leave Ioni's car parked here and her dad can come get it. We only need my car. It'll take me five maybe ten minutes to finish packing and get out of here."

He started to walk back to Tristan's bedroom but decided that he didn't want to leave them alone with Ioni. He didn't trust that her hunger wouldn't get the best of her with him out of sight. He held a hand out to her, silently beckoning her to come with him.

"No, that's okay," Nathan said, stepping between Raber and Ioni. "Let us say goodbye to her."

"She wants to come with me," Raber said angrily.

"She wants to say goodbye to her best friends and Tristan," Arlie shot back.

"She has nothing to say to *him*," Raber said, seething.

"Yes, she does," Tristan said, looking away from the wall finally. "She has some meaningful things to say to me that have absolutely nothing to do with you. We're letting you go. We're letting you take her away from us. I suggest you learn a bit of gratitude, pack your things and get out of my home."

Knowing he had no footing in that argument, Raber looked at Ioni in a significant way, hoping she understood to not disobey him and walked to the back room. Almost immediately he could hear hushed voices. Ioni's was among them. They were actually getting her to talk. He wanted to listen in, but knew that they were expecting him to be finished with his packing quickly.

Raber began sweating profusely, the stress of the situation kept mounting out of his control. He was carelessly throwing their belongings into one of his duffle bags, going as fast as he could. When he'd slung the bag over his shoulder, he practically ran into the living room.

Nathan and Arlie were sitting on the couch next to Ioni and Tristan was still standing in front of her. Arlie was crying and Nathan was so pale that he was almost translucent.

"You said your goodbyes," Raber said. He turned to Tristan. "And I assume that you can see that your house is mostly still intact. Now we're done with each other."

"You're not very smart, are you? My mother was right." Tristan said.

"What?" Raber asked, fury building fast and lapping logic.

"All of that flowery talk, all of that bragging about your superiority," Nathan began. "You're so full of yourself that you aren't even self-aware enough to know you're an idiot. I'm guessing that Andrew person was the detail guy."

"Was," Raber said. "What the fuck are you going on about?"

"Have you watched the news at all? Read a fucking newspaper?" Arlie screamed.

"Dead people aren't rare in this town," Tristan began. "But three people drained of their blood in quick succession is completely unheard of. Oh, and dead and drained pigs? Nice of you to make it easier to figure it out. After the coven got a good look at her and knowing that her behavior was completely different, it wasn't hard to see that you had done something to her. Something dark."

Raber began laughing. He couldn't stop himself. He heard his high-pitched, manic cackling and knew he was near hysterics. Not knowing what else to do, he slapped himself. Nathan and Arlie were aghast, staring at him with their mouths wide open. Tristan glared at him levelly.

"I guess it's just my luck that your pussy coven shies away from that kind of power." Raber said.

"Don't underestimate the love that we all have for that girl," Tristan said fiercely. "Don't you dare. What we do, we do out of love for her."

"So you plan to do something?" Raber said, dropping his bag and taking a wide stance. "And what is your plan of action, you craven sack of skin? Just how much do you love my fucking girlfriend?"

"She broke up with you, you fucking psycho!" Arlie shouted, bolting up from the couch.

Nathan was up and had his arms locked around her, holding her back. He whispered something in her ear and she calmed down. When they resumed their seats next to his vampire, Raber returned his gaze to Tristan who never took his eyes off of Raber.

"You don't know enough of what I've done to help her," Raber said.

"You're wrong," Tristan said. "I know exactly what to do."

He hit Raber and everything went black.

Raber awoke in the backseat of a car. Ioni was sitting next to him, serene and still. He groaned and rubbed his jaw. It was swollen and his head hurt terribly.

"I guess you've taken some sort of fighting class to know how to knock someone out like that," Raber said sourly.

"I've taken a few," Tristan said.

"Aren't you the hypocrite?" Raber said. "A peace-loving hippie taking classes that teach you how to inflict harm on your fellow man."

"It's good exercise," Tristan said, shrugging. "And it teaches mental focus. A good Wiccan knows mental focus."

"How nice. We're suddenly best buddies," Raber said. "Want to compare sexual experiences with Ioni? I know when she was with me, she was all about oral sex. I can't tell you how many times my dick was in her mouth. Could you taste it when you kissed her?"

"How unlike you, Raber. I thought you were better than that. As it is, I'm not going to play into this childish game," Tristan said.

Raber snorted and slumped back into the seat.

Nathan was driving. Arlie sat between Nathan and Tristan in the front seat of some car he didn't recognize. He looked at Ioni and stroked her hair. She turned her head and looked at him briefly.

"Why didn't she attack you? She didn't try to defend me?" Raber asked.

"Oh, she did," Tristan said. "She's plenty strong, too, but we're three of us here and she was only one. It was a struggle but we subdued her."

Raber really looked at Ioni and saw that her hands and feet were tied with a yellow nylon rope similar to the one he had used the night he transformed her.

"We got it from the trunk of your car," Tristan said, watching him. "It's not the piece you used to kill her, but it's from the same roll. We didn't want her screaming and whimpering the whole ride."

Raber's vision went totally black with panic and he stopped breathing as the anxiety choked him. His hands flew to his throat and he doubled over, trying to calm down. When the initial wave passed, he focused on his breathing.

"That's right," Tristan said seriously. "I know. She may not remember what you did, but she heard plenty of what you and Andrew said and was very obliging in relaying that information to me with the help of a small incantation. You see, you monster, her coven and I have been working tirelessly making phone calls, writing emails and reading every piece of information we could find on vampires. We got very lucky."

"I thought your kind wanted no part in dark magic. Why would you know about something like that unless you're liars as well as hypocrites?"

"No, no, we want no doings with *practitioners* of black magic. We do, however, find it useful from time to time to keep a record of things we come across that your kind does. It's not a collection that we let just anybody see, you know. There's danger in chronicling what black magic brings about. Even a small amount of curiosity or apathy toward the dangers of going dark can be disastrous because someone can be easily impressed or romanced by those things. It takes a strong constitution to be able to see what black magic can do and not want to try it for yourself." Tristan said.

"I'm fairly certain that you just back-handedly called me weak," Raber said.

"Oh, I'm sorry," Tristan returned. "I thought that it was pretty palm-side of the hand. I see the blow to the head must have slowed your thinking, so let me be clear: it makes me sad that someone as spineless and unsure of themselves as you was ever a part of Ioni's life. It makes me sick that you tricked her into seeing anything in you that was valuable or worth her heart. You are and always will be a scared little boy who likes to pretend that you're a superhero, or in your sad case, a supervillain."

"Those are some pretty big words for a guy who's supposed to ignore my very existence," Raber said.

"I was happy to do just that until you started attacking members of my coven and wreaking havoc on my hometown.

But really, I'm not someone you need to worry about. I'm bound by my beliefs to not inflict any real harm on you. There's no way for you to answer to me or my coven for what you've done." Tristan said.

"Then why in the hell am I being kidnapped?" Raber yelled, tired of the all-too civil back and forth.

"Look out the window and see if you can guess where we're driving," Nathan said.

Raber looked out of the window and at first saw only dark and trees. Then a familiar turn of road, a prognostication of landmarks ahead, and he knew where they were going.

"She remembered this place?" he asked, shocked.

"Her memory since her murder is actually quiet flawless," Tristan answered.

"I call it the night of her transformation or rebirth," Raber said, smiling. "Of course you would call it a murder. She's not dead. She's sitting here next to me wishing that I would give her permission to drain one of you. She's quite alive."

"You're so delusional," Arlie said.

"Selfish," Nathan added.

"She broke up with me!" Raber screamed.

"My, my, I wonder why," Nathan said in a singsong voice.

"I know you two had her ear and didn't help matters. I also know you were sniffing around her pretty aggressively, you piece of garbage," Raber snarled, jutting his chin at Tristan. "The three of you turned her against me. So this? This is your fault. You couldn't just let her be happy. All that time that she was lonely while her supposed best friends rubbed her nose in their relationships. And then I came along and made her happy. I loved her and lifted her up!"

"You did at first," Arlie said quietly.

"That doesn't matter," Nathan said, hotly. "You could have been the best thing that ever happened to her at one time, but look at her now. You are the worst thing to ever walk into that girl's life, end of story."

"Not end of story!" Raber yelled. "I got her back and made myself her everything!"

"That's about to change," Tristan said.

Raber laughed.

"Andrew already tried that. As you can assume, that didn't work out too well for him."

"Hmm," Tristan said. "It's a shame he didn't have my connections."

The last few minutes of the ride were silent. Raber was trying to get his wits about him so that he could get away. He debated throwing all caution to the wind and putting the hungry vampire on them, but he still wanted to leave town quietly and cleanly. He debated taking them on physically, but Ioni's assertion that he was sickly bothered him. Intellectually, he knew that she was right. The long and hard drug use, mixed with a sporadic and poor diet, had taken a toll on his young body. Emotionally, it was hard for him to admit to any weakness.

The car stopped and pulled off of the single-lane dirt road about twenty yards before the crossroads. The three in the front seat all got out and went around to the door closest to Ioni. Raber considered bolting. He wasn't tied up and if he hit tree cover, in the dark, he had a great chance of evading them. He took a moment to look over at Ioni, her wrists and ankles bound. She was his and they knew that he wouldn't leave her with them. His mind raced with the options before him. He could run away, leave Ioni for the time being and retrieve her later. He could also cut all of his losses and just leave and not give a damn about what happened to Ioni. Or he could do a Hail Mary and come out swinging, do the heroic rescue of his vampire-lady-fair and steal their car and get out of town.

His ego was inclined toward the latter. Too many things could go wrong if he left Ioni with them. They might kill her, or cure her, or possibly even take her to the police. If Tristan had been able to use an incantation to get her to talk to him, surely he would be able to get her to talk to the police and implicate Raber in the dead bodies found in town.

When the door opened and hands gently grasped his vampire and lifted her from the car, Raber opened his own door and ran around to the other side. He encountered Arlie first. He punched her in the face and grabbed her by the neck. He spun her around so that she was facing her companions and held her to him. With his hand still around her throat, he began squeezing.

"Let her go!" Nathan screamed.

"A trade, then," Raber said, panting.

Tristan was standing behind Nathan, holding Ioni close to him, the way one might hold a child. She couldn't stand on her own, tied up as she was. There was affection in the way he was touching her and Raber became enraged. He squeezed Arlie's throat tighter. She thrashed in panic and Nathan ran at him. Raber turned and Nathan nearly missed, but he was able to grab Arlie as he tripped and fell, pulling her down with him. Raber turned to face them, looking down at the two sitting on the ground. Arlie was coughing and wheezing and Nathan was rubbing her throat.

"You sick motherfucker," Nathan said, looking up at him.

Raber took a moment to smirk at Nathan before turning to find Tristan. Tristan was already on him. Raber yelped in surprise and Tristan had his arm twisted up behind his back. Raber screamed, feeling that the tendons and ligaments in his shoulders would snap if he moved.

"I don't want to have to knock you out again," Tristan said, right into his ear. "You just calm down and do what I tell you to do." Tristan gave Raber's arm a violent jerk to send his point home.

Raber gritted his teeth and complied. He let Tristan walk him to where Ioni was sitting quietly, still bound by the yellow cord. Tristan released Raber and picked up Ioni, holding her close to him.

"Follow me. Don't make me chase you." Tristan said to Raber.

Raber followed as they walked to the center of the crossroads. Tristan gently sat Ioni down on the road and instructed Raber to sit about a foot away from her, also in the middle of the crossroads. Tristan stood over them quietly, waiting.

Nathan and Arlie came not long after, their arms loaded with bags and supplies. Raber smiled. He didn't fear their magic. If Andrew couldn't break him and Ioni apart with magic, there was no way that those idiots could do it.

They had six candles. Five of them were white. They were placed around Raber and Ioni in the five points of a pentagram and were lit. Then a yellow candle was set between and slightly in front of them. Tristan anointed the candle with oil before he lit it. Then Nathan handed Tristan a length of the yellow cord. Raber tensed. The noose at the end was still on it, he hadn't bothered to untie it. Tristan did what he didn't, he untied it right then and there, a sad look on his face. He then took one end and tied it around Raber's midsection. He pulled the cord tight and tied the other end around Ioni in a similar fashion. Ioni winced and whimpered, pulling away from the rope. Tristan looked up at Nathan and Nathan knelt down and held Ioni still as the rope was tied around her. Raber started squirming. The sounds coming from his vampire were pulling on every nerve within him.

When Raber and Ioni were joined by the yellow cord, Ioni whimpering the whole time, Tristan began with the circumambulation. He went counter-clockwise, or widdershins, Raber noted. He was performing a banishing ceremony, and Raber smiled. Tristan pulled out a pair of gardening shears and set them beside him as he knelt before the yellow candle. Tristan meditated on the flame of the yellow candle for an agonizingly long moment.

Still kneeling, he lifted his arms to the sky.

"Great goddess, hear my cries and favor my endeavor, I beseech you," Tristan said. "Here, in your place of power, hear me and save your child. Forgive my crossing of lines and help me to be strong. Lady, come with your dogs and your light and your goodness and help me, I beg of you."

Tristan stood and walked before Ioni. He held his hands out and over her, his eyes closed.

"I free you from your bonds.

"I call you to remember.

"You will remember pain and death."

Then Tristan poured a small amount of oil into the palm of his hand. He knelt before Ioni and rubbed the oil on her smooth cheeks. Ioni, still whimpering over the cord touching her, seemed not to notice. Tristan kept his face close to her and said the next bit of the spell softly.

"My love frees.

"My love kills.

"My love breaks the bond."

He stood again and picked up the gardening shears.

"Ioni, I call on you to draw breath and remember!"

Tristan cut the yellow cord and Ioni stopped whimpering and began screaming.

CHAPTER TWENTY-NINE

Throat raw and bleeding, she was screaming in pain and from the flood of memories slamming into her brain. Her whole body hurt. She was so very hungry. All the horrible things she had done...

She was still bound by the cord wrapped around her middle and her hands and feet were still tied up. Panting, she looked up at Tristan, who was looking down at her, a question in his eyes.

"It's me," she said to him.

Arlie started sobbing and Nathan wiped tears from his cheeks. Tristan sighed in relief and let his head hang down low for a minute. She watched as his eyes shifted to a place beside her. She followed his gaze and found Raber's white face. His eyes were wide and he was panting.

"I told you that you didn't have to worry about answering to me," Tristan said to Raber. "But that's not to mean that you could come out of this unscathed. You have to answer to *her.*" Tristan punctuated the last word by pointing the gardening sheers at Ioni.

"What have you done to her?" Raber snarled, panic still glistening in his eyes.

"I gave her back to herself," Tristan said, smiling. "She's still what you made her, she's just not tied to you anymore. And," Tristan walked close to Raber and bent so that his nose was almost touching Raber's. "She has all of her memories."

Raber swallowed hard. Ioni watched all of this quietly. She looked at Nathan and Arlie holding on to each other. She looked at Tristan, disconsolate and stalking about with a gardening tool in his grasp. She looked at Raber.

"Untie me," she said simply. "Then move away from me, Tristan."

"Ha!" Raber said a little too loudly. "See that? She doesn't want you after all!"

"No," Ioni said. "I don't. I want you, Raber. I'll untie you when I'm untied, baby."

Tristan untied her and stepped back, holding the shears before him in a defensive posture. Ioni stood and looked long at Tristan, her stomach rumbling.

"Just stay back," she said to him, softly.

She knelt down by Raber and gently freed him of the cord. When he was free, she held a hand out to him and helped him to his feet. She smiled at him, a gesture once meant to be sweet, but most of the people around her knew to be wary of a vampire baring their teeth. *Most* of the people knew that.

"Our bond is too strong to break," Raber said over her head to the people behind her.

Ioni stroked his cheeks and then moved down to the sides of his neck. Quickly, before Raber could entertain the thought of danger, her hands had a tight grip on his throat. Raber, shocked, clawed at her hands, and she marveled at how weak he was compared to her. She applied more pressure to the front of his throat with her thumbs and he fell to his knees before her.

"You killed me," she said to him. "And you used me. I'm dead. I am a monster. I have killed because of you!"

She moved her face down, completely intent on ripping at his throat with her teeth and draining him when she heard Tristan scream at her.

"NO, IONI, DON'T!"

Listening to the voice that she trusted, she used all of her willpower to pull her face back. Her hands were still locked around Raber's throat and his eyes were bulging.

"Ease up," Tristan said, not moving any closer to her.

"You know what he did," Ioni croaked, rage cracking her voice. "Everything I have, everything I am is lost because of him."

"Ioni, I'm not going to stop you from exacting revenge or justice on him. I'm not. But I need you to think about how things need to look when bodies are found. Think really hard. Look at me." Tristan pleaded.

She lessened her grip on Raber's throat so that he could breathe and turned to look at Tristan, a trusted person. Someone she could have loved. But all such possibilities were lost to her.

"Are you his accomplice or his victim? Don't answer. *Think*. Are you going to go on or stop? *Think*. Don't live in the moment on this one. Stop and think. Do you understand what I'm trying to tell you?"

Confused, Ioni shook her head.

"Listen carefully," Tristan said, intensity making his speech clipped. "Do you intend to survive this? Do you want him to be lumped into the same category as the other victims? Be smart about this. Make it so it is known who the real villain is here."

Ioni felt an idea begin to take root. She understood what Tristan was getting at. She tilted Raber's head so that he was looking into her face. His breathing was shallow, but there was nothing fatal happening to him just then.

"You're what's wrong with the world, you know," she said to him. "You couldn't just enjoy me and love me. No. You had to possess me. I was never a person to you, I was a thing. And when the thing dared to have a mind of its own, you felt that you were well within your rights to go to whatever lengths to put it in its place."

Raber opened his mouth as if to speak and Ioni squeezed his throat so that the only sound he made was a choked squeak. Her mouth gave an involuntary suck in his direction, the violence and close proximity to hot blood nearly wiping away her ability to think.

"You've spoken more than enough," she said to him. "I'm not interested in hearing your lies anymore, Raber. I've already failed to survive this." She turned her head and looked at Tristan, Nathan, and Arlie.

"I'm already dead." she said.

Raber made another choking noise and Ioni returned her attention to him.

"You draw your last breath tonight," she said to him. "And I'll end my own horrible existence and hope that any afterlife will forgive me of the horrible things that I've done with you. But I will also make sure that it looks like you killed me and then yourself. Do you understand? In death, you will be known for the monster that you are. You're not powerful, you're not some great mastermind. You're just some overpuffed twerp who throws an egomaniac's version of a temper tantrum when you're told 'no' and you deserve no better than what I'm going to give you. May the goddess erase our disgusting visages from these clean people's memories."

She turned and looked at Nathan and Arlie.

"Go get his car and make sure that the ladder is still with it. Bring it back here and park it right by the center of these crossroads."

"Ioni," Nathan began.

"No," Tristan said. "Please do as she says and be as fast as you can."

Without another word, Nathan and Arlie both sprinted off toward the rental car. Ioni let her gaze linger on Tristan.

"We all knew it would probably come to this," Tristan said to her.

"And the coven?" she asked.

Raber started to squirm but she squeezed lightly and shook him until he was still.

"Mom, Freya, Adare, and Mike all know about this. Your father, well he's not a believer. He thinks you're being drugged. We rose up to save you because you're one of us." Tristan said.

"And you?" Ioni asked him.

"I love you," he said simply. "I just wish I could have saved you completely."

"You did enough," she said. "Thank you. And make sure you thank Karen, Freya, Mike, and Sarah for me. Tell them that I knew of their help. Tell them that it touched me."

"It will take weeks to purify our circle," Tristan said. "But the goddess showed us that we needed to help her servant. We prayed and meditated and all five of us were doubtless that this is the path we were to take."

"Do you know how to kill me?"

"Yes."

"Are Nathan and Arlie aware that it has to come to that?"

"They've tried to fight me on it, but they know."

"Well then," Ioni began. "We've said all that we need to say. Raber, it's time."

Raber started squirming and fighting against her, but Ioni's strength kept him overpowered. She held him to her with one arm and scooped up the coiled piles of bright yellow nylon cord with her free hand. She started toward the ancient oak tree, her giant and reaching reaper. She felt her breath catching and scratching in her throat as she looked at the tree getting closer and closer to her, almost like she was having an allergic reaction. She could hear Tristan following while also keeping a safe distance away.

"Stop this! Let me go! Ioni! Stop it!"

Raber's senses had returned to him enough to rediscover his talents for speech.

"You just be quiet now," Ioni said to him calmly. "Talking time is over, my pet."

"Don't do this, Ioni!" Raber screamed. "Don't do this to me! Don't do this to yourself! Do you have any idea how valuable you are? The world needs you! Your fucking faith needs you! How could people fail to be faithful when they see proof of the power we can wield?"

"I never wanted to be this," Ioni said, not slowing her march to the tree. "I was a servant. I walked the right-hand path. Divinity is around me, not within me. I studied and I learned. I learned a self-awareness about Wicca that taught me that will and desire are two different things. That's something you never learned. You're selfish and you're wrong about everything. I'm nothing more than a cautionary tale. I'm a fucking after-school special on the dangers of abusive boyfriends, you piece of shit!"

Ioni threw him to the ground and kicked him smartly in the ribs before picking him up again and continuing toward the tree. When they arrived at the thick trunk, Ioni tossed Raber to the ground again and glared at him.

"If you move, I will tear you into pieces as slowly as I can muster," she said. He swallowed hard and sat back against the trunk of the tree.

She looked down at the yellow cord in her hands and looked at Tristan, who was still safely back.

"This thing was unbearable to touch before," she said, shaking the cord in her hand. "Now it's just like any other benign object. What changed?"

"That rope, being your suicide weapon, was a physical embodiment of your lost memories. The curse that he put on you that made you forget made you fear your truth, that's why the rope turned into a convenient protective talisman against you." Tristan smiled sadly. "When you had your memories returned, the rope lost all of its power over you. It's just rope now."

Ioni glared down at Raber.

"It's about to become a recycled murder weapon," she said.

"Please, baby," Raber said. "Please don't do this. We can still be together. We can still go away. Please, Ioni. Please."

"You dare to beg me?" Ioni asked coolly, looking down at Raber. "My, my, Raber. You just don't know when you've lost, do you?"

"I haven't lost!" he screamed. "You just need to stop listening to *him* and fucking remember who got you all amped up for your super serious religion in the first place!"

"Raber," Ioni soothed, smiling. "I'm not going to fight with you. The fight is over. Quit screaming like a scared child and take your punishment like a big boy."

Raber shrieked and scrambled to his feet. He clumsily started running for the total darkness beyond the trees, beyond the field, and to the thick forest. Ioni watched him gain some distance before giving chase, toying with him. She was on him in a moment. He was panting and wheezing, while she was barely even breathing. She marveled at her superior physiology, looking down at her terrified murderer.

"You poor, scared little thing," she cooed. "You don't need to worry about it. I'll take care of everything. I'll do more for you than you did for me, baby."

He started sobbing. Ioni laughed.

She wrapped her arm around Raber's neck in an almost chummy way and dragged him back to the tree, laughing the whole way. She noticed Tristan stepping away from the tree as she got closer. He had a canvas tote bag slung over his shoulder and she thought that she had seen him slip something inside.

"Nathan and Arlie are taking too long for my liking with that ladder," Ioni said.

She picked up the cord and tied a sloppy, looped knot at the end. Using a surprisingly accurate aim, she threw the length of rope over the same branch that had seen her demise and draped the loop over as she held the other end. She slipped the loop over Raber's head and jerked the rope with a hard, sharp pull.

Raber's body heaved off of the ground and then fell limp in a pile, his neck broken, his life ended. Tristan gasped in surprise.

"There," Ioni said, releasing the end of the rope and letting it dangle from the branch. "Now maybe we can have some quiet."

"I knew it would come to that, but you just *did it*," Tristan said, panting lightly and staring at the lump that had formerly been Raber Belliveau.

"Quick and painless was better than he deserved," Ioni said, shrugging. She went to sit, propped up against the oak tree, but grunted and shot back up to a standing position, facing the tree.

"What?" Tristan asked her.

"I don't like touching it," she said. "It doesn't really hurt, but I don't like it touching me."

She turned her blue eyes to Tristan and blinked in a flirty way, smiling crookedly.

"Why is that?" she said in a low but sweet voice.

Tristan took a step back from her and began answering her question, but she wasn't listening to him. She was smelling him and looking at his delicious skin and listening to his heart thumping in his chest. She could hear small whooshing noises with every heartbeat as the blood rushed through the veins in his body. She found herself smiling widely and walking toward him.

"Stop," Tristan said loudly, snapping her out of her focus. "You're not doing this."

"I'm not doing anything," Ioni said casually.

"We're not finished helping you yet," Tristan said.

"Oh, you mean you haven't killed me," Ioni said.

"Put you at peace," Tristan corrected.

"You have no idea how delicious you look, smell, and sound."

"You have no idea how serious I am about you staying back, away from me." Tristan said. He slipped a hand into the canvas bag on his shoulder.

"I'm just so hungry," Ioni whined. "It hurts."

"That's why you need to be put to rest," Tristan said.

"I could stay around, you know. We don't even know how long I might live. Maybe I'm immortal. Raber said that a vampire hasn't been made in about a hundred years."

"It's rare now, but it used to happen more often than you might think," Tristan said. "When they used to bury suicides outside of town at crossroads, it used to happen quite often. Every couple of years one would show up."

"And that's how you know how to kill me, Tristan Van Helsing?" Ioni smiled, and stepped closer to Tristan.

"I didn't know anything about real vampires or how to kill them until I saw you through the webcam. Like I said before, we have a network that spans the entire North American continent and some of South America and Europe and someone within the network had the information that we needed."

"Andrew said he found the spell in an old book given to him by a relative from Europe, I believe," Ioni said. "How come he didn't know my weaknesses? They performed a few tests that were based on lore and Hollywood."

"Andrew and Raber were like kids with explosives. Stupid kids with more firepower than they could handle." Tristan answered.

"And you can handle the heat, is that right?"

"I came prepared, that's all."

Ioni rushed him, but was stopped when a silver amulet was shoved into her face. The searing pain changed her focus and she screamed and stepped back. Tristan kept the amulet held before him. Ioni touched the side of her face where the silver had made contact with her skin. The skin was hot and tender, but unbroken.

"Have you decided to stop being cooperative with this rescue mission, Ioni?"

Ioni snorted haughtily and sat cross-legged on the ground.

"I'm so very hungry," she said softly.

It was true. Now that Raber had been dealt with, her focus was completely bent on her hunger. She was so overwhelmed with it that she barely understood what Tristan was talking about. What rescue mission? She couldn't concentrate on it for very long. The scent of Tristan was deep in her nose and the sound of the blood rushing around inside of him were dominating her attention.

"You have to have strength, Ioni," Tristan was saying to her.

"For what?"

Tristan frowned at her.

"Control, Ioni. You need to control your urges. I'm going to help you, but you need to calm down."

"I can finally eat?" She asked, hopeful. Tristan frowned again.

"No," he said simply.

"Then how are you going to help me? Raber starved me! I need to eat! I'm so hungry!"

"I'm so sorry this has happened to you," Tristan said quietly. "I'm so sorry that your life has been ruined and I'm even more sorry that the only help I can offer you, you can't understand right now because you're so out of your mind."

"I'll be better if I eat," Ioni said hopefully, rising to her feet. "I'll be able to think if I can just have a drink, Tristan! Just a drink!"

"I'm so sorry, Ioni," Tristan said again.

He dropped the silver amulet to the ground and Ioni rushed to him, her arms outstretched. Tristan was ready for her. As she sped the few feet to him, he caught her right arm and swung her around, using her own speed to toss her onto her back. She wasn't startled, but she was incapacitated long enough for him to reach into the canvas bag and pull out a large wooden stick. He used both of his arms to hold it over his head and bring it down with all of his strength, but she was

304

quick and rolled away. The stick caught her in the shoulder at the last second. The stabbing itself was extremely painful, but something about the stick was worse.

"It's from the tree!" she shrieked.

Panting, Tristan slammed Ioni back onto her back and pulled the stick out of her shoulder. This time, instead of holding the stick above his head, he placed it in the middle of her chest and leaned on it with all of his weight. He had to bounce once to get the stick to go through her breastbone but it went through. Ioni, screaming the whole time, felt every inch of the stick's journey to her heart in slow motion. Searing pain and disgust flooded her as she looked into Tristan's concentrating and determined face. When the tip of the stick touched her heart, she had time to gasp before the organ was pierced and everything went black for her. Again.

EPILOGUE

Tristan, Nathan, and Arlie did a lot of positioning and posing in order to make the grisly scene at the crossroads look like a murder/suicide. The gruesome task of pulling the rope so that Raber's limp body was suspended from the tree branch took all three of them, each perched precariously on the ladder. They put the ladder under his feet, making sure that it would have reached high enough, and then kicked it over, hoping that it would look as if Raber had kicked it himself.

They left Ioni where she was. It was obvious that she had been murdered. Nathan and Arlie were pretty broken up about her demise. Tristan sympathized with their horror and sense of loss when they returned with Raber's car and the ladder only to find that they had missed everything. He tried to relay the events to them as they worked together to set their macabre scene, but they were upset with him. They had hoped to save their friend, but he knew that that was impossible. That became clear to him when she lost all ability to focus on anything other than eating.

When the posing was finished, they walked back to the rental car and Tristan called his mother and let her know that the ordeal was over. The coven stood ready to serve as witnesses with Nathan and Arlie that Raber was abusing and drugging Ioni.

They had decided that they didn't want Wicca or magic in any form to come into play in the grisly scene, even though it very much was. For their own safety and comfort, they didn't want themselves scrutinized too closely. An abusive and controlling boyfriend was an easier sell than black and white magic and accidental vampires.

When they returned to Tristan's home, the trio cleaned and Tristan called the police. Two uniformed officers came to his home and took his complaint. The story was that Tristan had asked Ioni to house sit for him while he was in South America visiting his father, but returned early when he learned that her ex-boyfriend was living in the house with her. When he returned, he said, he found that Ioni seemed to be drugged and held against her will and that when he confronted the ex-boyfriend, things got violent. Tristan told the police that he demanded that the ex-boyfriend leave his house, but the ex-boyfriend took Ioni with him. Tristan was concerned that something had befallen Ioni because she wasn't answering her phone or returning texts (Tristan, Nathan, and Arlie all had called and texted her phone after they left her dead body in the field). Nathan and Arlie were there because they were worried about their friend as well and had noticed her strange behavior since the ex-boyfriend had come back into her life.

The bodies were found the next morning. There were questions about the authenticity of the scene, but ultimately it was the answer that made the most sense to the right people in charge. The town was afire with the horror of the crime. Candlelight vigils were held for Ioni and her face appeared on the front page of the local newspaper and on an inner page of a few national publications.

After all of the horrible things that sweet, naïve Ioni had had to endure during her ordeal, she became just as she predicted. She was a cautionary tale used to scare teenaged girls into being wary of abusive boyfriends. Raber, in a twist that might have pleased him, became a bit of a cult figure in line with slasher movie antagonists.

Those who knew the full truth of what had happened between Raber and Ioni lived haunted by what they had seen and heard. They didn't see any learning experience in the situation, nor did they feel that there was a hero to the story. Tristan was pitied, not celebrated. He wasn't revered as a true vampire-killer. The story, to those who knew it, was just fucking sad.

END

PUBLISHER'S NOTE

Thank you for reading *You're Mine.* Whether you liked it or not we hope you'll take a moment to leave a review on Amazon or your favorite book review site. Reviews are vitally important, both to help us market the book and to help the author improve their writing. Thank you!

ABOUT THE AUTHOR

Somer Canon is the Splatterpunk Award nominated author of works such as Killer Chronicles and The Hag Witch of Tripp Creek. When she's not wreaking havoc in her minivan, she's avoiding her neighbors and consuming all things horror. She has two sons and more cats than her husband agreed to have.